A Christmas Visitor

The Cape Light Titles

CAPE LIGHT

HOME SONG

A GATHERING PLACE

A NEW LEAF

A CHRISTMAS PROMISE

THE CHRISTMAS ANGEL

A CHRISTMAS TO REMEMBER

A CHRISTMAS VISITOR

A Christmas Visitor

A Cape Light Novel

THOMAS KINKADE

& KATHERINE SPENCER

**Doubleday Large Print
Home Library Edition**

B

BERKLEY BOOKS, NEW YORK
A Parachute Press Book

This Large Print Edition, prepared especially for Doubleday Large Print Home Library, contains the complete, unabridged text of the original Publisher's Edition.

THE BERKLEY PUBLISHING GROUP
Published by the Penguin Group
Penguin Group (USA) Inc.
375 Hudson Street, New York New York 10014, USA
Penguin Group (Canada), 90 Eglinton Avenue East, Suite 700, Toronto, Ontario M4P 2Y3, Canada
(a division of Pearson Penguin Canada Inc.)
Penguin Books Ltd., 80 Strand, London WC2R 0RL, England
Penguin Group Ireland, 25 St. Stephen's Green, Dublin 2, Ireland (a division of Penguin Books Ltd.)
Penguin Group (Australia), 250 Camberwell Road, Camberwell, Victoria 3124, Australia
(a division of Pearson Australia Group Pty. Ltd.)
Penguin Books India Pvt. Ltd., 11 Community Centre, Panchsheel Park, New Delhi—110 017, India
Penguin Group (NZ), 67 Apollo Drive, North Shore 0632, New Zealand
(a division of Pearson New Zealand Ltd.)
Penguin Books (South Africa) (Pty.) Ltd., 24 Sturdee Avenue, Rosebank, Johannesburg 2196,
South Africa

Penguin Books Ltd., Registered Offices: 80 Strand, London WC2R 0RL, England

A CHRISTMAS VISITOR

ISBN: 978-0-7394-8870-6

PRINTED IN THE UNITED STATES OF AMERICA

**This Large Print Book carries the
Seal of Approval of N.A.V.H.**

DEAR FRIENDS

EACH YEAR AS CHRISTMAS DRAWS NEAR, I FIND myself eagerly awaiting the precious time I will spend with my family and friends. What could be more special than spending the holidays with the people we love? Those whom we hold most dear always enrich this holy season. They show us the true meaning of love. They show us the true meaning of Christmas.

But as I think about this, I remember an exceptional Christmas when we welcomed a stranger into our home, and I am reminded of the blessings that visitors can bring with them.

So come with me now to Cape Light, our quiet town by the sea. Let us call on Miranda Potter, who will learn both the joys and sorrows of letting a stranger into her heart.

Let's spend some time with Reverend Ben Lewis, who will meet an unexpected visitor and find a renewed sense of faith.

And finally, let us visit Molly Willoughby, for whom a startling arrival will prove to be the most wonderful blessing of all.

Come with me to the town of Cape Light, whose residents will welcome us into their homes and allow us all to share in the delight of Christmas miracles and the joy this holiday brings.

Merry Christmas!

Thomas Kinkade

CHAPTER ONE

A BITING WIND SWEPT THROUGH POTTER'S ORchard. Miranda wrapped her arms around her waist, trying hard to ignore the cold. She watched the bare branches of the apple trees bow and sway like a row of dancers on a stage. The dusting of snow that had fallen at Thanksgiving had all but vanished the past week. But it was always colder up here, at the top of the hill, where the view below stretched out wide and unobscured.

This was her favorite place. She came here nearly every evening, just as the sun began to set. From this point, she could see the entire village tucked into the cape, the harbor dotted with boats and glassy chunks of ice, opening to the dark sea. Out past the harbor, where the sky and ocean met, low clouds were tinged purple and rose, predicting a clear day tomorrow.

It was hard not to be hopeful here. Hard not to see "the big picture," as her grandmother would say. Hard not to feel faith in something larger than herself, something positive and good, urging her forward, though her life seemed confused lately, with too many choices and no clear path to follow.

Miranda watched until the sunset faded and the sky above turned inky, midnight blue. White stars dotted the sky and the lights glowed below in the town of Cape Light, looking like a miniature village, set out under a Christmas tree. Finally, it was time to go.

"Dixie! Come!" Miranda called for her dog, but as usual at this point in their walk, when Miranda was most eager to get home, the dog ignored her. Instead, Dixie sniffed and licked at something on the ground. "Oh, great." Miranda groaned, and started toward the dog, hoping to reach her before she started rolling around in ecstasy and wound up smelling too awful to be let back inside.

"Dixie! Come now. Come on!" Miranda shouted and clapped her hands, trying to sound stern.

The dog glanced her way then lay down. Then she lifted her head and barked. Like a rebellious child, answering back.

Miranda sighed, and slowly walked toward her. Dixie was her darling, her pal, a bear-sized mutt with a stubborn streak as big as her heart. Generally calm and well-behaved but very independent, a trait they definitely shared.

Miranda drew closer, half expecting Dixie to leap up and play a chase game. But the dog didn't budge. "Stay, Dixie. Good girl."

Dixie stared up at her, panting, then barked again.

Miranda finally realized what was going on. The dog was keeping watch over a body—a man lying prone on the ground.

Was he dead?

Dear God, she hoped not. She ran forward and crouched down beside him. His head was turned to one side. She took off a glove and gingerly felt for the pulse in his throat. Though his skin felt icy, his pulse beat steady and strong. *Thank goodness!* she thought.

"Hello?" she said uncertainly. "Can you hear me?"

There was no response. Now what was she supposed to do?

In the pale moonlight, she could see that his face was streaked with dirt, and he had an egg-shaped bump on his forehead. The skin there was cut, and a thin trail of blood ran down his forehead and cheek. He didn't look like a drifter or derelict. The pants and tweed sports coat he wore looked new, definitely not mismatched items from a thrift shop. But his coat wasn't thick or warm. She hoped he hadn't been stranded out here long. The temperature was falling. She had to get him off this hill and inside the house. The sooner, the better.

"Hey." She tried again. "Can you hear me? Are you awake?" When he didn't answer, she touched his face and gently slapped his cheek. "Can you hear me?"

Nothing. Miranda began to get frightened. What if he were in a coma—or worse?

Dixie whined, then nuzzled him, her wet nose against his neck. This time the stranger stirred and gave a low moan. His eyes slowly opened. His dark lashes were incredibly thick. *How stupid to notice something like that,* Miranda thought as he stared up at her, looking shocked then panicky.

He made a quick, jumpy move, and she put her hand on his shoulder. "It's okay. Just stay still a moment. I don't think any fast action would be a good idea right now."

He stared back at her but didn't reply. Then he struggled to sit up and Miranda helped him, her arm around one shoulder. Despite his condition, she felt his strength, his arms and broad shoulders hard with muscle.

"My head . . ." He lifted his hand and touched the lump, his face twisted with pain. "Wow . . ." He looked at his fingertips, tinged with blood.

"You have a huge cut and a bump. Did you fall?"

He stared down, his mouth a tight line. "I don't think so . . . I don't remember."

A fall that would cause a bump and cut like that seemed to Miranda something a person would remember. Then again, it wasn't surprising that he was a little disoriented. He had been unconscious, lying out in the bitter cold.

"Does it hurt any place besides your head?"

"Not really . . . I don't feel much right now, just half frozen."

"Think you can stand? I'll help you. We need to get down to the house where you can warm up." She gave him a wry smile. "You happened to pick the one place in the orchard where I can't bring the truck. Even if I drive partway up the hill, you'll still have to walk some distance and in the opposite direction from the house."

"Don't worry, I can stand." He started to push himself up then nearly tipped over. Miranda grabbed his arm and slung it over her shoulder. She was a tall woman, nearly five feet eleven. But he was taller and heavier than he looked.

She listed to one side, supporting him.

The corner of his mouth turned down in a thin, strained smile. "Think we'll make it?"

"Guess we'll find out. Luckily, it's all downhill."

"Great. If the force of gravity takes over, just let me roll down like a log."

His joke, despite his obvious pain, surprised her. *A good sign,* she thought, reflecting on his overall condition and the kind of person he must be. She was a great believer in finding a ray of humor in just about any situation, and she felt an automatic kinship with anyone else who reacted the same way.

There was no more conversation as they stumbled down the path toward the house. Supporting him was real work. Every few steps Miranda felt him shudder and smother a grunt of pain. She sensed one of his legs had been injured, too—maybe his ankle or knee. She fixed her sights and her will on the warm, glowing lights of her grandmother's rambling Queen Anne, which grew closer with each step.

Dixie had stayed close by as they staggered down the hill but now ran up ahead, barking wildly. Through the bay window in the kitchen, Miranda saw her grandmother wipe her hands on her apron as she walked toward the side door.

Sophie Potter opened the door, sounding impatient. "Dixie, stop that barking. Silly girl . . ."

"Grandma, help me. Quick!" Miranda called.

Sophie stood in the doorway, peering into the dark yard. "Miranda? What's the matter? Is that someone with you?"

"Yes . . . He's hurt. Just come quick. Please . . ."

Sophie pressed her hand to her mouth and ran out to meet Miranda, and not a moment too soon. Miranda felt as if she couldn't hold him up another minute. The stranger's head hung down heavily, resting against her own. He seemed to have spent whatever energy he had been able to summon, and she felt about to crumble under his full weight.

"I got him. It's okay." Sophie quickly stepped to the other side of the man, helping to support him the last few yards.

Moving slowly, the two women managed to carry him in through the pantry and kitchen, then into the nearest sitting room. They steered him to the couch and set him down, with his feet and head elevated.

"That cut on his forehead needs attention. I'll get some water and antiseptic," Sophie said, and started off in search of first-aid supplies.

That was one of the many things Miranda loved about her grandmother. When there was a crisis or a job to be done, she didn't waste a minute. She jumped right in without a lot of questions or chatter.

Miranda dropped down in a chair next to

the couch, too tired to do anything except watch their unexpected visitor. He lay stretched out, his eyes closed, his skin pale as paper. She hadn't focused on his looks when they were outside in the darkness. Now she noticed the lean face with a shadow of stubbly beard, the long straight nose and square jaw, thick dark hair that curled a bit. She guessed he was in his mid-thirties, a few years older than she was. He was handsome. Very handsome.

Get a grip. The man is half-frostbitten and in serious pain, and you're sitting here, ogling him. You've been stuck on this orchard too long, Miranda . . . way too long.

He was shivering and she covered him with an afghan, then grabbed a quilt from the nearest bedroom and piled that on top as well. His eyes opened partway. He was watching her.

"My grandmother's going to get some antiseptic for your cut," Miranda explained. "But I think you're going to need to see a doctor as well."

He nodded.

"My name is Miranda Potter. My grandmother's name is Sophie."

She waited for him to reply, giving his own name, but he didn't respond. Miranda couldn't tell if he was blacking out or falling asleep. Or perhaps the pain was so bad, he couldn't talk.

Moments later Sophie returned with a bowl of water, a washcloth, and other supplies. "Where did you find this poor fellow?"

"At the top of the hill. He was lying on the ground. Dixie found him, actually. I wasn't even going to walk in that direction."

"How in heaven's name did he end up there?"

"I don't know. He didn't say."

He hadn't said much, she realized.

She did wonder how he had found his way to the middle of the orchard. Sometimes strangers wandered in among the rows of trees in search of help after a car broke down on the road that bordered the west side of the property. But the big hill wasn't near the road. If his car had broken down and he had started walking, looking for help, he wouldn't have ended up there.

But he had to have come from somewhere.

"He must have taken quite a fall." Sophie dabbed at the bump and cut on the man's head.

"He said he doesn't remember."

"Oh . . . dear. That's not good." She dipped the cloth and wiped the spot again.

"I'm going to call for an ambulance," Miranda said.

"Yes, you'd better." Sophie's voice was calm, matter-of-fact. But Miranda knew her grandmother well enough to sense that she was concerned. "He needs some medical attention, more than we can give."

Miranda picked up the phone in the kitchen, dialed 911, and quickly explained the situation.

"Keep him warm. Keep his head elevated and try to keep him awake," the operator told her. "If he's had a concussion, you don't want him to lose consciousness."

"Right. We'll keep him awake," Miranda promised.

Miranda returned to the sitting room, where her grandmother had put the cloth and water aside and sat on a chair, watching the stranger. His eyes were closed again, which alarmed her.

"The EMTs will be here soon," Miranda reported. "We're not supposed to let him fall asleep."

"Of course. What was I thinking? I remember when your father was five. He decided he was a superhero and dove off the roof. We had to wake him up all night long and shine a flashlight in his eyes."

It was hard for Miranda to imagine her father as a child, gleefully pretending he could he fly; he was so serious and rigid now. But she would have to ask her grandmother about that story some other time. Now Miranda walked over and gently touched the man's shoulder. "Hey . . . how are you doing?" She crouched down beside him and watched his face. When his eyes slowly opened she felt relieved. "The ambulance is coming. You'll be at a hospital soon."

"Thanks." His head moved in a slight nod and she saw him wince with pain.

"Try not to fall asleep, okay? It's bad if you have a concussion."

"Okay. I'll try," he promised quietly.

Dixie pushed her way between them and rested her head on the edge of the sofa cushion, her muzzle touching his leg. "Dixie, go away." Miranda gently pushed the dog's head aside.

"That's okay. Let her stay." The stranger glanced at the dog, who was staring at him with the look of complete adoration that she usually reserved for Miranda.

"Do you have a dog?" Miranda just wanted to keep him talking, to keep him alert until help arrived.

He looked confused by her question. "I'm not sure."

Before Miranda could reply, Dixie suddenly pulled away and ran toward the door. She started barking just as Miranda heard a heavy knock.

"I'll stay here. You get the door," Sophie said.

Miranda headed for the foyer. It seemed too soon for the ambulance to have arrived.

The orchard was several miles from the village and the EMS crew in Cape Light was all-volunteer, working out of the firehouse.

She quickly opened the door. Officer Tucker Tulley from the town's police force stood on the porch, his notepad in hand.

"Hey, Miranda. I heard a call on the radio for an ambulance. You have a problem here?"

"I found a man up on the hill behind the house. He seems to have struck his head. He was lying on the ground, out in the cold. I don't know how long he was out there. He's in the sitting room now."

Miranda led him through the house to the sitting room. Tucker nodded at Sophie briefly, but his attention was fixed on the stranger lying on the couch.

Sophie looked up at Tucker. "He seems to drift in and out. We just tried to get him comfortable."

The man's eyes opened. He stared up at Tucker wordlessly.

"That's a wicked-looking cut on your head, sir. Did you have a fall?"

Miranda saw an anxious look shadow the man's dark eyes. "I guess I must have . . . I can't seem to remember how it happened."

"That's all right. It'll come back to you." Tucker picked up his pad and wrote something down. "May I have your name, sir?"

Tucker waited, his pen poised over his pad.

The man didn't answer. Finally, he let out a long sigh. "I'm sorry. I can't remember. It's just . . . strange. I can't seem to remember anything. My name. How I fell . . . how I got here. . . ."

Tucker stepped forward and rested a hand on the man's shoulder. "It's all right.

Just stay calm. You must have some ID on you, a license or something."

"Yes, I must." The man started to sit up, and Tucker helped him. The man reached into the breast pocket of his muddy sports jacket, then checked both outside pockets, then finally, the pockets in his pants.

"I don't seem to have a wallet. There's some change and a key . . . and a matchbook."

"Mind if I take a look?" Tucker reached out and took it from him. "Regatta Bar. Charles Hotel. That's in Boston, near Harvard. Nice place," he said to the stranger.

"I wouldn't know," the man answered.

Tucker made a note on his pad, then handed the matchbook back to the stranger.

No identification? And he doesn't remember his own name? Miranda couldn't quite believe it. What did they do now? She looked at Tucker, who showed no reaction at all, something she suspected he had learned from years of police work.

Tucker stuck the notebook in his back pocket. "Could be you left a car on the road somewhere. Might be some ID or belongings there."

The stranger nodded. "I hope that's the case."

A knock sounded sharply on the front door. The ambulance. Finally.

"I'll go," Miranda said.

"I'll come with you. I need to talk to the EMS crew." Tucker followed her out of the room.

When they were a good distance from the sitting room, Miranda turned to him. "Tucker, he has no ID. He can't even remember his name. Will the hospital even treat him?"

"He'll be taken care of, don't worry. I still think there must be a vehicle out there somewhere." Tucker glanced at her. "Listen, I know you're a decent, trusting person, ready to help anybody. And that goes double for your grandmother. But have a little caution. This guy may not be as harmless as he seems."

"He doesn't even have a wallet. He was probably mugged or something."

"Maybe. Or maybe he's only acting as if he's been mugged. Or as if he can't remember. You don't know anything about this man. You took a big chance taking him in, with just you and your grandmother alone out here."

"He was hurt," Miranda said. "What else could we do? We couldn't leave him outside to freeze to death."

Tucker touched her arm. "I would have done the same. But just remember, people aren't always what they seem."

Miranda didn't answer. She knew what Tucker said was true, but she didn't believe the stranger was purposely hiding his identity. She had a feeling about him, and Miranda always trusted her feelings—sometimes more than she should.

She opened the front door and led the two EMTs to the sitting room. They asked the man a few questions, examined his head wound, then bundled him on a stretcher and began carrying him out of the house. It all happened so quickly, Miranda didn't even have time to speak with him before the stretcher was whisked out of the room. He caught her eye for a moment, his dark gaze locking with her own. Then they carried him out of the house, and he was gone.

She turned to Tucker. "Where are they taking him?"

"Southport Hospital."

"Are you going, too?" she asked.

Tucker shook his head. "No, they'll take good care of him. I'm going to start looking for his car, try to figure out how he ended up here. I'll call the hospital later to see how he made out."

"I'm going to follow. I want to make sure he gets good care."

Tucker seemed surprised. "I'm sure he'll get the right medical attention, Miranda."

"I think she should go if she wants to," Sophie said. She was folding the blankets the man had used. "Hospitals are complicated places these days, and that man has no one to look out for him." She lifted her chin and faced Tucker. "I think I'll go, too."

Tucker looked as if he were about to argue, then stopped himself. He put on his hat and closed his heavy jacket. "I'm not sure where that fellow came from. But he was darn lucky to be rescued by you two."

"Thanks for your help, Tucker." Sophie opened the door for him. "We'll let you know how it turns out."

"I'll be waiting to hear from you. Good night, ladies."

"Good night, Tucker." Sophie closed the door and turned to her granddaughter. "We ought to bring him some clean clothes. He can't put on those wet, muddy things again."

"A heavy jacket, too. I think there's one out in the mudroom that would fit." Miranda

headed for the mudroom as her grandmother headed upstairs.

"I'll get some pants and a shirt from the
cedar closet," Sophie called. "Your grandfather's things will go swimming on that man,
but that's the best I can do."

Miranda's grandfather Gus had died three
years ago. Miranda knew her grandmother
had held on to some of Gus's clothes and
other possessions, unable to give them all
away to charity. It seemed a good thing now
that she was so sentimental. *At least your
things are being put to good use, Granddad*,
Miranda told Gus silently.

WHEN IT CAME TO SERVING HER FAMILY A NICE
dinner every night, Molly Willoughby Harding
knew she had it easier than most working
women. She could just bring something
home from her gourmet food shop,
Willoughby's Fine Foods and Catering. On
any given night, half the town seemed to be
eating her cooking, so why shouldn't her
own family do the same?

"Because the shop menu gets boring,"
Lauren, her eighteen-year-old, explained
when Molly made her usual call home at four
to check on everyone. "We want pizza. No

gourmet pizza, with artichokes or truffle oil or those gross anchovies. Just plain old pizza."

"Totally plain!" Jillian, the thirteen-year-old, chimed in.

"Basic. Bare. Generic. No frills." Lauren clarified the order with the sharp authority only a high school senior could possess.

"Extra cheese?" Jillian added. Jill was a cheese fiend. It figured.

"Okay, a basic, no-frills pizza. And a big salad," Molly added, pushing the green food. "I'll be home around six. Jillian, no IM-ing until you finish your homework."

"How can I IM anybody? Lauren is totally hogging the good computer with her iPod!" Jillian complained.

Lauren laughed at her. "Chill, Jill. Shouldn't you be working on a report about Babylonia or something?"

"Shouldn't you be working on a college essay or something?" Molly cut in.

She heard Jillian laugh. "Nice one, Mom."

"Jill, finish your homework. Lauren, give her a turn on the computer when she's done." Molly sighed. "Where's Amanda?"

"She's upstairs, practicing for her voice lesson," Jillian reported.

"At least somebody is doing what they need to do without being reminded. Please empty the dishwasher before I get home and pick up your rooms."

After a few more instructions and heavy teenage sighs, Molly finally said good-bye.

It figured that her stepdaughter Amanda would be out of the fray, occupied with some useful activity. Not that Amanda didn't enjoy giggling and getting silly as much as Jill and Lauren. But she was the most responsible, a stabilizing force among the three.

Ninety-five percent of the time, the three got along surprisingly well. But they were three girls in various stages of adolescence. Mood swings abounded and hormones were raging. Still, whenever her patience felt stretched to the limit, Molly tried to step back and take a deep breath. And just appreciate that she had them with her at all. It wouldn't be too long before the nest was empty.

The three years since she and Matt had gotten together had passed so quickly. Jillian was still her baby, but Lauren and Amanda had grown up in the blink of an eye. They would both be off to college next fall. Molly would miss them so much. The house would seem empty and quiet. She tried not to think about it and instead, looked for the number she needed to order the pizza.

A few minutes after six, Molly pulled into the driveway and parked her white SUV behind her husband Matt's black sedan. They had moved in about three months ago, but she still felt a thrill driving up to their new house. She still couldn't quite believe she lived here.

The custom-built pale brick colonial was set on two landscaped acres in a new development just outside the village. There were five bedrooms, four baths, a formal living room and a dining room, along with a stadium-sized kitchen and an adjacent family room. Beyond the glass sliders of the family room, a two-tiered deck and a kidney-shaped pool created a perfect setting for summer entertaining.

Some might call her new house a mini-mansion. To Molly, it was the Taj Mahal, the kind of house she had believed forever beyond her reach. The kind she would gaze at longingly as she drove past, feeling like an interloper in the neighborhood. It used to be that Molly never even entered a house like this unless she was hired help, the cleaning lady, cook, or dog walker.

Four years ago when Molly met Matt, she and the girls had been living in a small apartment above a store in town. She had been struggling to support them—with no help from her ex-husband—cleaning houses, driving a school bus, baking for restaurants, and doing any odd job she could find. She had struggled through the hard times, eventually following her bliss and talent as a cook. Soon after she met Matt, she established a wildly successful food store and catering business. She sometimes thought she might like to go back to school and get a real degree. But who had the time? She barely had time to sleep and shower between taking care of her family and keeping her business running smoothly.

Lately, she had been feeling even more stressed. Maybe it was just a bad case of PMS, she told herself. Overall, life was more than good. Sometimes she woke up beside her husband and wanted to pinch herself, sure she must be lost in some wonderful dream. Molly didn't want to think about what her life would be like if she had never met Matt. She couldn't imagine her life without him.

Now she walked up the long curving path

to the front door, keys jangling in one hand, pizza box balanced on the other.

Yes, you live here, Molly. This is really your house.

You're not just delivering the pizza.

She dropped her purse and keys on the table by the staircase, then headed back to the kitchen. The table was set for dinner, and Matt was unloading the dishwasher, carefully placing clean glasses in the cupboard.

"Hi, honey. One of the girls was supposed to do that."

"They claim to be engrossed with their homework. Such studious children," he joked.

"Especially when you ask them to do some housework."

She studied the controls on her new oven for a moment before putting the pizza in to warm. The oven was a high-tech, top-of-the-line model, sold mostly to restaurants. Molly still felt a bit guilty about her self-indulgence. But she was a professional now, so she could justify it. Besides, as Matt reminded her, they could afford the best and she deserved it. It hadn't taken too much persuading for her to give in.

The stadium-sized kitchen was her playground, with all the latest equipment, special pots, and gadgets she could ever need. "You could film a cooking show in here," her friend Betty Bowman had teased her. "Including a large, live audience."

Ironically, since they moved in, Molly hadn't had much time for home cooking. It was hard to believe she had all this state-of-the-art equipment at home and usually ended up re-heating something from the shop.

She was shutting the oven door when she felt Matt sneak up behind her. He put his arms around her waist and kissed the back of her neck. "Hmm. You smell good."

"It's probably just the pizza."

"Perhaps . . ."

She turned in his arms and gave him a kiss. "I missed you today."

"I missed you, too. I thought you were going to stop by for lunch."

"Oh, right. Sorry, I totally forgot. Why didn't you call?"

"I figured you were busy. It's okay. I was busy, too."

"That goes without saying."

Although Matt had taken over Dr. Elliot's practice four years ago, folks in town still called him the "new" doctor. New or old, he was the only doctor within twelve miles, and his waiting room was always packed.

"How about tomorrow?" she said.

"Let's see. I think I can fit you in. I'll have to check." He sounded very serious, but his dark eyes sparkled.

Molly held him closer. "You *think*? Thanks a bunch."

Matt laughed and kissed her. Molly closed her eyes and melted in his arms. She loved him so much. Sometimes it hurt just thinking about it.

"Ugh . . . gross."

Molly looked down to find Jillian standing nearby, rolling her eyes with disgust.

It was a big house. But sometimes, not quite big enough.

She drew apart from Matt and straightened out her sweater. "Everything's ready for dinner. Why don't you call your sisters?"

"No problem." Jillian turned on her heel and headed back toward the stairs. "But try to behave while I'm gone, okay? You guys . . . geez."

Matt started laughing and Molly shot him a mock glare. "Stop laughing. You're encouraging her."

"I'm sorry. I couldn't help it." He tried to stop, but when he caught her eye, she started laughing, too.

Dinner flew by in a flurry of talk and laughter. The girls devoured the pizza in about five minutes flat, notably faster than they ate her gourmet food. It didn't matter, Molly decided, as long as they were together. She had never been big on saying grace at the dinner table, but tonight she sent up a silent prayer of thanks for her wonderful family and all the blessings in her life.

"So, Mom," Lauren said, "have you and Aunt Jessica decided who's having the big Christmas Eve party this year?"

"Oh, I forgot to tell you," Molly said, wondering how she could have let this major detail slip. For the last three years her brother Sam and his wife, Jessica, had held the annual family Christmas party at their house. "This year," Molly said happily, "the party is coming to our house!"

"What about your mother?" Matt asked. "Wasn't she saying that she wanted to have the Christmas Eve party at her house this year?"

"She's claimed Christmas Day," Molly explained. "I think my folks are still cleaning up from Thanksgiving. They're fine with coming here for Christmas Eve."

Molly had grown up in a big family, six children in all. Most of the Morgan clan still lived in New England, though Molly was closest to her brother Sam. Holidays had always been important in their house. Their parents seemed to love any excuse for a family party. Her mother, Marie, was a fabulous cook, and her father, Joe, had been a professional chef, working on cruise ships and in hotels. Molly sometimes felt intimidated cooking for them, but they always applauded her efforts and never seemed to criticize or offer unwanted advice. Well, practically never.

"Won't that be difficult for you?" Matt asked. "I thought you said you were totally overbooked with all the seasonal parties and had to hire more help."

"Honey, parties are my business. I can certainly do one for our own family. Besides, it's our first Christmas in the new house. Don't you want to entertain?"

He didn't look totally convinced. "Of course I do. I just don't want you to get exhausted. I know how you go crazy if we're having company, especially if it's your family."

"I won't go crazy. I promise. Besides, the

girls will help me. Right, girls?" Molly looked at her three daughters. They exchanged wary looks.

"You do get sort of intense, Mom," Jillian said. "I mean, remember last year when you made, like, a hundred of those little liver cakes with the little flowers on top for Aunt Jessica's?"

"That was pâté, Jill. With edible nasturtiums. Everybody loved it."

Matt made a face, as if he agreed with Jill. "Look, Molly," he said diplomatically, "we just want you to have fun on the holidays, too, and not be stuck in the kitchen all night. It's not a black-tie charity ball at the historical society. It's just . . . family."

"But we have a big family. Can I help that? I can't just send out for buckets of chicken."

Matt laughed. "As if a bucket of chicken would ever cross the threshold in this house."

"How many people are coming?" Amanda asked her.

Matt didn't have much family, just his parents in Worcester and a sister in Newburyport. Amanda still wasn't quite used to the big family parties Lauren and Jillian had grown up with.

"Oh . . . you know, honey, the usual. Just family," Molly said. "I haven't called anyone yet. I'm not sure who can come." That was true, though a quick mental tally that afternoon had put the list at over fifty. Molly reminded herself that they had plenty of room now in their grand new house. Fifty people wouldn't feel crowded at all.

"We have plenty of time before Christmas to figure it out," she added. Matt stared at her doubtfully. "I won't go crazy. I won't get all fussy and nutty, I promise. I won't cook complicated foods that take two weeks to prep and keep me stuck in the kitchen all night, okay?"

Matt nodded then reached across the table and touched her hand. "I know it means a lot to you to have your family here for Christmas. I want them here, too. I'm sure it will be wonderful. All I ask is that you try to keep it in perspective, okay?"

Molly nodded. "Okay."

That's what she loved about Matt. One of the things, anyway. He genuinely wanted her to be happy.

When dinner was finished, the girls helped clear the table and clean up the kitchen. Then they scattered, escaping to their private spaces upstairs to finish homework, talk online with friends or wash and blow out their hair, a never-ending project.

Molly spent the rest of the evening washing and folding laundry while half-watching TV with Matt. Finally, around eleven o'clock, Matt handed over the remote. "I'm going upstairs. I have to be in early tomorrow."

"I'll be there in a minute." Molly glanced at him. "I just want to straighten up."

He leaned over and kissed her on the cheek. "Don't be too long."

She heard his footsteps on the stairway, then a short time later, heard their bedroom door shut. She walked to the foyer and peeked up the stairs. It seemed very quiet. Jill had gone to bed around ten, and the two older girls were occupied, their bedroom doors shut.

Molly opened her purse, which she had left on the table near the staircase. She took out a small white paper bag and carried it into the downstairs bathroom. With the bathroom door closed and locked, she took out the slim box that was inside the bag, tore it open, and read the instructions.

It seemed pretty simple. Not the complicated test and doctor's appointment she had gone through when she was pregnant with Jill. But that was nearly fourteen years ago. Now, you could find out in five minutes if you were pregnant.

She stood at the sink, staring at the tiny window on the plastic stick. Then at her watch. It wasn't taking very long. Not very long at all. The dot was blue and got bluer and bluer.

Molly felt her stomach clench with nerves. She couldn't believe it. There had to be something wrong. Maybe these home tests weren't that reliable?

She took out the other plastic stick and tried again.

Blue. Almost instantly.

Dark, undeniable blue.

She felt her head spin for a minute, as if she were going to faint.

She *couldn't* be pregnant. Not now. She didn't have time to be pregnant, to have a new baby. She had just started her business. Everything was going so well.

But a baby! Now? That would change everything.

She would be back to square one.

The diapers, the bottles, the waking up in

the middle of the night for bad dreams, fevers, false alarms.

She had spent the last eighteen years raising her daughters, concentrating on them instead of herself. She had lost so much time and was just starting to make up for it. Just getting her life back and achieving something of her own.

Just when she was making some progress. Now she would be homebound again, sitting by the sandbox, watching kiddie shows on TV, mistaken for a grandma at Gymboree.

Molly sat down and held her head in her hands. She started to cry, then quickly grabbed a towel and covered her mouth so no one would hear her.

When she was cried out Molly splashed her face with cold water. She hid the pregnancy tests at the bottom of the kitchen trash, then shut off the lights and went up to bed.

Matt was sound asleep when she crept into their room. She didn't have the heart to wake him. She pulled on a nightgown, brushed her teeth, then slipped into bed.

Just when things were going so well.

It just didn't seem fair.

* * *

THE DOCTORS AND NURSES CALLED HIM JOHN Doe. *The name doesn't fit,* Miranda thought. She and Sophie sat in waiting-room limbo in the Southport Hospital's emergency room. The big clock on the wall opposite the TV showed it was nearly midnight. When they arrived the area had been crowded, almost every seat taken. But as the hours passed, the crowd had thinned. They were practically the only ones left. Sophie thumbed through worn-out magazines while Miranda sipped a cup of cold coffee.

"I'm not sure we should wait." Sophie put the magazine aside. "They'll probably want to keep him overnight."

"They might," Miranda agreed. "If only someone would tell us what's going on."

The admitting nurse had told Miranda and Sophie that as strangers, they were not actually permitted to see the patient or be given access to his medical information. Miranda explained how she had found the man in the orchard and that he had apparently lost his memory, and the nurse's officious attitude seemed to soften a bit.

"Can you let him know that we're out here?" Miranda had asked.

"I can, but I'm not sure you'll be allowed to see him. It's usually only family."

"I understand. I just wanted him to know he wasn't alone. How is he doing?"

The nurse glanced at her over the top of her slim reading glasses. She appeared to be weighing how much she could say. "He's just been admitted. I doubt if there's anything to report. If you want to wait, I'll try to get some information later."

Miranda smiled at her gratefully and took a seat to wait.

And wait. And wait.

The updates had been brief and spaced apart by hours. John Doe had gone upstairs to have his head x-rayed and downstairs for an examination by a neurologist. The nurse added it was sheer luck a specialist had been in the building at this hour. There had been a car accident during rush hour, and a neurologist had been called in to assist with emergency neurosurgery. John Doe wouldn't be examined until the surgery was over, which would take a while longer.

That was the last they had heard, almost two hours ago. The nurse didn't seem to know anything more and Miranda was wary of seeming like a bother.

She was also starting to worry about her grandmother. Though Sophie never complained, Miranda was sure she must be uncomfortable sitting in the hard, plastic chair all these hours. Now Miranda saw her lean her head back against the wall and close her eyes.

Miranda touched her arm. "Grandma? I think you're right, maybe we should go. I don't think there's anything we can do for him."

Sophie sat up with a start and blinked. "I'm all right, honey. I was just resting my eyes."

Miranda smiled at her. "Let me try that nurse one more time. Maybe if she sees that we intend to go, she'll finally tell us something."

Miranda headed off to confront the supervising nurse again, expecting another brushoff. Sophie followed a few steps behind.

The nurse was talking on the phone and Miranda waited until she had hung up. "Miranda Potter, right?" The nurse glanced at a note on her desk. Miranda nodded, surprised that the woman remembered her name. "You can go back and see the patient now. Here's a pass. He's in area three."

"Area three. Okay. Thanks." Miranda took

the stick-on pass and pasted it to her jacket. *A badge of honor for waiting out the system*, she thought. She turned to Sophie. "I won't be long."

"Take your time. I'm not going anywhere." Sophie gave her a hug and headed back to the waiting area.

Miranda stepped through the swinging doors. A busy nursing station was at the center of the floor. No one paid attention to her or stopped to check her badge. She saw a few rooms on the far end of the floor, but mainly beds separated by curtains and movable dividers. She noticed numbers on the dividers and soon found area three.

John Doe, as the hospital now called him, was lying in a bed with its backrest raised almost to sitting level. There was a large white bandage on his head. Miranda guessed that he must have had stitches to close the cut.

His expression brightened as he saw her. "Miranda . . . I didn't even know you were out there."

"My grandmother and I wanted to make sure you were given good attention."

"I've been rolled from one end of this place to the other. I think this bed is going to need new tires."

Miranda smiled. He still had a sense of humor. "What does the doctor say? Has your memory returned at all?"

"No, nothing yet." His expression turned serious again. "They say it's just a concussion. I had an X-ray and they ruled out a brain tumor."

"Well, that's something to be thankful for."

"Sure, I guess." He let out a long sigh. "But if they could find something that was causing it, at least they could fix it."

A doctor pushed back the curtain and walked in. He wore green scrubs and carried a clipboard. "How are you feeling? Has that medication helped your head any?"

"I'm doing all right."

"Good. Let's check your eyes again." The doctor leaned over, took hold of his patient's chin, and peered into his eyes. Then he took out a small flashlight and aimed the beam directly into his right eye, then his left. "No progress with your memory?"

"No, not at all."

"Do you know this woman?" the doctor asked, stepping back and looking at Miranda.

The stranger's expression brightened, almost making her blush. "If it wasn't for her, I would still be out there, frozen to death."

The way he put it sounded so dramatic. Had she really saved his life? *Well, maybe,* Miranda thought.

"It's good you remember that much. I'm not an expert, but most memory loss is temporary when it's triggered by head trauma."

"Falling down you mean?" Miranda clarified.

"I don't believe the wound I saw was caused by a fall," the doctor told her. "It looked more like a blow to the head—with a blunt object. Of course, you found him on the ground and he had obviously fallen. He could have struck his head again at that point."

"But you think he was hit on the head before he fell?"

"That's right." The doctor glanced at John Doe again. "We've already talked about this. It's possible he was mugged and his attackers hit him on the head to subdue him, then took his top coat and wallet, et cetera. Not unusual in that sort of robbery. That kind of blow and emotional trauma could cause a memory loss. It's what we call stress-induced."

"How long will it take to come back?" the man asked.

"Hard to say. Your memory could return in a few hours, days, or even months. I'm not sure even a specialist could predict it with any accuracy. It's a tricky situation, memory loss. Not too much is known about it, really."

"I see." Miranda could hear the discouragement in the stranger's voice. "Do I need to stay here any longer?"

"I can admit you . . . but we're short on beds," the doctor replied. "The only place we can put you tonight is in the psych ward."

The psych ward? Miranda thought that sounded depressing. "Does he really have to stay? You just said the concussion isn't that serious."

"I can release him if I'm sure he'll have responsible care," the doctor said. "He needs to be woken up every few hours to see that his pupils are dilating. You just use a flashlight, the way I did."

She looked over at John Doe. "I can do that," she told him. "You can come back to our house."

"Thanks . . . but I don't think so. I've been too much trouble for you already."

"It's not any trouble, not at all. We would feel a lot better if you came back with us."

He didn't answer but looked about to refuse again.

Miranda couldn't leave him here. He didn't

belong in the psychiatric ward. Or sitting out in the waiting area, sleeping on a plastic chair. What would he do tomorrow morning? Who would be here to help him sort things out if his memory hadn't returned?

"Lots of people say the Potters are crazy . . . but it's still a better choice than the psych ward. You'll get a better breakfast, too," she promised.

He stared at her thoughtfully. Then, finally a small smile turned up the corners of his mouth. "Okay, I'll go back to the orchard with you," he said. "But just for tonight."

"Sounds like that's settled." The doctor wrote some notes on his clipboard. Miranda had almost forgotten he was still in the room. "You're free to go. Just give this to one of the nurses at the desk."

He handed John Doe several forms. He also handed Miranda a note, instructions on checking the patient's concussion, and a number to call if his condition took a turn for the worse.

An aide with a wheelchair came for John Doe, and Miranda accompanied them out to the waiting area. She found Sophie sitting with her eyes closed in the seat farthest from the big TV.

"Grandma?" Miranda touched her grand-mother's shoulder. "We can go now." Sophie opened her eyes, sat up, and smiled at her granddaughter and the stranger. "I've asked . . . John . . . to come back with us," Miranda explained.

She didn't know what else to call him. She hoped he didn't mind.

Sophie stood up and buttoned her coat. "Of course you did," she said to Miranda. She glanced at her house guest. "That's an impressive bandage. Hurt much?"

"Not too much." From his expression, Mi-randa guessed it actually hurt a great deal.

"I'll make you an ice pack as soon as we get back," Sophie told him. "Sometimes these things hurt more later, after the numb-ing drugs wear off."

John got to his feet at the hospital door, and they started across the parking lot.

Sophie took his arm in a friendly, comfort-ing gesture. "I bet you didn't get a thing to eat, either. We'll have a bite when we get in, a midnight snack. I have some chili and john-nycake . . . Oh, and there's an apple crumb pie. I just baked it this afternoon."

"Some snack." He laughed. It was the first

time, Miranda realized. "What would you call a real meal?"

"I'm just a plain, Yankee cook. Nothing fancy. But you won't leave the table hungry, I can guarantee that."

"You're very kind." He glanced at Miranda, and their gaze held for a moment. "I'm very grateful. To both of you."

"Nonsense." Sophie waved her hand at him as she climbed into the front seat of Miranda's small car. "It wouldn't have felt right, leaving you here. You're doing me a favor, young man. Now I can get a good night's sleep."

There is no greater wisdom than kindness, Miranda had once read. If that was true, then her grandmother had to be the wisest woman in the world.

As she drove out of the parking lot and headed back to the orchard, Miranda thought again of Tucker Tulley's warning. Perhaps they were taking a risk, bringing this stranger home. Even for one night. But it didn't seem right to leave him stranded here. Not to her or her grandmother.

That was all there was to it.

CHAPTER TWO

~~~

"I WOULDN'T HAVE ASKED YOU TO HELP, REVerend. But the plumber will be here any minute, and I'll never get these boxes cleared with my bum hand."

Carl Tulley, the church sexton, held out his bandaged hand to show Reverend Ben. Carl had been replacing a broken pane of glass in one of the Sunday school classrooms a few days ago and accidentally slashed his left palm.

"I don't mind helping," Ben assured him. "Just show me what you want moved and where."

"The pipe froze and busted right here."

Carl pointed to a thick copper pipe near the low ceiling. "All the boxes on this end need to get moved. A lot of the stuff got wet. You'll have to tell me what to throw out, though. I don't want to toss out anything valuable."

"I'll have to sort through it all later." Ben wasn't looking forward to that. He hated going through old files and correspondence, even when it was dry. Dealing with wet boxes full of moldering church records was his idea of serious penance. "For now, let's just move it all out of the way."

Ben lifted a large cardboard box from the basement floor and carried it to the far side of the basement—the high and dry side, Carl called it. Ben would be the last one to deny the visible difference between one side of the basement and the other. The church had been built in the Colonial era and was now sinking in various directions, as old buildings tended to do. The wooden floors upstairs were wavering and so were the walls.

The basement was little more than a hole in the ground, which had been reinforced from time to time with solid-looking layers of gray concrete on the walls and floor. The original beams, clearly recognizable as tree trunks, had been reinforced in the 1960s but never removed.

Ben liked to look at the tree trunks and think about how old they were, how many church services they had supported, how many holidays, baptisms, weddings, and droning church council meetings—even church crises.

How many pastors they had held afloat, unconditionally.

Ben came back for another load. He could tell Carl was struggling to carry a carton one-handed but preferred to manage on his own. "Did you see a doctor about that hand?"

"I had a visit with Harding. He put in a few stitches, gave me some ointment. Swelling's gotten worse, though."

"You might have to go back and see him again. Sounds like it might be infected."

Carl grunted, dumping his load. Ben doubted the sexton would take his advice. Carl was the type to tough it out, never asking for help or taking much care of himself. He had grown up in Cape Light, then disappeared for over twenty years, spending part of that time in prison for accidentally killing a man, and the rest wandering, taking odd jobs or going homeless. No one really knew the whole story—not even his stepbrother, Tucker Tulley, who had served on the village police force most of his life.

Carl had never really thanked Ben for the sexton job. Still, Ben knew the job meant the world to him. Carl worked hard at it. He hadn't walked out or messed it up, as he had with so many other opportunities.

Working together they managed to clear the space in a short time.

"That should be enough space for the plumber, don't you think?" Ben brushed the dust off his hands with a rag.

"I think so. I just want to get this last box out of the way." Carl was leaning forward, trying to slide a large wooden crate across the floor. He stopped and stood up. "What do you think this is, Reverend? It's sort of heavy."

Ben walked closer and looked the crate over. It was old, made of wooden slats nailed together, not the type of storage or shipping container used anymore. Bits of yellowed newspaper and straw poked through the spaces between the planks. He noticed stamp marks on the top and sides, the ink and printing so faded he couldn't read them.

There was no label, like the ones on most of the other boxes, describing the contents.

"I don't know what it is," Ben admitted. "I never noticed it down here before."

"Can I open it? Maybe if I take a few things out, we can move it easier."

"Go ahead, good idea."

Carl began to pry the lid off the crate with a screwdriver. It took a few minutes for him to loosen the old nails and lift off the wooden lid. Ben moved closer and they both started pushing aside the straw and newspaper that filled the crate.

Ben withdrew a piece of yellow newspaper, noticing the masthead. The *London Times*, April 21, 1951. It practically crumbled in his hand.

Carl pulled out more of the old packing material then gave a low whistle of surprise. "Look at this."

Ben peered down into the crate where Carl had cleared a large space. Buried in the pile of stiff yellow straw, he saw a face— feminine and round, yet not distinctly female. Fine-featured, it looked like carved wood that had been painted in rich flesh tones. But he couldn't be sure what it was made of in the dim light.

"It looks like a statue of some kind. . . . Let's lift it out." Ben reached into the crate on one side and Carl took the other. "Carefully now. We don't want to break it."

"Whatever it is." Carl grunted. He had to use both hands, Ben noticed, gingerly managing with just the fingertips of his injured hand.

Finally, the statue was lifted up and out of the crate. "Let's set it down over there where we can get a better look." Ben nodded toward a table on the dry side of the basement.

It was an angel. Carved in wood, it had been painted and varnished, though the sheen was worn away in most places and the paint was faded and cracked. It was clearly very old, but amazing to look at, Ben thought. Remarkably beautiful.

The face uplifted, gently smiling, seemed to radiate light from within. A royal blue cape, and beneath it, a long scarlet tunic trimmed with gold that flowed across the graceful body. Large golden wings sprouted from its shoulders. The angel appeared to be stepping forward and carried a banner between its hands. But the message it had come to proclaim was now faded beyond recognition.

"Wow . . . Isn't that something?" Carl looked at Ben, then back at the statue. "Not like the plaster statues they make nowadays. That looks like the kind of thing you'd see in a museum."

Ben guessed the statue had been made in Europe. He didn't know much about religious art, but there was something about it that didn't seem American.

"I wonder why we never noticed it. Did you ever see that crate before, Carl? You must have."

Carl shrugged and shook his head. He picked a bit of straw from his sweatshirt. "No, sir. I don't recall. It must have been down here, though. Didn't appear out of thin air this morning."

"Yes, of course not." Ben said slowly. He looked at the statue and walked around the table, to view it from all sides. "Do you think we could carry it up to the sanctuary?"

"The crate weighs half a ton, but the statue isn't so heavy."

"What about your hand?" Ben asked.

Carl held out his injured hand and flexed his fingers. "It doesn't feel so bad now. Maybe it was just stiff."

Carl took the top of the statue and Ben took the bottom. They carried it through the basement and up the stairs, then down the hallway to the sanctuary.

"Where do you want it, Reverend?"

"Up at the front. Opposite the pulpit, I think." Ben directed him to the corner opposite the pulpit and they set the statue down. "I think there's a pedestal back in the sacristy. It would look better displayed up higher."

"I'll get it. Here, I brought a rag to clean it off." Carl handed Ben a dusting rag and headed off in search of the pedestal.

Ben gently started wiping off the dust and bits of straw. The varnished finish looked a bit brighter, though the colors were still mellow with age.

Where had it come from? Perhaps some family had donated it. Ben didn't remember anyone ever mentioning such a piece. There was a record book someplace in the church office where gifts and donations were recorded; maybe he would find it listed there. If it had been a gift to the church, it must have been given years ago. It seemed odd that someone might have donated such an extraordinary statue, and yet no one had ever asked why it wasn't displayed.

The church was very simple in design, inside and out. There was little decoration, no statues. Just the stained-glass windows and two tapestry banners that hung up front, behind the altar.

During Advent, the sanctuary was decorated for Christmas with a tree, a nativity scene, and the traditional Advent candles on the altar. Ben thought that the angel statue could be trimmed with some boughs of holly and pine at the base for the holiday. He wondered if anyone would protest its appearance. Some of the congregants had strict ideas about what was appropriate in their church and didn't mind saying so.

Carl brought out the wooden pedestal, and they lifted the angel up and balanced it on top.

"Perfect," Ben said, stepping back.

"Yeah, it does look good up there. Looks like she's smiling right down at you, don't it?" Carl stared up at the angel, his expression almost mesmerized.

It did have a powerful effect, Ben thought. He was almost unable to take his eyes off it.

Shafts of sunlight filtered through the long windows, bathing the angel in colored light. The touches of gold on the wings and robe were fairly glowing. The painted eyes and expressive face seemed animated, as if about to speak.

"Carl? Hey, fella. I've been looking all over for you."

A tall man in coveralls stood at the back of the sanctuary. He carried a bucket in one hand and a toolbox in the other. Ben guessed it was the plumber.

"Hey, Milt." Carl raised his bandaged hand in greeting. "I didn't hear the truck. We cleared away those boxes under the pipe. You can start anytime you like."

The two men walked out of the sanctuary, and Ben heard their voices fade down the hallway. He stood a moment longer with the statue. An interesting way to start the day, that was for sure. As he turned to leave the sanctuary, he felt himself smiling. Finding the crate had been like opening an unexpected gift. The statue was surely a forgotten treasure.

Mysterious and beautiful.

He hoped the congregation would approve.

BEFORE LEAVING THE HOUSE THAT MORNING, Miranda peeked into the parlor to check on their overnight guest. He was asleep on the couch in the sitting room, his feet poking out from under the quilt.

"Let him sleep," Sophie whispered, closing the door again. "He must be exhausted. It's not as if he has anywhere to go."

True enough. Though Miranda wondered if somehow in the middle of the night, he had magically regained his memory.

"Aren't you tired, too, Grandma?"

"Me? I'm fine. I'm going to make some pancakes and bacon. I promised him a good breakfast."

Sophie tied an apron around her ample middle and then cracked several eggs into a yellow bowl. Miranda watched her grandmother, marveling at her energy. Not only had Sophie been up late the night before, but she was the one who had woken up every hour to check the stranger's eyes with a flashlight.

"It's easier for me. My bedroom's on the first floor," Sophie had said when Miranda argued she should be the one to care for him. "Besides, you have work to do tomorrow. I can nap."

Miranda had a funny feeling about this— that Sophie was being protective, not wanting her granddaughter to nurse the stranger.

Did Sophie sense she found him attractive? Miranda guessed that she did. But what of it? It wasn't as if he would be around here long enough for that to matter.

Miranda filled a big mug of coffee, then headed outside with Dixie. The morning air was chilly and damp. She lifted the collar of her tan barn jacket and closed the button at her neck. Under the jacket she wore an old yellow sweater, paint-splattered jeans, and work boots. Her long thick red-gold hair was tied back in a ponytail.

She stopped as she reached the big shed where they sorted, packed, and stored the apples during the picking season. A few of the outbuildings needed fresh coats of paint before the winter set in, and she had started on the shed earlier that week. She knew that if the temperature dropped any lower, the paint wouldn't stick. She was trying to finish all the painting before the first week of December, but that looked like an impossible deadline now.

She set up her ladder and popped open the paint can. She stirred it, then poured some into the roller pan. She had been painting so much this week, her arm was sore. But she started in quickly, determined to get most of the big wall done before she went back inside for breakfast.

Miranda had been running the orchard with her grandmother for the last three years, ever since her grandfather Gus had died. Miranda had come for a visit, to help her grandparents get through the final days of Gus's life. She had ended up staying on, giving up her life in New York City, leaving behind a faltering acting career and a failed relationship.

Everyone in her family believed Miranda was making a huge sacrifice, offering to run the orchard and live alone with her grandmother in such a remote place. Miranda knew she had gotten the better part of the deal. It had been the perfect place to regroup and renew, to regain a sense of balance and even self-worth that city life and career struggles had stolen from her.

Now, though, she felt restless, at a crossroads. She couldn't help feeling that her retreat had come to a close and it was time to come out of hiding and get on with her life. Her grandmother would be all right. Miranda would make sure of that. She would find enough hired help and negotiate with her family to keep Sophie's place secure.

But where would she go? What would she do?

Returning to New York didn't seem a good idea, and setting up in Boston wasn't that enticing either. She hadn't totally abandoned acting. She had taken classes in Boston and still showed up, head shot in hand, for select auditions. There had been a call just two weeks ago for a part in a very experimental production of *King Lear*. Miranda had auditioned for the part of Cordelia and had been called back for a second reading.

It wasn't a huge role but a very good one. If she got it, it would put her back on the acting track and would be a big commitment. The play would run a few weeks in the summer on Cape Cod, then travel around the country for almost a year. Her grandmother knew about the auditions—and the consequences of Miranda winning the role—but she hadn't said a word for or against it. Only that she would miss her company. It would mean leaving the orchard . . . and leaving Greg Cassidy, the man Miranda had been seeing since September. She had mentioned the callback to Greg, though they hadn't really discussed it. But they would— soon, she promised herself. It was just that, at present, they were in a sort of holding pattern. They enjoyed spending time together and got along well, but neither had mentioned the word *commitment* yet.

Christmas was coming, a difficult time to decide anything important. The holidays were a time to put real life on hold. Miranda decided to give herself the New Year to sort things out, about Greg, about acting, about everything.

She had worked her way halfway across the wall when her rumbling stomach told her it was time for breakfast. She put the roller and pan away and started back toward the house. She could smell the pancakes and bacon as she drew closer.

Miranda walked into the kitchen and saw their houseguest seated at the table with her grandmother. He smiled at her. "Good morning."

"Good morning." She quickly looked away and poured herself a mug of coffee.

Despite his disheveled appearance—the growth of beard on his cheeks, his uncombed hair and bandaged forehead—she couldn't help noticing his good looks.

Or maybe it wasn't his looks exactly. She had been around plenty of handsome men.

It was something more, some special light in his eyes, in his smile. Some energy that connected with her, big-time.

It was probably just some "rescuer infatuation" syndrome, she decided. There must be a word for it. Maybe if you save someone's life, you automatically get a crush on them? The daytime talk shows must have covered it. She would have to check for a rerun.

She added some milk to her coffee and sat down at the table.

He met her glance and smiled. "Don't tell me . . . painting something red?"

She laughed, looking down at her hands and clothes. "How did you guess?"

"The whack on my head made me psychic. Did you get any paint on the barn?"

"It's not a barn. It's a shed," she told him. "And yes, there's plenty on the building. It's been breezy this morning."

"It's almost too late to paint anything out there. It's getting too cold," Sophie said. "You ought to just leave it, Miranda. Leave it for the spring."

"It's not that cold today. I'll see how far I get. I'm sure I can at least finish the shed."

Sophie stirred her coffee and turned to their guest. "She's stubborn. Hard worker, but once she gets her teeth into something . . ." She shook her head.

Miranda felt a flush of embarrassment; she wished her grandmother wouldn't talk about her as if she weren't in the room. Their guest, however, seemed to be enjoying Sophie's revelation. He smiled at Miranda and said, "Stubbornness can be a good thing at times. It keeps people from giving up."

"Exactly," Miranda agreed. "Edison tried ten thousand different materials before he perfected the lightbulb. Nobody called him stubborn."

"Maybe not to his face they didn't. After all, he was Edison." Sophie passed her the platter of pancakes and Miranda put a few on her plate.

She poured on some syrup and started eating. How had they gotten onto this odd subject?

"Do you remember Edison?" Sophie asked quietly.

The stranger forced a smile. "Actually, I do. Thomas Alva. Though I still don't remember my own name."

Miranda could see her grandmother felt bad now for asking. "At the hospital they called you John Doe. Should we call you that?"

"To be perfectly honest . . . I don't like the name John. But there didn't seem much point to telling the doctors that last night."

"How about Jack?" Sophie asked.

"It doesn't really matter. Anything will do. John. Jack. Whatever," he said. But Miranda could tell he didn't care to be called by either name.

"Look," she said, wanting to make him feel better, "you have a unique opportunity here. How many people get to choose their own names? Besides celebrities, I mean."

"That's true," he said, looking intrigued.

"We can start at the beginning of the alphabet. . . . How about Adam?" Sophie offered. "I think a guy named Adam met up with a gal under an apple tree once. Remember that story?"

Miranda thought her grandmother was being silly. If he was Adam . . . did that make her Eve? The image made her cheeks redden, though their visitor didn't seem to notice.

"Adam's not bad. The first man, a blank slate. He had to head out into the world empty-handed, too. A lot like my situation."

An interesting analogy. He had a way with words. Miranda was impressed.

The phone rang and Miranda rose to answer it.

Tucker barely bothered to say hello. He sounded upset. "I called the hospital last night to follow up on that John Doe. They said you took him back to the orchard. I thought you were going to call with an update."

"Sorry, Tucker. It got very late. I guess we just forgot."

"Do you think that was wise, Miranda? Taking in a complete stranger? He could be a con man. He could be dangerous. Excuse me for being so blunt, but I worry about you and Sophie being all alone out there."

"Thank you, Tucker. We appreciate that, but everything is fine here, really. I don't believe the man poses any danger." Miranda worded her reply diplomatically. She knew Tucker was just doing his job. "Did you find his car?" she asked.

"We didn't find any abandoned vehicles near the orchard—or anywhere around town, for that matter. I still can't figure out how he ended up in the middle of your place." Tucker sounded exhausted and frustrated. "How about his memory loss?" he asked. "Any progress?"

"He seems to recall information most people know. But nothing about himself. Not yet anyway."

"He can come down to the station, and I'll fingerprint him then run a computer check. We have access to a few different data banks. They cover the whole country. Anyone who's ever worked for the government, or even been a consultant, has their prints on file. We might find his identity that way. I've called a detective from the county who knows more about these things. We have a few avenues to try . . . if he's willing."

"That's great," Miranda said. "I'm sure he wants to do everything he can to find out who he is and where he belongs."

"Miranda." Tucker hesitated. "If he has a police record and is wanted for a crime, the computer will spit that out, too."

Miranda hadn't thought of that. When she didn't reply, Tucker added, "I want you to pay attention to his reaction when you suggest the fingerprinting. He might make an excuse not to come down. Or you might turn around and find out he's disappeared. Poof! Just like that. Don't be surprised."

Somehow she was sure that Adam would be fine with the prospect of being finger-printed. Then again, if he did have a criminal record, there was a good chance he didn't remember.

"I think we can get to town by noon. Does that work for you, Tucker?"

"Noon would be fine," Tucker said. "If something comes up, just call the station."

He meant if his prediction came true.

When she walked back into the kitchen, her grandmother was clearing the table and Adam stood at the sink, washing dishes. He was wielding a big soapy sponge, his sleeves rolled to his elbows. He was wearing one of her grandfather's old flannel shirts. Though Adam was tall, the shirt hung practically to his knees, and Gus's old jeans sagged on his lean frame. He didn't look the least bit dangerous.

Overriding Tucker's sensible warnings— overriding the fact that she knew firsthand looks could be deceiving—Miranda felt something deep down inside that simply told her this man was not a threat in any way . . . except perhaps to her own heart.

"That was Tucker Tulley, the police officer who came here last night," she explained. "If you want to go to the station and give them your fingerprints, he'll run a computer check. It might turn up your identity."

Adam turned to her. His dark eyes brightened. "How long does it take for them to check the prints? Did he say?"

"Tucker said the prints are run through a few different data bases—federal jobs and government contractors or consultants. Criminal records, too."

"Sounds as if that takes a while then. But it's a start."

It certainly didn't seem as if Adam was afraid of uncovering his identity. Still, Miranda felt relieved by his response.

Sophie stepped forward and took the sponge out of his hand. "I can finish up in here. You get cleaned up. I left you some towels and a plastic razor. There are more clothes in your room, too—on the chair. I know my husband's clothes don't fit very well," she added, trying to hide a smile, "but you can pick up a few things in town. Miranda will take you."

"These clothes are fine. I don't need anything more." He looked at Sophie and then at Miranda. "You've both done enough for me. I don't want to bother you anymore. If you can give me a ride to town, I'll find some help from a social service agency. Maybe stay in a shelter until I can figure things out. Someone at the hospital said that could be arranged."

Miranda knew that was the logical solution. Especially after Tucker's warnings. But she didn't want Adam to go into a shelter. But before she could say anything, her grandmother turned from the sink, looking appalled.

"No, sir. I won't hear of it." Sophie shook her head, her swirl of white hair nearly coming loose from its pins. "Miranda will take you into town, and you'll do what you need to do with the police. Then you must come back here and stay as long as you need to. We don't mind having you stay here. It's no trouble at all, is it Miranda?"

"Not at all. Honestly," Miranda told him. "Besides, it probably won't be for long. You might find out that someone is already looking for you, if not today, then maybe tomorrow."

Adam looked as if he was about to protest, then seemed to reconsider. "If I stay, I have to work. There must be some way I can help out here." He looked back at Miranda. "I don't know what kind of painter I am . . . but I can probably meet your standards."

Was he teasing her? Miranda didn't mean to smile, but couldn't help it.

"Probably," she admitted.

"All right, we have a deal," Sophie cut in. "You stay and we'll put you to work if you feel up to it."

"I do," he insisted.

"I need to change." Miranda glanced at her watch. "We'll leave in about half an hour, okay?"

He met her eyes and nodded. "I'll be ready."

Upstairs in her room, Miranda tried to change quickly, but struggled with the choice of what to wear. She settled on a blue sweater with a shawl collar, jeans, and boots. She brushed out her long hair, leaving it down, then put it back in a ponytail again. She did her usual amount of makeup for a trip to town, which was next to none. Finally, she slipped on some thin silver bracelets and a pair of earrings set with blue topaz, her own creation. Nothing she wouldn't usually wear to town, she kept telling herself, but all the while, conscious that she was going to spend time with Adam and wanted to look a bit better than usual.

She grinned at her reflection as the reality of the situation hit her. *This is so not a date,* she reminded herself. *You're taking the man to a police station to be finger-printed, remember?*

When she came back downstairs, Miranda found Adam waiting for her in the front parlor. He sat in an armchair with Dixie leaning against his leg, staring up at him adoringly. He petted her head in an absent-minded way, his expression pensive.

"Waiting long?" Miranda asked. "Sorry I was so slow."

At the sound of her voice, his expression brightened. She could tell he was surprised at the change in her appearance. She was equally surprised by his. Adam's face was smoothly shaven, his hair slicked back wet from a shower, emphasizing his rugged features, large, dark eyes, wide mouth, and strong jaw. He wore a gray pullover with a black T-shirt underneath and a pair of jeans that were oversized but not comically baggy.

She was suddenly glad there weren't any clothes around that actually fit him. That would have been a real problem.

She cleared her throat. "We'd better go. I told Tucker twelve."

"Sure. Let's go." He quickly slipped on the big parka she had found the night before.

Sophie peeked into the room. "Miranda, you had a phone call while you were upstairs. A jewelry shop in town, the Golden

Moon or something or other. I wrote down the name and number for you."

Miranda walked over and took the slip of paper. She recognized the name of the caller, Krista Mullan. A few weeks ago, they had met at a crafts fair and Krista took some of Miranda's jewelry to sell in her shop.

"Thanks, Grandma. Maybe I'll stop by while we're in town."

"All right, see you later," Sophie said.

Miranda led the way outside to the orchard's truck, and they climbed in.

"How far are we from the town?" Adam asked as they started out.

"Oh, about fifteen minutes." She headed down the private road from the house and turned onto Beach Road that led to the village.

He gazed out the window as she drove. "If I had to get lost somewhere, I sure picked a beautiful spot."

The comment made her laugh. "Yes, you did. It's very pretty here. Unspoiled. We're not too far from Boston—two hours, maybe less. Depends on your driving."

His dark brows drew together and she could see him struggling with something she had said.

"Boston. In Massachusetts," she prompted. "Do you ever remember being there?"

"Yes, I do. There's the Old North Church, where Paul Revere saw the lights in the tower that meant that the British were coming. The state house, with a gold dome roof . . . and the swan boats in the Public Garden."

She nodded, staring out at the road. "That's right. Sounds as if you know it well. Maybe you live there?"

He considered this for a moment. "No . . . I don't think so. I don't get that feeling anyway when I think about the place."

He looked out at the passing scenery. There were very few houses visible on the winding road, even in winter. The road was a tunnel through bare arching branches, fragments of blue sky visible in between. Vines twined around the old trees, hanging in clumps like decorations. Brush along the roadside grew dense and wild in the summer, but now there were only bare brown stalks.

"Did you grow up around here, Miranda?"

"Down in Connecticut. I've always loved it

here, though. My parents would bring us up around the Fourth of July, and then they'd leave us with my grandparents for a long visit. My grandmother would let us run wild. It was better than sleepaway camp."

"How did you end up here? Living with your grandmother?"

She glanced at him, surprised at all the personal questions. But maybe it was easier for him to be interested in her story right now than focus on his own. She actually didn't like being asked these types of questions much. They made her uncomfortable. Her life was almost as confusing as his was right now, she thought.

"Let's see, there were a few reasons. Mainly, because my grandfather died a few years ago and my grandmother was left alone. No one in the family wanted to help her run the orchard and she was too old to do it on her own. Everyone—my dad, my aunts—thought she should put the place up for sale. And she eventually agreed it was the most reasonable thing to do. We even packed all her things. But she didn't want to go. I could see it was breaking her heart."

He had asked a simple question and here

she was, going on and on. Delivering a Shakespearean monologue. She had to be boring him silly with the personal details.

But Adam didn't look bored. "So you volunteered to stay with her," he filled in. "That was very generous."

"It worked out for me, too. I had been living in New York and I had reached sort of a dead end there. City life wasn't working out for me, but I didn't know where else to go, what to do."

"What kind of work did you do there?"

"I was trying to make it as an actress. But I was mostly waiting tables or doing temp work in offices." She glanced at him and smiled. "I got some small parts, Off-Off Broadway, a TV commercial, a few lines in a soap opera. But I never got that big break that makes the difference."

"I guess that could wear you down."

"After a few years . . . yeah, it did. I probably wasn't thick-skinned enough. You try not to take it personally when you miss out on a part. But it's hard not to."

The cattle call auditions, the constant judgment and rejection, the fierce competition, even with friends. And boyfriends.

During most of those struggling years,

she had been in love. Miranda met Jake in an acting class when they were matched by their teacher to prepare a scene from *A Streetcar Named Desire*. The chemistry had been instantaneous. After that, they were together constantly.

They shared their work and understood each other. Or so Miranda had thought. She expected that they would marry sooner or later but had never pushed Jake for a real commitment. They had to establish their careers, he kept saying. It was foolish to make plans before then. She wasn't the type to pressure a man or lay down ultimatums. Then he left for someone else, a woman who was an attorney and married her six months later. He had been drawn to her self-confidence, he told Miranda. She knew what she wanted and went after it. Miranda guessed he meant that she was the opposite. Too nice. Too easygoing.

Well, maybe she was all that. She couldn't change herself. She didn't want to. Maybe she wasn't tough enough for acting, for city life.

It wasn't a very original plot and not one she cared to share with Adam. The betrayal had hurt her deeply and it was hard for her even now to trust men.

"Are you still involved with acting?"

"A little. I'm more selective now, though." She paused, deciding not to mention her callback or her own conflicted feelings about it. "I also make jewelry—simple pieces, my own designs. I sell a little at flea markets and shops in town, but mostly, it's for fun."

He glanced at her and smiled. "So you keep pretty busy. Running an orchard, acting, making jewelry . . . rescuing people."

She shrugged. "The rescue work is just a hobby, too. I don't think you should include it in my resumé."

"You're good at it. You might want to reconsider."

The way he looked at her made Miranda feel self-conscious and strangely happy. She fixed her eyes on the road and tried not to show her reaction.

"So, we're two hours from Boston; north or south?" he asked, changing the subject.

"Southeast. It's a fairly direct route on Highway 95, which runs north, through New England. I guess you don't remember where you were coming from?"

He sighed. "That would be too easy."

"I'll show you a map when we get home. Maybe that will jog your memory."

"Maybe," he agreed, but he didn't sound hopeful. "You would think I would have left a car somewhere around here. I couldn't have just dropped down from the sky."

"I think we can safely rule out that possibility. Tucker said the police were still looking. If you were lost and drove off onto one of the side roads around here, it might take a while for them to find it."

"I suppose that's possible." He sat staring out the window again, seeming to sink into his own thoughts. Miranda felt bad for him. She couldn't imagine being so lost, so unanchored by everything familiar in your life.

"I'm sure someone out there must be looking for you," she said. "Even if your memory doesn't return for a few days, I think we'll find out very soon who you are and where you're from."

He glanced at her, a warm look in his eyes. "There must be someone, right?"

"Yes, I'm sure there is." She smiled back, feeling that connection again, but knowing that there had to be someone—a girlfriend or even a wife—searching for him.

When they reached town, Miranda parked on Main Street in front of Village Hall, which also housed the police station.

They stopped at the front desk and gave their names to the officer on duty. Tucker soon came out to greet them and lead them back to the squad room.

He was friendly and efficient, Miranda noticed. If he still believed Adam's fingerprints might reveal a criminal history, he didn't show it. Tucker took a photo of Adam, facing forward and then sideways. Then he took his fingerprints, pressing Adam's inky fingertips one by one onto a white card.

"The prints and photo will run through different data banks, nationwide," Tucker explained. "We'll also send your photo and description to all the police stations in the state, over the Internet."

Adam sat back, wiping the dark ink off his fingers. "How long does it take for the computer search?"

"A few days. Maybe less, maybe more. Heck, you could get lucky and we could hear back in an hour. I made a note about that matchbook in your pocket. I was right about the Charles Hotel. It's a fancy place in Cambridge. The Regatta Bar is one of its restaurants. I'm going to call over there, ask if someone remembers you. I'll send them the picture, too."

"Sounds good." Adam looked encouraged. "What about a car? I guess you would have told me if you had found one by now."

"Still working on that. We've widened the search and are checking with the highway patrol. It's possible your car broke down someplace on the main roads, far from here and you hitched a ride."

"I didn't think of that," Adam admitted.

"We haven't found a missing persons report that fits your description. But that might come through today or tomorrow. From the looks of the clothes you had on last night, I would guess that you haven't been lost very long."

"Probably not," Adam agreed. "It just feels like a long time."

Tucker looked sympathetic, but when he spoke again his tone was all business. "I was talking to Roger Lester this morning. He's a county detective who works on these kinds of cases—missing persons and all that. He suggested you go public, get some news coverage. Sara Franklin, a reporter at the paper here in town, already picked up the story from the police blotter this morning. Said she would put it out on the Associated Press wire and send a copy to the TV and radio stations."

Miranda noticed Tucker watching Adam's reaction. Did he think Adam was about to bolt again? Adam did look uncomfortable. He didn't answer right away.

"What do you think?" Tucker persisted. "Want to try it?"

"It makes sense. But I feel a little odd, talking to a reporter. I don't have much to say." He shook his head. "I never thought I would end up being some believe-it-or-not news story."

"Sara is a great person," Miranda assured him. "She won't make you feel like a freak."

Adam nodded and glanced at Tucker. "I guess I can't pass up any ideas right now."

"I'll call her and give her a heads-up." Tucker called the newspaper and had a brief conversation with Sara. "She said you could drop by anytime today," he told them. "Listen, before you go, that detective gave me the name of a psychologist in Newburyport. Says he might be able to help you if your memory doesn't come back in a day or so." Tucker handed Adam a slip of paper with the doctor's name and phone number.

Adam glanced at the information and slipped it in his pocket. "Thank you. And thanks for all your help, Officer. I appreciate all you're trying to do."

"You don't have to thank me. It's my job. I hope we have some news for you soon."

"You can call the orchard if you hear anything," Miranda said. "He'll be staying with us and doing some work around the place. We can use the help for a few days."

Tucker didn't look pleased by the plan. He jotted a note in his file and then closed the folder. "Sounds like you have that all settled. I'll call you if I hear anything."

"That would be great," Miranda said, though she couldn't help hoping that it might be a while before Tucker called.

They left the police station, stepping out into the wintry air. "The newspaper office isn't far. It's just down at the end of Main Street," Miranda explained. "Want to take a walk and see the village?"

"Sure, I can use a walk," Adam agreed. "I've decided I probably wasn't in law enforcement. I don't like hanging around police stations much."

"Me, neither," Miranda admitted, falling into step beside him. "Tucker's actually a really good guy, but that sort of gets hidden when he's in cop mode."

Adam looked at her curiously. "Does everyone in this town know each other?"

"I don't know everyone," Miranda admitted. "My grandmother, though, has lived here all her life, and sooner or later everyone stops by the orchard for her apples or pies. So I guess everyone knows Sophie."

Miranda liked walking quickly, but whenever she walked with a man, she inevitably found herself slowing her natural pace. Jake had complained about her "speed-walking," and even Greg would ask if she could please slow down a little. Adam was taller, with long legs and a loose, easy stride. He seemed to travel at the same brisk pace that came naturally to her.

Miranda didn't talk much as they walked, letting Adam take in the sights. The village was decorated for the holidays, with displays in all the store windows and wreaths and bows on the gaslight street lamps. Even the parking meters were covered with red and white tape to look like candy canes. The coastal village, with its well-preserved Victorian-era architecture, was picturesque any time of year, but it looked particularly charming during the holidays, and Miranda hoped the scenery would help cheer Adam.

"Does any of this look familiar to you?"

she asked. "Maybe you came to town to meet somebody?"

He paused at the corner and looked around. "It all looks like a beautiful Christmas card, one I may have seen before. But I don't feel as if I've ever been here."

They were standing right near the Golden Moon jewelry store. "Do you mind if we stop in here a minute? I need to talk to the owner," Miranda said. "She saw some of my jewelry at a craft fair and offered to sell it in her store. So I guess I'm about to find out whether or not she did."

Adam nodded. "No problem." Miranda entered the store and he followed.

Krista Mullan stood at a counter in the back arranging some items for display. She smiled as Miranda walked in. Krista was in her mid-thirties, a few years older than Miranda, but the two women had hit it off from their first meeting. Miranda admired Krista's sense of style, from the way she dressed to the colors and displays in the shop. The Golden Moon sold a different type of jewelry from the other shops in town—arty, handcrafted items, hipper and more daring styles that one might find in Boston or even New York.

"Look who's here . . . I just called you this morning. Did you get the message?"

"My grandmother told me. I was on my way to town so I thought I would just stop in."

"I sold everything you gave me at the fair. I have a check for you. But I also wanted to order more—for the Christmas rush."

"Oh . . . that's great. Thanks." Miranda was both thrilled and a little daunted by the news. Krista and her husband, Michael, also owned jewelry shops in Newburyport and Provincetown, which meant the order could be a big one. And Christmas was less than three weeks away! "Uh . . . What exactly did you have in mind? I mean . . . How much and how fast do you need it?"

Krista laughed at her. "Take a calming breath, Miranda. We can figure this out."

Adam touched her arm and she suddenly remembered he was there. "I'm going to walk around a little outside. Meet you in a few minutes, okay?"

Miranda glanced at him. "Sure. I won't be long."

Krista watched Adam go. "Who's your friend?"

"Oh, sorry I didn't introduce you. That's Adam. . . . He's staying with us for a while."

"Cute." Krista nodded with approval then seemed all business again. "Here's what I'd like, in a week if you can do it. I can take less, of course. . . ." She pulled out a pad where she had written down some numbers and item descriptions.

Miranda stared at the list, mentally calculating what it would take to complete it. The earrings were no problem, but she wasn't sure about some of the necklaces and bracelets. "I'm really glad you want so many pieces," she told Krista, "but I'm not sure I have all the necessary materials. I'm running low on silver wire and seed pearls, as well as some of the gemstones. Let me take this home and I'll check my supplies. Can I call you tomorrow?"

"That would be fine. Oh, and here's the payment for what I sold," Krista added, handing her an envelope.

Miranda smiled, realizing she had just made her first big sale. "I'll talk to you tomorrow. Thanks again."

"Thank you, Miranda. I'm excited to be selling your work."

"I am, too. I mean, excited that you're selling it," she said honestly.

Miranda stepped outside, feeling light-headed with happiness. She glanced around for Adam. She saw him about halfway down the block, gazing into the window of a clothing store. She walked toward him, thinking they probably ought to go in and find him some new clothes.

Adam looked away from the window and smiled at her. "You look happy. Did it go well in there?"

"I'll say. She sold everything I gave her at the crafts fair last month and asked if I can make up a big order . . . and I got a check," she added with a grin. "My first real sale."

His smile widened. He looked truly pleased for her, forgetting his own problems entirely. "Congratulations. You must be very proud."

"Amazed is more the word for it."

"You're too modest, Miranda. I'm sure the jewelry is beautiful. Can I see some of it when we get back?"

She shrugged. "Of course you can. You might be seeing a lot of it if I agree to fill this order." She took out the yellow sheet with Krista's notes and looked it over again. "I'm not sure if I can do this, especially by her deadline. She needs it really quickly for Christmas shoppers."

"That is a tough deadline," he said. "But you should think it over carefully. It sounds like a good opportunity. I mean, if you want to build a business from your hobby."

That was the question, wasn't it? Adam, who didn't know her at all, had hit the nail on the head. Did she want to make a real commitment to jewelry-making? With clients and orders and deadlines, and letterhead and business cards . . . and maybe even a Web site down the road? It felt overwhelming to think about all that right now. But it appeared that she could make a go of it, with some focus and effort.

Or did she want to return to acting? And maybe even leave Cape Light?

"You're right. I need to think about it carefully . . . but not right now." She sighed and stuffed the note into her pocket. "See anything you like in the window here?"

"It's nice stuff, but I'm fine. I don't need anything new."

"Of course you do. You can't walk around in my grandfather's old clothes. You look like . . . a time traveler from nineteen sixty-two."

He struggled to keep a straight face, but couldn't quite help smiling. "Well, when you put it that way. But you have to promise you'll let me pay you back. Every penny, okay?"

"Yes, you'll pay me back, every cent. Now let's get in there. We still have to go see Sara."

Inside the store, Adam went straight to the sale rack. "How about these?" he said, holding up a pair of dark green pants.

"Um, I think there's a reason they're on sale." Miranda pointed to a small stain on the knee. "Let's try that rack," she said, steering him over to the regular-priced clothing. While Adam looked at the jeans, she picked out two shirts, a black wool sweater, and a dark blue fleece pullover she thought might suit him. Adam refused the extra items at first, but she finally persuaded him.

It felt a little odd shopping with him. It seemed so . . . personal, creating a strange sense of intimacy. *A false sense*, she reminded herself. By this time tomorrow, Adam might be gone.

They set off for the newspaper office, walking to the end of Main Street, then turning onto a street that faced the harbor. "This must be the place," Adam said as they reached the building with *Cape Light Messenger* painted in gold letters on the wide plateglass window.

"Are you all right about this?" Miranda asked, hesitating before opening the door.

"I suppose I have to be," Adam said. "But I feel a little like a tabloid freak: 'Lost Man, Can't Recall His Identity.'"

"Sara won't write it that way," Miranda promised him. "She's a first-rate reporter. I know her story will help you."

He nodded, looking tense, and held the door open for her.

The newspaper office was a large room, filled with desks, computers, and filing cabinets enclosed in a series of cubicles. Artists' drawing tables covered with marked-up layouts lined the back wall. Miranda saw Lindsay Forbes, the editor in chief, sitting at her large desk. Sara stood at her shoulder, gazing at a computer screen, while Lindsay talked on the phone.

Sara looked up and waved, then quickly walked up to meet them. She greeted Miranda with a friendly hug and extended her hand to Adam. "Hi, I'm Sara Franklin. Thank you so much for coming by."

Adam seemed to relax at her words. "Thanks for helping me out. I'll tell you whatever I can. But I really don't remember much."

Sara smiled. "That's sort of the point of the story, though, isn't it?"

Without waiting for his answer, she led them back to her desk behind a partition in the middle of the room.

Miranda had always liked Sara. She was good with people, just like her mother, Emily Warwick, who was Cape Light's mayor. Although Miranda and Sara were friends, they didn't get to see each other much, mostly because Sara worked long hours and was often out on assignments. She had surprised her family about a year ago, eloping with her longtime boyfriend, Luke McAllister. They now lived with her grandmother Lillian Warwick in Lillian's huge house on Providence Street. Sara, Miranda knew, never felt comfortable inviting her friends there—Lillian, even at her best, was difficult—so when they had the rare chance to get together, it was usually for coffee or lunch in town.

After reviewing the basic facts of Adam's appearance in the orchard, Sara asked him some direct questions then took his photo with a digital camera. When she showed them the photo on her computer screen, Adam looked relieved. "Well, at least it's not as bad as the police mug shot."

"No, it's a much better likeness," Miranda said, thinking he really was incredibly handsome.

"I'm going to work on this right away," Sara promised. "I might be able to make some late editions and tonight's TV news. We'll put it out on the wire, too, and it will go out nationally. A lot of outlets will pick up a story on amnesia," she assured him. "We'll give a contact number at the police station, and they'll check out the calls to see if they're legitimate."

Miranda couldn't help a flash of apprehension. With Adam's photo on the news and in papers all over the country, someone was bound to come forward to claim him.

"Have you ever heard of this happening to anyone?" Adam asked.

Sara thought for a moment. "As a matter of fact, there was a story in the news last year, about a man who went out to walk his dog and out of nowhere, lost his memory. It was some sort of stress disorder; I can't recall the medical term. Anyway, he wandered around for about a month and walked miles from his neighborhood. He lived on handouts and what he could find in trash cans. People who saw him thought he was homeless. The police and his family were looking for him the entire time. Just by chance, someone he knew recognized him one day and brought him home."

Adam looked a little dismayed. "A month is a long time to be lost," he said. But I guess I'm a lot more fortunate than that poor guy. After a month with the Potters, I'll be too spoiled to go back to my real life."

Miranda laughed, secretly touched by his compliment. Sara glanced at her then, and something in her expression made Miranda blush. She was suddenly sure that Sara knew: somehow Sara had sensed that spark she felt with Adam.

"Thanks for stopping by. I'll call you, Miranda," Sara said with another meaningful look. "Maybe we can get together for lunch or something next week?"

"Absolutely. Call me and we'll figure out a time to meet."

When they finally left the newspaper office, it was almost two o'clock. Even though they had eaten a late breakfast, Miranda was hungry. "Want to grab some lunch before we head back?" she asked Adam. "The Clam Box diner down the street is okay."

"Maybe another time. I think we ought to

get back to the orchard so I can help you do some more painting. I'm still feeling guilty about this new wardrobe."

It wasn't much, she wanted to remind him. She could well afford it today, with her surprise payment from the Golden Moon. But she could tell that working and doing something productive would make him feel better.

"I think we got a lot accomplished," she said. "The word will be out soon, and someone you know will see the news article, or some police station will put things together."

"I hope so. I guess we've done all we can do for now. Except wait."

That was all she would be doing, she knew. She had known him less than twenty-four hours, and already she dreaded the moment when Adam would find out who he was and leave Cape Light. He had shown up like an unexpected gift, and suddenly her life had gotten brighter, more exciting. Even though he had been kidding around, just the idea of him staying a month at the orchard had made her deeply happy.

Get a grip, Miranda, she told herself. *He's got a life of his own, and you happen to have a boyfriend.* Okay, she resolved, she could be friendly to him, and even kind, but any other feelings would be inappropriate and pointless. More than pointless—totally ridiculous.

They headed back to the orchard, each lost in their own thoughts. Finally Adam turned to her. "Something Sara Franklin said made me wonder. What if my memory loss wasn't caused by the concussion? What if I lost it before that?"

"What do you mean?"

"When Sara was talking about that other case of amnesia, she said it was caused by psychological stress. It made me wonder if that happened to me, too. What if I was actually running away from something and the place I belong is a place I don't want to return to?"

"I suppose that's possible, too."

Miranda had never believed Tucker's suspicious scenarios about Adam's background. This was a bit different, though. The idea that Adam was running from something or someone was unsettling, and she didn't quite know what to think about it.

CHAPTER THREE

"I DON'T USUALLY LIKE CURRY, BUT THIS IS YUMMY. The spice is just right." Betty Bowman nodded and chewed, her eyes half-closed and her expression dreamy.

Molly dipped her fingertip in the sauce on her plate and tasted it again. "It's not too hot? You know how people around here feel about spices."

"You've been educating their palates, Molly. It's a public service to add these exotic dishes to your menu." Betty reached for a second curried shrimp kabob. "I'm going to have another."

"Save room for the spinach puffs. They should be done in a minute."

"I'm going to charge by the hour for these taste-testing sessions. One lunch break here and I need about five extra sessions with my personal trainer."

Molly knew Betty wasn't serious. She loved coming in to taste and review new dishes for the shop's menu. Molly had come to rely on Betty's critiques, which could usually predict which dishes would be popular and which would be duds.

The phone rang and Molly answered it. Another call, asking if she could do a party this month. Molly had to politely refuse. Willoughby Fine Foods and Catering was booked solid for December straight through New Year's Day.

"I can't believe you're turning down business." Betty rolled her eyes. "You ought to hire more help. You could probably be doing twice as many parties this season if you had more help here."

Normally Molly welcomed Betty's advice. Betty had always been her mentor as well as her friend; she had been the first person to encourage Molly to start a business of her own. Betty was also the most successful

businesswoman in town, the owner of Bowman Real Estate, and Molly had always admired that, hoping she could someday come
close to Betty's success.

But this morning, the casual comment
rubbed her the wrong way.

"It's not just waitstaff at the parties. I can
always find people to do that. It's all the prep
work and setup. There's no one but me to
oversee and manage everything. I can't be
ten places at once."

A timer buzzed. Molly stepped over to the
oven and took out a tray of spinach and
cheese puffs, slipped them onto a dish, and
set it down on the table.

Betty touched her hand. "I'm sorry. I didn't
mean to criticize. Most people in your position are complaining because they don't get
enough calls. My office is just dead right
now. We won't have any signs of life until the
end of January. If then. The real estate mar-
ket is completely flat up here."

"It will come back," Molly promised her. "It
always does."

"In my lifetime, I hope." Betty laughed and
leaned back in her chair. "Don't spread it
around, Molly, but I almost don't care. I've
sold every house in town, some of them

twice. I've seen every basement, attic, furnace and crawl space in town. I've been at it a long time, pal."

"And you're great at it. The best," Molly reminded her.

"Yes, but . . . I'm getting bored." Betty shrugged. "The problem is, I don't know what else I can do. I'm still way too young to retire, thank heavens. But it's hard to make a change at my age. It's hard to start over in something new. And what would I do anyway? Real estate is my life. Unfortunately," she added, making a face.

"How are the puffs?" Molly asked.

"Very good. Seem creamier . . . don't tell me. You added a touch of cream cheese? And a dash of nutmeg?"

Molly nodded. Betty couldn't cook her way out of a take-out container, but she had infallible taste buds.

"Aren't you having any?" Betty looked over at Molly's dish.

"Curry disagrees with me lately. I'm not really hungry."

Betty peered into Molly's dish. "Rice pudding?"

"I just felt like it." Betty was watching her, a curious light in her eyes.

Molly hadn't planned to tell anyone, not before she told Matt. Suddenly, she just couldn't help it. "The thing is . . . the funny thing is . . . whenever I get pregnant, I crave rice pudding. . . ."

"Pregnant?" Betty gasped. "You mean . . . Do you know for sure?"

Molly nodded. "I did a home test last night. Actually, I did about three of them."

"That's wonderful!" Betty leaned over and gave Molly a tight, quick hug. "Let's see, December, January, February . . ."—Betty counted down the months out loud—"that means the baby will come some time around August?"

"Probably more like July. I think I've been in denial about this situation at least a month. Hence, my clothes suddenly not fitting." Molly tugged on the waistband of her jeans, showing Betty how tight they were.

Betty's happy expression changed. She rested her hand on Molly's shoulder. "What's wrong? You don't seem happy. Don't you feel well?"

"Oh, I feel okay, I guess. It's just that I've been working so hard these past few years to build this business, to really do something with my life . . . and now I'll have to just put that all on hold." Molly looked down at the bowl of rice pudding and wiggled the spoon around. "Don't get me wrong, I loved having Lauren and Jill. But I thought I was done with all that. Changing diapers and watching feeding schedules is not what I was planning. I know new mothers are supposed to be bubbling over with joy but . . ."

"I hear you. It's sort of hit you out of the blue and seems like a major detour."

Betty was a true friend. Molly knew she could be totally honest with her. "Yes, a major detour. It's like I fell asleep on a train and just woke up at the wrong stop. This is so not where I planned on going." Molly sighed. "How am I going to run this business with a new baby? I just won't be able to do it. After all this work, I'll have to give it up."

"Of course you can do it!" Betty leaned over and patted her arm. "You can chew gum, change a diaper, and close a deal at the same time. You're not a man," Betty reminded her.

Molly had to laugh at that logic. It certainly rang true. Still, she wasn't convinced.

"I couldn't do anything while I was raising Lauren and Jill," she said. "Nothing worthwhile, anyway. Even when they went into school full-time, it was still a struggle to manage working and a child-care schedule."

"This is different. You're the boss. You don't have anyone to answer to if you need to be late or work from home. You can delegate and be less hands-on," Betty suggested. "That's the only way to grow your business anyway, Molly. You're certainly ready for it."

"How can I delegate when there's no one here who could manage things for me?"

Molly had always had a vision of her business and how she wanted things to be run. So far, she had been a very hands-on manager. Although she had finally hired more help to cook and run events for her, she still did a good share of both.

"I don't know," she continued. "I think I'd be better off just bailing out all together. This place will be chaos if I'm not around to tell everyone what to do."

"Typical control-freak management style. We have to work on that." Betty shook her head. "That's why babies take nine months. So you can figure this stuff out."

"I guess." Molly rested her chin on her palm and took another bite of pudding.

It was nice to have a friend like Betty, older and wiser. Someone you could talk to totally honestly, without fear of being judged. Molly did feel a bit better getting it all off her chest.

"Aren't you forgetting something, Molly? You basically raised Jill and Lauren on your own after Phil walked out. Now you have Matt. Doesn't that make a difference?"

"Matt doesn't know yet."

Betty's eyes widened again. "What do you mean he doesn't know? You've got to tell him. It's not fair."

Molly nodded glumly. "Yes, I know I do. I just found out last night, though, for sure. But I have to tell him." *Even if it's still hard to say the words out loud,* she added to herself.

"Promise me that you'll tell him tonight." Betty met her eyes and wouldn't look away.

Molly hesitated for a moment, though in her heart she knew it was the right thing to do. The only thing to do. "I promise."

"Don't worry. It will be better once you tell him."

"I hope so," Molly said.

"SO YOU'LL CALL BACK MRS. LARSEN AND GIVE her the price for the canapés?" Molly scanned the list she had scribbled. It was 4:48 P.M., and she had promised herself that she would leave the shop by five; she didn't want to be completely exhausted and harried when she talked to Matt. "And make sure the florist can get those orchids for the Finney party, though why she's insisting on orchids at this time of year, I'll never know."

"She doesn't like poinsettias," her assistant, Rita, said as she stirred a béchamel sauce. "Don't worry, I've got it covered."

"Oh, and we need to know if the lasagnas for the Gifford office party are vegetarian or meat. Lacey Gifford never said when she left that order."

"I'll call her." Rita glanced up from the pot. "Molly, go home already. I promise that I can handle things for the next sixty minutes."

"Okay," Molly said, putting on her coat and hat. "Thanks, Rita. I appreciate you closing up."

"No problem," Rita told her.

Still, Molly's feet dragged as she left the shop. She hesitated for a moment, wondering if she should ask Rita to start on the pastries for Mrs. Cantwell's order, then realized she couldn't. Rita had kids, too; she couldn't possibly stay late. *And I am procrastinating*, Molly realized. *Trying to put off the inevitable when I need to take charge of the situation.*

So on the drive home, she practiced telling Matt that she was pregnant.

"Honey? I have something to tell you. It's important . . ."

Nope. Sounded too ominous. Like she banged up the car.

"Honey? I have some great news."

Not quite. Sounded a little like she won a sweepstakes.

"Matt . . . you'll never guess. I'm going to have a baby."

Molly reached for a cheerful note. She almost made it, too.

It shouldn't be too hard. She would find a quiet moment when the girls weren't around talking nonstop and interrupting every minute. And she would tell him.

She tried to think optimistically. Matt would be surprised but happy and seeing him that way would make her feel happy, too. *Right?*

"HELLO," MOLLY CALLED AS SHE WALKED INTO THE house. "Anybody home?"

There was no answer but rock music blasted from the family room, the beat from the speakers so strong the entire floor was vibrating.

Molly walked to the back of the house and found Jillian and her friends, leaping about, twisting, twirling, and giggling.

"Hi, Mom." Jill waved. "We're practicing a dance routine for the school talent show. Remember?"

Molly didn't quite but knew she must have given her permission for the gathering at some point. "Oh sure . . . right. Looks great, girls. I wish I had that energy."

That comment at least was sincere.

"Where are your sisters?" Molly shouted to Jill over the music. "Are they home?"

"Amanda is upstairs, studying for a test."

With this racket going on? The poor thing. Amanda had started wearing earplugs so she could concentrate. Molly wondered if she should buy one of those heavy-duty noise-blocking headsets for her as a Christmas gift. The kind the workers on airport runways used.

"How about Lauren? Did she call at least?"

"She has a game, remember?"

Molly nodded, wondering how she could have forgotten the basketball game. She liked to watch Lauren play whenever possible. She felt awful about missing this one, but she had so much on her plate lately that she simply couldn't keep track of everything.

She went into the kitchen and started dinner. Herb-grilled chicken from her shop and string beans. She also made garlic mashed potatoes, which didn't look that great on her hips, but the girls loved them dearly. Besides, she told herself, garlic was filled with antioxidants; that made the dish healthy, if not dietetic.

Just as she started mashing potatoes, she heard someone knocking on the back door. *Brilliant timing,* she thought.

It was the contractor who had been working on their house. "Hey, Mrs. Harding," he shouted over the music. "We just stopped by to finish up that installation down in the basement."

"Now? I was just making dinner."

"Sorry about that. I called to give you a heads-up. Didn't your husband tell you?"

"No, he didn't. He must have forgotten." Matt could be so absentminded sometimes. He was so busy, worrying about so many people everyday, Molly really couldn't blame him. But it would have been nice if he had told her about this sneak attack from their contractor.

The contractor's helpers, carrying large bales of cottony material, stepped past her, heading for the basement.

"Do you think you could do this some other time . . . like on the weekend or something?" Molly was shouting back at him because of all the racket in the next room, but she tried to keep a pleasant tone. "We're sort of busy here tonight."

"What? Sorry, didn't catch that . . . First door on the left, Jack, just go straight down," he shouted to the worker. He turned to Molly, cupping his ear with his hand.

"I said, do you think you could please come back on the weekend? Please?"

"Oh, I get ya." He nodded then shook his head. "Sorry, no can do. I just started a big job down in Hamilton. It's sort of now or never. I don't know when I can make it back this way. Meanwhile, your heating bills are going sky high, Mrs. Harding. We're getting into the dead of the winter, know what I mean?"

"Good point," Molly conceded. "Go ahead down then. Thanks for remembering us."

She hoped they didn't make too much noise. That cottony stuff didn't look very noisy. It reminded her of a fluffy blanket and how tired she felt. She felt as if she could just close her eyes and fall asleep right now. Anywhere. That part of being pregnant she remembered.

She forced herself to stay alert. With the school dance group in full throttle, it wasn't all that difficult.

Then the noise from downstairs started, an erratic buzzing sound followed by a *boom-boom-boom.* Like little gunshots. Molly guessed that must be some kind of electric nail gun. It made her jump a bit, even when she expected it.

She returned to her cooking and pulled out the fixings for a green salad. She was deep in thought about her pregnancy, tearing lettuce leaves to the beat, when Matt snuck up behind her and planted a kiss on the back of her neck.

"Ahh!" Molly jumped with fright.

"Oh . . . sorry I scared you, honey. You just look so cute, I couldn't resist."

She turned in the circle of his arms and gave him a kiss hello. "Sorry, I'm just a little on edge."

He smiled down at her. "What's up? Anything happen at the shop?"

She shook her head. "Nothing out of the

ordinary. I'm insanely busy, but that's what you want this time of year, right? I'd be complaining if I wasn't."

"Yes, you probably would be." He stepped away and poured himself a glass of water. "What's with all the noise around here?"

"Which do you mean? The target practice in the basement? Or the disco divas?"

"Oh, I know about Bud. He's here for the insulation, right?"

"It was now or never, he said."

"I meant the music." Matt pointed to the family room.

"Jill's in a dance group. They're auditioning tomorrow for the school talent show." She glanced at the clock. "Don't these girls need to go home and have dinner?"

As if on cue, Jill popped her head into the kitchen. "Mom, could me and my friends order some food? Like tacos or something? Sidney and Karen can stay until eight thirty. Their parents said it was okay."

Eight thirty? They were going to be listening to that noise for . . . another two hours?

"Great. Why didn't you ask me? Aren't I a parent?"

Matt glanced at Molly then turned to Jill. "I know you want to practice longer, but you should have asked your mom first if it was okay."

"Oh . . . right. Sorry." She looked up at Molly with pleading eyes. "Is it okay, Mom?"

"Now she asks me," Molly mumbled under her breath. Jill was hot, sweaty, and desperate looking. Molly knew she would be disappointed if her group wasn't chosen. "Yes, it's okay. It's fine." She handed Jill a take-out flyer. "Here's the menu. Just order what you want."

"Thanks, Mom." Jill grabbed the flyer and vanished.

"Molly, is something wrong? You don't seem like yourself tonight." Matt was studying her, as if she were a patient he was trying to diagnose.

Molly let out a long sigh. *Should I tell him now?* she wondered. *Who knows when I'll have another opportunity.*

"Hi, everybody. Guess what? We totally whipped Winston. Katrina Newland scored twenty-five points. She was like, so hot. Now we're in second place."

Lauren swept into the house from the side door, talking nonstop and simultaneously cruising the room for anything edible. Molly imagined dinosaurs roaming the primeval forests in much the same manner as her voracious teenage daughters. Sweeping by the salad, Lauren picked out a handful of cucumber slices. Then stopped at the fruit bowl and picked up a banana, consuming it in three large bites.

"Second place? That's great." Matt was impressed. "How did you do?"

"The coach started me. I scored ten points and had some awesome passes. And a steal . . . it was great."

The coach started her? How many times had Molly sat through one of those games, balancing on a hard wooden bleacher for hours, just to see Lauren on the court for two minutes of play? She must have felt bad with no one there to cheer her moment of glory.

"A steal, wow. Honey, I'm so sorry I missed your game."

Lauren shrugged. "That's okay, Mom. The season just started."

Molly nodded, still feeling she'd screwed up. "Why don't you run up and take a shower before we eat? You have time."

Lauren disappeared, and Molly cut some more cucumber slices. Matt slipped up beside her and put his arm around her shoulders. "It's okay if you miss one game here and there, Molly. Nobody's perfect."

"I know, but the coach never starts her. She never had a steal before." She turned to him, her eyes filling with tears.

"Molly? Are you crying?" Matt's voice was filled with disbelief. "Because you missed Lauren's game?"

Molly sniffed and looked up at him. She knew that the extra hormones whizzing around in her body were making her all crazy and emotional. She just couldn't help it.

"It's not just the game. It's . . ."

Boom-boom-boom. The tack gun fired in a long series and then was followed by the whir and buzzing of a saw. It sounded as if the men were working right under their feet.

Molly looked around, then pulled Matt, by his shirt, over to the pantry—the huge pantry she had always wanted and had designed herself for her new kitchen. "Just come here a second, will you? I just want some privacy. . . ."

He looked confused but followed her into the closet, where she closed the door. He stared down at her, an amorous light in his eyes. "Hmmm, this is cozy. Very creative." He slipped his arms around her waist and kissed her neck. "Did you read about this in some women's magazine or something?"

Men . . . when they get home, they only think of one thing. Well, three things, if you include dinner and the remote.

"Matt, wait a second." She pulled back and looked up at him. "I have to tell you something."

"Go ahead, I'm listening." He leaned forward and pressed a kiss to her temple.

"I'm going to have a baby." Molly suddenly lost her voice and the words came out in a whisper. Yelling over the music all night had made her hoarse, she realized.

Matt pulled back. "What did you say?"

"I said, I'm going to have a baby. I'm pregnant."

She stared up at his shocked expression. He didn't answer for a long moment, but she felt him squeeze her tight.

"Wow! I can't believe it!"

"Believe it," she said quietly.

"Are you sure? I mean, really sure?"

She nodded. "Three home pregnancy tests all turned blue."

"Blue! Wow . . . Does that mean it's going to be a boy?"

He looked so serious for a moment, she didn't realize he was teasing her.

"Molly, I'm a doctor, remember? Of course I know you can't tell the gender like that. It's wonderful enough to hear it's a baby . . ." He pulled her close and kissed her deeply. "Oh, honey, this is such great news. I never dreamed we'd have a baby together."

"Neither did I," Molly answered honestly. He was so very happy. She had expected that he would be, but seeing it was different. At least one of them was over-the-top thrilled.

"I wonder what the girls will say? I can't wait to tell them."

The girls! She had almost forgotten that part. She knew they would be happy, too, but she just didn't feel up to it tonight. "Can we wait on that a little while? Telling you has been hard enough. I don't think the five of us will fit in here."

Matt laughed, and she could tell he didn't understand her reservations.

"I just want to wait until I see a doctor," she added.

"Okay, whatever you like. Let's get out of here. It's getting stuffy."

Just as he opened the door and they

stepped back into the kitchen, Molly spotted Amanda. She looked up from the newspaper she had been reading at the kitchen table.

"Hello? What were you guys doing in the closet?"

Molly felt her face go red. Matt laughed, looking equally embarrassed.

"I was helping Molly put some groceries away . . . and the door closed behind us." He glanced at Molly for backup.

She didn't dare look at him. Her darling husband couldn't keep a secret if his life depended on it. She had a feeling the girls would know before the night was out.

A few hours later, after the dance troupe had exhausted themselves, and Bud, the contractor, and his merry crew had thoroughly insulated the entire foundation, and their three daughters had each retreated to their separate rooms upstairs, Molly found the profound silence in the house almost deafening.

Matt had nearly slipped a few times during dinner, but miraculously, their secret was still safe. And all she could think about now.

She toted a basket of laundry into the family room and plunked down on the couch near Matt, who was in his reading chair, engrossed in a medical journal.

She always thought he looked awfully cute in his reading glasses. Now, though, it just reminded her that they weren't young. Not that old . . . but still, not really young. How could they be having a baby?

"Molly . . ." Matt looked up from his journal and put it aside. "I've been thinking about your big news all night, honey. I have to say, you don't seem that excited about it. Is there something wrong? Something you're not telling me that worries you?"

He meant something amiss medically. It made sense that he would think that way; he was a doctor.

Molly shook her head. "I feel fine . . . except for being tired and sort of cranky . . . and way too old for this."

"Old? You're not old. Women are having babies at your age all the time. And even older, well into their forties—their first babies, too. Why, you're an old pro at this. You won't have any trouble at all."

Molly's eyes widened. "See, you just said it yourself. You said I was an *old* pro."

"Molly, you know what I meant. Don't be silly."

"I'm not being silly. Our girls, my daughter

and yours, are going to college next fall," she reminded him.

"Well, that may be true, but I don't feel too old for a new baby. Look around, honey. We have this huge house now. It's going to feel very empty once Amanda and Lauren go away to school. A new baby is just the thing to liven things up. Come to think of it, I hope it's twins."

Molly stared at him, unable to find the words to respond. She burst out crying, tears running down her cheeks. "Do twins run in your family?" she sobbed. "You never told me that!"

She could see Matt was confused at her reaction. He still didn't get it. "Molly . . ." He moved over to the couch and put his arms around her. "What is going on? I just don't get it. Aren't you happy about the baby? I certainly am. I think it's the best news I've heard since you agreed to marry me."

Molly didn't know what to say, how to start.

He was so happy, happy enough for the both of them. She wasn't sure he would ever get it, even if she did try to explain.

She took a deep breath and forced a reasonable tone into her voice. "Matt, I'm glad that you're happy. I know I should feel the same. But it's different from when I had the other two. I feel as if I'm at a completely different stage of my life now. I worked hard to get here, too. While Lauren and Jill were growing up, everything was for them, for their welfare. Then, when I met you, I finally started having a life for myself. Using my . . . potential . . ."

"I understand all that," he assured her.

"But after all my hard work, it just feels like I'm being forced to go backward. Diapers, formula, feeding schedules . . . Been there, done that. I just can't see myself, sitting at the sandbox again, zoning out."

Matt softly stroked her hair. "Molly . . . it will be different this time. Completely different. We can afford help, a live-in nanny if you want. We can even pay someone to zone out at the sandbox."

Molly appreciated Matt's efforts to understand her feelings. It was true that they had the means to hire help, even a live-in nanny. But that wasn't the solution for her.

"Look," she said. "I know a lot of people put their children in day care so they can work. I know a lot of people have no other choice. But it seems to me that since we have the means for me to stay home with a baby, it wouldn't be right to pay someone else to take care of him or her all day. I'm sorry, I'm still old-fashioned. I don't want to pay someone to raise my child—to hear their first word or help them learn how to walk. What sense does that make?"

Matt sat looking at her, considering her words and her dilemma. "All right. I get your point. But why don't we try to table the big decisions for now and just focus on the happy news?"

It was more or less Betty's advice. Don't panic. You have nine months to figure it out.

Matt was so happy about the news— happier than she ever expected—she didn't want to ruin this moment for him. Even though it felt as if he hadn't really heard a word she'd said.

She sighed and rested her head on his strong, warm shoulder. "I'm happy, too. Honestly. I never expected to have a baby with you, Matt, but now that it's happened, I know it will be a great thing for us. A real blessing in our lives."

She wasn't just saying it. She loved Matt with all her heart and was thrilled to be carrying his child. At least, when she could stop thinking about how the baby would turn her present life upside down.

Matt kissed the top of her head. "Don't fret, Molly. You'll see. Everything is going to be just fine."

Molly didn't answer. She wanted to believe him. But he was so blindly optimistic, and she was a realist. She would keep a lid on her real feelings for now if that's what Matt wanted. But she couldn't deny her apprehensions forever. Even for her husband's sake.

THE STRANGE SOUND WOKE HER FROM A DEEP sleep. Miranda sat up in bed, listening. She heard it again—someone calling out. She couldn't make out the words, but realized it must be Adam.

She grabbed her robe and ran downstairs barefoot. Moonlight cast blue shadows in the empty rooms. She found her way to the back parlor where Adam lay in bed, groaning and shouting in his sleep.

"Adam?" She leaned over and shook his shoulder. "Wake up. You're having a dream."

He gasped, waking with a start. Then he jumped up and grabbed her. His hands dug into her shoulders, and he held her as if defending himself, about to push her down.

"Adam, it's me. Let go!" She pushed back, struggling against his strength, but he held on.

Suddenly, he pulled back and released her, staring at her with wild eyes.

"Miranda . . . I'm sorry."

She didn't move at first, just waited for her own pulse to return to normal. She was certain that he hadn't meant to hurt her.

Adam turned away from her, as if ashamed, and walked over to the window. He stood there silently, gazing out into the night. A full moon rose high in the winter sky and lit the room, giving everything inside the parlor a soft silvery glow. Miranda could see Adam running a hand through his thick, dark hair. She crossed the room and sat down on the edge of his bed. "It's okay," she said. "You obviously had a nightmare."

"Yeah, a bad one."

She reached over and touched his arm. "What was it about? Maybe there's something you were remembering from your past."

He sighed and sat down next to her. "It did

feel real. More like remembering something that actually happened to me than just a dream," he said. "It was so vivid. Everything was in that kind of high-relief you only get in dreams—or bizarre movies. And it wasn't good." She felt a shudder ripple through him. "I was running behind these buildings. I felt as if I was searching for a hiding place, and I was desperately scared. It looked like maybe a warehouse or a factory. It was nighttime, very dark. There were gunshots." His voice broke and he hesitated for a moment before continuing. "*I* was shooting a gun. I saw a man fall by the side of a car. Then I was running away, carrying a big canvas bag. I zipped it open and it was full of money."

Miranda felt him sitting tensely beside her, waiting for her to respond, expecting her to draw away. "It was just a dream, a nightmare," she said, trying to convince herself. "It doesn't mean anything."

"What if I was remembering something I really did? What if I'm . . . a criminal?"

"You aren't," she said. "You couldn't live like that, Adam. You're not a criminal. I just know."

He turned and faced her, his expression softening. "You can't possibly know that.

You've only known me . . . two days. But it's nice to hear you say it."

It was true. She barely knew him and what she did know was under the most bizarre circumstances possible. Still, she had a strong feeling about the kind of person he was.

He reached out and touched her, his hand resting gently on her shoulder. "I didn't hurt you before, did I? When I grabbed your arms?"

She shook her head. She couldn't speak. The soft light from the window cast his face in shadows. His dark eyes seemed large and bright. They captured her gaze and held it. He cupped her cheek. "I'm not sure of anything right now. What's real. What isn't. Maybe you're the dream. You . . . and this place. And the other is reality."

He leaned forward and she was sure he was going to kiss her—at that moment she *wanted* him to kiss her—but he pulled back. "I-I'm sorry," he said.

She didn't answer, couldn't. She felt as if she could barely breathe.

"I—" He hesitated, searching for words. "I need to find out who I am, where I came from. Until then—"

"I understand." She wasn't sure if she was

disappointed or relieved. She was, after all, seeing Greg, she reminded herself. And she certainly didn't need to add to Adam's confusion. She got to her feet. "I'm going back upstairs. I'll see you in the morning."

He nodded. "I think I'll stay up and read for a while. No sense in trying to fall asleep right now."

Did he mean because of the nightmare . . . or because of their almost-kiss? Miranda didn't dare ask.

She turned and headed up to her room. She passed her grandmother's door and heard Sophie's deep, even breathing, feeling grateful that Adam's cries hadn't woken her, too.

Settled back under her covers, Miranda stared up at the ceiling. Adam's confession disturbed her. Was his dark dream a memory? Or perhaps not an exact memory but something that held some truth about him? She knew she wanted it to be a dream. She didn't want him to have a dark past. But maybe he did. Maybe his real life was nothing like the way he seemed when he was with her.

Would she still care for him if he wasn't a "good" person? Would her feelings matter at all once his real life caught up with them? Or perhaps, she mused, the real question was: even if she learned the worst, would she ever be able to make herself *stop* caring about him?

CHAPTER FOUR

"REVEREND? SORRY TO BOTHER YOU. THERE'S something happened that I think you ought to know about."

Carl Tulley stood in the doorway of Ben's office. He had just arrived at church to start his workday. His green parka was zipped up to his chin, a gray knit cap pulled down low over his forehead, and thick wool gloves covered his big hands.

Ben stood with his coat on, his hat in his hand. He was on his way out to a monthly meeting of the local clergy and had come to his office early this morning to answer a few calls and e-mails before he set out.

"Come in, Carl. What's going on?"

Considering Carl's background, Ben knew it could be anything from problems with the law to the assorted ailments that plagued Carl's battered body. The man had been through so much and taken care of himself so little, it was a wonder he was fit for work at all.

"It's my hand, see?" Carl pulled off a glove and held out the hand that had been bandaged for the past few days. Ben could see the vague outline of the cut that had been stitched by Dr. Harding. The stitches had melted away to leave a neat, thin scar. Other than that, it looked fine.

"I don't see anything wrong," Ben confessed.

"Yeah, well, that's just it. I go to change the bandage last night, and there it was. All healed, good as new."

Ben still didn't get the man's meaning. "Why is that so surprising? You saw Dr. Harding, and he stitched the cut. Why wouldn't it be healed by now?"

"You saw me yesterday, trying to move them boxes. It was sore as anything. You said yourself that it might be infected and I ought to see the doctor again."

Ben remembered that now. "Yes, I did. Well . . . maybe it wasn't as bad as you thought. Maybe it just felt sore in the morning for some reason."

Carl shook his head. "No, sir. I looked underneath the bandage yesterday, and it was all red and swelled up, sort of oozing around the cut. I called Dr. Harding and was supposed to go in there today."

Ben didn't know what to say. He was glad Carl's hand had healed quickly but wasn't sure why Carl seemed so in awe of the situation. Carl had never talked much about any of his injuries. He wasn't the type to go on this way even if his hand fell off completely.

"I'll tell you what I think," Carl went on, "what I know, in my gut. I say it was the angel. I knew it the minute I touched it. I felt the power but I didn't say anything."

Ben couldn't believe what he had just heard. Was this really Carl Tulley talking? For a moment, Ben wondered if the man was mentally sound. Perhaps he'd had a minor stroke? But Carl looked and sounded perfectly normal. In fact, he sounded completely sincere.

"I don't understand, Carl. What are you talking about?"

"The healing power. Of the angel. Be honest, Reverend. I won't tell nobody. You must have felt it when we picked up the statue, or when you were cleaning it. I saw the look on your face. You can tell me the truth. I'm no snitch."

Ben was confounded. The angel had affected him emotionally, but that was to be expected. It was a fine and unusual piece of art.

Had he felt any special power? Anything supernatural? No, he could honestly say he had not.

He summoned a serious, respectful expression. "Carl, if that was your experience, if you had some special feeling while handling the statue, then who am I to contradict you? I think the statue is unique and quite beautiful. Personally, though, I didn't feel anything unusual at all."

Except that his lower back hurt a bit from moving the heavy crate. But he didn't want to sound as if he was making light of Carl's experience.

Carl didn't answer. He looked down to the floor, his cap in hand. Ben saw he was disappointed by his answer.

"Perhaps your hand was doing better than you thought," Ben suggested.

Carl shrugged. "Maybe it was. Sure, that must be it." He held up his hand again and looked at it. "It was coming along quicker than I thought."

He met Ben's gaze for an instant. "All right. Just thought I'd let you know. I better start work now."

Ben smiled gently at him, but felt unsettled by the exchange. It had taken a lot for Carl Tulley to make that unusual confession. Carl had looked to him for validation, but he honestly hadn't felt any strange power while handling the statue.

Ben checked the time. He was running late. He headed for the sanctuary to retrieve a folder he had left on the pulpit. He pushed open one heavy wooden door and walked in. The sanctuary didn't get much light at this time of day. Dim and shadowy, a few pale yellow beams filtered through the stained glass windows on one side of the church, the side where the angel statue stood, up near the altar.

Backlit by beams of light, it did look mysterious. Ben stood for a moment at the top of the center aisle and gazed at it. Could Carl's story have any credence at all?

No, of course not. It was Carl's imagination, a wishful-thinking sort of thing.

It was also exactly the opposite of what Ben would expect from their church sexton, a man who had been tried and convicted of second-degree murder, who had spent fifteen years in prison and many years after, living on the streets, a homeless drifter.

Carl was not exactly a warm and fuzzy character. And that was exactly what made his confession even harder to brush aside as some fantasy.

Ben looked up at the angel's face, her expression smooth as a placid lake, revealing nothing.

No, it couldn't be possible. What in the world was he thinking?

He found his folder on the pulpit and walked quickly down the center aisle to the door. He didn't look back at the angel again, determined not to give it another thought.

EARLY THE NEXT MORNING, MIRANDA SAT IN THE cottage, comparing Krista's list with her own stock of supplies—beads and gemstones and pearls, silver wire and clasps, crimp and spacer beads. There wasn't enough

time to reorder the things she was out of—
labradorite beads, for example. She wouldn't
be able to make the necklace that combined
black opals, rainbow moonstones, and
labradorite. Maybe Krista would accept a
substitution. She did have extra garnet. Miranda began a list of her own. She could definitely make the earrings, more than half of
the bracelets, and a few of the necklaces as
well. She hoped it would be enough.

Twenty minutes later, when Miranda returned to the house for breakfast, Adam was
already at the table, sipping coffee and reading the newspaper.

"Morning," he said, looking pleased to
see her.

"Good morning," Miranda replied. She
was keenly conscious of the night before, of
the way he had held her and of that moment
when they had almost kissed. Was he thinking about it, too?

Her grandmother stood at the counter,
cracking eggs into a bowl. She glanced at
Miranda over her shoulder. "I feel more snow
coming today. I feel it in my bad knee and I
could smell it in the air when I let Dixie out."

Her grandmother's sense of smell and her
famous knee rivaled any forecast made with

the most high-tech, sophisticated equipment. Miranda peered out the kitchen window. The sky was gray and heavy. They probably would get snow.

Miranda poured herself a mug of coffee and sat at the table opposite Adam. "I'm going to call the Golden Moon and start on their order today. But I've got a few hours before they open. How would you feel about working inside today?"

"Painting again?"

She nodded and sipped her coffee. "One of the other outbuildings. It's a guest cottage. It's not properly set up yet, but I want to use it as a studio for working on jewelry. Maybe I could even work on my theater parts out there, too."

"Miranda's been doing all her rehearsing in her bedroom," Sophie put in. "And most of her jewelry-making in the kitchen. I keep finding pretty little beads in the corners of my cabinets."

"You're very tolerant, Grandma," Miranda said with a smile. The problem wasn't so much losing beads, as it was taking out all her supplies and tools each time and putting them away again. She wanted one permanent work space, where everything was handy.

"Most of the work on the studio is done," she explained. "We just need to paint the walls and trim."

"That doesn't sound too difficult."

"It won't be as hard as the shed. But we'll have to tape the room first."

"Tape it?" Adam sounded puzzled. "You mean like, Scotch tape?"

"Masking tape. On the edges of the moldings and ceiling, and things you don't want painted." She couldn't help grinning at him. "Something tells me you never earned your living as a housepainter."

"Probably not," he agreed cheerfully. "At least that eliminates one possibility. I can cross house painting off the list."

Sophie brought a platter of scrambled eggs and a pile of toast to the table, then sat down in her place. "Adam might be more comfortable out in the cottage than sleeping here in the parlor," she said thoughtfully. "He can move over there tonight, if it's aired out enough. He'll have more room and some privacy." She looked over at Adam. "It's a nice space with a half bath. We just put some heat in there, too. Used to have it all set up for summer guests, but we let it get run down." She turned to Miranda. "Didn't we have a cot or a daybed in there?"

"Yes, it's in the alcove at the back."

Miranda wasn't sure she liked the suggestion. She had planned to have access to the studio anytime she wanted, not fit her work schedule around Adam. But considering their encounter last night, maybe it was a good idea to give him some space. She had already decided they needed to avoid any more intimate situations. Besides, she had been working on her jewelry in the kitchen up until now; a few more days wouldn't hurt.

Adam was watching her. She almost felt as if he were reading her mind, sifting out all the pros and cons. "If you wouldn't mind me being there, Miranda. I don't want to be in your way."

"It will work out," she said quickly. "Don't worry."

Sophie met her eye and nodded with approval. Had her grandmother been awake last night and aware of what was going on downstairs? It did seem an odd coincidence that she was now suggesting Adam move outside. Miranda had a funny feeling but couldn't be sure, and it wasn't a conversation that she was ready to get into.

Miranda and Adam headed for the studio right after breakfast, lugging cans of paint, drop cloths, a stepladder, and other necessary paraphernalia.

Adam walked slowly, gazing around the property. It was still early and a frosty mist covered the orchard, clinging to the rows of bare trees. Above the mist, a swath of thick, blue-gray clouds hung heavy and low.

"It's so peaceful out here in the morning," Adam said. "Any time of day, really." He glanced at her, his cheeks ruddy from the brisk cold air. "I like the country. But I don't feel as if I ever lived in a rural place, like Cape Light."

"The dream you had last night sounded as if you were in a city. Did you remember anything more about it?"

"After you went upstairs, I decided to write down what I could remember. I found some paper in the living room, in that secretary by the fireplace, and I started writing."

"How much did you write?" she asked, curious.

He shrugged. "About ten pages."

"Ten pages? Wow, that's a lot."

"Once I started, it was hard to stop. It wasn't just about the dream," he added. "It helped me feel better to write things down and try to sort things out. I wrote about going into town, talking to the police and that reporter. Waking up in the orchard." He paused for a moment. "I wrote a lot about you, of course."

Miranda felt herself blush, thinking he had just complimented her. Her common sense kicked in at once. *Don't get carried away,* she scolded herself. *He's just trying to get a handle on who he is, so he's writing down everything he can remember. It doesn't mean anything special that he included you.*

"Sounds like you started a journal," she said, hoping she sounded encouraging.

"I think I did. I'm going to keep at it. It might help."

They had reached the studio and she opened the door and led him inside. "I did some free-association writing in a poetry class once," she said. "We didn't try to order our thoughts or even write in sentences. We just put down anything that came to mind. The most amazing things would pop into my brain. Images and memories I hadn't thought about for years. Out of the clear blue."

"I'm hoping something like that will happen. I might not even recognize a good clue right now, but maybe in a day or two, if I read over the pages, something will jump out at me."

He sounded hopeful, almost optimistic, and Miranda found herself hoping he was right.

They worked together without speaking, spreading out the drop cloths and setting up the ladder and paints. She liked working with Adam. He was easy company. He didn't complain or criticize. He didn't need to talk and seemed perfectly comfortable with silence.

She thought about his dream again and its possible significance. She wondered if Adam should tell the police about it. There was nothing substantial to tell them, she reasoned, unless he remembered a street sign or something specific. But he hadn't mentioned anything like that; maybe it was best to just let it go for now.

"Okay, here's what you do with the tape. You run it along all the edges of the wall, like this." Miranda crouched down and stretched out a length of tape, then pressed it to the top of the wood molding near the floor. "That way, we won't get paint on the moldings, which are going to be another color."

"Right, I get it. I think I can handle it," he said very seriously, but she saw a smile playing at the corners of his mouth.

"This is a nice space for an art studio," he added as Miranda took another roll of tape and started on the other side of the room. "Is that your worktable over there?"

She nodded. "It will be. There's still so much dust in here from the renovation, I keep it covered with a tarp." She lifted the canvas and showed him her equipment and supplies. "This is what I use to make some of the earrings and necklaces, silver wire and beads. Those are seed pearls," she pointed out. "I cast silver, too, but all that equipment is put away for now."

He seemed interested, picking up an earring she had been working on that combined turquoise, amethyst, and peridot beads. "This is beautiful. No wonder that shop wants more."

"You've got good taste," she joked, not wanting to let on how much his compliment pleased her.

He set the earring down again, looking impressed. "We have to get this place painted, so you can get started on your big order." He dropped the tarp down gently and smoothed out the edge. "You're sure my staying here won't interrupt your schedule?"

"No, I'll be fine," she said. "I can work in here during the days and then get in some extra hours in the kitchen at night. It's not a big deal, really. I'm used to it. Besides, you'll be more comfortable in here. You'll have more privacy," she added.

She glanced at him. He didn't answer, but when he met her gaze she knew he was thinking of last night, and she realized the cottage was not a complete solution. Not for her. It was easy to put some physical space between them, but not quite as simple to put space between them emotionally.

The taping went quickly and Miranda was pleased. She was used to working on her own; it made a difference to have an extra pair of hands on the job. She started Adam on the painting and they worked together until she took a break to call Krista and confirm which parts of the order she would fill. She returned to the studio to find Adam still painting; the room was half done. *He's a hard worker*, she thought, as she took up her roller again.

Two hours later Miranda declared that it was time to break for lunch. Adam watched with curiosity as she covered the paint pans and wet rollers with plastic wrap. "Latex paint dries fast," she explained. "This keeps everything from getting gluey while we're eating."

"Ingenious." He shook his head as he pulled on his jacket. "Hey, look . . . it snowed. I didn't even notice."

Miranda walked over to the window. She had noticed the flakes start to fall but hadn't thought much about it. It looked as if a good three to four inches had piled up while they were painting. Although it had already snowed once, before Thanksgiving, it melted soon after. It was colder now, and Miranda expected this fall to stick for a while.

She buttoned up her jacket and started off toward the house. Halfway there, she realized that Adam wasn't keeping up with her. She turned to see why he was walking so slowly and spotted him standing a few steps behind her, sticking out his bare hand to catch the flakes.

"Do you remember snow?"

"Of course I do. I just like it, that's all."

He turned and grinned at her. He hadn't put his hat on and his dark hair already had a soft white coating. It was so tempting to just reach up and brush it off.

Instead she leaned over and scooped up a handful. "This thick wet snow is perfect for making snowballs. My brother taught me." She packed up a snowball then tossed it at him. It splattered on the shoulder of his parka.

Adam looked down at the spot in surprise then laughed. "I remember how to make snowballs, Miranda. Better than your brother taught you, too, I bet." He quickly reached down and made his own snowball.

Laughing, she started to run for the house. "No, you don't . . . Hey, I'm your boss, remember?"

He threw it anyway, hitting her back.

Of course, she had no choice but to make another snowball, or two, and retaliate. The oversized boots Sophie had found for him should have slowed him down, but Adam was surprisingly fast and nimble, dodging her by ducking behind a tree.

It feels good to run around out in the cold, Miranda thought. They had been through so much the past two days, so much stress and wondering. She felt giddy and silly as she ducked behind another tree, then got Adam right in the stomach as he ran past her.

"Direct hit! I'm winning," she teased.

"I didn't know we were keeping score." He chased after her, panting and laughing. "There's another thing you need to learn about me: I hate to lose."

He stooped to gather up more ammunition and Miranda ran from him, leading a chase through the rows of apple trees. The trees were bare and the thin trunks didn't offer much protection. His first shot hit a tree trunk, but finally, he cornered her, the snowball in his hand, as big as a grapefruit.

"Whoa . . . you are good. That's a beauty. Don't waste it now. . . ."

Just as he got close enough to toss it, Miranda spun and made a dash for the house.

She hadn't gotten very far, though, before she felt her feet fly out from under her. She fell with a thud on her back, landing hard on the snow-covered ground.

Adam was beside her in seconds, his expression serious. "Miranda . . . are you all right?"

"Sure. I'm okay. There's just some ice on the ground, under the snow." She sat up and he offered her his hand. But just as she took hold and he began to pull her up, he lost his balance and fell down right next to her, bringing her down again beside him.

Miranda was startled at first as she once again found herself, flat on her back, gazing up at the sky. Then she heard Adam laughing and she started laughing, too. He rolled over and looked down at her. His thick dark hair was wet, smoothed back from his brow. His eyes were bright and his cheeks red from the cold.

He smiled down at her. "You lose points for falling down."

"Okay," she said quietly. She could feel his warm breath on her skin. His looks were mesmerizing. He didn't answer. He leaned forward, and she put her arms around his neck. She drew him toward her and closed her eyes.

Dog barking. Loud and coming closer. Miranda's eyes flew open. Dixie galloped toward them through the snow, eager to get in on the game.

"Oh, no . . . get up. Quickly!" she urged Adam. "She'll jump right on top of us. . . ."

They scrambled to their feet, just in time. Dixie seemed disappointed and leaped up on Adam, trying to knock him down again. He laughed and petted her. Then he picked up a snow-covered stick and tossed it for her to fetch. "Here you go, Dixie. Go get it."

The big dog looked beautiful running through the snow, Miranda thought. She happily retrieved her prize and they took turns, tossing it for her as they walked back to the house.

"That dog likes you," Miranda said. "She doesn't take to everyone—especially men, for some reason."

"Well, she rescued me, so you know how it goes. Now she feels . . . responsible." Adam smiled at her, a dimple creasing his lean cheek, and Miranda was fairly certain he wasn't just talking about Dixie.

Miranda saw her grandmother through the kitchen window, and suddenly it all made sense. Sophie had been watching the snowball fight. Letting Dixie out when she did was no coincidence. Miranda shook her head, laughing to herself. Only her grandmother could make her feel like a teenager, getting caught with a forbidden boyfriend.

Inside the house, the air was filled with the scent of freshly baked bread. "Hang up those wet jackets in the mudroom, will you?" Sophie called from the kitchen. "I have some soup for lunch and a nice braided bread, just out of the oven."

Miranda and Adam didn't need to be

called to the table twice. Between painting all morning and running around in the snow, Miranda felt half-starved.

Adam rubbed his hands together as Sophie served him a bowl of beef and barley soup. "Wow, that looks delicious. Smells good, too." He leaned forward and reached for a slice of bread. He regained his composure easily, Miranda thought. She still felt a bit off balance from her fall in the snow. She looked across the table and met his glance. An intimate smile in his eyes told her his thoughts were still outside, too.

They had just started eating when the phone rang. Sophie was nearest and answered it.

"Miranda, it's for you," she said quickly. She gave Miranda a meaningful look. "It's Greg. He's called twice this morning."

"Oh . . . sure. Excuse me," she said to Adam. She rose and took the phone from her grandmother.

"Hi, Miranda. I'm just calling to see if we're still on for tonight." She felt a twinge of guilt. She had a date with Greg. And she had completely forgotten. "Tonight, right," she said. "I'm looking forward to it."

"I thought we would go into Newburyport

and have dinner at that French restaurant you like."

"That sounds great. I would love that," she added sincerely. Greg was very thoughtful and went out of his way to please her. She hadn't met many men who seemed so aware of her likes and dislikes.

Greg asked what she had been up to, and she told him about the order from the Golden Moon. "That's good news," he said, sounding genuinely pleased. "That should keep you busy for a while. Any word from the play people?"

That's what he called the director and producer she had auditioned for. Miranda bit her tongue, trying hard not to correct him. "No word yet. I don't expect to hear from them, though, for at least a week or so." She quickly changed the subject. "I've been doing a lot of painting, inside and out . . ."

She told him about finishing the studio, leaving out the help from Adam. That seemed too complicated to get into right then.

She had met Greg at a party a few months ago and they had been dating ever since. He was attractive and smart, a senior engineer at a local firm. He traveled a lot for business, and so they hadn't actually spent that much time together, but they genuinely liked each other and Miranda felt their relationship had the potential to be something serious.

Greg had been on Cape Cod for the last few days, supervising a project. Normally, she would have been waiting for his call. Now Miranda realized she had barely given Greg a thought for the past two days—not since Adam arrived.

". . . I'm so glad to be back in town," Greg was saying. "We've been having serious problems with that project in Wellfleet . . ." Greg started describing the situation in more detail, and Miranda tried to make the appropriate sounds of concern. The truth was, though, she found descriptions of engineering rather dull.

And she had a more pressing concern. She wondered if she should tell Greg about Adam now. Or wait until she saw him tonight.

"So I'll pick you up at six?" Greg asked.

"Perfect," she replied, deciding that was a sign that she should wait. Besides, she and Greg didn't have any sort of commitment. And nothing had actually happened with Adam yet, not even a kiss. Maybe she shouldn't say anything at all.

"Hey, I almost forgot. I read a story in the newspaper today about you. Did you really find a man with amnesia on your property the other night?"

So much for signs. "Dixie found him, actually," she admitted. "His name is Adam. Well, we call him that for now."

"So . . . he's still staying with you?"

"Yes, he is." Miranda felt self-conscious talking in the kitchen with her grandmother and Adam so nearby. They were having a conversation of their own and didn't seem to be paying any attention to her. But she still felt awkward. "I'll tell you all about it tonight, when I see you. Okay?"

"Sure . . . sure thing. I can hardly wait to see you, Miranda."

"Me, too," she said quietly. She liked Greg. She had missed him. She was looking forward to seeing him . . . wasn't she?

When Miranda returned to the table, Sophie and Adam were done with their soup and had moved on to dessert, which consisted of fudgey looking brownies and a bowl of yellow pears.

"Sounds like you won't be home for dinner tonight," Sophie said.

"I'm going out with Greg. He'll be by

around six." Miranda concentrated on her soup, and tried to resist checking Adam's reaction.

He was paging through the newspaper while eating a brownie and didn't seem to have heard her. He seemed addicted to reading. He had explained that he hoped some random place, name or photo in the newspapers might jog his memory.

"I'd better start on that order for Krista," Miranda said. "Adam, do you mind finishing the painting on your own? I'll work in here."

"I didn't think you trusted me enough. I'm deeply honored." He sounded serious, but the spark in his eyes told her he was teasing.

"It's washable paint. I can always fix the spots you mess up."

"Good point," Adam said, laughing.

Miranda went upstairs to change out of her painting clothes. She considered working in the cottage at the table she had set up there. The paint smell didn't really bother her. But Adam's proximity did.

No, she would cart it all inside and work in the kitchen. The break from his company would be a good thing. So would her date with Greg tonight. She needed to return to reality. She was starting to get carried away by her attraction—carried along to some place she didn't want to go.

WHEN BEN WALKED INTO THE CLAM BOX, THE diner was empty, as he expected it would be. It was half past three, the lull between lunch and dinner. He liked the place best at this time, when he could get a big table by the window all to himself and it was quiet enough to gather his thoughts.

He had been up to Southport Hospital, visiting an elderly woman named Vera Plante, a member of his congregation, who was in the hospital for an upper respiratory infection. Vera was active for her age and lived in a large house outside of town. She took in boarders to make ends meet and did all the housework and cooking herself.

One never lacked for conversation with Vera, not like some of the members of his flock. Vera would ask him questions then answer them herself. And even stranded in the hospital, she seemed to know everything about everyone in Cape Light. He didn't have to supply much at all, just the occasional, "Is that so?" and "Really? I'd never heard that. . . ."

He knew that Vera appreciated his visits.

She only had one daughter who lived down in Connecticut. Most of her friends were her age, too old to drive the long distance to the hospital. He actually didn't mind the routine much. But he had driven back to town through the snow with his head sore and his stomach rumbling empty.

He looked around for a waitress and was surprised to see Lucy Bates, the owner's wife, working behind the counter. She waved and smiled, signaling that she would be right over.

Lucy had waited tables full-time at the diner for most of her married life until she decided to go back to school for a nursing degree. Almost a year ago, she had begun her clinical training in Southport Hospital, and Ben couldn't help but be delighted at how it had changed her. The new Lucy seemed so much calmer and more confident.

She walked over to the table and handed him a menu. "Hello, Reverend. Stopping in for a late lunch, or just coffee?"

"Lunch. Finally. You know I don't need that," he added, waving away the menu. "I'll have a grilled cheese with tomato . . . on whole wheat. Carolyn says I need more whole grains in my diet."

"Your wife is right. As wives usually are. Fries or side salad?" She peered down at him, suddenly looking every inch a nurse.

"Is that a trick question?"

She laughed at his reply. "How about I bring both?"

"Good idea. And a coffee, decaf."

"Got it." She jotted the last bit down.

"By the way, what are you doing here today, Lucy? Not that it isn't a pleasure to see you."

"Charlie was in a pinch and I'm on the night shift at the hospital this month, so I came in to help out."

"You're going to work here all day then work all night at the hospital?" It sounded like Lucy. She could never say no when someone asked for help, especially to Charlie.

"I'll be okay. The floor I'm on is very quiet at night. I'm going to leave here soon and catch a cat nap before I head out. Let me put the order in and get your coffee, Reverend. I'll be right back."

Ben watched her go then glanced out the window. The snowfall had tapered off just as he had entered town. Shopkeepers were out, shoveling patches of sidewalk in front of each doorway. The bright white dusting was just enough to coat rooftops and treetops and give the village a genuine Christmas look, he thought. The holidays finally seemed real. The town had put extra lights on the trees along Main Street and pine garlands and tiny white lights on the gazebo-style bandstand in the Village Green.

Lucy arrived with a mug of coffee on a tray and set it down in front of him, the cup still steaming. "There you go." Then she set the tray on the table and sat down across from him.

Ben noticed that for once, she didn't look over her shoulder to see if her husband was watching. She just did it. My, things had changed around here. Bravo, Lucy! But something had to be troubling her. Lucy rarely stole the time for a chat with him unless there was a problem.

"I heard there's a special statue over at the church," she began. "A beautiful angel that looks like it's from a museum. I'd like to come see it. Is the sanctuary open all day during the week?"

Ben sipped his coffee, curious to see where this would lead. "Yes, of course. The sanctuary is open every day. You can come anytime."

She leaned closer, nearly whispering. "I

heard that this statue, this angel, has special powers. Is that true?"

Ben felt his mouthful of coffee stick in his throat. He put the cup down.

"Who told you that, Lucy? Was Carl Tulley in here?"

"Carl? He doesn't come in here much. Just to rattle Charlie's chain every once in a while. No . . . it wasn't Carl."

Ben didn't reply. He knew Carl and Charlie didn't get along. He also knew that if he waited long enough, Lucy would tell him. She had a bit of Vera Plante in her, she couldn't help herself.

"It was Tucker," she said.

Ben should have guessed. Tucker was Carl's brother and Charlie's best friend from childhood.

"Tucker told Charlie the story about Carl's hand. Did that really happen?" Her bright blue eyes were wide and curious. Ben felt a knot in his stomach.

Instead of answering her question he said, "What did Charlie think of the story?"

"What do you think? He doesn't believe a word of it, of course. Charlie says Carl must be cooking up some scheme, but he can't figure out what it is. Charlie's been telling everyone the story and warning them about Carl."

Ben wasn't happy to hear that. First of all, it didn't reflect well on the church, having Charlie Bates tell everyone that the church sexton was up to something. Not that he could defend Carl's story without sounding as if he believed it. But he did believe Carl was sincere.

"I'm sorry, Reverend. Did I talk out of line? I thought Carl had told you about his hand."

Ben looked up at Lucy. "Yes, he did tell me. You didn't say anything wrong, Lucy. I'm glad I found out he was telling everyone in town."

Charlie appeared from the kitchen and set Ben's order on the counter. "This is getting cold sitting back in the kitchen, Lucy. Why didn't you come get it?"

"I was talking to Reverend Ben."

She rose and tucked the tray under her arm, taking her time and not seeming the least bit intimidated by her husband. Ben was impressed. Lucy used to jump up like a rabbit when Charlie so much as looked at her.

She set the sandwich in front of Ben. "If it's cold, I'll reheat it for you, Reverend."

"I'm sure it's all right. I shouldn't be eating

a heavy lunch at this hour anyway." Hearing that Carl's story was spreading around town had definitely taken the edge off his appetite.

Charlie leaned over the counter and smiled at him. "I heard that wild tale about Carl Tulley's hand healing from touching a statue. Did you ever hear such a bogus piece of baloney in your life?"

Could baloney actually be bogus? Wasn't that a redundancy? Ben wondered vaguely.

The easy way out would be to agree with Charlie, Ben knew, or at least, make some mealymouthed reply that didn't commit one way or another. That was the way Charlie won most of his arguments, by intimidating his opponent before he even started.

"Carl did tell me about his hand. I was the first one he told, in fact." Ben sat back and looked at Charlie squarely. "I think he's sincere, and I can't imagine that he has any hidden motives."

"Oh, you think he's sincere, do you? That would be the first time in his miserable life, then. *That* would be the miracle." Charlie laughed at his own joke.

"You have no right to say that, Charlie," Ben replied, his voice even.

Charlie shrugged. "Hey, it's a free country,

last I heard. I can say anything I like. Can't say I'm surprised Carl conned you with that story, Reverend. With all due respect, folks in your line of work don't have much knowledge of what a guy like Carl is capable of. Me, I've known Carl all my life, and he always has some scheme going. I wouldn't be surprised if he starts promising cures and charging people to touch the statue."

The last suggestion made Ben's blood boil. He practically saw spots in front of his eyes.

"How dare you even suggest such a thing? The statue is in the church sanctuary. Anyone is free to walk in, anytime, and look at it. Touch it even, if they must. It's a plain wooden statue. There will be no schemes or charges or anything of the kind. Not by Carl or anyone else. I would appreciate it if you kept your speculations to yourself and stopped repeating the story altogether. The mere repetition of Carl's claim gives it validity."

Lucy stepped back and turned to her husband. "You're the one stirring up trouble about this story, Charlie, not Carl Tulley. You're totally out of line, talking to Reverend Ben that way, and I want you to apologize. Right now."

Ben had known Lucy to sass Charlie back

when he provoked her, usually under her breath. She would stick up for herself when he pushed too hard, but he had never heard her speak up so forcefully, demanding an apology no less.

Charlie looked shocked. He glanced at Ben, then back to Lucy. Ben saw a fire in his eyes and expected an angry retort. But Lucy stared him down, and Ben saw Charlie's defiance wilt. It reminded Ben of a lion tamer he had once seen at the circus when he was a boy, the look the tamer had given the big cats to heed his commands.

Charlie sniffed and looked up at the ceiling. "Reverend, my wife says I was out of line, speaking to you so frankly. Sorry if I offended. I was just calling it the way I see it."

It wasn't exactly an apology, but Ben knew it was the best he would get from Charlie.

"I understand the way you see it, Charlie. I'm well aware of that." Ben stared down at his cold sandwich. He pulled out some bills and tucked them under the side of his plate.

Lucy watched him, and he saw her face fall. "Do you want me to wrap that up, Reverend? You hardly touched it."

Ben rose from his chair and slipped on his coat. "That's okay, Lucy. I shouldn't be eating such a big lunch this late in the day anyway. It will ruin my appetite for dinner."

He gently touched Lucy on the arm and gave her a smile as he started for the door. "I'll see you soon."

"See you Sunday," she promised.

Ben glanced over at the counter, but Charlie was gone. Ben wasn't surprised. Charlie Bates was a hit-and-run sort of guy. He had done his damage for the afternoon.

Ben stalked back to the church, walking to the end of Main Street and then across the Village Green that bordered the harbor. A brisk wind blew off the water, raising the waves to white peaks. The path across the green hadn't been shoveled yet, and his boots crunched on the freshly fallen snow. The green looked beautiful with the sun just starting to set over the harbor and the boughs of the tall trees, covered with snow. The village Christmas tree sparkled with colored lights and the large golden star on top.

Ben's thoughts fixed on the statue and the gossip racing around town. He didn't blame Carl Tulley. He didn't have the heart. The man had been genuinely moved by . . . something. Some out-of-the-ordinary experience, real or imagined. How could Ben even begin to discern? Carl had told his brother, Tucker, which was understandable. Aside from Ben, who else did he have in the world to tell? Of course Tucker told Charlie. Tucker stopped in the diner every day. With Charlie owning the diner and Tucker working in the police station, the two old friends knew and discussed pretty much everything that went on in town. This was a juicy tidbit.

The old game of telephone. At least it hadn't been exaggerated to outrageous proportions. But what should he do about it?

Ben's first impulse was to march into the sanctuary and take the statue down. Then he realized that wouldn't help at all. It would just make people more curious. They would probably think there was something special about it for sure.

The thing to do was leave it up. Let them see for themselves. It was a lovely statue. He could never deny that. But totally and unequivocally ordinary.

GREG ARRIVED AT THE ORCHARD PRECISELY AT six. Miranda heard him at the door and heard her grandmother greet him, sounding even more pleased than usual to see him.

Greg was an engineer and extremely

punctual. The problem was, he expected Miranda to be punctual, too. Clock watching just wasn't in her nature. But she made an effort to please him.

She scurried to finish dressing, holding up one set of earrings and then another, finally choosing a long dangling pair of her own design, a pair he had once complimented her on. She lifted her hair and dabbed some perfume on her neck then took one last look in the mirror.

She was wearing a new dress she had bought for her audition, a wrap style, with long sleeves, a deep V-neckline, and a belt around her waist. The deep, blue green fabric brought out her sea-green eyes. Instead of her usual low pumps, she was wearing high black dress boots with heels. She thought they might make her taller than Greg, then decided it didn't matter. If it bothered him, it was his problem.

Miranda checked the time as she left the room. Five after six. Well, that wasn't too bad.

When she came downstairs she saw Adam, sitting in the living room, reading a book. Dixie lay by the side of his chair, like a loyal stone lion.

Adam looked up immediately. His dark eyes lit up with approval at the sight of her, and Miranda felt herself nearly blush.

Greg was facing away from her, talking to her grandmother, but he turned to her with a smile. "Miranda." He gave her a quick hug and kissed her cheek. "You look gorgeous, as usual."

"Thank you." Miranda felt slightly awkward talking to Greg in front of Adam. "Sorry to keep you waiting."

"It's nice to catch up with your grandmother . . . and to meet Adam."

"It's mutual," Adam assured him, then returned to his book.

Sophie walked with them to the foyer and said good night. "Have a nice time," she called before closing the door.

Miranda couldn't help but feel her grandmother was relieved to see her going off with Greg—and away from Adam.

It wasn't until they were in Greg's car, on their way to Newburyport, that he spoke. "So, that was Adam. He looks different from the photo I saw in the newspaper."

"It wasn't a very good likeness. But Sara did a good job on the article."

"It's quite a story. It was generous of you and your grandmother to take him in. Most people wouldn't go that far."

Miranda glanced at him. Something in his tone didn't match his approving words.

"We just want to help him. I'm sure his memory will return very soon. Or someone will see the news articles and get in touch."

Greg was quiet for a moment. "What does he do all day?"

"Well . . . it's only been two days," she pointed out. "He's been doing work around the orchard, helping me paint. He insisted on it, to pay us back."

Greg nodded. "He sounds like an ethical guy."

"He is." Miranda knew her reply sounded a bit more forceful than she meant it to be. "I mean, he seems to be."

"Yes, I guess it's hard for you and your grandmother to be sure of much. I mean, he's a stranger. One who doesn't even remember his name. So he says, anyway."

Miranda was surprised by Greg's insinuation. He was starting to sound like Tucker Tulley.

"Do you think Adam is faking his memory

loss?" she asked him point-blank. "Why would he do that?"

"I'm not saying he is. I don't know much about amnesia, though I do know it's quite rare. In fact, it's practically impossible to find someone with real *global* amnesia. I mean, you have better odds of being struck by lightning. I looked it up on the Internet," he explained.

Miranda wasn't surprised. "It might be rare. But people do get struck by lightning and people do get amnesia."

"You seem to believe him. You have no doubt at all?"

"No, I really don't." Miranda had been staring out the window. Now she turned to face Greg. "From what I can see, it's very painful not to know who you are or where you belong. I think Adam is handling it as well as he can."

Greg seemed to shut down at her words. She saw his body tense as he fixed his gaze on the road ahead. "How long do you think he'll stay with you?"

"I'm not sure. Until someone claims him or he remembers his identity."

"That could take a long time."

"I don't think so. I'm almost certain someone will come forward. He'll be back to his
normal life in no time, even if his memory
doesn't return."

Greg pulled into a parking space near the
restaurant. "I hope so," he said, sounding
serious.

Was Greg actually jealous? Miranda pon-
dered this idea as they got out of the car and
walked to the restaurant. Did he really care
that much about her? If that was the case,
she hadn't done much to relieve his insecurities. She promised herself that she would try
to put aside the tense conversation in the
car and be more attentive during dinner.

"So, how's Lily? What's she up to these
days?" Miranda asked as soon as they sat
down. Lily was Greg's seven-year-old
daughter from his now-defunct marriage.

"She's started piano lessons. She plays
her lessons for me over the phone," he said
with a laugh. "You cannot imagine how many
times I have listened to, 'The Eensy Weensy
Spider.' And acted thrilled about it."

Miranda laughed. She genuinely loved
hearing about Lily. Greg adored his daughter
and was a wonderful father, and that had
touched her from the start.

Greg took out his latest photos of Lily, and the conversation drifted from his daughter to his latest project and complicated problem. But many of their conversations drifted that way, sooner or later.

Miranda tried to stay focused, but it was a struggle. She just didn't 'get' engineering. Perhaps Greg felt the same when she talked about acting or jewelry designs? Sometimes, she did feel he was bored by such conversations, but tried hard not to show it.

Greg was very grounded, a "just the facts" type, while she was more flighty and creative. Everyone said that opposites attract and compliment each other, but could she really be close with someone who was so different from her?

You have to be open-minded and flexible, she reminded herself as Greg began to talk about his latest project. After all, she was old enough to know that no man was going to be perfect. She just had to fall in love. Was that so hard?

". . . So, I had this idea of reinforcing the foundation by placing a grid of steel H-beams underneath"—Greg was drawing a geometric formation on the napkin—"to support the additional loading from the water . . ."

Miranda watched Greg sketch out the situation on a paper napkin, all the while studying him. He was very good-looking. He worked out in a gym several times a week and was an avid long-distance runner. Miranda had cheered him across the finish line at the last Boston Marathon.

"The long course suits me. I'm the slow and steady type," he had once told her. "Long-distance running is about focus and persistence and stamina. That's more my style than a short, flashy sprint. Also, I like the pasta dinner the night before a big race," he had joked.

He had a runner's physique, with lean, muscular legs and arms. Straight brown hair, blue eyes and an even-featured face. More than that, he was confident. The fact that he had singled her out at that party and kept calling felt to Miranda like a great compliment. He was the type who would never have trouble finding a date, and out of everyone, he had chosen her.

More important, he was considerate, sweet, and tried hard to please her. Miranda knew that she trusted Greg. He was the kind of man you could build a life with, a good life. Maybe she wasn't in love with him yet, but

Miranda believed that in time she could fall in love with him. Maybe it wouldn't be that head-over-heels feeling, but something deep and grounded. Something that would last.

Adam's image popped into her head—right in the middle of her favorable inventory of Greg's qualities. *Go away,* she thought crossly. But her mind wouldn't cooperate. She was sitting right across from Greg, trying to concentrate on him, and seeing Adam. She couldn't help it. Miranda gave a silent sigh. She wondered what was wrong with her sometimes. An attraction to Adam was like purposely sabotaging herself, purposely avoiding a real relationship.

Greg was the real deal.

Adam was . . . a fantasy. A blank slate that she could fill in, any way her heart desired.

Then why was she so drawn to him? It wasn't good for her and it didn't make any sense. Then again, that type of attraction rarely made sense. That was just the problem.

". . . So, enough about my H-beams. I see your eyes glazing over, Miranda." Greg's words broke into her rambling thoughts, and she felt herself flush. She had been zoning out on his conversation. But when she met his eyes, he was smiling at her. He reached over and gently brushed a strand of hair from her cheek.

"Any more news about your audition? You haven't mentioned it." His tone was casual, but she sensed his keen interest.

"I won't hear anything for at least a week, maybe more. One of the producers or some-one is away, and they're waiting for him to get back east before they make a final deci-sion. I might even have to read again before it's all over."

Greg didn't say anything at first. Then he reached across the table and took her hand. "I guess I'm more interested in your feelings about the situation. If they offer you the part, will you take it?"

Will you leave here? is what he meant. *Will you leave me?*

Miranda wished he hadn't framed it as such a black-and-white choice. But he was an engineer. That was the way his mind worked.

"I really don't know. I wish I did," she added sincerely. "I haven't figured it out yet. It's not a huge role but it's an important one. Playing Cordelia can get you noticed."

"And that's what you still want?" He was

asking the right questions, she realized. Questions that showed he cared about her.

She took a sip from her water glass. "Sometimes, it seems foolish to keep chasing after that kind of success. Maybe I need to just put it all behind me. But it's hard," she admitted. "And I know that even if I get this role, it won't necessarily lead to a big breakthrough. I might find myself on the same old treadmill again."

"Even so, I guess it's the kind of opportunity that's tough to pass up."

She could tell that he was trying to see it from her point of view, trying to be supportive even if it wasn't what he wanted.

"It is," she told him. "And I have to admit, it feels good to know I'm in the running. The pay is good, there will be publicity, a couple of big-name actors in the cast, nice theaters. . . . After all the times I've been passed over, this time they're really interested. This could be the one."

"I understand. It would be a validation for you. Something you've worked for but never quite achieved."

"Exactly." She nodded, grateful that he understood. "But if I take it, there will be real consequences in my life. It would be the way it was when I lived in the city, always on the move. Back then, if I needed to go out of town, I didn't even have to worry about a houseplant. Now it's different. There's my grandmother and the orchard and . . . there's you . . ." She broke off, unable to continue.

"A year is a long time, Miranda. I've thought about it, too. I don't think I could manage a long-distance relationship with you far away all that time."

If she took the role, they would break up. She had guessed that. But still, it was hard to hear him say it.

"I understand," she said simply. "I do."

"I'm sure it's confusing. I don't mean to make it harder. I just thought you should know how I feel about it, that's all."

She looked up at him. "I think it's good that you've told me, Greg. I'm glad you've been honest."

"I do have feelings for you, Miranda. I think our relationship has a real future. . . ."

"I do, too," she said.

He smiled softly at her, then leaned forward and kissed her, a sweet, tender kiss that told her more than his words could say.

Greg drove her back home after dinner and walked her to the front door. "Would you like to come in for some coffee?" she asked.

He smiled, seeming pleased at the invitation, then shook his head. "Some other time. I have an early meeting tomorrow."

"Sure, it's getting late. Dinner was terrific. Thanks again."

"You're very welcome. I was really looking forward to seeing you tonight. I missed you while I was away. I know it was only a few days, but I was thinking about you. A lot."

"I missed you, too," she said. It was true. She had missed him. Until Adam appeared.

Greg put his arms around her and gently kissed her cheek, then her lips. The kiss was full of longing. It might have been even more passionate, except that Miranda felt a little awkward because her boots made her a shade taller than he was. She made a mental note to wear lower shoes next time they went out.

"Can I see you this weekend?" Greg stood close, his arms looped around her, waiting for her answer.

"I think so. I'll have to see how the jewelry-making goes. Krista needs everything before Christmas."

"Okay, I'll call you." He kissed her on the forehead and stepped back. "Good night now."

"Good night, Greg." Miranda unlocked the door and stepped inside.

She entered the house quietly, not wanting to wake Adam or her grandmother and heard a noise coming from the back parlor.

She walked in, and Adam looked up at her from the couch. "I couldn't sleep," he explained. "Thought I would watch some television."

There wasn't a TV in the cottage, she remembered, so he would have to watch in here. Was that really the problem—or was he waiting up for her? Miranda didn't have the nerve to ask.

"Find anything interesting?" she asked instead.

"Not much. I thought something might trigger my memory. Maybe the mention of some different part of the country. Or a TV show. I'm sure I used to watch something. Besides all these commercials, I mean."

"Didn't anything seem familiar?"

"I did remember that I don't like fast food." Miranda laughed at him.

"Channel surfing was fun," he admitted.

"I can't say I'm surprised. Typical male be-havior," she assured him.

Adam laughed, his eyes sparkling, and she felt that connection again, that spark that she only felt with him. She considered sitting down beside him then decided it was better to stay on her feet.

"How about you? Did you have a good time?"

"Yes, I did. We had a great time. Greg's a wonderful guy," she said, a bit more force-fully than she intended.

"How long have you been seeing him?" Adam asked.

"Oh, a few months now. Greg travels a lot for business. So we don't see each other as much as we'd like, I suppose."

Why had she said that? To give Adam the idea this was a serious commitment and he ought to leave her alone? She felt so trans-parent. She turned her back on him and pulled out a book from the bookcase, as if she had never seen it before.

Adam shut off the television and put the remote on the coffee table. Miranda noticed a notebook on the table. His journal, the one he started the other night after his nightmare.

"Have you been keeping up your journal?" she asked.

"Yes, I have. It's been helpful." He picked up the book and stood to face her. "I've been thinking things over, Miranda, and I don't think I should stay here any longer. You and your grandmother have been very kind. But I don't like putting you out, disrupting your life."

"You're not putting us out. We don't mind having you here. It's been . . . interesting," she added. The truth was, he was a more-than-interesting interruption in an otherwise quiet and routine life.

Adam was not convinced. "I know I am. I can see it. You've got a lot going on. You don't need me here. I'm going to pursue some other options, like trying a shelter. It might not be so bad. Maybe someone can set me up with a job, and I can rent a room somewhere."

"You can't go into a shelter. I won't let you. And neither would my grandmother," she added, a little embarrassed by the strength of her reaction.

"I can't stay here forever. Let's be realistic."

"It's only been two days. Have some patience." Miranda tried to meet his gaze, but he kept looking away from her. "You can stay as long as you need. But it won't be that long. I can almost guarantee it."

"I wish I felt the same way," he said bleakly.

Miranda felt her heart go out to him. Gently, she touched his arm. The slight contact was electric. His eyes locked on hers, and she felt something starting again between them, an attraction that couldn't be denied. She quickly took her hand away and stepped back.

"You have a life somewhere, people who miss you." Her voice was low but firm. "Someone will come to find you. They're looking for you right now."

She believed what she said, but she was also reminding herself of his situation, trying to rein in the feelings that were threatening to race out of control.

Adam glanced at her and nodded, his face unreadable. "All right. Let's see how it goes. There must be something more I can do, though. Go to the library, check the newspapers, check the Internet." He pulled on his jacket, preparing to head back to the studio. "Maybe I'll call that detective who works on missing person cases. Maybe he has some ideas for me."

"I can take you into town tomorrow. Anytime you like."

"All right. Good night, Miranda." He walked past her, heading for the kitchen and the side door.

"Good night," she said quietly. She watched him go, feeling there was something more she should say—and not having the slightest idea of what it was. She shut off the lights in the parlor then headed up to her room.

Of all the men who were perfectly suitable, why did she have to feel drawn to Adam? A man who could be married. With ten children. Who could be . . . anyone.

There must be something wrong with her, Miranda decided. She wondered if she would see him in the morning. She wouldn't really be surprised if he was gone. And if he was, she wasn't sure if that would be a fortunate, or unfortunate, end to their story.

CHAPTER FIVE

~~~

THE GIRLS LIKED BACON. EVERY TIME MOLLY served it, Matt reminded her that it wasn't exactly from the nutritious-choice column. It was loaded with sodium, clogged your arteries, and had all kinds of unhealthy side effects. But they were teenagers and didn't give a hoot about their arteries. All Molly knew was that the smell of bacon cooking on Sunday morning was enough to lure her pack of sleeping beauties out of bed in time for church. Once a week wouldn't hurt them, she reasoned. All for a good cause.

The scent was usually appetizing to her, too, though she rarely indulged in more than a bite. This morning, though, the sight of the sizzling, fatty strips on the hot pan sent her stomach churning. She made it to the bathroom just in time.

She heard Matt coming down the stairs, then his sharp knock on the door. "Molly? Are you in there? Are you all right?"

When she didn't answer, he tried the door. He opened it to find her kneeling next to the toilet. "Oh, dear . . ." He made a move toward her and she waved him away.

"Just . . . go. I'll be all right in a minute . . ."

Her body immediately contradicted her.

Matt looked torn between his desire to help and her desire for privacy. Finally he retreated and quietly closed the door, leaving her to her misery.

Molly lifted her head as the sharp bleat of the smoke alarm cut through the quiet house. She heard the girls pounding down the stairs, asking what was going on. She already knew what had set it off. The unmistakable smell of burning bacon filled the air, along with Matt's shouts.

"Lauren, get me the fire extinguisher. Amanda, hand me that salt . . . Hurry, girls! Jill, open all the windows and try to shut that thing off!"

Brilliant doctor, but not much in the kitchen.

Although Molly normally rushed in and handled any household calamity, she decided to let her husband take over for once. She waited until her wave of sickness was clearly past, then she washed her face and pulled herself together.

In the kitchen, Matt and the girls were gathered around the table. Her chattering family suddenly stopped talking as they all turned to look at her.

"Good morning," Molly said, trying to sound cheerful. "Sorry I burned the bacon. I'll make it up to you. At least the fire department didn't show up."

She sat next to Matt in her usual seat. A platter of something that was a sickly yellow—it might have been scrambled eggs—sat in the middle of the table. Molly immediately looked away, feeling her stomach start to churn again.

"How are you doing, honey? Feel any better?" Matt patted her hand comfortingly. "I made you some tea and dry toast. Maybe that will settle your stomach."

"Are you sick, Mom?" Jill stared at her curiously, crunching down on a bite of toast. "If you're sick, do we still have to go to church?"

"I'm not sick and yes, you still have to go." Molly looked down at her weak tea and stirred in a spoonful of sugar.

"Geez, no offense but it sounded like you were barfing your brains out. Are you sure you aren't sick?" Jill asked. "I absolutely do not want to catch that. It sounds pretty nasty."

"Don't worry, honey. It's not catching." Matt shot Molly a glance. Molly looked back at him warily.

She had been to the doctor on Wednesday. Her pregnancy was confirmed. They had already discussed telling the girls sometime this weekend, though Matt had left the how and when to her. She had missed a number of choice opportunities and here it was, Sunday morning.

Molly sipped her tea again, feeling Matt's steady gaze fixed on her.

She set down her cup and looked at each of the girls. "The thing is, kids, we have something to tell you. I'm not sick. I'm pregnant. I'm going to have a baby."

Jill rolled her eyes, seeming unimpressed. "We know what pregnant means, Mom."

Lauren's mouth hung open in shock. She

didn't say a word, just stared across the table, as if her mother had grown two heads.

Amanda was the only one smiling. "Wow. Really? That's great!" Amanda sat back and looked over at her father. "I always wanted a lot of sisters and brothers."

"I know you did, honey. Looks like you're finally getting your wish."

"A baby wouldn't be so bad," Jillian reasoned aloud. "I mean, that's sort of cool to have one at your age."

Molly laughed. "Thanks a lot. You sound like I belong in the *Guinness Book of World Records*. I'm not *that* old."

"I don't get it," Lauren said. "Amanda and I are nearly in college, and Jill is already in middle school. What do you want to go and have a baby for?"

Good point, Molly nearly replied. *I don't get it myself.*

When she didn't answer, Lauren added, "Guess it was an accident, right?"

Molly saw Matt's head snap back and felt her own do the same.

Matt was the first to react. "This baby is a blessing. Not an accident. Don't ever say that again," he told Lauren. "We didn't plan on expanding the family, but we're grateful and happy about the news." He looked over at Molly and covered her hand with his own.

Molly knew he expected her to jump in and back him up, but this was one of those rare times that she found herself at a loss for words. "Sometimes . . . these things just happen, honey," she finally managed to say. "You have to . . . accept it."

She could tell from the look on Matt's face that she had given the B answer.

"Wait a second. Does this mean I get stuck with all the babysitting?" Jill turned to her mother, looking stricken. "There goes my social life."

Lauren laughed. "What social life?"

Jill just glared at her. Molly realized that her point was totally valid. With Amanda and Lauren away, Jill was going to be their only built-in sitter.

"Don't worry. We'll let you out of the house once in a while," Molly promised. "We don't want you to end up going to a therapist over this."

Even Matt had to laugh at that. "All right, girls, help clean up. We're leaving for church in half an hour," he said.

Molly was glad for the abrupt interruption.

She had felt like a high-level politician, holding a press conference. She thought she had come prepared, but some of the questions had been rough.

"You sit. Finish your tea," Matt said, using his firm, doctor voice.

For once, Molly stayed put and watched as he and the girls cleared the table and cleaned up the kitchen. They ran upstairs to change, and suddenly, she was alone with Matt.

He came back to the table, and she could see that he was upset. She knew why, too.

"How do you feel—any better?" he asked as he sat down again.

"Somewhat. My stomach seems to have settled down." The truth was she still felt queasy, but she didn't want to sound like a complainer. She wasn't the first woman to get morning sickness and she wouldn't be the last.

"Why don't you stay home? I'll take the kids to church. I'll take them out for lunch after, too. You can just relax."

He really was so thoughtful, trying to make things easy for her.

"Lunch is a good idea. Better take them someplace where they can all order BLTs," she added with a small smile.

His expression was serious. "I know you don't feel well, Molly. But you could have sounded a bit more positive about the baby. Even if it was just for the kids."

Molly winced at that. Basically, she agreed with him, and at the same time she couldn't help feeling a little resentful.

"You're right," she said. "I should have sounded more upbeat. Spending the morning in the bathroom, hugging the toilet bowl may have drained my enthusiasm."

He gave her a reluctant smile. "Okay. I understand. This is just the first family conversation about it. We have nine more months to sound more upbeat. Right?"

She nodded. "Absolutely."

She wished she did feel upbeat about the pregnancy. Then she wouldn't have to act. It wouldn't feel like such a strain—or such an issue between them.

He looked as if he were about to say something more then seemed to change his mind. "So, why don't you head back up to bed? I'll bring you the Sunday papers and some more tea before I go."

"That's okay, honey. I'm just going to sleep," she said. "I'm sure that will make me feel better."

"Yes, I'm sure it will, too. I think you're just tired and overworked. You'll feel better if you sleep."

"Thank you, Doctor." Molly rose and kissed him on the cheek. "You're the sweetest and most handsome doctor I've seen in a long time. Your patients must be lined up around the block."

He hugged her close. "I love you. And I don't say that to all my patients . . . only a very, very few," he teased.

The phone rang. Molly didn't budge. She knew the girls would pounce on it.

A few seconds later, Amanda called down the staircase, "Molly . . . it's for you. Sonya, from the shop."

"Don't answer it," Matt said. "Let me. I'll tell Sonya you're not feeling well."

"Don't be silly, I have to answer it. We have a big party going on today."

Molly glanced at her watch, trying to gauge the stage of preparations. Normally, she would have called to check in by now. But what with feeling sick and then talking to the girls, she had lost track of time.

She picked up the extension in the kitchen. "Hi, Sonya. What's up?"

"Sorry to bother you at home. But it's a

disaster. This client . . . this Mrs. Norris . . . she's driving me crazy. Did you promise dendrobium orchids in the centerpieces? Because we didn't get dendrobium, just plain old white ones . . . and she's going bananas. And that's the least of it . . ."

Sonya was a terrific cook, extremely creative and hardworking. She was Molly's best employee and a potential first lieutenant if ever she had one. But Sonya was not great with clients and all their seemingly impossible demands. She tended to lose her patience with women like Mrs. Norris, and quickly.

"Sonya, don't worry. Put her on the phone, will you? Is she around?"

"She just took a break from beating up on me. She's out, getting her nails done. I pity the poor manicurist."

"Okay, hold tight. I'll be right over."

"Thanks, Molly. I don't want to end up as a headline in the *Messenger* tomorrow—if you know what I mean."

"I know what you mean. If she comes back before I get there, just . . . hide in the van or something. Tell her I'm coming."

"Will do. See you later." Sounding relieved, Sonya hung up.

Molly took a deep breath. She looked like a wreck and felt even worse. Even a fast shower and makeup wasn't going to help much. But there was no help for it.

She got up from her chair and headed upstairs. Matt was in the family room, reading the paper while he waited for the girls. She had a hunch that he had overheard every word and tried her best to sneak up the staircase before he noticed.

"Molly, you're not going out, are you?"

She turned and tightened the belt on her robe. "Well . . . it looks like I have to. Sonya is having trouble with an important client. She can't handle it. I have to go and bail her out."

Matt rose and came toward her. "Just talk to the client over the phone. Tell her the truth. Tell her you're sick and that you trust Sonya to run the party."

That was the problem. Molly didn't really trust Sonya to resolve things.

Mrs. Norris was a new client and an important one. If she recommended Molly to her friends, it would open up an entire new business territory. A territory monopolized by her larger, established competitors, and one Molly had been trying to edge her way into.

"Look, I just have to go. Yes, Mrs. Norris is

throwing a hissy fit over nothing. But she wants me to handle it. If that's what it takes to win her over, I'm there."

Matt shook his head. "I can't stop you. I know that by now. But sooner or later, you're going to have to draw the line, Molly. You're going to have to make some tough choices."

She stared at him but didn't answer. She knew that already, thanks very much. Wasn't that the very reason she had been unhappy about getting pregnant?

Twenty minutes later, Molly climbed into her car and headed for the problematic party. Mrs. Norris lived in the heart of the village, in a large Victorian on Mariner's Way, one of the loveliest streets in town. The house, which faced the bay, was restored to perfection and beautifully decorated. Mrs. Norris was forever reminding people that her house was on the historic register and that her ancestors had come across on the *Mayflower*. This only made Molly feel great sympathy for the other *Mayflower* passengers.

Molly tried to center herself, summoning her game face. Normally, she could deal with the Mrs. Norris–type without blinking an eye. But today she felt her force field down, her energy low. It didn't help at all that normally unnoticeable smells in her car—the leather seats, the heater, the scent from the engine coming through the air ducts, some traces of perfume on her scarf—were setting off her stomach again.

Molly opened the windows and felt the cold bracing air sweep in. She took in a few deep, gasping breaths. But it seemed a losing battle.

"Don't get sick again. Do *not* get sick again . . ." she told herself over and over.

Her mantra did not prevail. She pulled over just in time and ran out of the car, sticking her head in a bush. Luckily, it was vacant property. She stood up and wiped her mouth with a bunch of tissues then ran back to her car.

Matt had been right. She was too sick today to run around and put out fires. She should have handled the whole thing over the phone. Now what was she going to do? She was too far from home to run back and change her clothes. If she called now claiming to be sick, Mrs. Norris would think she was lying.

She was so close, too. The house was just up the hill and over a few streets.

Suddenly she realized that so was her best friend, Betty. That's what she would do.

She would clean up at Betty's house, then plow on.

Molly pulled out her cell phone, punched in Betty's number on speed dial, and started the car. She sent up a quick prayer of gratitude as Betty picked up on the first ring.

"Betty? It's me. I'm so glad you're home. Can I stop by for a minute? I'm having a little emergency."

"Sure, come on by. What's going on?" Betty sounded concerned. "Are you all right?"

"Not really," Molly admitted. "I'll tell you when I get there."

"Should I come pick you up? Can you drive?" Betty sounded worried now.

Molly tried to soothe her. "I'm fine to drive. I just have bad morning sickness."

"Then come right over. I'm here for you." It was a much used and even over-used saying, but Molly knew Betty really meant it.

Less than five minutes later, Molly found Betty waiting for her at the front door. "You poor thing. Come into the living room and lie down on the couch. . . ."

"Do I look that bad? I just want to use the bathroom and maybe borrow a blouse."

Betty took Molly's coat. "You're pale as a

sheet. You can't just run in and out of here. How about some tea?"

Why was everyone always offering her tea lately? Molly didn't even like the stuff, and it had never once settled her stomach.

"I'll have some ginger ale if there's any handy."

"Coming right up. My mother used to say it had to be flat to do any good for an upset stomach."

Molly took a seat at the kitchen table and watched as Betty poured some ginger ale into a glass then added a drop of tap water.

Betty handed her the glass. "Where in the world are you going in such a panic?"

"Sonya called. Mrs. Norris is throwing a hissy fit over the centerpieces. She's just annoyed because I didn't do her party personally."

"Oh, Madeline Norris. Say no more. That woman makes a fetish out of bullying the hired help. I was at a luncheon once and she made a huge scene about finding a minuscule crack in her soup cup. I mean, you needed a microscope to see it. Drove the waiters crazy."

"Sounds about right. So, you know her?" Molly asked.

"We were on some board together. The historical society, I guess it was." Betty knew everyone in town, especially Cape Light's high society.

Betty found a box of plain crackers and brought them to the table. She sat down across from Molly. "If you don't have an upset stomach before you deal with Madeline, most people get one during or after."

"Thanks. That makes me feel much better." Molly sipped her soda and took a bite of a cracker.

"I just call 'em the way I seem 'em, honey."

Molly knew that by now. It was one of the reasons she and Betty, who seemed so opposite in many ways, got along so well.

"Hey, I've got an idea. Why don't you send me? I know her. I can deal with her, board member to board member."

"Oh, that's a tempting suggestion," Molly said. "And I'm sure you could deal with her, but, no offense, you don't really know anything about catering. She might get even angrier if I sent you to sort things out."

"Don't be silly. I've been to parties. I know a canapé from an entree," Betty teased. "Bread dish on the left, beverage on the right? Besides, I've been hanging around your shop so much lately, I feel as if I'm already on the payroll."

"True," Molly said. She sometimes felt that way, too. While Betty hung around, taste testing, Molly often got her involved in some question or little business problem. Betty was always either helping her work out the staff schedule or revising her ad copy.

But, no . . . It wouldn't work.

Molly felt a sudden surge in her stomach that sent her running to the bathroom. When she emerged a few minutes later, Betty had a cold cloth ready for her face. "Come on," she said. "You need to lie down."

Betty led her upstairs to the quiet, dimly lit guest room. Molly gratefully stretched out on the bed, two pillows stacked beneath her head and a rubber bucket at her side.

"Case closed," Betty said, pressing the cool cloth to Molly's brow. "Don't worry. I can handle Mrs. Norris. She'll be calling you tomorrow, thanking you for my visit."

Molly doubted that would happen. The best she could hope for was that the problem with the centerpieces would be resolved and the party would run relatively smoothly. But she knew Mrs. Norris would never call her again, and certainly not to thank her for Betty's visit.

Molly grinned at her friend. "Check all the soup cups for cracks, now that I'm thinking of it."

"Will do. You know me, I was born to manage. It doesn't take much more than that." Betty leaned over and tucked an afghan around her shoulders. "Should I call Matt, tell him you're here?"

Molly shook her head. "I'll tell him." *Later*, she thought. *Much later.*

Betty headed toward the door. "If you decide to go before I get back, just close the front door. It will lock behind you."

"All right. I'll remember . . . Betty?"

Betty stopped by the doorway to look at her. "Yes?"

"If it's a girl, we're naming her after you," Molly croaked.

Betty grinned. "I'm touched. But what are friends for?"

Molly didn't answer. Betty disappeared and she closed her eyes.

There are friends, and there is Betty, she thought. *That's the difference.*

THE CHOIR LED THE CONGREGATION IN THE CLOSing hymn as Ben made his way to the back of the church. When the hymn was over, he raised his hands and delivered the final blessing over the rows of worshipers who stood with heads bowed.

". . . and let us now go forth and live the faith we've proclaimed here today. Amen."

Even before the introit had ended, the pews began emptying. It was interesting the way the congregation members who regularly attended the Sunday service always sat in the same places, almost as if the church had assigned seating. Or perhaps it harkened back to the days when each family owned their own "box" in the old New England churches.

Lillian Warwick, the village's reigning grande dame, was not old enough to remember those days, but she had often told Ben of the box her Brahmin ancestors claimed in one of Boston's "best" churches. She made a point of always sitting up front on the pulpit side and usually had some member of her family with her. Now Ben noticed her coming down the aisle. Her daughter Emily Warwick, the town's mayor, was at her side. Emily's husband, Dan, and their adopted daughter, Jane, followed. Jane was in her terrible twos, Ben had noticed, but managed to last for most of the service. Her father only had to take her out twice.

Matt Harding, on the other hand, sat in the back, along with his daughter and two step-daughters. The three girls were all growing so tall and lovely, Ben hardly recognized them from week to week. He didn't see Molly, but knew that her work often conflicted with Sunday service. She got to church when she could and that was fine, too.

Sophie Potter sat toward the middle, near the aisle, alongside her granddaughter Miranda. Ben had read about the man they found on the Potter Orchard, the man with amnesia, but he didn't see anyone fitting that description sitting near them. It appeared that even Sophie, with her powerful talent for persuasion, had not been able to lure her houseguest to church.

He couldn't help but notice Lucy Bates with her bright red hair and her two sons sitting in a back row. Tucker Tulley and his wife, Fran, sat next to her. Unlike his buddy Charlie, Tucker was an active member of the church. He was the senior deacon now and usually came early to help set up.

Ben had been looking for him this morning, hoping to have a word about Carl and the angel story. But it wasn't Tucker's turn to serve so he had slipped in late, during the announcements. Ben decided that if he missed Tucker this morning, he would give him a call. After all, Tucker had been the first to repeat his brother's story. He could have told half the town by now.

The weeks before Christmas usually brought new faces into church, but there were many more today than the holiday could account for. Ben had noticed it from his pulpit view. As most of the congregation lined up to greet him, he also noticed how many hung back and collected around the angel.

Some sat in the nearby pews to pray. Others reached out to touch it. He noticed more than one person tuck a little piece of white paper under the statue's base. A prayer petition, he guessed.

What was happening? Had Carl's story started a real rumor here?

Grace Hegman was the first in line to greet him. "Excellent sermon, Reverend. Dad enjoyed it, too. What he could gather," she added in a quieter voice.

Grace turned to her father, Digger. The old seaman nodded and stroked his long beard with a thick, gnarled hand. Digger was famous as the best clammer on the cape in the last fifty years. Sadly, his memory and mind were slowly failing these days, and he often seemed to drift into some other world.

Digger stuck out his hand and Ben shook it. "Good to see you, Digger. How are you today?"

"Faring well. Listing to the side a mite." He leaned to one side and made a gesture with his hand, imitating a sailboat that was off balance.

"Dad's knee is acting up. His arthritis," Grace interpreted. She drew closer. "That statue over there"—she glanced over her shoulder and pointed at the angel—"we heard Carl Tulley touched it and it healed an infection on his hand. Is that true?"

Ben didn't know what to say, though he had fully expected he would be asked that question this morning.

"I believe the statue is totally ordinary, Grace. Lovely, but just carved and painted wood. I would say that Carl's healing was most likely a coincidence."

Grace looked down, as if now embarrassed to have asked at all. She touched a button on her sweater. "Well, you hear these things around town, especially running a store. You don't know what to think. Right, Dad?"

Digger nodded sagely. "Oh, yes. Don't know what to think. We'll have to wait until the tide goes out, right, Reverend? It all washes out with the tide."

Ben smiled gently and touched Digger's arm. "Yes, Digger. That should make it clear."

"Thank you, Reverend. Our best to your wife. I hope she's well?" That was Grace's way of asking why Carolyn wasn't at church this morning.

"She has a cold. I think she needed some extra sleep to kick it."

"Tell her I said hello. Come on, Father."

Grace took Digger's arm and led him away. Not out to the narthex, Ben noticed, but back into the church. Toward the statue. Obviously, he had not convinced Grace of the statue's ordinariness. Or perhaps she just wanted a closer look. It was, indeed, beautiful.

Ben watched as Grace and Digger joined a group gathered near the angel. Some were members of the congregation, but many were visitors.

Among them, Ben recognized a woman he had seen at the statue before. He was almost positive she didn't live in town. She was slim with thick white hair in a stylish cut.

She always wore a dark red coat with a large, patterned silk scarf around her shoulders; that's how he recognized her. He wondered where she came from, how far away. There was something elegant about her. If he had to guess, he would say she lived in Boston. If that was the case, then why had she come so far? Why was she, too, drawn to the angel?

Ben had been right, Carolyn decided. The extra sleep had done her good. So had the slow Sunday morning, in the snug, warm rectory. She'd had a late, leisurely breakfast, read the newspapers, then dressed, and straightened up the house.

Her music room seemed in a perpetual state of disorder. She could never seem to keep it neat. She had read somewhere that a neat desk was the sign of a unproductive person. Perhaps the same applied to her profession. After all, there were students coming in and out all week, and her own last-minute searches for misplaced sheet music.

Carolyn sorted out some music books that were piled on the top of the piano. Then she dusted off the keys, creating a brash, discordant sound. She sat down and stretched out her fingers. She lifted both hands to play, the right moving nimbly through the first notes of a simple version of "Fleur de Lis," the left, resting heavily on the edge of the keyboard, striking a bass key or two if she really focused.

The physical therapist said to keep at it, but Carolyn felt she had hit a wall. It had been almost three years since the stroke. She had spent hours in physical therapy and doing exercises at home, and she had recovered some degree of use of the left hand. But it had been months since she'd made any progress at all. Deep inside, she knew it would never get any better than this. It seemed foolish to keep pushing herself. Why pretend? She knew it was wisest now to just accept it. To count her blessings.

The stroke could have robbed her of much more—the use of both hands, the ability to walk, to speak, to function independently. To even be alive today after what her body had been through was a miracle in and of itself.

She tried to remind herself every day, especially when she sat down to give a lesson, that she was lucky just to be here. She really tried to be grateful.

After all, almost all of her students had come back, which was a great compliment. She realized that she had never appreciated those children enough. She had never appreciated what a gift it was to be able to pass on her knowledge and to see them come into their own talent. Once she had played effortlessly in grand concert halls. Now her touch was almost as faltering as those of her students. But somehow, she enjoyed it more.

One needed to be flexible in life, to revise one's expectations. "Blessed are the flexible," her husband had once said. "They don't get bent out of shape."

She had laughed at the time, but it was true.

She sighed and shuffled through the sheets of music, finding another piece to play. A simplified, bare-bones arrangement by Bach. She did the best she could, without any illusions that her playing would ever sound better.

BY THE TIME BEN GOT HOME FROM CHURCH, IT was after two. He let himself in the front door and hung his coat and hat on the coat tree in the foyer. Beautiful notes drifted through the house from the music room, though even his unschooled ear could discern that there was something lacking.

He wished he could stop thinking that way, comparing what she was now to what she had been. He knew better. After her stroke, it was a wonder Carolyn could play at all. She rarely complained about it. Still, he knew it must pain her deeply to remember how she used to play so flawlessly, how her fingers once glided and danced over the keys, calling up the most divine sounds from the instrument.

He walked into the kitchen and poured himself a cup of coffee. Then he leafed through a section of the Sunday paper he found on the table. Carolyn appeared in the kitchen doorway. "Ben, I didn't hear you come in. Have you been home long?"

"Only a few minutes."

She walked over and kissed his cheek. "How was church this morning? Sorry I had to miss it."

"The Hegmans asked for you. I told them you had a cold."

The minister's wife was expected every Sunday, a permanent fixture front and center, smiling and friendly and pious. Ben knew it could be stressful to have to live up to those expectations. He hadn't married Carolyn because he thought she would make the perfect partner for a man of his calling. He married her because he loved her, because he couldn't imagine his life without her. Because the ways they were different made him whole. He still felt the same, too, after all these years.

"How are you doing?" he asked. "Feel any better?"

"Oh, it's nothing. I'll be fine in a day or so. I've been taking a lot of vitamin C and those zinc lozenge things. Rachel says they really work. Rachel's so sweet. She's going to drop off something for dinner so we don't have to cook."

"You mean, so that you don't have to cook," Ben said wryly. He was a disaster in the kitchen and could barely call for take-out. He and Carolyn were lucky that their daughter, Rachel, and her family had chosen to live nearby. Ben's grandchildren—Will, who was four, and Nora, who would soon be one—were among the great joys of his life.

"Rachel does so much," he said, "even with two little ones to look after."

"Jack helps her. She's very organized."

"She didn't get that from me," he said with a laugh.

Carolyn smiled but didn't disagree. "I'll be making Christmas Eve dinner this year," she told him, "and they're going to Jack's family's for Christmas Day. We're invited, too. Rachel just mentioned it."

"That will be something new for us." Ben didn't know Jack's parents very well and didn't like the idea of spending the holidays away from his own home. But now there were the grandchildren to consider. One had to be gracious and share them, he supposed.

"Have you heard from Mark?" Carolyn asked. Their son Mark was away at school in Portland, Oregon. "Will he be home for Christmas?"

"I'm afraid not," Ben said gently. "His last e-mail—I just opened it this morning—said he might stay for intercession and take some extra credits. He has that girlfriend now from California. I think her family has invited him there for the holidays."

"Well, I suppose I can't be too upset about that," Carolyn said. "I've been waiting a long time for Mark to settle down with a nice young woman. And I thought Erin was lovely when we met her last summer. Do you think they'll get engaged for Christmas?"

"How would I know? He never talks to me about those things. I didn't even think of it," Ben answered honestly.

"Of course you didn't, you're a man." Carolyn grinned. "I'll bet Erin expects a ring by now."

"They both have to finish school first. I think Mark should wait before he makes that kind of commitment."

"He only has a year left. And he is twenty-five, Ben. We were married by then, you know."

"People married earlier when we were young. It was expected and we were more mature than kids these days . . . or something."

Ben wanted Mark to find real love and settle down in a solid relationship, too. He sometimes thought that's what the boy needed more than anything. But these things couldn't be rushed. He wouldn't ever dare even suggest it.

"If he does come home, I don't think we should talk about any of this with him," Ben warned. "He can't feel pressured . . . or as if we're too nosy about his personal life. You know how he hates that. He'll do just the opposite of anything we say."

Carolyn nodded. "I won't say a word. Promise."

Ben knew her promise was sincerely given but wondered if she could keep it. Maybe it was just as well if their son spent Christmas in California.

Eager to change the subject, he said, "Listen, something happened at church today. I'm not quite sure how to handle it." His wife lifted her chin, listening with interest. He didn't know where to begin. "Carl's story about that statue has really made the rounds. It's started something, Carolyn— there were a lot of new people in church today, people I didn't recognize."

"How do you know they came because of the statue? It is almost Christmas, and you are an excellent preacher. Maybe word is finally getting around?"

He knew she was teasing him. "I've been at that church for nearly forty years. I say, it's high time," he joked back. "But as much as I would like to agree with you, I know it's not me. It's not even Christmas. After the service quite a large group gathered around the statue. They gazed up at it and prayed and stuck little bits of paper with prayers . . . calls for help, really . . . at its base. I've never seen anything like it. Not in our church anyway."

Carolyn's expression was serious again. "That's really something."

"I'm always trying to bring new members into the congregation, heaven knows. Maybe I should just sit back and encourage the rumor. It seems to be the best advertising campaign we've hit on so far."

"Ben . . ." Carolyn cast him a look. "I know you're not serious."

"Of course not." He rubbed his forehead, realizing he had been tense all morning. "You know how serious and matter-of-fact Grace Hegman is. She believes it, too. She cornered me right after the service to ask about Carl's story. Even when I told her straight out that there was nothing to it, I could tell she wasn't convinced. She went right back into the sanctuary and sent up a prayer or two."

"Maybe just in case?" Carolyn offered.

Ben shook his head. "When people want to believe something, it's hard to change their minds. What do you think? Should I make some statement next Sunday? Should I write something for the bulletin?"

"What would you say?" Carolyn asked. "I mean, what do you think is going on?"

"I honestly don't know," Ben admitted. "It's a slippery slope, especially for a minister. You should have seen the look on Carl's face when he showed me his hand. He believes it was a miracle. He truly believes, and who am I to argue with him?"

"But you don't believe it," Carolyn said.

"I believe he's sincere," Ben answered carefully. "But no . . . I don't think there's been divine intervention here. There are just too many logical explanations."

Carolyn looked thoughtful. "Well, if that's so, why make any comment at all? Wouldn't it be giving the statue too much importance? I'm sure once people realize that nothing really happens if you touch the statue or even leave a little note there, Carl's story will die out. Don't you think?"

Ben mulled it over. "Yes, I think you're right. Why give it too much attention? Sooner or later, everyone will decide that Carl was just imagining things. Or that it was all a coincidence."

"Just give it a few days," Carolyn advised. "I expect they'll forget all about it."

The phone rang and Carolyn rose to answer it. Ben heard her talking to Rachel, but he couldn't stop thinking about the statue. What Carolyn said made sense. Still, the situation troubled him. It stirred up so many ideas and questions about spirituality. Ben had often heard stories of divine or spiritual intervention. Prayers were answered. Miracles sometimes occurred. After all, he reminded himself, there were numerous mentions of angels in the Bible. And Ben had always believed that God does answer prayers, and that spiritual power—perhaps even in the form of angels—does intervene in earthly lives.

Had it really happened in his church? To Carl Tulley? Despite his own faith, Ben couldn't quite believe that it had. And yet, no matter what he had told Lucy Bates or Grace Hegman, or anyone else who asked him, he knew in his heart that he could never be absolutely certain that it hadn't.

CHAPTER SIX

MOLLY GOT STUCK AT THE SHOP ON TUESDAY
night, supervising dishes that were to be
served at a school board holiday luncheon
on Wednesday. It was a full three weeks until Christmas, but the parties were in full
swing. It was hard to believe that anyone in
any office in town got anything done for the
rest of the month, she thought. But it was
good for her business.

She didn't get home until nearly nine and
when she walked in, the house seemed
eerily quiet. She walked back to the family
room and found Matt alone, reading the
newspaper while he watched TV.

"Hi, honey." She bent to kiss him. "Where is everybody?"

Usually, she treasured a rare moment of quiet and calm. One look at Matt's expression and she longed for the cover of her noisy, demanding children.

"Upstairs, doing homework. I think Jillian went to sleep. Hard volleyball practice." He kept his eyes on the paper, then finally looked up at her. "What happened? You told me you would be home by seven."

Molly shrugged and flopped down on the couch. She was beat, but resisted showing him how very tired she truly felt. "Oh, the usual. Rita and Dawn stayed but Sonya made some excuse at the last minute and they needed me. Sonya's a great cook but temperamental."

He glanced at her but didn't say anything. Molly knew that look. She didn't like it. He was mad. Steaming to be precise. Matt rarely lost his temper but when he did it was more of a slow-rising simmer . . . until finally the pot boiled over.

"I'm going in late tomorrow," she offered. "They're going to run the whole thing, and we don't have to open until eleven."

"Why don't you just take the day off? In

fact, why don't you take a week off? I'm pretty sure you could sleep straight through, given the opportunity."

"Matt, you know I can't do that. Don't be silly." He wasn't pleased with that answer, she realized too late. She had just managed to turn the heat up even higher. "I can take some time off after the holidays," she added in a more soothing tone. "Maybe I'll even close the shop a few days." The idea had suddenly come to her, though she wasn't at all sure she would ever go that far.

"Guess who came to see me today? A client of yours, Mrs. Norris."

Molly heard a distant alarm sounding. "I didn't know she was one of your patients."

"She isn't. But her regular physician is on vacation and she twisted her ankle. She didn't want to drive all the way to Southport and sit in the ER if it was just a sprain. Which it was."

"Oh . . . Well, I hope she's doing better. Good thing she didn't hurt herself before the party."

"Yes, good thing." He nodded and put the paper aside. He looked straight at her. "I asked about the event. She said that after a bumpy start, it all went very smoothly."

"Good. I'm glad she was pleased." Molly shrugged and avoided his gaze.

She hadn't told Matt about her stop at Betty's and how her friend had helped out. She didn't like keeping secrets from him and usually never did. But she was afraid that if she confessed her collapse on Betty's guest room bed, Matt wouldn't let her out of the house until the baby was born.

"Mrs. Norris said that if it wasn't for Betty Bowman, the whole affair would have been a complete disaster." He paused and stared at her. "Good old Betty. Sounds like she saved the day. Where were you all morning, may I ask? At Betty's house, getting sick?"

"I wasn't that sick. I was resting, in her guest room . . ." Her words trailed off on a weak note. "I'm sorry I didn't tell you what happened. That was wrong. I shouldn't have kept it from you. I just didn't want you to make a big thing about it."

Matt rose and paced around the room. "Well, excuse me. I'm just the father of your child and a doctor, to boot. Of course I'm going to make a big thing about it. You need to slow down, Molly. What is it going to take to convince you?"

Molly couldn't stand for anyone to give her

orders. Even Matt. Even if he was right. It just pushed her buttons.

"That's easy for you to say," she snapped. "How can I slow down? It's Christmas, my busiest season. I'm booked with parties practically every night of the week, straight through New Year's Day. What should I do, call up some of the clients and say, 'Sorry, I can't do that party for you. I'm slowing down'?"

"I know it's complicated. I know you have commitments. But you need to think of the baby first now. You can't keep up this pace day after day. You can't overdo it."

Molly made a face, rolling her eyes at him. "I have to overdo it if I'm the only one doing everything. The business, taking care of the house and the girls. Even with the cleaning service, there's still a lot to keep up on around here, Matt. I don't get a lot of help from the kids. They're always too busy. And I don't get that much help from you either, come to think of it." She bit back her next sentence, wondering if she had gone too far.

Matt sighed and rubbed the back of his neck. "I know we all need to help more. I know I should be more available, spend less time at the office. I've been thinking about how much I missed with Amanda, because I was always working. I don't want to make the same mistake with this child. I don't want you to either," he added.

He had a good point. *At least he's thinking about these things,* she reflected.

"Before we found out about the pregnancy, I started looking for a partner to bring into the practice. Now it seems like a necessity, so I can have more free time to help with the baby."

"That's a great idea." Molly was both surprised and encouraged by this news. "Have you found anyone?"

"Yes, I think I have. An old friend from med school, Alex Cole. She might come to visit next week and make a decision."

She? Molly was surprised to hear that Alex was a woman. When Matt had said he was thinking about a partner, she had automatically pictured another guy. But, of course, that was silly. Lots of women were doctors these days. And anyone willing to take some of Matt's caseload was welcome.

"Wow, that's great. I mean, if it works out."

"Alex is a terrific doctor. I hope it works out, too."

Molly gazed at him, feeling suddenly sorry

for the nasty things she'd said. He was only trying to take care of her and the baby. "I'm sorry, Matt. I promise I'll try harder to delegate at work and cut back on my hours. You're right, I have to think of the baby right now."

Matt slowly smiled. "Okay. You got my point. Now I want to see you stick to those words, Molly."

"I will," she said. She stood up and faced him, raising her right hand and looking very solemn. "Caterer's honor."

"Caterer's honor?" Matt grinned and shook his head.

"Well . . . I was never a Girl Scout. I didn't want to fib to you again."

"I'll have to take what I can get, I guess." He pulled her close and kissed her.

Molly kissed him back, glad he wasn't angry anymore and that they had resolved things so easily. At least for now.

THE FIRST THING THAT OCCURRED TO MIRANDA when she woke up on Thursday morning was that it had been a week since she and Dixie had found Adam. Funny how it seemed much longer.

She'd had another date with Greg the night before. Again, he had asked how long she thought Adam would be staying, and again she had no clear answer for him. Thankfully, Greg let the matter drop. They had gone to see a movie and then Miranda had come straight home to work on the jewelry order. That made it a short date with not much time for conversation, and Miranda was relieved to have escaped another discussion about Adam or their relationship.

She and Greg had made plans for Saturday, their usual date night. But as she got out of bed and started to dress, Miranda had to admit, she wasn't really looking forward to seeing Greg again so soon. She wasn't really sure why, either. In a way, she almost felt as if the date was an obligation, something she had to do, because it would be good for her. Like eating some healthy vegetable she didn't like.

But that was silly. She liked Greg. They had a good relationship, a good rapport. She couldn't just toss that all away because Adam had swept into her life . . . and would soon be sweeping out.

Every morning, she wondered if Adam would even emerge from the cottage and come into the house for breakfast. Or if he would just disappear in the middle of the night. When he did show up, her heart did a little leap in her chest, a reaction she tried hard to conceal.

Miranda had been concentrating on her jewelry-making the last few days. She had been working so hard on the Golden Moon order that she hadn't seen much of Adam. He had been spending nearly all of his free time on the Internet, looking at maps and pictures of nearby towns, trying to find some clue to his past. Just last night he told her that some of the images of New England seemed familiar to him. He was fairly certain that he had been living somewhere in the area.

Adam also spent time at the library, skimming old newspapers and magazines, searching for any mention of a lost vehicle or petty crimes that might be connected to his disappearance. Sophie had done most of his chauffeuring, driving him back and forth to town whenever she did errands.

They had finished painting the cottage, and Sophie had put Adam to work in the house. With Christmas coming, Sophie was expecting most of their huge family to arrive; guests would be sleeping in every available space. A leak in the roof last fall had stained the ceiling and wallpaper in two rooms, so

Sophie set Adam to work stripping the wallpaper—a messy, time-consuming job—then painting.

Miranda walked into the kitchen and headed straight for the coffeepot. Adam was on the phone.

"Detective Lester," her grandmother explained. "He called so early, we both thought it was good news. But I don't think it's anything important."

Tucker Tulley had passed Adam's case on to a county detective, Roger Lester. The detective had been in touch a few times by phone, following up on the fingerprint database search, which had turned up negative. *Good news and bad news,* Miranda thought. The bad news was they still didn't know his identity. The good news was that he wasn't a criminal. Or at least, had never been arrested.

The Cape Light police department had received a few calls in response to the news article, but so far none of the inquiries had held up. Miranda was still hopeful, but she could see Adam's optimism fading day by day.

"Yes, Detective. Thanks for the number. I guess I'll call and see if it's worth a try."

She heard Adam say good-bye and hang up the phone.

"Morning, Miranda," he said, helping himself to the orange juice.

"Good morning." She was dying to ask him what the detective had said but didn't want to pry.

Sophie, though, had no such scruples. "Adam, dear, do you have any news? Why did Detective Lester call so early?"

Adam glanced at her, then spread some of Sophie's homemade apple butter on a warm biscuit. "Um, two things. The first is that they showed my photo to the staff at the Regatta Bar and in the Charles Hotel. No one remembers me." Adam gave a bitter smile. "Maybe amnesia is contagious. The second thing is Lester thinks I should see a psychiatrist in Newburyport who knows a lot about memory loss. He thinks maybe that would help."

"Of course you should go," Sophie urged him. "I was watching my show yesterday and there's a character who's had amnesia for weeks now. He got hypnotized by accident, and he snapped right out of it. Just like that, he remembered that his evil half brother . . ."

Adam listened patiently to the soap opera plot. Miranda could tell he was struggling to keep a straight face.

How could someone get hypnotized *by accident*? She didn't even want to ask.

Adam smiled gently at Sophie. "Yes, Detective Lester mentioned hypnotherapy. I've read about it, too. It can work. But it's very rare that a person's entire memory comes back in a snap. It usually takes quite a few sessions to break through." Adam sounded discouraged, frustrated.

"Well, it may be a long process," Sophie said, "but you really shouldn't leave any stone unturned. Do you have the doctor's name? I think you should make an appointment."

"Grandma's right," Miranda said. Much as she didn't want Adam to leave, she did want him to recover his memory. "I could take you there."

Adam glanced at her. The warm look in his dark eyes seemed to fill something inside her. She was going to miss that. "Okay," he said, and she got the distinct feeling that he was agreeing because she wanted him to go. "I need to speak with the doctor first, to find out if he can even see me."

Suddenly, Miranda understood his hesitation. The doctor wasn't going to treat him for free, and Adam was too proud to ask them for any more help. Perhaps he hoped to work out some deal with the doctor, without them knowing.

Her grandmother realized it, too. "Don't worry about the cost, Adam. For goodness sake, you'll pay us back when you're able. This is important. That's all there is to it."

A look of something like awe flickered across Adam's face. "Sophie Potter, I will always remember you as the most generous person I've ever known. I'm sure that even in my past, there could be no equal."

Sophie beamed. "Well, you see this doctor, and maybe we'll find out if that's true."

"Maybe we will." Adam smiled at her, then headed back to the phone. Miranda could tell his spirits had lifted. He had some hope again. Didn't everyone need hope in their heart about the thing they wanted most?

Funny how, while he had more, she was left with less.

THE BRAMBLE ANTIQUE SHOP DIDN'T OFFICIALLY open on weekdays until eleven, and it was exactly five minutes before the hour. Ben knew Grace Hegman stuck to her schedule and made few exceptions—perhaps not even for him.

The small Victorian house at the end of Main Street stood on its own amid the other shops and buildings. The Bramble was decorated beautifully for Christmas. There was a wreath on every window hanging by a thick red ribbon, and a long white candle in every window, too. A larger pine wreath hung on the front door, studded with holly, dried white roses, and a few tiny ceramic angels. Ben couldn't help wondering if the angels were a recent addition.

He knocked on the front door, using the vintage brass knocker in the shape of a sea shell. Ben had not called in advance; he assumed they would be in. They rarely went out these days, except for doctors' appointments. Now he wondered if he should have called. He tried to peek around the lace curtain behind the glass, then quickly stepped back, hearing footsteps on the stairs. Finally he saw Grace coming to open the door.

"Reverend Ben, what a surprise."

"I was just in town and thought I would drop by to say hello. How is Digger feeling? He mentioned his knee was acting up on him again. Is he still in pain?"

Ben was sincerely interested in Digger's welfare. But he was even more interested in finding out if the Hegmans had witnessed another miracle cure. Word around town was that they had and were telling everyone who came into the shop.

Ben could easily imagine Digger saying such things. The old man's mind was so foggy lately, he couldn't tell real life from his dreams or memories. But Grace? Ever level-headed, no-nonsense Grace Hegman? That part, Ben could not believe.

"He's much better, thank you." Grace nodded and smiled. She held an account book to her chest, and a handful of yellow pencils, the points very sharp.

"Good to hear." Ben nodded. "I know on Sunday, he told me it hurt something fierce. Has he been taking any special medication?"

"Just his usual brand of liniment. But he's been using that for years, ever since I was a little girl."

Ben knew what she meant. He was familiar with the strong menthol scent that often lingered around Digger.

"Grace, I'll be honest with you. A report has reached me that your father believes his knee has been miraculously healed, that he was helped by the statue at church—the statue of the angel. Has Digger been telling people that?"

It was hard for Ben to put it so bluntly, but he had to know if the gossip was true.

Grace shifted on her feet and looked out at the street, over Ben's shoulder. "My father does believe that, Reverend. We visited the angel on Sunday. We sat and said a prayer. He woke up on Monday and said the pain was gone. The angel had fixed it for him. He said he saw it all in a dream."

Visions in dreams? What next? Ben felt his blood pressure rise and took a deep breath.

"Grace . . . you don't really believe that, do you?" he asked quietly. "Couldn't it be that Digger is just having a good spell with his knee? Perhaps he's feeling better because of the dry weather or maybe because of those new supplements he's taking?"

The rational possibilities were endless. Didn't Grace see that? Didn't everyone?

Grace met his gaze with her typical, level look. "Well, Reverend, I suppose any of those could be the reason. But I believe Dad. He wouldn't make up a story. It's not in his nature, you know?"

Ben nodded, fearing he had offended her. "Yes, of course. I'm not saying he purposely made up a story, Grace. But his mind isn't sound. I'm sure he tells you a great number of things all day that don't quite make sense."

"Yes, he does," she admitted. "It's the dementia. He's better some days. But it's pretty much a steady decline." Her eyes filled with a sad light.

Ben suddenly wished he had not pursued this face-to-face confrontation. He wanted to get to the bottom of this story, but not at the cost of hurting Grace's feelings.

Ben reached out and touched her arm. "I'm sorry. Let's not bother about this anymore. Digger feels better and that's the main thing."

Grace nodded. "I know what your point is, Reverend. But I also know my father. I can tell when he's . . . off somewhere. Or lost in the past. When he told me about the dream, why, it was the most lucid I had seen him in months. Perhaps it was just his imagination. But he did convince me."

Ben didn't know what more to say. He thanked Grace for her time and headed down Main Street, toward the church. He never would have guessed that Grace Hegman would side with the angel-believers. Now who would convince Digger that perhaps the angel had not really healed him and that he should stop repeating the story?

Ben wrapped his muffler around his throat and pulled his cap down lower. The wind off the bay whipped up the wide street, cutting right through his wool overcoat and thick sweater. He shielded his eyes with his hands and suddenly found himself walking straight into Emily Warwick, who had just come out of the Village Hall.

"Emily . . . I'm sorry. I nearly knocked you over."

"The wind is wicked today, isn't it?" Emily gave him an apologetic smile. "Sorry, Revered. Perhaps I shouldn't have put it quite that way."

"That's all right, Emily. I'm permitted to hear the word. It won't corrupt me."

Emily laughed and fell into step beside him. She wore a long brown coat and an elegant scarf, a paisley pattern on velvet. She hugged the coat closer around her slim figure. "Are you headed this way? I'm running down to the newspaper office."

"Yes, I'm on my way back to church. I was

just over at the Bramble, visiting the Heg-mans."

"Oh? Something wrong with Digger?"

"No . . . not exactly. He's feeling unusually fit, in fact." Ben glanced at her, trying to decide how much of his morning business he should confide. Emily was sensible, intelligent, and unfailingly discreet. He knew she would be a good sounding board for his dilemma.

"Digger believes he's had a cure from the angel. The arthritis in his knee is miraculously improved. He saw it all in a dream, he says. And whether through Digger or Grace, I'm not sure, but the story is making its way through town."

"You seem worried about it," she said, sounding surprised. "We all know that Digger's reasoning powers are failing him. Who would actually believe the story once they know the source?"

"But people do believe it. I know it sounds absurd, but the word is spreading like wildfire. Visitors are coming to the church every day. They come to see the angel. I've no idea how they've heard about it. They tuck notes under the statue's base, even on the floor at the bottom of the pedestal. It's very touching really . . ."

He could see that Emily was taking him seriously now. "Yes, that is touching. . . . What do you do with them, the notes I mean?"

"I don't read them. I feel they're private, written to the angel. Or maybe they're notes to God. I'm not sure the authors would want someone reading their requests. But I do pray over them. That seems the least I can do."

He had been spending time lately collecting the notes. The little folded bits of paper were important to him, each one holding a prayer, perhaps a desperate plea to God. He had spent not only time but emotional and spiritual energy on these petitions. He really had no choice in the matter—he felt it was his duty to pray over them. In all his years as a pastor, he had never experienced anything quite like it. Watching the visitors come and go, some who looked as if they didn't have a care in the world, reminded him that everyone suffered in some way. Everyone had a burden to bear. At the very least, the angel statue had served to remind him—reteach him—that lesson.

He looked at her again. "The thing is, Emily, you're the mayor. I think you ought to have some say in all this—where it might lead, what we can do to stop it."

"Stop it? Why would you want to stop it? It seems harmless enough to me."

"Think about it, Emily. Do you really want your town known as some sort of holy shrine? One that many people will believe is totally bogus. Is that what Cape Light will be famous for? Aside from Charlie's clam rolls, I mean."

Emily smiled a bit. "Normally, I'm in favor of anything that might deflate Charlie's ego. And I see your point. But I don't know what I can do about it, Ben. Don't you think it's just the holiday season inspiring these stories? Maybe after Christmas, it will all die down."

"Carolyn predicted something like that. But the interest has only grown as far as I can see. It's going to get worse before it gets better, and I'm not sure I should wait. It might be too late by then. We'll be stuck with a local legend we can never undo."

Emily didn't answer for a long moment, and Ben thought that was the end of the conversation. "Have the deacons discussed it yet?" she asked finally. "I think they would be the appropriate group to call upon for some guidance."

The deaconate. Why hadn't he thought of that? He had been too mired in his own spiritual debates and anxieties. The deacons were leaders of the church, helping him oversee the spiritual life of the congregation. They should be consulted about this situation before he took any action.

"Yes, you're right. The question is complicated. I need to hear what the deaconate has to say. Thank you, Emily. You've been a big help."

"Oh, I didn't do much," Emily assured him. "You've sorted out my problems plenty of times, Ben. I owed you one."

They had reached the end of Main Street. They said good-bye, and Emily headed toward the newspaper office and he headed toward the church.

As he walked across the green, he noticed a white minivan parked in front of the church. A middle-aged man, who appeared to be the driver, helped the passengers out. They were all seniors, some quite infirm. *Oh, no,* he thought. *Not again!* He knew why they had come and where they were headed.

Normally, he liked to meet visitors, but today he walked around to the side entrance, purposely avoiding them. He went straight to his office to call a meeting of the deaconate. Clearly, there was no time to waste.

FRIDAY AFTERNOON, MIRANDA AND ADAM SAT side by side in a small waiting room at the office of Dr. George Carter. It was a cloudy day and the room was dimly lit. Adam had hardly spoken on the ride to Newburyport and now sat paging through a magazine. Though he was taking pains not to show it, Miranda could tell that he was nervous. Usually, he read things thoroughly, devouring information. Now he was flipping through the magazines, as if he had just completed a course in speed-reading.

At exactly three minutes past four the door to the doctor's office opened, revealing a friendly looking man, who appeared to be in his early fifties. He was neatly dressed, wearing corduroy pants and a yellow wool vest over a pale blue shirt and patterned tie. He peered at them from behind wire-rimmed glasses. "Adam? I'm Dr. Carter. Please come in."

Adam rose from his chair in the waiting room. "Thanks for seeing me on such short notice." He turned to Miranda. "This is my friend Miranda Potter. I told you about the Potters when we spoke," he added.

"Yes, I remember. Hello, Miranda." Dr. Carter smiled at her then turned back to Adam. "Would you feel more comfortable if Miranda joined us?"

Adam looked surprised by the suggestion. "I guess I would. Do you want to come in with me, Miranda?"

"If you'd like." Miranda hadn't expected to be included, but didn't mind. If it would help Adam, it was fine with her. If Adam felt he wanted more privacy, she could always leave, she reasoned.

They walked into the office and Dr. Carter shut the door. There was a large wooden desk near the windows. Shelves filled with books and Native American pottery lined one long wall. Dr. Carter sat in an armchair in front of his desk. Miranda and Adam took chairs that faced him.

"I've read your story in the newspaper, Adam," the doctor began. "But why don't you tell me everything you can remember, starting with the night Miranda found you."

"All right. No problem." Adam sat back. He told how he woke up on the cold ground, hearing a dog barking, then opened his eyes to see Miranda. He recounted how she helped him up and down to the house, how Tucker had arrived, and how he had been taken to the hospital.

"Is that similar to your memory of the night?" Dr. Carter asked Miranda.

"Yes," she said. "It's completely accurate."

Adam told the doctor about visiting the police department and his interview at the newspaper. "For the past week I've been at the orchard, waiting for some news. I've been visiting the library in town, too. Looking through the local newspapers, and checking out ideas on the Internet—just random subjects that catch my interest. I've printed out anything that seems significant and started a file," he added.

"What else have you been doing, besides visiting the library?"

"Working for the Potters. Painting mostly. And I've been reading and writing in a journal at night."

The doctor nodded. "That's good, that's all good. This journal—whose idea was that?"

Adam shrugged. "My own, I guess. One night I had a very vivid dream. A nightmare I guess you'd have to call it. Writing it down seemed to help get it out of my system. I've been writing every day since, hoping the writing will help me remember something."

"Has it helped, do you think?"

"Not yet. Not really," Adam admitted. "But it does make me feel better somehow. As if I have some control over the situation, sorting it out. It's hard to explain."

"I think you're explaining it very well. The journal is a good idea. You can try just letting your mind wander, almost in an imaginary state, not editing or judging at all. Just writing the first thing that pops into your head. You may not realize it at the time, but ideas or images that come to you can be valuable clues to your past. Sometimes a person in your situation needs only one image, like a key, that will unlock the door to your memory."

"I'll keep at it then," Adam said. "Maybe I've been too analytical. I'll try to let my thoughts wander more, try to relax and not force it so much."

"Let's get back to the dream," Dr. Carter said. "Why was it so frightening?"

Adam described the nightmare much the same way he had described it to Miranda the night it woke him.

"I guess the worst part about it was that it felt so real. More like a memory than a dream. It made me think I've been involved in some kind of crime. I was surprised the police didn't find a record of my fingerprints. Maybe that's just a matter of time," he added, his voice troubled. "Or maybe I've just never been caught."

"Maybe," the doctor said. "How are you behaving day to day, Adam? Do you feel the urge to act unethically? To steal money from Miranda's purse, for instance?"

Adam shook his head. "No, not at all. The thought never crossed my mind. I could never do something like that."

Adam turned to Miranda, and in that instant she was sure she could read his mind: the only vaguely unethical urges between them were romantic ones. Yet they both knew that he probably had commitments and ties elsewhere. And she, of course, was seeing Greg.

Dr. Carter sat back in his chair. "Some people are prone to guilty feelings, Adam. Ironically, these are often people who have nothing to feel guilty about. I suspect you fall into this category, and the images in your dream that seemed so vivid were not actual memories but just a hodgepodge from your subconscious. Like debris on the ocean floor stirred up by a storm, these images were stirred up by the trauma you experienced that caused your memory loss."

"So, you're saying the dream has nothing to do with my past? It wasn't a memory?"

Dr. Carter tilted his head to one side. "There's no way in the world to be sure. I can say that until you have a distinct, clear memory about some event, or some person, it's impossible to know what your life was like. If you're really experiencing fragments of memory returning, then more distinct memories will emerge. Not just in dreams, but in your waking life. Or someone will find you and your past will emerge that way."

Adam nodded, seeming somewhat comforted. "What about hypnosis? Does that ever work?"

"In some cases." Dr. Carter paused, adjusting his glasses. "It depends on the subject, how well their psyche is protecting against the trauma. Sometimes we have a clue or some fragment to work with, to lead us forward. That helps. There doesn't seem to be any in your case, except the nightmare."

"So you're advising against it?" Miranda asked.

"No," the doctor told them. "I'm only cautioning that it could take a while. Sometimes the first session of hypnosis doesn't break through, but a second or even a third might be successful. Hypnosis doesn't work in every situation, though. There's no magic bullet, I'm afraid."

"I understand," Adam said, and Miranda could tell he'd hoped for something more.

Dr. Carter waited a long moment before speaking again. "We can try a hypnotherapy session today. Are you still interested?"

"Yes, I am. Definitely," Adam said, sitting up straight and alert in his chair.

Dr. Carter nodded. "All right. I think Miranda should wait outside though. It will help you focus better."

"Yes, of course." Miranda rose from her seat. She glanced down at Adam and lightly touched his shoulder. "See you later. Good luck."

He met her glance and smiled briefly.

Miranda left the two men alone and quietly closed the door.

Out in the waiting room, she picked up a magazine but didn't open it. She could only think of Adam, what he was going through. She knew how much he wanted this to work, how frustrated he felt, how nearly hopeless. With all her heart, she wanted it to work for him. She wanted him to remember his place in the world, his identity. No matter that it would mean him leaving her, probably forever.

That probably meant she loved him, she realized, if she wanted his happiness more than her own. The realization surprised her. And made her somehow feel happy and sad at the same time.

Adam watched Dr. Carter draw the wooden blinds so that there was hardly any light in the room. "Do you know anything about hypnosis, Adam?" the doctor asked.

"I've read a bit about it."

"Perhaps you've read that the word *hypnosis* comes from a term that means 'sleep of the nervous' system. It has been described as a partial sleep, one in which the subject can listen and respond to the hypnotist. Generally, hypnotized people are more receptive to suggestion, though it's believed the hypnotist can never make anyone do anything they wouldn't do in waking life."

"I guess that's a common fear. But I trust that you won't tell me to go out and rob a bank," Adam replied with a wry smile. "I'm pretty desperate to get my memory back, so I'll have to take my chances."

Dr. Carter smiled back. "Yes, I guess you will. But the state of hypnosis is a familiar one, which people experience all the time. It's very similar to being lost in thought, when you're thinking so deeply about something that you lose track of your surroundings. Have you ever felt like that?"

"All the time." If he was writing in his journal or even painting at the Potters', his mind slipped into that meditative state very easily.

"Excellent. That's the sign of an imaginative mind, which is good for this sort of therapy. When you're hypnotized, the body is totally relaxed and focused. All logical levels of thought are bypassed, and the brain is in an altered state. Hypnotherapy is most commonly used to end some type of undesirable behavior, like overeating, or smoking, or phobias. Athletes use it to improve their performance. We're going to use it for memory regression," he added. "Though I must tell you that there is no way to distinguish an imagined or false memory from a true one. Only after you leave here, when you're able to research some name or bit of information that surfaces, will you know for sure."

"I've read that, too," Adam said. The doctor's words made him think of his dream again. Would he talk about it once he was hypnotized? And was it real, or a false memory, as Dr. Carter believed?

"I'm going to make a recording of the session. Then I'll give you a copy of the tape when you go. You can listen to it on your own, and you might hear something that rings a bell for you." Dr. Carter turned in his chair and began the tape player. He first gave the date and time and Adam's name.

"Okay, Adam, I'd like you to watch this pendulum. Just focus on it and relax your body completely. . . ."

Adam did as Dr. Carter asked, focusing on the small silver object that swung from a string over the tabletop. His eyes followed it right, then left, then right again. That was all he remembered.

Suddenly, Dr. Carter was calling him. "You can open your eyes and wake up now, Adam."

Adam opened his eyes. He felt embarrassed. He shook his head, as if to shake himself awake. "Wow . . . That was strange. I feel as if I've been sitting here, totally asleep."

"You just felt as if you were. You were an excellent subject. Very verbal."

"What did I say?" Adam leaned forward in his chair. "Anything important?"

"Well, you didn't remember your real name or where you live—or anything that definitive, unfortunately. You talked about an orange car. The number fifty-three came up a lot. Maybe that's part of your address?"

"What did you ask me?"

"A list of questions devised for this type of session." Dr. Carter lifted his yellow pad and Adam saw the long list. "It's all on the tape. I asked you how you found your way into the orchard. You told me you just jumped."

"I jumped?"

Dr. Carter nodded. "That's right. . . . You weren't wearing any skydiving gear when they found you, were you?"

Adam smiled. "No, I think someone would have noticed that." He grew serious again. "Did I mention anything about the nightmare? Any of those places I described from the dream?"

"No, nothing at all."

Adam wasn't sure if he was relieved or disappointed to hear that. The vivid dream was the most substantial clue he had. He felt suddenly deflated. He watched as Dr. Carter removed the cassette, packed it in an envelope, and handed it to him.

"When you listen to this, try to keep your mind open. Be nonjudgmental. Don't dismiss anything as meaningless, even if it sounds strange or illogical."

"Like jumping into the orchard?"

"Exactly." Dr. Carter gazed down at him a moment. "Do you have any more questions for me, Adam?"

"No, I don't think so." Adam tucked the envelope into his pocket and rose from his chair. His legs felt strange and heavy. He suddenly longed to get moving again. "Thanks for the information. You've been very helpful."

"I'm not sure I've helped you all that much. Take some time to listen to the tape and think it over. Keep working with your journal. If you would like to try hypnosis again, we can set up another session. If you'd like to return and talk some more, we can do that, too."

Adam thanked him again for his time. The two men shook hands, and Dr. Carter walked him out to the waiting room.

Miranda jumped up from her seat when

she saw the door open. She couldn't help it. The magazine she'd been reading slipped from her lap and fell to the floor. She quickly read Adam's expression and guessed that the hypnosis session had not been a miracle cure.

She felt disappointed, too, she realized with a touch of surprise. Maybe she was ready to learn the truth about him.

"How did it go?" she asked quietly.

"I'm not really sure. I was out like a light." Adam sighed. "The doctor said I didn't come up with any real breakthrough, like my real name or my address. But he asked me a lot of questions and gave me a tape, so I can listen to it and try to figure out if I mentioned anything important."

"Well, it's a start." They walked out of the office and got into the elevator. She stood next to him and he stared straight ahead. He looked so dispirited, she fought the urge to put her arms around him in a comforting hug.

When they stepped outside, it was nearly dark. The streetlights shone against the frosty air. They had been in a rush earlier to park and find the office on time. Miranda hadn't even noticed that they were in the very heart of Newburyport. The town was much bigger than Cape Light but just as beautifully decorated for the holidays, with garlands and lights across the main street and all of the shop windows filled with decorations.

On a Friday night, the streets of Newburyport were bustling with restaurant- and moviegoers, and at this time of year, it was even more crowded than usual, with people Christmas shopping or meeting for parties.

"Do you mind if we don't go back right away? I'd like to check out the windows of some of the jewelry stores," she told him.

"Sure. I can use a walk. I feel as if I've been sitting for hours."

They strolled down the main street for a while and Miranda stopped at a store window, looking over the jewelry display. "That piece is nice," she said, pointing to a rose-gold bracelet set with pink and green tourmalines.

"Yeah," Adam agreed. "But your work is just as pretty. Even nicer," he added.

Miranda smiled at him. She wasn't sure if he was just trying to be encouraging or if he really meant it. Perhaps a bit of both.

She turned from the window, and they started walking again. "Do you remember anything about the holidays, Adam? Or does all this fuss look very strange to you?"

"I remember something about it. More of just a feeling, I guess. Not any specific day, where I spent it, or who was there." He glanced at her and forced a smile. "You would think something like Christmas would stick in your memory."

"Yes, you would," she agreed. She thought it was sad that he had no real memories of the holiday. Some of her favorite memories were of waking up on Christmas morning, rushing downstairs to open her presents, or sharing the day with her family.

"I think you're making progress." She was trying to find something positive to say, something that wouldn't make him feel worse. "Even if you haven't unlocked any memories yet, visiting Dr. Carter was important."

"Thanks for coming with me," he said. "That was important to me, too."

He slowed his step and looked down at her. Miranda met his gaze. She felt there was so much she wanted to say to him, so much in her heart. But she looked away quickly.

They walked on for a few moments until Miranda paused in front of a small café. "This is a great place, not expensive either. Want to stop for a bite to eat?"

"Sounds good." Adam smiled at her. "Being hypnotized works up an appetite—who would have guessed?"

Miranda laughed as he held the door open for her and they walked inside. The little café was cozy on a winter night. They had arrived well before the dinner rush and practically had the place to themselves.

They sat at a table near the window and ordered dinner, with Miranda suggesting her favorite dishes. They didn't talk at all about Adam's memory loss or even his visit with Dr. Carter. It was as if they had made an unspoken pact to take a break from Adam's problem.

Adam asked her questions about her family and about her past, the years she'd lived in New York and worked as an actress.

"So, you haven't mentioned anything about a boyfriend, down in New York, I mean," he said finally. "There must have been someone."

"There was a someone, another actor," she admitted. "It was pretty serious for a while. But he . . . Well, eventually it fizzled out." She shrugged.

"Is that when you came up here?" Adam asked.

"More or less."

"You must have been very disappointed."

"I was heartbroken, to be perfectly honest about it. But looking back, I'm relieved. Jake wasn't right for me. It was all for the best."

"And what about Greg? Is he right for you?"

Whoa, he cuts right to the chase, doesn't he? Miranda wasn't sure what to say. "I like Greg. We get along . . . But we don't have a serious commitment yet, if that's what you're asking."

Adam didn't say anything for a while. He filled her cup with more tea, then poured some for himself. "You're a special person, Miranda. It sounds to me like that guy Jake didn't appreciate you. Or deserve to be with you. . . . I'm not sure Greg really appreciates you either."

Miranda gave a nervous laugh. "You make me sound like some sort of . . . prize."

"You are a prize. You're an amazing woman. Don't ever forget it."

Miranda felt embarrassed. She wasn't used to such compliments. He sounded sincere, too, which made it even harder to handle.

Jake had not really understood or appreciated her. That much was true. She wasn't sure about Greg. Greg liked her and was attracted to her, but he didn't really "get" her completely.

Adam did, though. Maybe more than any man she had ever met. She felt good with him, as if he connected to the deepest part of her. It was easy, just for tonight, to pretend that a future between them was possible.

Once they had finished eating, Miranda paid the check and they left their table. Just as they reached the door, a hostess stopped them. "Miss, is this your glove? I think you dropped it."

Miranda turned. "Oh, thanks. It must have fallen out of my pocket."

Adam stood staring at the woman. Petite, with curly black hair that touched her shoulders, she was very pretty. But Miranda sensed that Adam's intense interest in her had to do with something else altogether.

Miranda touched his arm. "Do you remember her?" she asked quietly.

He shook his head. "Not really. Though there is something so familiar about her."

"Maybe we should ask her if she recognizes you?"

He stared at the hostess, thinking about it for a moment. "All right. I guess I should."

The hostess had been seating a couple at

a nearby table and now returned to the front of the restaurant. "Excuse me, miss," Adam began. "You look very familiar, but I can't remember where we may have met." *That much was true,* Miranda thought. "Do I look familiar to you?" he asked hopefully.

The woman looked confused, staring first at Adam and then briefly at Miranda. Miranda realized that the woman was wondering if Adam was trying to pick her up and couldn't quite figure out how Miranda fit into the picture. Miranda smiled at her encouragingly until the woman looked back at Adam.

"I'm pretty sure I don't know you," the hostess said. "Maybe you've seen me here?"

"Sorry, I must have mistaken you for someone else," Adam said.

Adam sighed as they stepped outside. "Another red herring."

"More of a brunette herring," Miranda corrected him. She glanced his way and he smiled, then slipped his arm around her shoulder.

"Let's walk down to the water," he said. Miranda fell into step beside him then slipped her arm around his waist. She knew she shouldn't, but couldn't stop herself. It just felt right to be close to him.

The waterside was chilly, but there was no wind. The sky was an inky blue-black color, studded with tiny pinpoints of lights. A thin crescent moon hung above the dark water. The harbor was nearly empty. A large white boat, trimmed with lights, drifted some distance from the shore.

"It's beautiful here," Adam said quietly. "I can see why you don't want to leave."

"I still might," she said quietly. "Sometimes I feel as if my life is just as confused as yours. And I know my name and remember my past. Too much of it," she added.

He turned his head and smiled down at her. "You'll figure out the right thing to do. I have faith in you." When she didn't answer, he added, "I'm certainly not in any great position to give advice, but trying to figure out my identity has made me see something really important. I could be . . . anything. An insurance salesman, a brain surgeon, an astronaut. People have a lot more choices than they realize or even want to consider. Just figure out what will make you happy, Miranda, and follow your heart."

Miranda winced, unable to help thinking that the expression was a cliché.

"Did that sound sappy?" Adam asked her, a hint of laughter in his voice.

"A little," she admitted.

"It's the right thing to do anyway," he said. "That's about the only thing I'm sure of."

Miranda didn't answer. She turned her head against his shoulder and looked up at his strong profile. He was right. All these choices were unnerving to say the least. But the right choice would emerge, if she could sort out her true feelings.

Right now, her heart was leading her to Adam. He was not the right choice, but the one she wanted.

Just for this moment, he was here. She was close to him, in his arms, and she willed herself not to think about what might happen tomorrow. Or even an hour from now.

Adam turned, so that they stood face-to-face. He put both arms around her and touched his lips to her forehead. When she lifted her head to look at him, he kissed her on the mouth. Softly at first, then deeper. It was as wonderful as Miranda had ever imagined a kiss could be. Even better. She felt perfectly in tune with him, as if their minds and souls were merging in a graceful dance.

She had never felt so right with anyone. Certainly not with Jake, or even Greg.

She wasn't sure how long they stood there together. It might have been minutes, or hours. Out at sea, a foghorn sounded, calling her back to reality.

She pulled away slowly. Adam seemed reluctant to let her go but finally did. "That wasn't an accident," he said softly.

"No," she agreed.

"I have strong feelings for you, Miranda. You must know that by now. And not just gratitude, either."

"I know that," she said simply. "I care for you, too. I know I shouldn't," she added. "But I do."

He took her hand. "I'm sorry. I never meant for this to happen. I would give anything if things were different. I don't have anything to offer you, Miranda. I have no idea of who I am, or what my obligations are. But I can't imagine feeling any happier with anyone. I feel . . . *right* with you. I feel as if you were meant to find me, to just . . . wake me up and lead me to a new life."

Miranda pressed her fingers to his lips, willing herself not to cry. "You don't have to say any more. I wish it were different, too.

You have a life somewhere, people who love you. Who miss you. You belong there, not here with me. We need to remember that."

"I'm trying to. But it isn't easy."

Miranda didn't answer him. It wasn't easy, not for either one of them.

MIRANDA STOOD AT THE KITCHEN SINK THE NEXT morning, washing the breakfast dishes, and thinking of what Adam had said the night before. She couldn't remember ever feeling so elated and at the same time, so achingly sad. She couldn't even bear to think about the kiss. That was something she needed to forget, and quickly. Remembering the touch of his lips on hers was overwhelming. It made her feel as if she would never be happy again.

Fortunately, Adam was upstairs now. He had woken early and he and Sophie were already working on the ceiling in one of the guest rooms. Miranda was glad to have missed them. She wasn't quite ready to face Adam again. The phone rang and she answered it, welcoming the distraction.

"Good morning," Greg said, and her heart sank. This wasn't the distraction that she wanted. "I know it's early but I'm going to be out all day on a job, and I wanted to make sure I caught you," he explained.

It took Miranda a moment to make sense of that, and then she remembered. They had a date for that night. Her first impulse was to make some excuse, to say she didn't feel well or needed to do something for her grandmother. But she hung tight, feeling that would be dishonest. Greg deserved better.

After the usual small talk, Greg brought up their plans for the evening. "I hate to cancel on you at the last minute, Miranda, but my ex has to go out of town to help her sister. She asked if I could pick up Lily and bring her to an ice-skating party tonight. I'm really sorry, but parenthood calls. I hope it's all right?"

"Of course it's all right. Don't even think about it. Lily needs you. I totally understand." Greg didn't suggest that she come along to the party and keep him company, and Miranda understood that, too.

Greg had mentioned introducing her to his daughter sometime soon, but he didn't want to confuse Lily and introduce Miranda unless he felt it was a serious, long-term relationship. Right now their relationship seemed headed in that direction, but wasn't quite there. Miranda could hardly argue. As much as she wanted to meet the little girl, she knew it was a big step, one that she didn't take lightly either.

They talked for a few more minutes, then Greg said, "Look, the next couple of days are going to be busy for me. How about if we don't make any plans right now, but I'll call you during the week? My calendar should be clearer then."

"That's fine," Miranda told him. She was hoping that in a few days, her feelings would be clearer, too.

THE DEACONATE ASSEMBLED AT A LONG TABLE set up in Fellowship Hall on Saturday morning, with eight of the ten members responding to Ben's call. He thought it was a good showing for such short notice.

Tucker Tulley, the senior deacon, called the meeting to order. "Sorry to put a kink in everyone's Saturday plans, but this is an important situation. We need to discuss it and devise some plan to handle it. Reverend, do you want to get us started?"

Ben shook his head. "Actually, I called you all here because I wanted to hear your opinions. I have very conflicted feelings about this situation, so if you don't mind, I'm just going to listen for a while."

"Fair enough." Tucker turned to address the group. "I'm sure by now you've all seen the statue in the sanctuary. Reverend Ben found it in the basement about two weeks ago and thought it would make a nice Christmas decoration. The very next day my stepbrother, Carl, claimed that a pretty serious cut on his hand was healed by just touching the statue. Digger Hegman says the angel cured his arthritis, and there are other people making similar claims." Tucker paused and looked down at his notes. "We also have folks from out of town coming to our church just to see the statue. They pray by it and leave written petitions. The church is getting pretty full on Sundays, which I suppose is the upside," he added, glancing at Ben. "But do we want our church filled with folks looking for a miracle? Do we want to be known as the church with the magic angel?"

Harry Reilly spoke up. "Guess that depends on whether or not we think those claims are true. I mean, what if people start to say it's a hoax? Then we're known in a different way. Why risk it? I say we just take the statue down and forget about it."

"We certainly don't want the reputation of the church to suffer, but there's another, more serious dimension here," said Arthur Hinkle, who did surveying for the county. "What if someone stops chemotherapy because they think the angel is going to cure their cancer? That's the kind of situation I'm wary of."

Isabel Englehart, a librarian at the high school, rose and asked to be heard. Most of the other deacons respected her opinion, and Ben was interested to hear what she had to say.

"Arthur has a point," she conceded, "though I think if someone's going to give up on their medical treatment, they'll do it with or without the angel. To me, it's a blessing to have so many visitors drawn to our church. Maybe that's the miracle of this statue after all. Maybe people come to see the angel, but they end up staying for the service. Next Sunday, maybe they'll come again. I think anyone who prays to a statue realizes that their prayer might not be answered, so they aren't going to blame our church. Meanwhile, the congregation is growing. And we all know that's a good thing."

Now there was a point Ben had never

even thought of. Maybe the angel's purpose was to bring new members to his church.

"All that might be well and true," Tucker countered. "But I say it's sort of sad if we need to resort to using some cheap trick to build our membership. I don't think that's a very good way to grow the congregation."

Sam Morgan had been atypically quiet, Ben noticed. Now he rose to speak. Sam was a modest man who earned his living as a woodworker. He was younger than many of the other deacons, but had many friends in town and was well respected. He was more than a carpenter, too, Ben knew. Sam was an artist, able to form rough hunks of wood into beautiful pieces of furniture, his own one-of-a-kind designs. Perhaps he appreciated this statue in a different way, Ben thought, as an artist.

"I've been listening to everyone's point of view," Sam began. "I think most of you raise some good questions and have some valid concerns about how outsiders see our church. But what I don't understand is, what's the harm if people come to visit this statue? If they want to pray or even leave petitions? Isn't their expression of faith the important thing? Wouldn't it be wrong to deny or discourage that?" He paused and looked around. No one interrupted him, Ben noticed.

Sam glanced over at Tucker. "Sure, they're coming to see the angel because they heard the stories. I don't think we can ever say for sure if those stories are true. But aren't all these people really coming because they want to communicate with some greater power? Not just the angel. They're looking to heaven for help with their problems. I don't think that hope should be taken away, especially not at Christmastime."

Sam's simple point hit home with Ben. It seemed to score a bull's-eye in his very heart. Maybe he had been wrestling with the issue logically, with practical and even theological questions that entirely missed the spiritual essence of the situation.

People came to the angel, seeking help from God with their problems. Their expression of faith was the important thing. The most important thing.

Ben rose and looked around. "I've been confused about this situation, which is why I called you together to discuss it. Now Sam has reminded me of one very crucial point. In the midst of all the fabricated holiday cheer, the TV commercials and store decorations, there are so many people who are privately hurting, even people who may seem as if their lives are carefree. People who are, as Sam says, carrying some secret burden. Carrying it all the way to our church in the slim hope that this statue will help them communicate their need to God. Can we take that away from them? At Christmastime? That seems very wrong to me, too."

Ben looked around at the group, noticing some disgruntled faces and others nodding in agreement.

When no one spoke, Ben added, "I think we should leave the statue up, at least until the holiday is over. Can we agree on that much?"

A few of the deacons exchanged glances, but no one objected. Ben felt they had reached a conclusion to the discussion, if not a consensus.

"Since there's no further comment, I'll take that to mean you all agree to this plan," Tucker looked around the room. "So the statue stays up until the holidays are over. Which actually, won't be too much longer."

Ben thanked them all for coming, and the deacons quickly dispersed, eager to get back to their Saturday routine and errands. Ben shut off the lights in Fellowship Hall and closed the doors. He was about to leave the church himself, dressed in his coat and hat, when he decided to detour into the sanctuary.

He peeked in the doorway. There were three worshipers present, all kneeling near the statue, each looking absorbed in their private prayers.

He quietly walked closer and looked up at the angel, trying to figure out its remarkable appeal. There was an eerily human look of faith in the angel's expression, a calm courage in her eyes.

He felt a calming energy settle into his very center, soothing his anxieties. He suddenly felt clearheaded about the entire issue.

He wouldn't remove the angel or make any statement about its alleged powers. Sam had been right. People were coming to the church seeking help, with hope and faith. Not just from the angel, but from God above. He shouldn't worry about the gossip or the negative judgments some might make about the church. Or even about himself, for that matter.

Expressions of faith and hope and yearning toward the powers above shouldn't be discouraged. Especially at Christmas.

CHAPTER SEVEN

MOLLY WAS UP TO HER ELBOWS IN A SPINACH AND cheese mixture. Betty grabbed a spare apron so her silk blouse wouldn't get spattered and watched carefully.

It was late Tuesday afternoon and Betty had left her office early. She had stopped by to pick up some takeout and ended up hanging out back in the kitchen, watching Molly cook. It was her favorite entertainment lately, Molly had noticed.

Molly picked up a shaker of nutmeg and carefully sprinkled it over the large bowl. "My secret ingredient," she whispered. "Even

Sonya doesn't know. A bar or two of cream cheese gives a nice rich flavor, too."

"It looks pretty good from here. I bet you can use that filling with a lot of that stuff. Not just the spring rolls." Molly was going to use the spinach to fill slim, cigar-shaped rolls of crispy pastry, one of her signature hors d'oeuvres.

"I want to try it in miniature ravioli. I just haven't had the chance to experiment."

"Things should slow down after Christmas," Betty predicted. "My office is dead. I'm going to close Christmas week. It's not worth the bother to stay open, and my staff appreciates the break."

"What are you doing for the holiday, Betty? Any plans?" Molly knew the topic was a sensitive one for her friend. Betty had been divorced years ago and had a grown son who was now in law school in Chicago. Her ex-husband had remarried and had two small children. Other than that, Betty had no relatives nearby and sometimes spent the holidays with whichever current boyfriend was hanging around. Once in a while, she was entirely alone.

"Good question," Betty said. "Brian is going to Ted's house this year," she said, mentioning her son and ex-husband. "I'll get him after the holiday, for a few days I hope. I might take one of those last-minute cruises to the Caribbean. I keep seeing great deals online."

Oh, the giddy freedom of single life. A cruise to sun-drenched, tropical islands. Being waited on day and night. Your every whim satisfied by a snap of your fingers. Massages, pedicures, chocolates on the pillow . . .

Still, Molly wouldn't give up her own hectic, crazy, triple-tasking lifestyle for a thousand Caribbean cruises at Christmastime. She admired Betty in so many ways and yet felt sorry for her. It was hard to believe that a woman who was so successful and accomplished had so few strong, emotional connections. Molly knew Betty didn't want it to be that way. It was just the way her life had turned out and now that she was older, it seemed harder every year to find a long-term relationship.

"Want to come to our house Christmas Eve? I mean, if you don't do something wonderful and exciting? It's just family. But we'd love to have you."

Betty looked a little hesitant. "Your parties are always wonderful—"

"—if you don't mind being surrounded by the whole, ginormous Morgan clan," Molly put in. "I do understand that it's not everyone's idea of Christmas bliss."

Betty laughed. "Let me think about it, okay?"

"No problem." Molly stirred the mixture, carefully scraping the sides of the huge bowl. "Hey, listen to this. Guess who called me this morning and asked if I could do a last-minute New Year's Day brunch? Madeline Norris." Molly grinned at Betty. "Guess you handled her just right. I owe you one."

"Yeah, you do." Betty nodded. "Listen, why don't you let me handle that party? I know you're totally overbooked. It will give me something to do while my office is closed." A good distraction from Christmas and everyone else being happy and focused on their families, Molly silently translated. Still, could Betty really do a whole party? An emergency flat tire was one thing. But an entire party?

"Gee . . . I don't know. These things are more work than they seem. Do you really want to spend your time dealing with that fussbudget Norris?"

"I do," Betty assured her. "I have some really great ideas, too. I was thinking of having a big party myself this year but never got around to it. It will be fun to pull it all together."

"Fun? You think this job is fun?" Molly rolled her eyes.

"You used to think it was fun," Betty reminded her. "Before you started working yourself half to death."

That was probably true, but Molly didn't want to get into that discussion right now.

"Come on, Molly. You just said you owed me one. This could be my Christmas present and payback all in one. I know how to handle Madeline Norris. I had her wrapped around my little finger on Sunday."

Betty was in fine form, a naturally persuasive person, Molly thought. She felt herself starting to crumble, like a chunk of blue cheese.

She could use the help. She had nearly refused the Norris job because she wasn't sure she could handle it. Now she had accepted and still didn't know how she would pull it off.

When she thought about it that way, Betty's offer looked like a godsend.

"So, what do you say? Do I get the assignment?"

"Okay, you wore me down," Molly conceded. "But you have to let me pay you." Betty made a face but Molly continued, "And we have to brainstorm. We need to offer Mrs. Norris some brilliant ideas we can do easily. I don't have unlimited help and resources around here."

"I agree. You're an awesome cook, Molly, but I'm loads more efficient," Betty pointed out. "Don't worry, you'll know about everything that's going on."

That made Molly feel a little better. Betty was great at client relationships. And she was efficient, amazingly so. The rest of it could be learned, Molly reasoned.

The phone rang and Molly heard Sonya answer it in the shop. "Molly, it's for you. It's Matt," she shouted back into the kitchen.

"Tell him to hold a sec' . . ." Molly shoved the bowl in Betty's direction and handed her a long spoon. "Stir this around awhile, will you? Your first official duty."

Betty took the bowl and spoon and set to work, looking excited to be given a real job. "Clockwise, right?"

"Either direction would be fine," Molly said patiently. She washed her hands quickly and then picked up the phone. "Hi, honey, what's up?"

Her husband rarely had a minute to call and when he did, it was usually something important.

"Great news. Alex Cole is here. We're going to look around the town for a while, see the sights. Then we can all meet for dinner. I don't want you to do a thing. We'll go out— some place nice. Spoon Harbor Inn?" he suggested.

Wow, this was news. Matt's potential partner had arrived and was checking things out. Molly had her fingers crossed. "That sounds perfect. What time?"

"Oh, something early. Six o'clock. Alex is driving back to Lexington tonight."

Molly did a quick calculation. She could leave here as soon as she hung up. Do a drive-by, change her clothes, put on makeup, and leave the girls something to eat. They would be fine on their own. "Sounds good," she said.

"Great. Alex is looking forward to meeting you," he added.

"Same here," Molly assured him.

She hung up the phone and practically

skipped across the kitchen. "Guess what? Matt's bringing a partner into the practice so he can have more time with the new baby. He's asked this old school friend. She came to town today to check things out, and we're all going out for dinner tonight."

Betty looked a bit sweaty, a strand of blonde hair plastered across her forehead. She stopped stirring and rubbed the top of her arm. "That's good news. See, Matt's really listening to you."

"Yes, I think he is," Molly said cheerfully. "It was all his idea, too."

Molly did feel encouraged by Matt's looking for a partner. It changed her vision of the future. "I feel a lot better about things," she admitted. "I'm even starting to remember some of the fun parts of having a baby— decorating the room, buying tiny clothes."

"They have the cutest baby clothes now," Betty agreed. "The styles are just adorable. Do you want to find out the baby's sex in advance, or do you want to be surprised?"

"I want to know. There are enough surprises," Molly added. "I hope it's another girl, but I think Matt might want a boy."

"I'm sure he'll be happy with either, as long as the baby's healthy."

"Yes, you're right. That's the way I feel, too." Molly's hand unconsciously rested on her stomach in a tender, protective gesture. "We have a long way to go," she said with a sigh.

"Oh, the time will go quickly. You'll see. Everything will be fine."

Betty was unfailingly positive. Molly sometimes teased her about being a former cheerleader in high school. But things were looking up, Molly couldn't deny it.

She smiled at her friend and checked the contents of the mixing bowl. "You did a very good job. A-plus for stirring."

"See, I told you I'd be a help around here."

Molly patted her arm. "Betty, sometimes I don't know what I'd do without you."

MOLLY RAN HOME FOR HER QUICK CHANGE, GOT the girls in order, and reached the restaurant at exactly five after six. She peered into her rearview mirror, whisked on an extra coat of lip gloss and fluffed her hair. Hmm . . . her face looked fuller. Had she gained weight in her face with the last two pregnancies? She didn't remember. Well, there was nothing she could do about it now. She gave her hair a final pat and swept into the restaurant.

The hostess greeted her with a menu in

hand. "I'm meeting my husband," Molly said quickly. She looked around and spotted Matt at a table in the rear. "There he is. I'll just go on back."

Wearing her best "Welcome to the neighborhood" smile, Molly sailed toward Matt. She glanced across the table, eager to meet his friend and soon to be—she hoped—partner.

She wasn't exactly sure how she had pictured Alex Cole, but the woman sitting across from Matt was not even close to anything she had imagined. Alex was slim and attractive with shiny, shoulder-length dark brown hair and big brown eyes. She was quite pretty and very well-dressed, in a pale gray wool suit with a pink sweater underneath. Tasteful pearl earrings brought out her fair complexion.

Okay, so she's pretty, Molly admitted to herself. *I can deal with that.*

Matt stood up as Molly reached the table. He leaned over and kissed her hello. "Hi, honey. We were just talking about you."

"Only good things, I hope," Molly said. "Hi, I'm Molly." She stuck out her hand and Alex shook it, smiling warmly.

When she smiled, Molly realized, she was a complete knockout. Not almost. Not partial. But complete.

"We passed the shop today and wanted to stop in," Matt explained. "But I figured you were too busy to talk, and we didn't want to bother you."

"It's a beautiful shop," Alex said. "Looks like you have a great business there."

"Yes, we're very busy. Especially with the holidays." Molly heard her voice as if from far away. Why should it bother her if Matt's partner was gorgeous? It was just this pregnancy getting her down again. She had been feeling fat and dowdy for weeks and meeting Alex Cole suddenly seemed to intensify all those feelings.

Alex was talking about Cape Light, how she found the town so pretty and charming. "Then we went out to the beach. It was cold, but just breathtaking. You're so lucky to live here. It's such a perfect spot."

"Oh, you guys went out to the beach today, too? It must have been windy." Molly forced a smile. "Sounds like you were out all day. Who stuck around to see the patients?"

Matt laughed. "I had a few cancellations

and got Amy to switch around a few appointments. I wouldn't be a very good salesman if I let Alex wander around town by herself."

Molly snapped open her menu and stared at it blindly. Normally, she loved this restaurant. Tonight everything on the menu seemed overly rich and fattening. By the end of the meal, she would probably weigh twice as much as Alex. She felt as though she was in the recap of a bad sitcom: *Matt's gorgeous new partner meets his wife, the Blimp.*

Molly knew she was being ridiculous. She was pregnant, not fat. And Alex was here to help them. It was time to stop acting like an insecure teenager. *Be welcoming,* Molly told herself.

Molly put her menu down and looked across the table at Alex. "So, how did he do, Alex? Are you sold?"

Alex looked over at Matt with a glowing expression. "Well, I really was thinking of a job right in Boston. . . . But this town is so incredibly lovely. And the people seem so nice, and relaxed. And the city is less than two hours away," she added. "What more could you ask for?"

Matt glanced at Molly curiously. "Are you feeling okay, honey?"

"I'm just dandy," Molly murmured.

"Molly's expecting," he announced happily. "She's been having some bad morning sickness, though, and not just in the morning . . ."

Molly felt herself flush red with embarrassment. "I'm fine," she said. "It was just one time. Basically, I'm just great. So . . ." she said, wanting to change the subject, "how did you two get in touch again? The college alumni newsletter?" Molly picked up a roll, tore it in half, then slathered it with butter. She felt like a whale anyway, and at the moment, she needed a bit of comfort.

"Yes, that's right," Alex said. "Matt had a posting about an opening in his practice. I felt a little awkward at first, getting back in touch with an old boyfriend. You know how that is . . ."

Molly felt something cold and clammy seize hold of her heart. "You two dated?" she managed to say. "You never told me about that, Matt."

"Oh, that's because it's ancient history." Matt put his arm around the back of Molly's chair in husbandly fashion. "We dated for a while in med school. We both knew it wasn't right, but we managed to stay good friends. Right, Alex?"

Alex nodded. "Right. That's it exactly."

Her tone was reassuring, but why did there seem to be a special light in her chocolate-brown eyes as she glanced at Matt? Was she regretting the road not taken? Wanting to backtrack and try again? Molly's eyes scanned Alex's hands for a ring—nothing, no diamond, not even a friendship ring. The gorgeous doctor was definitely not taken.

"So, Molly, tell me about your girls. Matt says you have a houseful. It must be very challenging, running your business and taking care of everyone. And now you have a new baby on the way," Alex added. She leaned forward, looking interested and charming.

Give her a chance, Molly told herself. *Just because she's beautiful and single doesn't mean she's after Matt.*

Molly answered Alex's questions but was mostly quiet for the rest of the dinner.

Alex and Matt didn't seem to notice, she realized. They were too busy discussing Matt's practice and the logistics of having Alex join him and move to Cape Light.

Finally, the waiter brought the check and

Matt pulled out a credit card. "It shouldn't be too hard to find a nice place in town," he told Alex. "Molly's best friend is a real estate broker. She'll help you, right, Molly?"

Molly nodded. "Absolutely. Just say the word and Betty will take you out anytime."

"Gee, thanks. You guys are great. It's so nice to know I'll already have friends here," Alex said brightly as she slipped on her coat.

Molly felt a prickle of guilt. Some friend she was turning out to be. *I'll do better,* Molly promised herself.

Finally, they said good-byes in the parking lot. Molly felt herself stiffen when Alex hugged her and then hugged Matt. Still, she managed a wave and yet one more smile as Alex's car left the parking lot.

She was quiet as she led Matt to her own car and opened the door.

"Give me the keys, honey. I'll drive. You look a little tired," Matt said.

"That's not tired. It's . . . I don't know what it is," she admitted. She got in on the driver's side and slipped behind the wheel. Matt got in the passenger's side and fastened his belt, all the while looking at her with a puzzled expression.

She started the engine, but he turned off the key. "I don't think you should drive right now. You seem . . . upset."

"Okay, maybe I'm upset," she admitted. "Mildly upset. Why didn't you tell me Alex was so . . . so . . . attractive? And an ex-girlfriend? And don't say it doesn't matter, because it does."

"Molly . . . come on . . ." He shook his head, as if he couldn't believe what he was hearing. "I'm sorry, but does it really matter? She's a good doctor and a very nice person. I think if you weren't so . . . hormonal right now, you would actually like her."

Molly's eyes narrowed. "It's not my hormones, okay? You should have been upfront and told me what was going on."

"What was going on? I told you I was trying to bring someone into the practice, an old friend. We only dated a few weeks in med school. Alex broke up with me . . . and it all seems like a hundred years ago. She saw my name on some alumni newsletter, so she called. End of story. You're not really jealous, are you?" He seemed amused and even flattered.

"No, of course I'm not jealous. By the way, George Clooney called me this morning. He wants to be my new chef. The kitchen in the shop will be close quarters, but I think I can stand it."

Matt laughed. "Okay, I get the point, though I think you're being silly. But before I tell Alex to stay in Lexington, I have to tell you that I'm not sure who else I'm going to find willing to come out here. This town is great, but it is an acquired taste. I didn't get one other response to that ad, and I really want to off-load some of my work so I can spend more time at home. Helping you," he reminded her. "Alex has agreed to come in as a partner. I don't think I should just do an about-face on her. I may not have another opportunity like this for a long time."

Molly knew what he said was true. And she did want Matt to have more time for her and the kids, especially the new baby. More time for himself, too.

She knew she would be acting selfish if she asked him not to take Alex as a partner. It would feel so childish and petty to object to her just because she was an old girl-friend. And smart and pretty. And sweet . . . and thin.

Molly sighed and looked over at her husband. "All right. I'm sorry if I was being a nut.

Besides, it's your practice and your choice, after all."

He smiled at her and rubbed her shoulder. "Don't look so glum. Things are going to be much easier for you."

Molly started the car and didn't answer. As far as she could see, things were going to be harder, thinking of Matt working with Dr. Alex Cole every day. But there didn't seem to be much she could do.

WHEN MIRANDA CAME IN FROM THE COTTAGE ON Wednesday evening, she found her grandmother sorting through boxes in the living room. The Christmas tree they had bought together over the weekend was set in its stand, the long green boughs sticking up a bit from being so tightly bound.

"Grandma, you didn't have to do all this by yourself. Why didn't you call me?"

Sophie stood up, rubbing her lower back with her hands. "That's all right, honey. Adam did the heavy lifting. I just gave instructions. He got a lesson in putting up a Christmas tree today. And a break from scraping wallpaper," she added with a laugh.

Miranda noticed Adam, hidden behind the tree. He was carefully taping a nail in the wall behind him. "Sophie's afraid the tree will get knocked over," he explained. "She told me to tie a few safety cords."

"The tree gets knocked over every year, with or without the safety cords," Miranda informed him, some of the more rambunctious youngsters in the family coming to mind.

"Oh, kids like to play. They can't help it. They're children. They're just doing their job," Sophie said.

Her grandmother had to be the most indulgent grandparent—or great-grandparent— on the East Coast, Miranda thought. That was one of the reasons her family loved to gather here. The kids were in paradise, running wild around the old house from cellar to attic and eating all the cookies they could hold.

"Come on," Sophie said, "let's get into these boxes. Miranda, you do the lights. I can't reach high enough."

Her height did come in handy at times, Miranda reflected with a private smile. She carried the box of lights to the tree and began stringing them around the branches. Before she realized it, Adam was close beside her, his hands touching her own as he helped arrange the decorations. She turned her head to look at him. Their faces were so close, close enough to kiss. She felt her heartbeat start to quicken as she remembered their first kiss. Would they ever have another?

"Thinking about that call from Detective Lester this morning?" Sophie asked him. Miranda decided her grandmother had a positive talent for defusing romantic tension.

Adam nodded, a flush rising above his collar. "He said he had a lead on a possible contact. Someone called about me."

"And?" Miranda asked. Her already frantic heartbeat seemed to have doubled its pace. Why hadn't her grandmother or Adam told her about this earlier?

Adam shrugged. "Lester said he had to investigate further, to see if the lead was valid. But he expects to call back before the end of the day with more news."

Miranda nodded, struggling to hide her feelings. It was the call she knew had to come. Still, her stomach felt jumpy with nerves as she realized this could very well be his last day at the house.

"Oh, now this is a real treasure." Sophie carefully removed the tissue-paper wrapping from an ornament made of colorful wooden beads and pipe cleaners. "Miranda made this for me when she was in grade school. Do you remember, honey?"

"Of course I do." Once again, Miranda realized, her grandmother was steering things, this time trying to get them all to concentrate on trimming the tree. Well, it was better than concentrating on losing Adam.

"Anyone could see how artistic she is," Sophie went on. "Miranda always had that creative flair . . ."

Sophie handed her the ornament and Miranda held it up below her ear.

"This would make a nice earring design," she joked. "You can see that interest emerging in my early work, right?"

Adam smiled gently at her. "Not quite my taste. But everything looks good on you."

Miranda felt herself blush as she met his warm gaze then realized her grandmother was watching. She turned quickly back to Sophie. "Here, let me hang those snowflakes," she said, taking a bunch of ornaments from her hands.

Her grandmother seemed to have a story about each ornament in her large collection, particularly the handmade gems, crafted by her children and grandchildren.

"I knew you had a big family, Sophie. But I honestly had no idea it was that big. Are they all coming here for Christmas?" Adam asked.

"Practically. Una's son, Kurt is in the service," she said. "Audrey, that's my other daughter's youngest girl, she's studying in London, so we won't see her until the spring. Other than that, they're all coming." She had hung the last Christmas ball and stood back admiring the decorated tree. "They fill up the house, sleeping on every horizontal surface. The little ones bring sleeping bags and I have a few air mattresses up in the attic. . . . Maybe you can get those down for me tomorrow and I'll clean them up?"

"Sure, I'll get them later," Adam said, seeming conscious that he might not be here tomorrow. Her grandmother seemed to have forgotten, Miranda noticed.

"I remember one holiday, my grandson Kurt, the one who's in the service now, when he was a teenager he could sleep through an earthquake. He conked out in the pantry after our Christmas Eve party. Just took a pillow and blanket and curled up on the floor. Well, that child didn't wake up until one o'clock the next day, and no one even noticed he was missing. He stalked out of that closet with the blanket wrapped around him, looking like a mummy."

Adam laughed and Miranda laughed, too, though she'd heard the story a thousand times. It suddenly struck her how many of her grandmother's bits of conversation started off with the words *I remember.* How much of everyone's character was the sum—and memory—of their past experiences. How hard it must be for Adam to hear all these stories and have no past of his own to draw on.

The phone rang. They all turned toward the kitchen, but no one moved. "I'll get it," Sophie said. She bustled into the kitchen, moving faster than Miranda imagined she could.

Miranda looked at Adam. He stared back at her, his eyes filled with a world of words, words that would never be spoken between them.

"Adam, it's for you," Sophie called out. "Detective Lester."

Adam abruptly looked away and went into the kitchen to take the call. Miranda meant to stay in the living room, but couldn't help following. She entered the kitchen to hear Adam say, "Well, thanks very much for following up on it. . . . Sure, I understand . . . All right . . . I'll keep in touch."

He set the phone down, a bemused expression on his face. "The person who had called was looking for a man who disappeared ten years ago. The photo and age didn't match at all."

"Oh my . . ." Sophie shook her head, her expression full of sympathy. "Well, there'll be another call. You'll get the right one sooner or later," she assured him.

Adam nodded, but didn't say anything. Miranda could see he had mixed feelings about the news. So did she. She felt a crashing wave of relief . . . and then a stab of heartache. She almost wished Adam had been found. How long could she stand this, having him here and all the while, knowing he would go?

"Well . . . I'd better take Dixie out for her walk," she said briskly. She headed to the mudroom, grabbed her jacket and called for the dog, who eagerly ran to her side.

She was only a few steps from the house, when Adam ran up to meet her. "Mind if I come? I could use some fresh air."

"Of course not."

They didn't talk, but seemed to know

where they were going. With Dixie running circles around them, they walked up the hill behind the house and into the orchard. To Miranda's favorite spot. They stopped and looked out at the harbor and the town below, tucked into the coastline. It was a clear night and beams of moonlight shone on the inky water.

Adam turned and looked over at the orchard. "That's the spot where you found me, right? Under that tree."

Miranda nodded and dug her hands into her pockets. "You must be disappointed about the call. You must have had your hopes up."

"Yes. For a while I really thought that was going to be it." He turned to her, his expression hard to read in the darkness. "Now I feel . . . relieved," he admitted.

"I do, too," she said quietly.

Before she knew what was happening, he'd moved toward her and surrounded her in his strong embrace. Miranda pressed her face to his chest and felt herself crying. He held her very tight and kissed her hair, then her cheek, finally finding her lips with his own.

Miranda gave herself over to their embrace, to their silent communication of all the feelings she held inside.

Somewhere in the distance, she heard the sound of a train passing. The whistle blew low and mournful, echoing through the night. The sound made her feel sad. It seemed to contain all the loneliness she would surely soon feel.

She pulled away slowly from Adam's embrace and stepped back. He didn't say anything, just watched her. "I'm going back now," she said.

"All right. I'll be down in a minute."

She nodded and turned away. Dixie stayed with Adam, staring after her with a puzzled expression.

Miranda concentrated on not crying as she strode back to the house. *This just isn't fair,* she thought. *Finally, I really know what it is I want. And it's something I just can't have.*

CHAPTER EIGHT

~

IT WAS THE THIRD SUNDAY IN ADVENT, JUST A week before Christmas Eve. Church attendance usually grew at this time of year, no doubt. But as Ben practiced his sermon in his office, he noticed a large blue bus pull up behind the church. The words *Shady Brook* were written in curly white letters on the side.

Was it a group trip that had gotten lost, stopping to ask for directions?

He watched from the window as Tucker Tulley ran out to speak to the driver. Then Tucker ran back inside, and the bus began emptying. More seniors. An entire busload.

Dressed in his robes, Ben swept out of his office and trotted toward the sanctuary.

He met Tucker in the hallway. "We've got some visitors," the deacon explained. "Big group. I'm getting a crew together to set up some folding chairs at the back of the church."

"Good idea," Ben said. "Where are they from?"

"Peabody," Tucker said, mentioning a town about twenty-five miles south. "They're all from the same senior community, Shady Brook. They heard about the angel statue on the Internet and got a group trip together."

"The Internet? How did they see it there?"

"On a chat board about angels," Tucker said simply. "You know, people post stuff about a topic and other people respond? Seems someone who thinks the angel granted him a miracle wrote about it on some 'Talk About Angels' site and . . . here they are."

Ben blinked in astonishment. He was no stranger to the Internet. He checked e-mail every day and occasionally did some online research. But he had never gone into a chat room, and the idea that people from who-knows-where were online discussing the statue in his church floored him.

As Tucker headed to Fellowship Hall for a

cart of extra chairs, Ben proceeded toward the sanctuary. Carolyn had just arrived and walked over to meet him.

"Ben? You don't look well. . . . Are you okay?" she asked quietly, touching his arm.

He did feel a little shaky. And alarmed. Why he should panic about a busload of retirees was the question. It just seemed as if his church was . . . out of control.

"Did you see that large group that got off the bus?" he asked his wife. "They came all the way from Peabody. They heard about the angel on the Internet."

"Oh." Carolyn considered the information a moment. "It would be nice if you acknowledge them in the announcements. They did come a long way."

His wife was right. Why was he getting so ruffled about it? *All are welcomed here*— wasn't that his church's motto?

Just as he tried to focus on a calm and centered attitude, Lillian Warwick stalked into the church, accompanied by Emily Warwick, Emily's husband, Dan Forbes, and Dan and Emily's two-year-old daughter, Jane.

"Good morning, Lillian." Ben greeted the most contentious member of his congregation with a smile.

"What has drawn the crowd today, Reverend? Are you giving away something for free? Toaster ovens? CD players?"

"We have some visitors from Shady Brook Village in Peabody, Lillian. You know that visitors are always welcome here."

"Welcome to put some money in the plate," she snapped back. "I know what they are, a group of elderly fools, visiting this benighted little burg to pay homage to a chunk of painted wood. With wings."

"We all have a right to our beliefs, Lillian. You do . . . and they do," Ben said evenly.

Emily, who had been putting their coats away, now caught up with her mother and the conversation. "Mother, come with me. Reverend Ben has to get ready for the service and you'll miss out on your seat."

Emily handled her mother as one would a spoiled child. She did a good job of it, too, Ben thought, though Lillian's high maintenance had to get tiring.

"I don't know about you, Reverend," Lillian said, "but I don't like the idea of my church turning into a sideshow spectacle."

"Mother!" Emily said in a low, outraged undertone.

"It's all right," Ben assured her, somehow

managing to smile. "I'm always interested in the views of all members of the congregation." He gave her mother a courteous nod. "Thank you, Lillian, for being so clear."

"It's not the last you'll hear of it," Lillian promised as Emily nearly dragged her away.

No, I'm sure it's not, Ben thought as he went to take his place at the pulpit.

AFTER HIS ENCOUNTER WITH LILLIAN WARWICK, Sunday's service had been blessedly uneventful. But on Monday morning, Ben found himself in his office, wondering how many people felt the way Lillian did. Was their church turning into a sideshow spectacle? And how many people were chatting about the angel on the Internet? Ben had an uneasy image of groups of seniors from the farthest points of the globe suddenly organizing trips to his church. Perhaps he should call his superior, Reverend Hallock, and give his side of the story before the angel wound up on *Entertainment Tonight.*

The phone rang and his secretary answered it. "It's Sara McAllister, at the newspaper office," Irene said. "She'd like to speak with you." Ben stared at the phone a moment, then picked it up.

"Good morning, Reverend," Sara said. After asking how he was, she got to the point. "I'm writing a story on the angel statue. I've done a lot of interviews and would like your point of view for the piece. Would you talk to me about it? I need to take some pictures, so I can come see you at the church."

Ben wasn't surprised by the query. The only wonder was that she hadn't called sooner. "Of course, Sara," he said. "I'll answer your questions if I can. I'll be here all morning. Stop in anytime."

A short time later, Ben saw Sara from his office window, walking across the green. He left his office and went to meet her at the front entrance of the church. They went into the sanctuary first, taking seats in the back, some distance from the statue. There were already a few visitors near the angel.

"Do you think it's all right if I take a picture?" Sara asked quietly.

"Yes, I think it's fine," Ben said. The visitors at the statue sat with their backs toward Sara and they were so far away, Ben didn't feel a photo compromised anyone's identity.

Sara took out her camera and snapped a quick picture.

Then she pulled out her long notepad.

"First, I'd like to get the basic facts of when and where you found the angel. I've already spoken with Carl Tulley, so I'm just asking now to verify," she explained.

Ben recounted his version of the story, then Sara told him about the people she had contacted who claimed their prayer petitions had been answered by visiting the statue. Ben's eyes widened as she described prayers for health, romance, financial worries, and even victory in a high school basketball game. It sounded as if Sara had interviewed an army of believers.

"So, what do you think, Reverend? What's your position? Do you think there's something to all these testimonials?"

Ben didn't know what to say. He hadn't heard about the other "miracles," beyond his own congregation. With all these witnesses coming forward, the phenomenon seemed harder to dismiss.

Still, where was the proof? The indisputable evidence? He had been doing some reading on these types of accounts—from statues that wept healing tears to the face of the Blessed Mother in a pizza. He knew how easily these claims fell apart with the slightest probing. He believed he had a duty to err

on the side of skepticism or at least a reserved opinion. The last thing he wanted to
do was offer false hope, and yet how could
he dismiss the very real power of faith?

"Reverend Ben?" Sara prompted.

"I'm sorry," he said. "But the issue is so
complex that I don't have a simple answer
for you. All I can reasonably tell you is that
the mind is powerful. If a person believes
hard enough, has enough faith, then anything is possible, I suppose."

Sara scribbled on her pad. "Can I quote
you on that?"

"Yes . . . I guess so." Did he really want to
be quoted in the newspaper when he didn't
really know what to make of any of this?
In for a penny, in for a pound . . .

"Well, thanks for your help. I'll take some
more pictures now." Sara rose with her camera and walked closer to the statue. The visitors had gone and they were alone in the
sanctuary.

She lifted the camera and focused. "It is
beautiful. It's very . . . unique. Do you have
any idea where it came from?"

"I've checked the church records of gifts.
There was a notation about a statue that
seemed to fit this description, donated in the

1950s. None of the donor's descendants are church members, and the record gave no information about the statue's origins—how old it was, where it was made, that sort of thing. I don't have much time right now to dig deeper, but perhaps after the holidays I can find out more."

"The church should hire an antique or art appraiser," Sara suggested. "They might be able to figure out its origins."

"I'd thought of that. But the church council will need to approve that kind of expense, and they won't meet again until the new year."

By then, I might be run out of town over this. Especially if Sara's grandmother has her way.

"By the way, did you interview your grandmother for this piece? She had a lot to say about the situation yesterday."

Sara and her husband, Luke, had lived in Lillian's huge house ever since last winter when Lillian had fallen and needed care. Now they remained there, keeping her company and allowing her to live more or less independently.

"Oh, don't pay any attention to Lillian. She always needs something to be outraged about. Otherwise, she gets low blood pressure," Sara joked.

"She did have a point," Ben allowed. "I've been wondering if others in the congregation feel the same way."

"Well, if they do, they're certainly not in the majority. I've interviewed dozens of people, and my grandmother is the only one who was so negative. I just chalked that up to Lillian being Lillian." Sara packed up her camera and notebook in a big leather sack that seemed to double as both handbag and briefcase. "Thanks for your help, Reverend. It's hard to say when we'll run the story. Could be as soon as tomorrow. Definitely before Christmas," she promised.

Ben walked with her to the big wooden doors. "I'll be interested to read it."

Not that he was looking forward to the publicity. But what could he do? The situation seemed to be spinning out of his control.

As the day progressed, the idea of the news article coming out weighed on Ben's mind. He decided he needed to call Reverend Hallock and explain what was going on, before his superior read about it in the paper.

At the end of the day, after his secretary, *Irene*, had left, Ben dialed Reverend Hallock's office number, half hoping he would find Hallock gone for the day. But surprisingly, Reverend Hallock answered the phone himself.

Ben greeted him. "Sorry to bother you so late in the day, Thomas. But something's come up here. You may read about it in the newspaper soon, and I wanted to give you a heads-up."

"Good to hear from you, Ben. What's going on?"

"Well . . . It's a unique situation, really. Nothing I've personally come across before, though, of course, you do hear of these things from time to time. . . ." Ben paused. He wasn't digressing on purpose, but it was hard to explain. He took a breath, willing himself to just get to the point.

"There's a statue in our church. It's an angel. Very old, a beautiful piece of workmanship. The sexton and I found it in the basement a few weeks ago and put it up as a Christmas decoration. Since then, several people have come forward, claiming that the angel has answered their prayers and possesses . . . miraculous powers."

There. He'd said it.

"Miraculous powers? What sort of miracles has this statue performed?" Thomas didn't sound shocked or even that impressed, Ben thought. He sounded skeptical.

Ben described the claims from Carl, Digger, and Grace. "I've heard those firsthand, from members of our congregation. There are others, too. People who have visited the church and left prayer petitions. There have been a lot of visitors lately."

"I see. This will all be reported in the newspaper?"

"A reporter from the *Cape Light Messenger* stopped by today. She said the story would run before Christmas."

"Perfect timing. Should sell a lot of papers."

"Yes," Ben agreed.

Reverend Hallock didn't speak for a long moment. Ben waited, wondering now if he should have called sooner, asking for permission to speak to the newspaper.

Finally, Reverend Hallock said, "And what do you think about all this, Ben? What's your position?"

Ben took a breath. "I think that there are many explanations for these events— logical, mundane explanations. Yet the peo-

ple who say they have experienced a miracle seem to believe it. I find it hard to deny
their personal truth unequivocally. Who am I
to say what they've experienced, Thomas?"

"True enough." But there was something
reluctant in Hallock's tone.

"I don't encourage it in anyway. Except
perhaps to keep the statue in the sanctuary,"
Ben allowed. "The deaconate met and discussed the matter. An excellent point was
raised that has become a touchstone for me.
One of the deacons pointed out that people
come to the statue to communicate with
some higher source, with God. They come
with faith that their prayers will be heard. We
felt that it wouldn't be right to remove the
statue right now and to deny those prayer-
fully seeking help and guidance . . . Not at
Christmas."

"I hear what you're saying." Reverend Hallock sighed.

Ben sensed that his superior felt uncomfortable with the entire situation. Especially
the impending publicity. He wondered if he
should have mentioned the Internet chat
board, then decided it was probably better if
Thomas learned about that on his own.
Sara's article was sure to mention it.

"After Christmas, we'll probably put it away again," Ben said. "We brought it out as a holiday decoration, not for permanent use."

"Well, that's some compromise. To be honest, I would prefer that the statue was removed immediately. But since you feel so strongly and your church deaconate has decided upon it, I agree it can remain until the holidays are over."

"Thank you, Thomas. I do think that's the right thing to do," Ben added.

"It's sounds as if you've thought this through and given the question full consideration. It's a complicated issue, Ben. Please be careful about what you say, what you endorse. Otherwise, we might both be starting the new year looking for new jobs."

Ben laughed, though he knew Hallock was serious beneath his joking tone.

"I will be careful, Thomas. But thanks for your advice."

Ben hung up the phone and straightened out his desk. He felt relieved now that the phone call was over and he was eager to get home. He retrieved his hat and coat from the closet, shut the office lights, and locked the door. Then he made the rounds to be sure all the lights had been turned off and the thermostat in the sanctuary turned to its low setting. It was really Carl's job but one Ben needed to double-check. They were not a rich church and had to watch their pennies.

He entered the sanctuary and was about to shut off the lights when he realized the church was not completely empty. A woman with elegant silver-gray hair stood near the statue. Ben watched as she slowly walked around the pedestal, studying it up and down. She wore a dark red coat, a patterned scarf, and black leather gloves. He recognized her. She had come to visit the statue several times before.

When she came around the front again, she stood before it, looking up into its face for a long time. Then she knelt in a nearby pew, her head bowed at a graceful angle. Ben sat in the rear of the darkened sanctuary, waiting for her to finish. Finally, she rose, picked up her purse, and walked down the center aisle, passing him.

He walked to the wall switches and was just about to turn off the lights, when she suddenly returned.

"I forgot my scarf," she explained, starting back to the pew where she had left it. She spoke with a slight accent, he noticed, possibly French. Her silver hair was thick, in a stylish cut, and her coat and large silk scarf looked expensive and chic.

Ben walked over to her and smiled. "Did you come from very far to visit the statue?"

"From Boston. I heard about it from a cousin, and I wanted to see it. I've come a few times. It calls me back." She looked up at the statue again, her eyes lingering on its lines. A gentle smile formed on her face. "We are old friends, this angel and I."

Ben was puzzled, wondering if she was yet another pilgrim with a vivid imagination about the statue.

"How is that?" he asked gently

"Do you have a minute, Pastor? I will tell you."

Ben nodded. "Please, do." He motioned for her to sit and then he did, too.

"I was born in a small village in the south of France. During World War Two, my family belonged to the Resistance. A young American soldier came to the village. He was to help the underground to prepare for the great invasion, D-day. Disguised as a bike mechanic, he worked in my father's shop. I was sixteen and the soldier, only nineteen. We knew each other only a brief time but had a great love." She paused and smoothed the silk scarf through her hands. When she looked back up at Ben, he could see that her wide brown eyes were glassy, filled with tears. She took a breath and continued.

"The church in my village was a meeting place for the Resistance. The Germans discovered this. Our village was bombed, the church destroyed one night when our group had gathered for a meeting. The American soldier and I were the only survivors. We took shelter in a small side chapel, near this statue." She pointed up at the angel. "It was as if her wings had spread above us. But not everyone was so protected. When it was over, I saw that my father was one who died, buried alive."

"How terribly sad for you," Ben said. "What an awful thing to witness."

She smiled grimly. "There were many awful sights in wartime, Pastor. We learn to go on. Not to forget but to live as best we can."

"How true. And what happened to you then, to your family?"

"The soldier and I managed to take the angel with us. The statue was amazingly unharmed. We knew the Germans would come and sift through the rubble of the church, looking for anything of value. We didn't want them to have it. We carried it to my house and hid it there for safekeeping. Of course, the Resistance group had been decimated. The soldier was sent to another part of the country. We made all the promises young lovers do, to be faithful and find each other after the war. I received one letter some months later. Then not a word. Then I learned he was captured and killed by the enemy."

Ben sat back, speechless. She had endured so much yet seemed to possess a great spirit. A great faith.

"After the war, my family left France. My mother had relatives in London, and we lived there for a time, then came to the U.S. My mother had tried to return the angel before we left France, but there was no church left to return it to. We took it with us to England, and there, she took it to an art dealer to raise money for our emigration. I believed I would never see it again."

"And you're sure it's the same statue?" Ben asked carefully.

"I know it is. I would recognize her anywhere. See the right hand, where she grips the banner? Her little finger was broken off in the explosion, the only harm done."

Ben looked at the statue closely. It took him a moment to find the damage she mentioned. He would not have noticed it otherwise.

He turned to her. "Tell me, do you remember what the banner said? The paint is faded and I can't make out the words. It appears to be written in French, so I wouldn't have been able to understand it anyway," he added.

She smiled at him, her eyes shining. "It says, 'Do not lose heart.'"

He nodded. Of course. That made perfect sense.

"So, tell me about your life. How did it turn out here in America?"

"Oh, very happily, to be sure. I'm a widow now but had a long, happy marriage. We raised three children and had many grandchildren. My life has been long, filled with blessings, Pastor. But I never dreamed I would see that statue again, not in this world. I do believe she is a miracle."

He had heard that said before. But this time Ben did not counter with some rational, debunking explanation. He let it be.

* * *

THAT EVENING BEN TOLD CAROLYN THE STORY AS they ate dinner. He could see from her expression that she was as moved by the woman's story as he had been.

When he was done, neither of them spoke for a long time.

Finally Carolyn said, "What was her name? You never mentioned it."

"Marie-Claire Perretti. I asked her to sign the visitors' book when she left."

"How do you feel about the statue now? Do you still think there's nothing special about it?"

"Honestly, I'm not sure," Ben admitted. "There have been so many odd stories from so many people, some of them people I've known for years. And now this woman, coming from so far . . ."

"And me, too," Carolyn added quietly.

Ben searched her face to see if he had understood her correctly. "You experienced a miracle?"

"I believe I've had some experience that was out of the ordinary after visiting the statue."

"Are you serious?"

Carolyn's calm gaze told him that she was. "It was last week. I was waiting for you to change and finish in your office," she explained. "The sanctuary was almost empty. I sat there a moment and prayed. About a lot of things—our children, you . . ." She shrugged. "I'm not sure I even remember everything."

"That's all right, you don't need to tell me."

"About two days ago, I was giving a lesson. I started to play the piece, to show my student some fingering. It took me a minute to realize, I was playing with my left hand, too. After all these years . . ." She paused and dipped her head then held out her hand—her left hand, the one that had been partially paralyzed by her stroke. She wiggled her fingers. "The movement has returned, Ben. The doctor said it would never happen."

Ben could hardly believe it. He reached out and took her left hand in his. Her hand clasped his, all their fingers interlocking. He had never thought he would feel that again. "Oh, Carolyn," he said, blinking back tears of gratitude. He lifted her left hand and pressed it to his lips.

"I know." Carolyn smiled at him through her own tears.

Ben folded her into his arms and for a

long while they just held each other. Silently, he sent up a prayer of thanks.

Carolyn was the one who broke the embrace. "Tell me, Ben," she said, pulling back a little and looking up at him. "Can you possibly doubt the angel now?"

Ben took a breath, sensing that his wife wouldn't like what he was about to say. "I don't mean to answer a question with a question, Carolyn, but can you remember what the doctor actually said? Did he say you would never regain full movement in that hand? Or did he just say that it was highly unlikely?"

"What's the difference?" Carolyn asked. "What's the point of splitting hairs? You've got the proof in front of your eyes, Ben. After three years, I've suddenly regained the movement in my hand!"

"Maybe it was your faith that made the difference," he said finally. "You believed so strongly, it's possible that your mind cured your body."

"Maybe," Carolyn replied. "But I'm not sure I would have believed if it wasn't for the statue. I believe that there is something special about it, Ben. Something . . . blessed."

Ben met his wife's clear blue gaze, and

wondered if he wasn't starting to believe it, too.

DR. ALEXANDRA COLE JOINED MATT'S PRACTICE on Tuesday. Molly tried her best to keep a low-key attitude, asking Matt only a few questions that night about how the new partnership was going. He was annoyingly spare with his answers.

Despite her own hectic schedule, Molly kept finding herself distracted by the thought of her husband and Alex Cole, working side by side.

By Thursday afternoon, she couldn't stand it anymore. She packed up a basket with some of Matt's favorite foods, pulled on her coat, and headed for his office.

In the old days, when they were dating and then engaged, she used to bring him lunch nearly every day. They would take a break together, sometimes even having a brief picnic on the Village Green, or they would find a bench along the harbor. It was sweet . . . and romantic. She had not appreciated those days, Molly realized now. How did they ever get here from there?

Molly swept into the office, the basket hooked under her arm. The waiting room was empty except for one man reading a magazine. Molly greeted Matt's receptionist. "Hi, Amy. Is Matt around? I brought him some lunch."

"How thoughtful. He hasn't had his lunch yet. He's in back, with Dr. Cole. I'll give him a buzz."

"Oh, that's all right. Don't bother." Molly waved her hand. "I'll just run back there. He won't mind."

Amy gave her a puzzled look but didn't pick up the phone. Molly headed for Matt's office.

She quickly knocked then walked right in. Matt was sitting behind his desk and Alex stood nearby, looking over his shoulder at a file. Beneath her open white lab coat, she wore tapered wool pants and a close-fitting cashmere sweater, both of which accentuated her slender build. *She's probably all of a size four,* Molly thought.

"Hi, everyone," Molly said, managing to sound cheerful. "I had a minute so I brought you some lunch, Matt. Amy said you haven't had a break yet today. You must be famished."

Matt looked surprised to see her. "Hi, honey . . . sure, lunch sounds great." He glanced at his watch. "It is late. . . . Alex, why don't you eat with us? I'm sure Molly brought enough to feed an army."

Gee, Molly thought, *that made me sound so . . . motherly.*

"Oh, I don't know." Alex hesitated, and Molly wondered if she was picking up on Molly's need to be alone with her husband. "I think I'll just grab a cup of yogurt at my desk."

Matt rose and put his hand on her shoulder. "No, you stay. Come on, let's all sit over at the table. Here, Molly, I'll take that." He picked up the basket and pretended to stagger under its weight. "Wow, what do you have in here, a turkey dinner?"

"It's the water bottles," Molly said quietly.

"It's good to drink plenty of water." Alex nodded, taking a seat at the table. "Especially when you're pregnant. It fills you up, too, so you won't overeat."

Molly smiled at her. *Thanks for the diet tip.* Was that a subtle insult aimed at her size?

Matt spread the pretty yellow and blue checked tablecloth Molly had brought, then set out the paper plates and plastic utensils. Molly took out the food, which she had arranged on attractive plastic platters.

"There are some roll-up sandwiches—

your favorite, Matt—roast beef and herbed goat cheese with watercress."

Looking pleased, Matt put a sandwich on his plate. "Yum. Haven't had one of these in a while."

"Glad to hear it," Alex said with a laugh. "That's a cholesterol bomb if I ever saw one."

Matt had been biting down with a contented expression but his face suddenly turned sour. He chewed and swallowed a bite. "That's true," he said to Alex. "I'm getting to the age when you really have to watch your fat intake." He glanced up at Molly. "It's really good, honey. . . . Here, why don't we split this one?"

He set half of his sandwich on Molly's plate. She stared down at it. When had Matt ever eaten half a sandwich for lunch in his life?

Molly glanced across the table at Alex. So far, she hadn't touched a bite of food. *Fine,* Molly thought. Fortunately, she had brought things besides the "cholesterol bombs."

"Let's see, we have some arugula salad with pears and walnuts . . . and some berries in this bowl." Molly set out the healthy choices then watched Alex help herself to a few spoonfuls of salad—no dressing—and a flat-bread cracker.

And about a quart of water, Molly noticed. The woman had to be half camel.

"So, how are you enjoying it here, Alex?" Molly asked in a pleasant tone. "Is Matt working you hard?"

"Oh, no . . . we're having a great time, aren't we Matt?"

"Alex is fitting in just fine. The patients love her."

Of course, Molly thought.

"Mrs. Kruger was cute this morning, wasn't she?" Matt said to Alex.

Alex laughed. "Yes, she was. But I think she ought to see an eye doctor."

Molly smiled politely, feeling left out of the joke. "What happened?" she asked finally.

"Oh, nothing . . ." Alex shook her head, looking embarrassed.

"When Alex went out into the waiting room to introduce herself, Mrs. Kruger thought she was one of our girls. She called her Lauren."

Molly knew that Alex had to be around Matt's age, but she didn't look it at all. That was probably one of the great benefits of not having children running you ragged: you had all the time in the world to work on yourself. Molly thought of a sarcastic comeback—she could agree that Mrs. Kruger certainly did need to get her eyes checked—but restrained herself. She didn't want to be mean and petty. She wanted to take the high road. After all, Alex was here so Molly could have more time with Matt; that was the thing to keep in mind.

The intercom buzzed and Matt rose to answer it. Alex looked over at her. "That was a nice treat. Do you and Matt do this often?"

"Oh, we used to," Molly said. "I know he enjoys it."

"It's very thoughtful. Matt says you're unbelievably busy at your shop right now."

"I always have time for my husband," Molly replied, knowing it wasn't exactly true. She loved Matt madly, but lately she had hardly had any time for him. He was a priority in her heart but not in her day-planner. The arrival of Dr. Cole, however, had given her a wake-up call.

Matt returned from his phone call. "Got to get back to work, honey." He took hold of her shoulders and gave her a quick kiss. "Thanks for lunch. That was great. See you home tonight, okay?"

Molly nodded. "Sure."

Alex started to clean up the paper plates.

"That's okay. I'll clean up," Molly offered. "You probably have patients waiting."

Alex dumped a few plates in the trash can. "Actually, I do. Thanks for including me. I'll see you soon, okay?" She stood at the door a moment and waved.

Molly waved back. Then heaved a sigh of relief when Alex disappeared.

Alone in the office, she dug down into the basket and found a package of thick, chewy brownies. She hadn't dared produce them in Alex's sight, fearing another lecture on triglycerides and blood-sugar highs. She picked one out and took a big satisfying bite. And then another.

One for me. One for the baby.

She gently rubbed her tummy and thought about the tiny being growing inside her. "Now, that's really tasty, right, baby? Chocolate is actually not bad for us at all. It's a proven fact. It's an antioxidant, as good as drinking green tea or eating bags of broccoli, and it puts you in a good mood. Mommy feels better already."

MOLLY RETURNED TO HER SHOP TO FIND BETTY waiting for her. Betty had wanted to stop by for lunch that day, but Molly explained where she had to go—and why.

"So, how did it go?" Betty asked. "Did Matt like his sandwich?"

Molly dumped her basket on the counter and pulled off her coat. She felt as if she'd just auditioned for a role as *Little Red Riding Hood* and hadn't been picked for the part.

"He did like it. He liked it a lot. But Dr. Anorexia disapproved of his food choices and took all the fun out of it, for goodness sake."

"She had lunch with you?"

"Matt insisted on it." Molly turned to her friend, looking grim. "Betty, maybe I'm just being paranoid, but I can't help worrying that there might be something going on there."

"You are being paranoid," Betty said at once. "Matt adores you."

"Maybe," Molly said. "But I'm—motherly. And she's beautiful, smart, sweet . . ."

"Maybe she is all those things, but so are you," Betty reminded her. "That still doesn't mean Matt is attracted to her and they're going to run off and have an affair."

"I'm not sweet," Molly corrected her. She opened the basket and began unpacking it. "I'll bet he is attracted. He just won't admit it, of course. Did I tell you they were an item once? He said Alex broke it off. He's probably been pining for her all these years. They're both doctors, for goodness sake. I didn't even finish college. Maybe that's starting to bother Matt, even though he said it didn't matter to him. . . ."

Betty touched her arm. "Molly, you're getting carried away with yourself. You're letting your old insecurities and self-image problems take over. I thought you were over all that."

"Okay, maybe I'm exaggerating," Molly conceded. "Maybe he hasn't been thinking of her. But the man isn't blind. Look at me, I'm turning into a blimp. None of my nice clothes fit anymore. I'm starting to go into the 'big shirt and black pants' stage. After Jill was born, I didn't emerge until she was in fifth grade."

"Molly, you're worrying yourself sick over nothing. Matt isn't going to run off with Alex Cole. He knows you're growing his child in your body. He knows you're going to gain some weight. Hey, some men love it when women look pregnant. He's certainly wild about the baby coming," she reminded her.

Molly sighed. "Here, let me pack this stuff up for you. You take it home, have it for dinner tonight." Without waiting for Betty's answer, she packed up the leftover sandwiches and salads. She even gave Betty the brownies, feeling horribly guilty now for her impulsive indulgence.

"I know what you're saying is true," Molly admitted. "I know I'm letting myself get carried away. But every time Matt talks about Alex, he sounds as if he's talking about Uma Thurman and Madam Curie, rolled into one. It just . . . drives me crazy!"

"Okay . . . but that's still your problem. It has nothing to do with Matt."

Molly glared at her. Sometimes Betty could be so . . . so . . . honest. And sensible. It was really annoying.

"I haven't even told you the worst of it. The other night, I was talking to him about Christmas Eve. You know, we're going to have that big family party. It'll be the first time we're really entertaining in our new house. I want it to be . . . special." She sighed. "So far, he's let me do all the planning. His only suggestion? 'Why don't we invite Alex? She'll probably be all alone for Christmas.'" Molly made a face. "I know it sounds mean and totally lacking in Christmas spirit but . . . I'm dreading her showing up. It will be this glaring contrast between Uma and the whale."

Betty looked at her sympathetically. "Oh, honey . . . don't get so bent out of shape. Matt didn't mean anything by that." Betty caught her eye and smiled. "Actually, I think you should invite her. In fact, I think it's a great idea."

Molly was confused. "Why?"

"Because this is the perfect chance to meet her on your own turf and show Alex how solid your marriage is. You're a wonderful hostess, a fabulous cook, your entire family adores you. If she is even remotely thinking of stealing your husband—and I *don't* think she is—she'll see that she doesn't have a chance. And if she is just Matt's partner, who doesn't know anyone else in town and could use an invite on Christmas Eve, then you'll have done a really nice thing. Either way, you win."

"Maybe you're right." Molly sat up straighter and smoothed out her blouse. "I'm going to call Matt's office right now and invite her."

Betty beamed. "That's the spirit, kid. Go for it."

"You just have to promise me one thing. Now you really have to come to the party— for moral support. I don't think I can pull this off without you."

"I'm sure you can," Betty told her. "But I'll come anyway. I wouldn't miss it for the world."

MIRANDA HAD DELIVERED HER PRE-CHRISTMAS order to the Golden Moon, only to have Krista give her a new order for Valentine's Day. At least that gave Miranda time to order some of the stones she was missing. And it gave her something to occupy her own time while she waited for Adam's old life to reclaim him. She knew it would happen any day now. She had seen him listening again and again to the tape that Dr. Carter had made of the hypnotherapy session. She hadn't asked him about it, but she was sure that there was a clue in there somewhere.

Now there were only four days until Christmas. Miranda had finished her Christmas shopping and was working on the new order. Krista had asked for more of Miranda's signature pieces—the necklaces and earrings that contrasted dark and light stones. But she had also specially requested pieces made with rose quartz, garnets, pink tourmaline, and even a few with rubies—all the red and pink stones that reminded people of their hearts and love.

As if I could forget, Miranda thought. She

felt as if her own heart had been aching for days now. At least it was easy to immerse herself in her work, probably a form of self-hypnosis, she decided, considering the way Adam had explained it.

Miranda had never thought about it much but now considered it a blessing, the way she lost track of time and even a sense of her surroundings while she worked. The long strands of colored beads—deep lapis blue, burgundy garnet, violet amethyst, and golden topaz—were mesmerizing. Forming the intricate shapes of silver wire, beads, and iridescent seed pearls to create a harmony of design required her total focus and concentration. Even paging through art history textbooks for inspiration transported Miranda to a distant, meditative place.

She came into the house for some coffee midafternoon and found her grandmother sitting at the kitchen table, writing out Christmas cards. Not that there was much time for the cards to reach their destinations. The way the post office looked this week, it would take four days standing in line just to mail them.

"Greg called," Sophie said. "I told him you were out in the cottage and I would run out and get you, but he said for you to call him back when you were able. I guess he didn't want to bother me. He's so considerate."

Miranda had to agree. Greg was considerate. She had noticed lately that her grandmother rarely missed a chance to comment on any of Greg's good points.

"Okay, I'll call him in a minute. Did he leave a message?"

Sophie shook her head. "Just to call him back. But we did have a chat. I hope you don't mind, Miranda." Sophie glanced up briefly at her granddaughter, a sheepish look on her face. "We started talking about the holidays, and he said he was picking up his little girl on Christmas Day . . . but didn't have any plans at all for Christmas Eve . . ."

Miranda knew where this was going. She braced herself. She loved her grandmother dearly, but Sophie had a habit of treating everyone like family.

". . . So what could I do? Before I even thought about it, I invited him to our party. I know I should have left that to you. But you've been dating Greg for a while now. I didn't think you would mind." Sophie shrugged and glanced at her again, a deeply penitent look on her face, designed to elicit sympathy, Miranda suspected.

And they say I'm the actress in the family. It's got to be genetic.

"I guess it's all right," Miranda said finally. "Thought it does create . . . expectations, Grandma."

Did she really want Greg here on Christmas Eve, with all her family around, including her father? When you brought a date to a family Christmas party, didn't it imply the relationship was serious? What would Greg be thinking now? That she had given her grandmother the impression their relationship was serious—or she hoped it was?

And what if Adam was still here? Christmas was only four days away. It was possible he would be here, and then the day would be an emotional tug-of-war for her. The whole situation gave Miranda a headache.

Sophie seemed to sense that Miranda was upset and shook her head dolefully. "I'm sorry, honey. I just wasn't thinking."

Miranda couldn't stay mad at her. "What did Greg say? Is he coming?" she asked finally.

"He thanked me for asking and said he

would let us know. Maybe he's waiting to hear it from you," she added.

"Maybe," Miranda agreed, though the idea of repeating an invitation she wouldn't have made in the first place didn't exactly fill her heart with holiday cheer.

Maybe Greg would decline, deciding for himself it would be taking a step he wasn't ready for. Or maybe he would get a better offer. Miranda decided there was nothing she could do about it. The situation already seemed out of her hands.

She watched her grandmother for a moment, writing a personal message in each of her cards, pausing to think of what she wanted to say, a slight smile on her face as she worked.

"Grandma, if you're done with those cards today, I'll take them into town for you later," Miranda offered.

"Oh, don't bother, honey. Anytime before New Year's is okay with me. It's the idea of it, you know. I always think I start early enough. Then I end up writing a note inside each one."

"Why don't you just write one of those chatty catch-up letters and send it out to everyone? Wouldn't that be more efficient?"

"Efficient maybe, but those things annoy me. Most people tell more than you ever wanted to know. First they brag about their grandkid graduating from medical school. Then they describe their husband's kidney stones. That's not my idea of a holiday greeting."

Miranda had to smile. Her grandmother was the most clear-sighted person she knew. She hoped some of those genes had trickled down to her, though it didn't seem likely. After all, it wasn't very clear-sighted of her to have fallen so hard for Adam.

The phone rang and Miranda picked it up, thinking it might be Greg again. But it wasn't Greg. It was Detective Lester. "Hi, Miranda. Is Adam there? I have some news."

"Yes . . . He's upstairs. Just hold on, I'll call him." Miranda felt breathless, as if all the air had suddenly been sucked out of the room.

This might be it. The news Adam had been waiting for—and she had been dreading.

Miranda called to Adam from the bottom of the stairs and then heard him pick up the extension. She hung up, giving him privacy. She glanced at her grandmother. Sophie had stopped writing, her smile transformed into a worried frown.

A few moments later, Miranda heard Adam coming down the stairs. He walked into the kitchen, his expression dumbstruck.

"Detective Lester says he's solved my case. He's found . . . my fiancée." Adam glanced at Miranda for a fraction of a second, then looked away.

She felt as if her heart had turned into stone. She wasn't sure if she could breathe, if she could feel. Her body felt thick and numb.

Her grandmother looked surprised, too. "Is he sure this time? I wouldn't want you to get your hopes up again for nothing."

"Yes, he's sure." Adam nodded. "He said he's been following the lead for a while, but didn't want to tell me until he was sure. A woman who says that she's my fiancée got in touch with him a week or so ago. She missed my photo and story when the news article first came out. But somebody showed it to her and she tracked me down."

"That's good news then. I knew it would happen. We just needed to be patient." Sophie stood up, sounding breathless and letting her reading glasses hang from the cord around her neck. "When will she come? Sometime tomorrow?"

"She's here, in Cape Light, right now. She's at the police station, giving proof of our relationship." Adam swallowed hard. His eyes looked glassy. "Lester says I live in Portland, Maine. She's taking me back there. Tonight."

"I'll take you to town, Adam." It nearly killed Miranda to make the offer, but she knew she had to say something.

"Detective Lester is coming here. With . . . Lisa. He thinks that will be best."

Sophie lifted her chin. "Well, it's all very sudden, but I guess it couldn't happen any other way. We'll miss you, Adam. It won't feel the same without you around."

Adam swallowed hard. "I'll miss you, too. Both of you," he said, glancing at Miranda. "I don't think you could ever know how grateful I am. Or how much I value your friendship."

Sophie walked over and patted his arm. "Portland's not far. We'll keep in touch. You can come back and visit us anytime. I'll put you to work out in the orchard next time. You might like that better than painting."

Adam gave her a small smile. "I might," he admitted. Then he leaned over and hugged Sophie tight. Miranda couldn't stand to stay in the room another second. If he hugged her like that, she wasn't sure she would be able to let him go.

"I have to . . . go back out. I left the burner on in the cottage . . ." She raced out of the kitchen and out the side door, then started walking swiftly up the steep hill, into the orchard.

When she got far enough away from the house so that no one could hear her or see her, she sank down against the trunk of one of the apple trees. Sitting on the cold ground, her knees drawn up to her chest, her head cradled on her arms, Miranda finally let herself cry.

MIRANDA DIDN'T KNOW HOW LONG SHE HAD BEEN sitting in the orchard when she saw the detective's car pull into the driveway. She wiped her eyes and her tear-streaked cheeks, feeling torn between the need to see Adam one more time and say good-bye, and the urge to hide until he was gone.

Finally, she walked down to the house. As she slipped in the side door, she heard voices in the living room. She drifted quietly into the room and saw her grandmother and Detective Lester standing together. Adam stood a short distance away, his expression grim. A woman stood next to him, staring up adoringly. Miranda didn't need to be told that was his fiancée, the woman who had come to take him.

Strangely, Adam wasn't looking at his fiancée. His eyes roamed the room until he caught sight of Miranda, then he looked at her as if he were drinking in her image. Miranda stared back, unable to look way. She couldn't just stand there gazing at him; she knew that if she did, she would burst into tears again.

Instead, she walked closer, coming to stand next to her grandmother. She studied the attractive woman who stood by Adam's side, her arm around his waist, squeezing him close, as if she could hardly believe he was real.

Miranda knew she would act the same way in her place. She felt a sudden unexpected pang of sympathy for the woman, realizing that she must have been out of her mind with worry these last few weeks. Miranda also felt a reluctant curiosity—this was the woman whom Adam had fallen in love with. What was she like?

As Miranda studied her, the first thing she realized was that they were almost complete physical opposites. Adam's fiancée was petite with curly black hair and—Miranda nearly gasped as she made the connection. The woman's hair was the same color and length as the café hostess's in Newburyport.

Oh, I was such a fool, Miranda thought. *I should have guessed then that Adam was remembering his significant other. Instead, I downplayed the moment, even made a joke about it.* She had been in denial, blinded by her own feelings for him and the chance to spend one carefree night in his company.

She and Adam had had a few precious hours alone together. This woman would be with him for the rest of her life.

"This is Miranda," Adam said to his fiancée. "She's the one who found me. Miranda, this is Lisa," he added.

Adam's fiancée extended her hand, and Miranda had no choice but to shake it. She drew on all her training as an actress, struggling to keep her expression relaxed and friendly. "Great to meet you, Lisa. What a happy day for you. For both of you."

"I'm so thrilled!" the other woman told her. "I can't believe it. I finally found Eric! You can't imagine how I worried."

Eric, Miranda thought. *His name was Eric.*

"I'm so grateful to you both," Lisa went on. "How can I ever thank you two?" She turned to Sophie, taking her hand. "You must let us pay you back for your trouble, for the medical bills at the very least. I hate to think of what could have happened to him if he had just been left to . . . to wander around . . . homeless . . ."

"We didn't do so much," Sophie said, patting her arm. "We're just thankful that he's going home now. I'm sure once you're both back in your own routine, his memory will return."

Miranda felt sure of that, too. From what she could see, Lisa was a bright, caring woman and he must be happy with her. Now that they had been parted and reunited, they would probably be even more eager to get married. When Miranda could stop feeling sorry for herself for a second or two, she actually felt happy for him. And even for Lisa, who, she reasoned, must love him, even more than she did.

Once he regained his memory, the time at the orchard would seem like a crazy aberration, something as strange and isolated as his period of memory loss. *And that's the way I've got to see it, too,* Miranda decided.

He was quiet, she noticed, barely responding to all the attention. He seemed to be in shock as he gazed over Lisa's head at Miranda.

Their eyes met again, and she held his gaze for a long, breathless moment.

Then Sophie reached up and embraced him again. "Good-bye, Adam . . . I mean, Eric. You know you're always welcome here. You come back and visit sometime, all right?"

"Yes, Sophie. I will. I promise," he said as he let her go.

He stepped back and faced Miranda. She didn't move toward him, though her spirit willed her to. Her feet felt like two bricks.

She couldn't say good-bye to him. Not with all these people watching. Especially not in front of his fiancée. She wouldn't be able to hold herself together. She was just barely hanging on as it was.

He made a move forward, as if to hug her, too. But she quickly took his hand and forced a smile. "Good-bye, Adam." She realized her mistake at once, but somehow she couldn't bring herself to call him by his real name. To her he would always be Adam. She tried again. "Good-bye and good luck."

"Good-bye, Miranda . . . and good luck to you."

He stood staring at her a moment, then Lisa touched his arm. "Is this all your stuff, honey?"

He looked down as if he had forgotten she was in the room. "Yes, just that one shopping bag."

Miranda noticed he carried his journal, which had grown to three notebooks.

"Okay, I'll take you two back to town. It's getting late," Detective Lester said.

He herded the couple out of the house and into his car. Miranda and Sophie watched from the front door as they drove away, headed back to town and back to Adam's real life.

"Well, that's that." Sophie shut the door and turned to her granddaughter. "I knew when he got the call, it would happen suddenly. But I didn't think he would be gone that fast."

"No, neither did I," Miranda said honestly.

"His fiancée seems nice. Seems devoted to him."

"Very nice," Miranda agreed. "I think he'll be fine."

"I think he will, too." Sophie walked into

the living room and lowered herself into a favorite armchair. She made a sound as she sat down, as if her body ached. Miranda realized that all this excitement was probably wearing on her as well.

Miranda followed her into the living room but didn't sit. She needed to be alone. She needed to absorb the reality of what had just happened. She felt the loss keenly, like a knife slicing into her side and leaving a big gaping hole. She wanted to cry, to scream and rail against fate, which had been so cruel to offer a man she could love, unequivocally, then just snatch him away.

Her grandmother glanced at her and sighed. "I know you're hurting, honey. But in time, it will get better. You won't be the same. I'm not saying you'll forget. But somehow you'll put the broken bits back together and keep going."

Miranda didn't answer. She just nodded and headed out to the cottage.

The big empty studio was eerily quiet. She noticed the blank places where Adam's belongings had been and looked away, the sight painful.

She had the place all to herself now. She

could spread out her materials and take over, without worrying about his schedule. Of course, that change gave her no satisfaction at all.

Miranda sat at her table and forced herself to pick up the necklace she had started that morning. The design was influenced by the jewelry of the Ancient Egyptians and very intricate. She strung one bead and then the next, as if in a trance, stopping every now and then to wipe her eyes.

She wasn't sure how long she had been working. She glanced out the window and realized it was dark outside. A while later, her grandmother poked her head in the door, asking if she wanted any supper.

"Not right now, thanks. I'm not very hungry."

Her stomach hurt from crying so much. Her broken heart made her feel as if she would never want to eat again.

"I'll save something for you on the stove. You can heat it up later if you like," Sophie said.

A few moments later, Sophie was back, a little breathless. "There's a phone call for you, Miranda. Want them to hold, or should I take a message?"

Miranda's heart beat double time. She had a wild impossible hope that it was Adam, calling to say he couldn't live without her.

But, of course, her grandmother would have recognized his voice.

"Is it Greg? I forgot to call him back." Adam's departure had distracted her from everything. She knew Greg would be wondering why she hadn't returned his call.

"No, it's not Greg. I know his voice by now." Sophie started toward the door. "I'll just take a message for you."

"It's okay. I'll come and get it."

Miranda walked quickly into the house and picked up the phone, which was sitting on the kitchen counter. "Hello?" she said cautiously.

"Is this Miranda Potter?" a man's voice asked.

"Yes, it is. Who is calling?"

"This Alan Halpern, with the New City Theater Company."

"Yes, of course. Mr. Halpern. How are you?" Miranda heard her words come out in a rush. She supposed it was better to play it cool with these directors, but she was out of practice in that area.

He was finally getting back to her about *King Lear*. Would he be calling if it were bad news? She didn't think so, but nearly everything about a life in the theater was notoriously unpredictable.

Halpern laughed. "I'm fine. I'm just calling to follow up on your audition. I'm sorry it's taken so long for us to make a decision, but our producer, Dick Winston, has been in London the last few weeks. He's finally returned and we've finalized our decisions. We'd love to have you join the company, Miranda, to play the role of Cordelia, if you're still available."

Available? She had never felt more available in her life. Like a helium balloon cut loose and floating far up over the trees and houses, into the sky.

"Well," she said, "I'm not under contract for any other roles right now."

"Good, just what I wanted to hear. I'll go over the offer with you right now, if you like."

"Yes, of course." Miranda grabbed a pad and pencil and began jotting down notes as the director outlined the contract. The pay was even better than she expected, definitely more than what she had been getting when she lived in New York.

Part of her wanted to accept immediately. To pack her bags and run away from all the poignant reminders of Adam. He would never come back here, come back to her. And staying here without him suddenly seemed so bleak and painful.

The offer seemed a blessing, just the ticket out she needed.

But another part of her counseled her to take her time. To think it through. All the angles and consequences. This show wasn't going to run for a weekend or even a week. It was a huge commitment, nearly a year on the road. She would be putting all her eggs in the acting basket again. Giving up her fledgling business, her relationship with Greg, her promise to help her grandmother, and her life in the orchard—among the trees at the top of the hill, the place that had restored her.

Finally Halpern was done. "So . . . how does that sound to you?"

Miranda paused. "It's a great package. But it's hard to make a big decision on something like this over the phone. I'm sorry. I just need to think it over a bit . . . if that's okay."

"Is it the money? I can speak to Dick. Maybe we can do better."

"No, it's not the money. The salary is fine," she said honestly. "I guess I just didn't expect you to offer me the part. It's sort of a shock."

A stunning shock. The second in one day.

"Of course. I understand, Miranda. I'll send the contract overnight mail. You take your time, look it over. Call me if you have any questions. Can you give us a decision the week after Christmas?"

"That would be fine. And thank you . . . I feel really honored that you asked me."

"You're a very talented actress, Miranda. We'd be thrilled to have you join us."

Theater people were known for hyperbole, over-the-top compliments. Miranda tried to keep the director's comments in perspective. But it felt good to hear the words from someone who was at the top of her field, someone she respected.

They wished each other happy holidays and Miranda hung up. She sat back in her seat, feeling stunned. Miranda knew she should share the good news with her grandmother and maybe even ask for some advice.

But her first thought was to tell Adam.

And he was gone.

CHAPTER NINE

~~

IT WAS A VERY BUSY WEEK AT CHURCH FOR BEN. Christmas Eve fell on Monday, and Christmas Day, on Tuesday. Counting the usual Sunday service, he would be preaching three days in a row, a marathon of services and sermons.

On Sunday, the church was full, but cleared out quickly, the congregation taking an abbreviated coffee hour afterward. Everyone seemed to be rushing around, eager to find the last items on their Christmas lists.

Ben was also eager to get home. He and Carolyn were having their own family gathering on Christmas Eve, and his wife had a long list of jobs for him to do. Tucker Tulley was in charge of closing the church today, so Ben didn't feel he needed to stay until the building was empty.

He returned to his office to remove his vestments and pick up his hat and coat. He was halfway out the door when he remembered he had left some notes on the pulpit. With a sigh, he returned to the sanctuary. He grabbed his notes and headed down the aisle. Just as he drew even with the last row of pews, he felt a heavy hand on his arm.

Ben turned to face a tall man, well over six feet, with broad shoulders and a tuft of white hair around his bald head. He wore a long, dark blue overcoat and a dark red muffler. Ben had noticed him at the service, another visitor drawn to the angel statue.

He appeared to be in his late seventies but he looked fit, and the single touch on Ben's shoulder hinted at undiminished strength. His blue eyes were sharp as he gazed down at Ben. "Excuse me, Reverend. May I speak to you a moment?"

Ben nodded and pushed his wire-rimmed glasses a bit higher on his nose. "Can I help you with something?"

"That angel statue. I read about it in the

newspaper. Do you know where it came from? The newspaper didn't say."

"I believe it was donated to the church sometime in the early 1950s, though no one in the family who gave the gift is still a member here. I have good reason to believe the statue was once in a church in France," Ben answered, watching the man's expression. "A long time ago, before World War Two."

The man didn't answer at first. "I have good reason to say you're right, Reverend."

"And why is that?" Ben asked, somehow anticipating his answer.

The man hesitated a moment, as if deciding how to answer. "During the war, I was drafted into the army. My family is originally from Quebec, so I spoke French fluently. I was sent to the French countryside to aid the Resistance and gather intelligence for the allied invasion. That's where I saw this statue, in the church in that village. She saved my life," he added.

Ben felt stunned, even though at the sight of this visitor he had felt a premonition of the connection. "Can you tell me the story?" he asked. "I would like to hear it."

"All right. It's a bit unbelievable, but every word is true." The man looked down a moment, as if gathering his thoughts—or perhaps getting hold of his emotions. When he looked up again, his eyes were bright, but his voice steady.

"The army placed me with a family. I worked in the father's shop and lived in their small house behind the store. They had a daughter, Marie-Claire. She was a few years younger than me but brave. And very beautiful. We fell in love. She was also part of the Resistance group. The group rarely met, for safety's sake. But when it was necessary, we gathered late at night in the village church. One night during a meeting, the church was bombed. A traitor must have tipped off the enemy. Marie-Claire and I ran to a side chapel and huddled together. The church fell down around us, just about every stone. But by some miracle, we survived. When I looked up, I realized that we had been kneeling in the shadow of this angel. Hovering over us, she had saved our lives. We couldn't leave her there, so we bundled her up in some tapestries that had fallen and we took our protector with us."

"You didn't want the Germans to get the statue," Ben added.

The man glanced at him in surprise.

"That's right. We knew they would ransack anything that was left. It was a dreadful time. My sweetheart had lost her father in that explosion. I wanted to stay with her, to protect her. But a few days later, I got my orders. I was sent to another village to continue my mission. It just about broke my heart to leave. I even thought of going AWOL, but she wouldn't let me."

"It sounds as if she was a very honorable young woman."

The man shook his head. "She was . . . remarkable. I promised that I would find her after the war. But I was never able to. I tried everything—the Red Cross, refugee groups. I even went back to France, to the village where she'd lived. Her family was gone. No one knew where to. I often wondered if she even survived the war," he said sadly.

Ben could hardly speak. "She did survive," he said slowly. "I know where she is. She came to see the angel, too, and told me the same story."

The man stared at him, his mouth gaping open, his eyes wide with shock. "She's alive? Marie-Claire? Are you sure?"

Ben nodded. "I'll show you how she proved it." He walked to the front of the sanctuary, straight to the angel. The visitor followed closely behind. Ben stepped closer and pointed to the injured hand. "She showed me the one bit of damage from the explosion, how the angel lost her finger."

The man lifted his chin, his mouth quivering. He whisked a big hand over his eyes and blinked. "Do you know how I can find her? Did she leave an address?" His voice was choked with emotion.

"Yes, I have her address. Come with me, I'll write it down for you."

The visitor followed Ben through the sanctuary doors to the narthex, where Ben opened the guest book and copied down Marie-Claire's address. "Will you also sign? I haven't even asked your name. I'm Reverend Ben," he added.

"Gerald Martin," the man said. He finally smiled, and Ben caught a glimpse of the handsome young soldier he had once been. He held out his hand and Ben shook it. "I don't know how I can ever thank you for this, Reverend."

"Don't thank me. Thank the angel," Ben said.

Then he wondered about his response. Did that mean he'd become a believer, too?

* * *

ON CHRISTMAS EVE MORNING, MOLLY STAYED home from the shop. She had booked the delivery of several dinners around town but no major parties that required her supervision.

Matt could hardly believe it when he found her in the kitchen, still in her bathrobe and fuzzy slippers. "No work today?"

"Nope." She shook her head, barely looking up from her list. Which was actually color-coded. "I have my own party to work on. Betty is helping out at the shop. Then she's coming over here later."

"Good plan." She could tell he was pleased to see her cutting back on work.

He looked very handsome, she thought, setting off for his day, his dark hair combed back with a slight wave on top, his cheeks smooth from a fresh shave. He wore a dark blue sports jacket and gray pants with a pink oxford cloth shirt and a patterned tie.

Did he always look that good in the morning? She was usually too busy to notice, she realized. He leaned over and kissed her cheek, his travel mug of coffee in one hand and his overcoat in the other.

"We're closing the office early. I'll be home

soon enough to help you," he promised. "So don't try to do everything yourself. The house already looks like a magazine layout. I don't think there's another inch left to decorate."

Matt always had good intentions when it came to their entertaining. But his idea of getting the house ready for a party was to clear any dirty glasses, socks, and shoes from the family room and set out some bowls of pretzels and chips.

Hers was a little more elaborate.

He kissed her good-bye on the cheek and she clung to him a bit longer than usual. He gave her a look, but only said, "Call my cell if you want me to pick up anything at the store."

"I will," she promised. Once he was gone, Molly sprang into action. She ran upstairs, showered and dressed in her comfy, work-around-the-house clothes. Then she ran down to the mudroom where she had stored boxes of ribbons, pine branches, and holly to make her own centerpieces in the beautiful brass urns she'd found in a thrift store. The day before, she had picked up armfuls of fresh flowers at the florist, red and white roses and large white lilies and long strands of ivy that would trail down the urns.

She set to work, snipping, trimming, sticking and arranging. But she soon found the scent of the flowers and florist foam riled up her stomach.

"Oh . . . drat. Not this again." Molly stuck with it, arranging through her discomfort until, finally, she couldn't last a second longer. She ran into the half-bath and got sick.

The girls had all been sleeping late. Amanda was the first one downstairs. "Molly, are you okay?" She ran into the bathroom and helped her up. Then she dampened a washcloth and handed it over.

"Oh, honey, thanks." Molly wiped her face, nearly crying with frustration.

"You don't look so good. Want me to call Dad?"

"Oh no, honey. Don't do that. I'll be okay," Molly said quickly. "I have so much to do today for the party. I don't want to worry your dad."

Amanda grinned. "He'll make you go back to bed—and he'll order out for Chinese."

"Something like that," Molly said glumly. She started to stand and felt her head spin, but forced herself up anyway.

Amanda grabbed her arm and led her out of the bathroom. They made it to the kitchen, where Molly dropped into a chair, swallowing back the sour taste in the back of her throat.

"Sit there." Amanda handed Molly her list of things to be done before the party. "Just tell us what to do. We'll help you," Amanda promised, speaking for her stepsisters, who weren't even awake yet.

Molly gazed back at her dear face. Amanda looked a lot like her father. She was growing up to be a beautiful young woman, with a certain quiet manner her own daughters didn't share. They were all like flowers in a garden, Molly thought. It was impossible to say which was the loveliest. Their new baby sister—or brother—would be still another variety.

"Let's see," Molly didn't think the girls were capable of doing half the tasks, but she tried to find one anyway. She started with setting her tables. The long dining room table sat twenty when fully extended. Then she had two long folding tables, to be set up in the family room. She had red and gold patterned tablecloths and matching china and silverware.

And cloth napkins. Heaven forbid Lillian Warwick dabbed her mouth with a paper napkin. Especially at a family party. Molly had learned that the hard way.

No, this party was going to be perfect. Her "coming out" soirée. She was going to show her entire family she was a success, that she had arrived. Even Lillian Warwick would finally have to acknowledge her.

LATE THAT AFTERNOON, MOLLY FINALLY SURRENDERED. She simply had to accept that she wasn't going to last for more than five minutes in a vertical position without a visit to the bathroom. She lay across her bed, practically crying with frustration, but holding back for the sake of the girls, who had been working hard, following her orders for hours and hours.

At noon, she had tried Matt's office, but he had closed early as planned. She tried his cell but kept getting a funny beeping sound and couldn't even leave a message.

It was about three o'clock when Lauren came upstairs for a visit. She brought a tray with ginger ale and crackers. "We set up the garlands and little candle holders just the way you said," she reported. "What's next?"

Molly scanned the list. Only food-related jobs remained, and none that the girls could do. "I think that's it for now. I'll be down in a little while and start cooking."

Lauren rolled her eyes. "You'd better wear nose plugs or an oxygen mask or something. This is not going to be pretty . . ."

"Lauren, give me a break," Molly pleaded. "For once, think positively."

"Think positively . . . but carry a big bucket." Her daughter had a way with words. Molly would have laughed if the advice wasn't so apt.

"Okay, kid. It's now or never. Watch out, I'm coming downstairs."

"Suit yourself," Lauren said. "I'll take the bucket." She grabbed the bucket by the side of the bed and followed her mother out of the room.

Molly climbed down the stairs and gingerly began to walk around the first floor to see what the girls had accomplished. She felt her throat tighten with horror. Absolutely nothing looked the way she had planned.

The garlands were hanging in all the wrong places, at all the wrong angles. The candleholders were bunched in a stiff little row. Her wonderful, creative flower arrangements looked a total mess, each worse than the last.

She wandered from room to room, as if in a nightmare. Her guests were due to arrive in less than three hours. Everything was either half-done or a decorating disaster. She took a few deep breaths, trying to control her distress. The girls had been trying so hard to help her, working all day when they could have been goofing off, starting their vacation.

But she couldn't help it. Nothing looked the way she had imagined it, the way she had planned. She had spent so much time and gone to so much expense to bring it all together, and now it was too late to even try to get it right. She felt so frustrated, she wanted to scream.

She sat in a chair at the head of the dining room table, which was set with dishes and a smattering of silverware. No forks, she noticed, the napkins folded any which way, and half of them on the wrong side of the dishes.

She could make everyone else's parties look perfect. Why couldn't she do it in her own house? She held her head in her hands, feeling sick and tired and filled with disappointment.

"Mom . . . Do you feel sick again?" Lauren was standing behind her. Her hand rested on Molly's shoulder. "Do you want the bucket?" she asked quietly.

Molly shook her head, struggling to hide her tears from her daughter. "I just feel a little dizzy, honey. You go wait for me in the kitchen. I'll be right there."

Lauren left her and Molly snuck a tissue from her pocket and dabbed her eyes.

She knew she was being silly. Vain and petty. For most of her life, she had just about despised the type of women who acted as if table settings and centerpieces and linen napkins folded like swans were important. Had she turned into such a person? She was making a career out of it, she realized.

But still, this was *her* big party. Couldn't it be nice? For once? She would never make such a fuss again, she promised the powers above. It just didn't seem fair.

She heard the front door open and Matt call out hello. The girls ran out of the kitchen to greet him.

"Wow, the place looks great!" Matt exclaimed. "You must have been working all day."

"Yeah, we were. Mom's feeling sick again," she heard Lauren say in a hushed tone.

"Well, you've done a great job. You've been a huge help. This is what I love to see. . . ."

Molly pulled herself together and walked out to meet her husband. She managed a smile, but she could tell from his expression he wasn't fooled.

"Hey, what's going on? Feeling sick again?"

She nodded. The girls ran upstairs, and she and Matt walked back into the kitchen.

She sat down at the table and rested her head in her hands. "Don't even look at me," she told him. "I'm a complete disaster! This house is a disaster. Nothing looks right."

"What are you talking about? Everything looks great."

Molly raised her head to stare at him in disbelief. "Are you kidding? The table isn't set. The decorations are all a mess. Oh . . . I wish I wasn't such a big pregnant wreck. I can't get out of my own way . . ."

Matt's sympathetic expression hardened. "It doesn't matter, Molly. We'll all have a good time. You're being too fussy. And driving everyone crazy."

She swallowed hard and looked at him. Okay, admittedly, she was driving everyone crazy. But he was upset because she was complaining again about being pregnant. Even Matt's long-lasting patience was wearing thin, she realized.

Matt took a deep breath and she could almost see him searching for another shred of patience. "Now, why don't you just go up and rest some more?" he suggested in a relatively calm tone. "I know what to do. You can come down later, when the guests get here."

That was the last thing she wanted to do. But she knew that arguing with him would start an even bigger fight. The truth was, she felt weak on her feet again, and her stomach was churning.

"All right. The list is on the table. Most of the appetizers are in the fridge. They just need to be put out on trays so they can come to room temperature. And the desserts—"

"Molly, go to bed. Now," Matt said firmly. He stared her down and she didn't say another word. Just picked up her bucket and headed back upstairs.

SHE HADN'T MEANT TO FALL ASLEEP. SHE HAD planned to stay in the bedroom for a little while, just to satisfy Matt, then dress and come down around five, with an hour to work in the kitchen before her guests arrived.

She was awakened by the sound of the

doorbell and her sister-in-law Jessica's cheerful, "Merry Christmas, everybody!" echoing up the stairwell.

Molly sprang up out of bed and immediately regretted the move.

It was too late for a shower, so she quickly washed up, dabbed on some makeup, and pulled on her hostess outfit—a big satin blouse in a deep forest green and the ubiquitous black pants. But these were velvet and looked very classy, she thought. Especially with her new pointy leather slides that were very much in style this season. Molly decided she looked almost . . . sexy. Well, at least from her ankles down.

She took the stairs slowly, holding on to the handrail, a smile plastered on her face.

"Hi, everyone. Merry Christmas!" Her brother Sam and her two nephews looked up at her and smiled. Sam was surrounded by bags of gifts, and the girls were helping him take them to the living room and place the boxes under the tree.

Jessica met her at the bottom of the steps and gave her a hug. "You look great. The house looks beautiful, too."

Molly waved away her compliment.

"Please. Everything is a disaster. The girls tried to help me today, but nothing came out right," she confided quietly. "But they did try," she added.

"Everything looks very pretty," Jessica insisted. "You can see their hand in it and that makes it even nicer, don't you think?"

Now that Jessica had pointed it out, Molly could see the handiwork of her girls and their good intentions in the awkward decorations. She did feel touched by their efforts, but suspected that wouldn't count for much with everyone else.

"What can I do to help? Just point me in the right direction," Jessica said. "See, I even brought my own apron."

"God bless you, Jess," Molly said sincerely. "Come with me. I have no idea what I'm going to find in here," she whispered, leading the way back to the kitchen.

She and Jessica hadn't gotten along when Sam first started dating his future wife. Molly had gone to high school with Jessica and thought she was not only Little Miss Perfect, but a perfect snob. She suspected the high and mighty Jessica Warwick had no intention of marrying a lowly carpenter like

Sam, and was only using her brother for a fling that would break his heart. Even after they got engaged, Molly still didn't approve of the match. Neither did Lillian Warwick, who ironically became Molly's ally in trying to break up the couple.

Jessica, though, had stood up to her mother and changed her entire life to be with Sam. *You misjudged Jess,* Molly now reminded herself as she accompanied her sister-in-law into the kitchen. *And you promised yourself that you would give people— that means Alex Cole, too—a fair chance and not jump to conclusions.*

Molly and Jessica found Matt and the girls in the kitchen trying to sort out the food. Was this her worst nightmare, or what?

The cold seafood platters, laden with shrimp, crab claws, and a marinated seafood salad drifted by, headed for the living room. Molly gasped, noticing that everything was still in little plastic containers and aluminum tins and had not been arranged on her beautiful ceramic trays, molded in the shape of fish.

"Hey, wait . . . Hold up with that!"

Jillian stopped short and a shrimp rolled out of its container.

Molly sighed out loud. Jessica took the food from her niece and placed it on the table. "You have trays for this stuff, I assume?"

Molly pointed. "They're all in a pile on the counter. I even labeled them."

"Whoa, so efficient."

"Right." Molly fought off an attack of wooziness and looked around to see what else was going haywire. Betty appeared and gave out holiday hugs all around.

"Everything went great today in the shop. You would have been proud of me," she boasted. "I guess you finally trust me. You didn't even call."

She hadn't called, Molly suddenly realized. Wow, that was amazing.

"Of course I trust you."

Betty smiled. "Well, what can I do in here? Need any help?"

There was more than enough work to go around. Molly put Betty to work on the appetizers that were still straggling out of the fridge. Molly had rescued the seafood platters, but somehow a plastic bowl of plain old potato chips was being passed around the living room, instead of the silver platter of pâté and French bread rounds.

"Hi, honey, sorry we're late." Molly's

mother swept into the kitchen and gave kisses and hugs to anyone she could reach. "Your father drove so slowly. He was afraid of jostling his tiramisu."

"Merry Christmas, honey." Her father tried to kiss her but a huge dessert bowl got in the way. "Where do you want this?"

"Oh, in the extra fridge, out in the mudroom, Dad. I think there's some room in there."

"What should I do, honey? Want me to take care of these roasts?" her mother asked, eyeing the filet mignon roasts that were lined up on the counter.

"Good idea, Mom. They need to be timed perfectly—"

"I know, don't worry." Her mother waved away Molly's concerns. "Smells like something's already burning though . . ."

"My spinach-cheese spring rolls!" Molly gasped. With all the confusion in the kitchen, she had forgotten all about them. She grabbed a pot holder, pulled open the oven door, and yanked out the pans, but it was too late. Burnt to a crisp. She sadly tossed them in the garbage.

"Oh dear, what a waste . . ." Betty looked genuinely sympathetic. "Do you have anything I can whip together to make a dip? Like some sour cream and soup mix?" she asked innocently.

"Quickie dip with sour cream? At my party?" Molly shrieked. "Sorry, Betty," she said quickly. She ducked into the fridge and emerged with a roll of herbed goat cheese. "Why don't you put this out? There's a nice marble cheeseboard in that cabinet next to the fridge."

As Jessica hovered over the oven while a tray of miniature crab cakes baked, Molly felt a familiar horrible feeling returning. The food smells, the noise, the sight of her beautiful party in shambles—it was all too much. She was going to be sick again.

"I have to go upstairs for something. I'll be right down," she fibbed.

Molly sprinted to her bedroom and made it to the bathroom just in time.

Then she lay facedown on her bed and cried, muffling the sound in her pillow.

IT SEEMED A LONG TIME LATER WHEN SHE SAW A figure in the doorway. At first she thought it was Matt, then realized it was a woman. Not Betty or Jessica. Amanda maybe?

"Molly, are you awake? I brought you some ginger tea."

Molly sat up. She couldn't believe it. The last person she wanted to see right now—Alex Cole. *Oh, well.* Some things, it seemed, just couldn't be avoided.

Molly leaned over and turned on the bedside lamp. "Come on in. I'm awake now."

Alex walked in, holding out the mug of tea. "It's an old wives' remedy, but it seems to work. Neutralizes the stomach acid."

Molly could barely look at her. She felt so embarrassed to be such a basket case.

She picked up the tea and took a sip. It tasted good. A little spicy, but it had a pleasant scent, one that didn't bother her stomach.

"This isn't bad. Maybe it will revive me." She tried to get up, but started to feel sick again.

Alex helped her settle back on the bed. "Just rest, everything is going well. Your guests are having a great time."

"Gee . . . thanks. I hope someone is taking a video."

Alex laughed. "I'll make sure it's covered. You've had a lot of morning sickness with this pregnancy, haven't you? Matt told me."

Molly winced at the thought of them talking about her.

"Yeah, morning, noon, and night," she admitted. "I had some with the girls. A few crackers and ginger ale would do the trick. But nothing seems to work this time around. This baby is a tough one. Guess it takes after me," she added ruefully. "They can send people into outer space. You would think someone could figure out a cure for morning sickness. If men got pregnant, believe me, the best scientific minds would be working on it, night and day."

"You have a good point." Alex smiled. "No one quite understands the cause. There are probably many different triggers. Stress is a factor," she added. "You probably need to relax."

"I probably do. But it's hard with a houseful of people downstairs. On Christmas Eve no less."

Alex nodded sympathetically. "I'm sorry. But look at it this way: maybe you feel awful at the moment, but I know plenty of women who would trade places with you in a heartbeat. They'd do anything to be in your shoes, having a baby."

Having Matt's baby? Is that what she meant?

Molly didn't answer. She couldn't help wondering if Alex counted herself among those women. Molly took another sip of her tea. "Thanks for thinking of me. I guess I'll try to rest now."

"I hope you feel better soon," Alex said and left.

Molly turned out the light. Her stomach seemed to settle in the darkness.

She had been acting perfectly awful tonight. Totally ungrateful for all the good things in her life. Maybe her centerpieces weren't the most important thing in life. Maybe even serving pâté out of a plastic tub wasn't cause for great heartbreak. She knew Alex was right. She ought to consider herself lucky and count her blessings, instead of fretting over every tiny, meaningless thing that had gone wrong.

This baby was a blessing, as Matt had told the girls. She needed to remember that instead of being so petty.

If only she wasn't stuck upstairs, unable to budge off the bed, while her husband was downstairs, entertaining with Dr. Gorgeous by his side.

What a Christmas . . .

THE POTTER TRIBE INVADED RIGHT ON TIME, ARriving at the orchard the afternoon of Christmas Eve and filling the house from top to bottom. Sophie, who looked forward to this mayhem every year, was in her glory. She had stationed herself at the stove and started cooking when the first group arrived at lunchtime and hadn't stopped since.

Miranda was having a harder time of it. She was glad to see everyone and was doing her best to take part in all the talking and joking, but she felt as if everything was happening at a great distance. It took all her energy just to act "normal," and keep from drifting off into her own sadness. Of course, all her cousins were curious about "the amnesia guy," but whenever the conversation came around to him, Sophie would find a way to change the topic, making light of it, as if men with amnesia sought shelter at her home every day. Miranda was deeply grateful.

Greg arrived at about five o'clock. He stumbled through the door with shopping bags of presents, a bouquet of flowers for her grandmother, and a box of fancy chocolates.

He kissed Miranda on the cheek and gave her a quick, sharp hug. "Gee, I missed you. I'm glad you asked me to come tonight."

"I'm glad you came," Miranda said, and hugged him back. She was happy to see him. There were a few cousins at the party her own age, but they were all married now with children, and Miranda felt out of sync with their lives. Now at least she had Greg here. There were no sparks, no lightning, but being near him gave her a warm, comforting feeling.

For the past few days she had wondered if she and Greg would be able to get back on track now that Adam was gone. She knew that she would never feel what she felt for Adam. *But maybe that's all right,* she reasoned. *Maybe things with Greg are fine just the way they are. I'm never going to find anyone like Adam, so that means I need to try again with someone else.*

Her cousin Sylvie nudged her out of these thoughts. "You need to look out for your guy," she said.

"What do you mean?" Miranda asked, misunderstanding at first, thinking Adam needed her help.

"Your dad's got Greg cornered in the living room," Sylvie told her. "Looks like he's giving him the third degree. You really ought to rescue him."

"Thanks, Sylvie," Miranda said. She rushed into the living room where, sure enough, her father had Greg nearly pinned against the wall. Her dad, she noticed, was the one doing nearly all the talking.

"Miranda," her father said as she drew near, "it seems Greg here has some pretty interesting projects going on, challenging field engineering. Big money to be made if you get hold of some of the government con-tracts." He turned back to Greg. "So you're a partner in the firm?"

"I'm a senior projects engineer, Mr. Potter, not a partner."

Greg glanced at Miranda. He seemed to be dealing with this interview well, secretly finding it amusing.

Miranda felt her face redden. Her father could be so pushy at times. She loved her dad but they didn't get along very well. A suc-cessful attorney, he was extremely status-conscious. He judged people—especially the men she had dated—by their title, in-come, or the type of car they drove. He had badly wanted his children to be successful in what he called "the real world," and Miranda knew she had never come close to hitting the mark.

Her father smiled at her and rested his hand on her shoulder. "Miranda, your grandmother tells me you've started your own business, and it's doing well."

"So far," Miranda said cautiously. She had an idea of where this was leading.

"Well, if you really want to make a go of it, you've got to get proactive and plan for the future," her father said. "You ought to be thinking about hiring staff, selling a line to the department stores. Debra knows all the buyers at Neiman Marcus. Should I ask her to set up a meeting for you?"

Debra, another status-conscious attorney, was the woman her father had been seeing lately.

"Dad, I don't think my jewelry is suitable for Neiman Marcus," Miranda said, trying to keep a straight face. "And I'm not quite ready to hire a staff. A good part of the appeal is that all the pieces are made by me, personally."

He scratched his forehead and gave her a look. That "my kids just can't get out of the box" look she'd come to know. "All right," he said reluctantly. "If that's the way you want to handle it. I'm just relieved that you finally saw the light about acting. That was a losing proposition for you, Miranda. But you'd never listen to me."

Miranda took a deep breath. She was in a fragile emotional state as it was, and now her father was pushing her over the top.

"I don't think so, Dad. I've just had an offer for the role of Cordelia in *King Lear*. The New City Theater Company is staging a production. It will run through the summer out in Provincetown and then tour for about nine months."

"Really. I had no idea you were even auditioning anymore." Her father stepped back and sipped his drink, his eyes widened in surprise.

"I wasn't going to every audition in the world anymore, just a select few. I liked this role. I guess it worked for me."

"Seems so. Well . . . bravo," he said graciously.

She suspected he thought she'd made this all up, just to save face, to prove him wrong. She glanced at Greg, who also looked startled. She hadn't told him about the call, wanting to tell him in person.

"So . . . that's news." Greg stared at her. "And you're taking it?"

"I'm not sure. They've sent a contract. I need to let them know in a few days, right after Christmas." Her father had finally drifted away, snagged by her aunt to carve the turkey.

Miranda moved closer to Greg. "I was waiting until later to tell you. I thought we should talk about it in person, not just over the phone."

He nodded. "Sure, I understand. I was wondering if you had heard anything, but since you didn't mention it, I thought it had been a rejection and you didn't want to talk about it."

Miranda touched his arm. "I do want to talk about it. There's a lot to consider."

Aunt Evelyn appeared in the doorway. "Dinner's ready," she called out. "The food is set up in the kitchen, just grab a plate and some silverware, and find a place to sit down."

Miranda glanced at Greg. "We'd better get in there. I know for a fact we're quite a few chairs short. In a minute, it's going to feel like a game of musical chairs in there."

Greg laughed and put his arm around her shoulder. "Perfect, just the cozy family Christmas I imagined."

EVERYONE HAD EATEN HIS FILL OF SOPHIE'S delicious cooking. Miranda was loading

plates into the dishwasher while her grandmother put out a big pot of coffee and
started setting out desserts on the dining
room table. Greg had been helping in the
cleanup effort—one of the only men in sight,
Miranda noticed, as the rest were in the living room, gathered around the TV—when
Aunt Evelyn put him in charge of guarding
the desserts from eager little hands.

He faced Miranda with a mock grim expression. "It's a tough job, but somebody has
to do it."

"Good luck," she said, sending him off. He
really was a good sport and seemed to fit in
perfectly with her raucous, often eccentric
family. Which was saying something.

"He's a very nice fellow," Aunt Evelyn
whispered to Miranda once he had gone into
the dining room. "How long have you been
seeing each other?"

Miranda felt cornered. Not that she would
ever deny Greg was "nice." But she was sure
her aunt meant something more by this conversation. "Oh . . . I'm not sure. Just a few
months. Not that long," she added.

Evelyn smiled at her. "Well, that's long
enough to know sometimes. If it's right."

Miranda nodded numbly. She had known

Adam for just a little over three weeks. And she had known it was right almost from the start.

Her father suddenly appeared. "That fellow you found in the orchard, the guy with amnesia. They're going to have a news story about him. Come on in, quick."

"Really? Let's go see." Sophie wiped her hands on a dish towel and herded her daughter and granddaughter out into the living room.

Miranda stood back as her relatives talked and laughed all around her.

"Next up, an amnesia victim who wandered miles from home is reunited with his family. Wow, what a Christmas story that is," the newscaster added.

A moment later a picture of Adam appeared on the screen. *Eric*, Miranda reminded herself, though she found it almost impossible to think of him as anything but Adam. He looked different on TV but also the same. He was certainly dressed well and had a different haircut. He smiled into the camera, and she thought he looked happy.

"A man who was found in an orchard in

northeast Massachusetts with no memory of his prior life was reunited with his fiancée after being missing for almost three weeks. Eric Copeland is celebrating his homecoming in Portland, Maine, and slowly regaining his memory."

"It's nice to hear a happy story for once," the other newscaster said.

"Yes, that one does have a happy ending. His doctor predicts a complete recovery. He's a lucky man. We hope he's having a great holiday. And we hope you are, too," the news anchor said before signing off.

"I didn't realize he was so young. And handsome," Evelyn said. "I pictured him older somehow."

"Oh, he was young. A few years older than Miranda, I guess," her grandmother answered. "A nice young man, too. You could just tell."

"I think you both took a great risk having him here," Miranda's father cut in. "I wouldn't have permitted that if I had known what was going on."

"That's why I didn't tell you, Bart," Sophie said to her son.

"Well, you're just lucky nothing happened

and he didn't turn out to be some unstable type. All's well that ends well, I guess."

It hadn't ended well at all, Miranda thought. Not for her.

The unexpected sight of him brought tears to her eyes.

She turned to see Greg standing beside her. The look in his eyes was a mixture of sympathy for her and his own hurt. He put his hand on her shoulder. "Want to go outside and get some air?"

Miranda nodded. She led the way to the mudroom where they slipped on their jackets and stepped outside.

It was a clear, cold night and a thin layer of snow crunched under their footsteps. Miranda breathed in the chilly air, trying to clear her head and hold back her tears.

Greg took her hand but didn't say anything. She felt herself walking aimlessly, then realized they were headed up the hill behind the house, to the place where she had found Adam.

They reached the top of the hill and Greg stared out at the view. "Wow, this is breathtaking. I don't think I've ever been up here before."

That's because I never brought you here,

Miranda realized, feeling a little guilty. Why hadn't she ever thought to show Greg her favorite place in the world? She would have shown Adam if he hadn't already known about it.

"Greg . . ."

"Miranda . . ." They both spoke at once.

"You go first," she said.

He looked at her for a moment then said, "I know the past three weeks have been hard for you. I know there was something between you and . . . Eric. I'm not accusing you of anything, honestly. I take some responsibility here, too. I travel so much for my work, we don't get to see each other nearly as much as I would like. My divorce has made me very cautious, I guess," he admitted. "Some women have told me I'm distant, I don't get close easily. If you think of it as an engineering problem," he added with a small smile, "there was definitely a gap there for Eric—or someone else—to step in."

"Greg, you're being too nice about this," Miranda began.

"I'm not saying that's the only reason. But it's true," he insisted. "I haven't made a commitment to you. I haven't stepped up. So what did I expect? You're a special person,

Miranda. I'm not the only guy in the world who's going to notice that."

It was very honest, even noble of him to take some responsibility for her attachment to Adam. She kept thinking she hadn't been fair to Greg, but it was true—there was a gap there that had allowed her feelings for Adam to develop. Then again, Miranda knew that her feelings for Adam would have grown anyway, no matter what. It was actually fortunate that she and Greg hadn't made any formal promises to each other.

"Listen." He took her hands and looked down into her eyes. "I don't believe in wasting a lot of time talking about what's past and done. I'm willing to move on if you are, Miranda. We had a chance at something good. It seems a waste to throw that all away. I don't even care if you take that role you've been offered. I know I said I wouldn't wait around for you. But I would," he admitted. "We could find a way to make it work. I'm willing to try."

He wanted to continue their relationship, on any terms she needed. He wanted to move on and pretend Adam—the comet that had streaked across her heart—had never happened.

Miranda didn't know what to say. She looked up at Greg, then out at the view below. She knew with utter certainty she couldn't do it. It would never work. It would always feel not quite right, second best, as if she had merely settled.

"Greg . . . you're such a great person. I care for you, very much. But I'm sorry. I don't think I can just pick up where we left off and keep going, as if nothing ever happened. Something did happen to me. Inside. I feel different. Changed."

Greg sighed. "Please don't answer right now. Think about it. In a few days, you might see this all very differently."

"I don't think so. I think you deserve more," Miranda said. "Someone who feels more than I do. It might work, for a time. But there would always be that gap you were talking about. I don't want to shortchange you. I don't want to shortchange myself. . . . Do you understand?"

He nodded slowly. "Yes . . . I do. Thanks for being honest, at least."

"No. Thank you. Thank you for trying. For being so understanding and patient with me. I think you're one in a million."

"I think the same about you." He leaned

over and dropped a kiss on her forehead. Then they started down the hill, walking side by side.

"I don't think I'll join the party," he said when they got to the house. "Please thank your grandmother and make some excuse for me?"

"Of course."

He stepped forward and hugged her. Miranda hugged him back, clinging for a moment, but knowing she had done the right thing.

"Merry Christmas, Miranda," he said, stepping away.

"Merry Christmas," she answered. She hoped he would find happiness very soon, with someone new. She wasn't sure she ever would.

Molly came down the stairs slowly, trying not to draw attention to herself. Betty was the first to spot her and called out from the living room. "Molly's back, everyone! How are you doing? Feeling better?"

Molly crossed the foyer and entered the living room where her guests seemed to be carrying on fine without her. They were sitting on the couches and armchairs, her fine china plates balanced on their laps as they ate dinner. It was not the formal sit-down meal with place cards she had prepared, but everyone seemed to be having a good time.

"Great grub, Molly," Sam called out, raising his fork.

"Glad you're enjoying it," Molly said sincerely. "There's plenty, so help yourself."

Jessica appeared at her side and rubbed her arm. "Do you want to sit? Can I get you something? Maybe some plain pasta? I saved some in the kitchen."

"My food could have been a little plainer," Lillian Warwick piped up before Molly had a chance to answer. "There are far too many spices. Anyone would think we were dining in Bombay, for pity's sake."

Molly had not actually prepared any truly exotic dishes, but she knew that Lillian considered a dash of cinnamon "overdoing it."

She decided to take the high road, to play the perfect hostess and cater to her most finicky guest. "Lillian, I'm so sorry you aren't enjoying your meal. Let me get you something else."

Lillian looked caught off guard as Molly

whisked her dish away. "Well, all right. Perhaps a buttered roll. Nothing with seeds," she added briskly.

Jessica glanced at Molly. "I'll get it for her."

"No, let me. I'm going to the kitchen anyway." Molly smiled and headed for the kitchen.

"A cloth napkin would be nice," Lillian called after her. "These paper items irritate my skin."

Molly struggled to keep from laughing, though she also felt a prickle of exasperation. After all her preparations, Lillian had ended up with paper instead of linen.

Let that be a lesson to you, Molly. Keep up these fussy ways and you'll end up like Lillian Warwick.

Molly found a fresh china plate and a linen napkin in the dining room. She searched through the bread basket and picked out an acceptable roll, a soft egg twist, no seeds. The butter dish, however, was nowhere to be found, so she headed for the kitchen.

The kitchen was surprisingly empty, except for her nephew Darrell who was pouring soda for himself and his little brother.

"Hey, Aunt Molly, do you have any more root beer? This one ran out."

Darrell held up the empty bottle as his little brother stared at her mournfully.

"No problem, guys. I have cases of root beer. Hang tight, I'll be right back."

She set down Lillian's dish and headed to the mudroom, where she had left the extra soft drinks in cartons. As she walked down the narrow hall, the voices from the living room seemed very distant. Yet, she suddenly became aware of other voices, much closer.

She paused, listening for a moment. It sounded like people whispering, not wanting to be heard. Then she heard someone crying very softly. She couldn't imagine who it could be. Was it one of the girls, getting into some sort of mischief back here? Maybe they had teased Jill and made her cry, Molly thought. Weren't they getting too old for that by now?

She turned the corner and walked into the mudroom, looking around for the culprits, a motherly scolding on the tip of her tongue.

The sight that met her gaze left her totally speechless.

In the far, dark corner of the room, half-hidden by the coat tree, she saw Matt. His back was turned to her and so was the back of his companion—Alex. Matt's arm circled

Alex's back and Alex's head was snuggled in his broad shoulder. She seemed to be weeping, and Matt was gently comforting her. Molly thought they would notice her, standing there. But they seemed totally immersed in a world of their own.

Molly took two quick steps backward, then walked quickly down the narrow hallway, back toward the kitchen. Halfway there, she paused and pulled open the door to a bathroom. She ran in and got sick all over again.

It took her a while to compose herself. While she washed her face and combed her hair, she heard Matt and Alex passing by, returning to the party. They probably thought they had never been missed.

Molly stared at herself in the mirror. How was she ever going to get through the rest of this party? She glanced at her watch. It was later than she had thought, past ten. She could either hide out upstairs again and stew—or keep herself busy and distracted down here. She decided on the latter and emerged determined to pick up the pace.

She returned to the mudroom for the root beer, then went back to the kitchen where she buttered Lillian's roll, arranged it on the dish with a fanned out strawberry. She drafted Darrell to deliver it. He didn't look pleased with the assignment—his grandmother scared him—but he didn't refuse.

Jessica and her sister Emily were in the kitchen, already busy getting out the desserts. Molly thanked them then went into the living room and surveyed the group. Matt sat with his parents. Alex sat on the other side of the room, talking to Betty. Both looked very calm and collected, Molly thought, all things considered.

"Hey, everyone, time to open the presents!" she announced.

Within minutes, the room was a frenzy of gift giving, with Sam and Matt sorting through the presents and calling out names. For a while, it seemed to be snowing inside as wrapping paper and bows flew in all directions. Guests called out thanks, oohing and ahhing over their gifts. Some were surprises, others fulfilled requests, but all seemed a great success.

Finally, the pace slowed and only a few small presents were left to open. Amanda and Lauren brought in big trash bags and began cleaning up. "Just make sure you don't throw out any presents," Molly warned.

"That's why I've been extra careful with

mine," Matt said, appearing beside her. He whisked a small box from his pocket. It was wrapped in gold foil paper and tied with a large white bow. "For you," he said, presenting it to her.

"Oh, wow . . ." Molly looked down at the tiny box, obviously jewelry. She felt a burst of excitement and pleasure . . . then remembered Matt with Alex in the mudroom and felt all the joy sucked out of the moment.

"Aren't you going to open it?" Matt tilted his head toward hers, so that they were almost touching.

"Yes, of course." She ripped off the paper and pulled open the box. It was a gold ring set with rubies and diamonds. She had admired it in a jewelry shop in Newburyport months ago and promptly forgotten all about it. Matt had remembered, though, and gotten it for her.

She put it on and held out her hand. "It's . . . beautiful. Really . . ."

"Do you really like it?" he asked eagerly. "We can pick out something else. I just remembered that you said you liked this one."

"Oh, yes. I do. I love it. Honestly," she assured him. She glanced at him, feeling con-

fused. He seemed to be confused by her reaction, too.

She leaned over and hugged him. "Thank
you, Matt."

He hugged her back. "I'm glad you like it,
honey."

"I love it. It's perfect," she said quietly.

It wasn't really. It was such an extravagant
gift, it made her wonder—had Matt gone to
all this trouble because he wanted to please
her and show her how much he cared?

Or was he just feeling guilty?

CHAPTER TEN

CHRISTMAS DAY AND EASTER SUNDAY ALWAYS drew the highest church attendance. Members of the congregation who were virtually invisible the rest of the year would show up for those two services. This Christmas, Ben noticed, attendance was almost literally through the roof. Every spare folding chair the church owned had been set up behind the wooden pews. Even so, the side aisles were filled with people standing. Ben wasn't sure he had ever seen so many in his church before. He felt excited and pleased—and somewhat anxious.

He stood at the back of the sanctuary behind the choir as they walked up the center aisle, singing the opening hymn, "Hark, The Herald Angels Sing."

Ben followed, walking at a stately pace, surveying the vast group gathered for worship, everyone dressed in holiday finery. Their energy and sense of expectation lifted him up.

While he always felt this way at the start of a Christmas service, somehow this morning, it seemed different. Even more intense. The church itself seemed brighter, more festive, with even more red and white poinsettia plants arranged on the altar than usual. More candles, more boughs of pine tied with white ribbons. This year the small but dedicated group of women who were in charge of such matters—Grace Hegman, Sophie Potter, and Marie Morgan—had outdone themselves.

His gaze came to rest on the angel, poised on the wooden pedestal just to the left of the altar. She certainly had a presence, he thought, silent yet undeniably powerful.

Suddenly, it seemed clear. The overflow of excitement and wonder this Christmas morning was all because of her. She was the one who had inspired the extra flourish of decoration. The one who had drawn this crowd of worshipers.

She seemed to be saying, "I've brought them all here this morning, Ben. Now, what do you have to say?"

What did he have to say?

He hoped his sermon was up to her standards.

He turned to face the congregation just as the choir finished the hymn. "Good morning, everyone. Welcome and Merry Christmas. A special welcome to any visitors at our church today . . ." He quickly reviewed the church announcements, reminders of committee meetings and other activities. The list was short; there wasn't much going on this week.

"Now, let us bow our heads, still our minds, and open our hearts, preparing ourselves to worship, and to celebrate a blessed miracle, the birth of our Lord, Jesus Christ. This day marks the start of new life. Let it also mark the renewal and rebirth of our spirits."

The congregation stood up, singing the next hymn along with the choir, "O Little Town of Bethlehem."

When the hymn was over, Lucy Bates rose and walked to the pulpit to give the day's reading from the Old Testament. Dressed in a satin blouse and a black velvet skirt, her red hair freed from its usual ponytail, she looked a bit nervous. Ben smiled at her encouragingly as she found her place in the large Bible.

Lucy began, reading from the Book of Isaiah, her voice steady and clear.

"The people who walked in darkness have seen a great light," she began, "those who lived in a land of deep darkness, on them a light has shined . . ."

When she finished and began walking back to her seat, Ben rose and took his place behind the pulpit. He looked out over the congregation a moment, then began the second reading, which was from the Book of Luke, chapter two, the passage that told the story of Mary and Joseph's travels to Bethlehem and the birth of Jesus in the manger.

About halfway through, he read, ". . . And there were in the same country shepherds abiding in the field, keeping watch over their flock by night. And, lo, an angel of the Lord came up upon them, and the glory of the Lord shone round about them; and they were sore afraid. And the angel said unto them, 'Fear not: for behold, I bring you good

tidings of great joy, which shall be to all people. For unto you is born this day in the city
of David a Savior, which is Christ, the Lord.
And this shall be a sign unto you; Ye shall
find the babe wrapped in swaddling clothes,
lying in a manger . . .'"

As Ben finished the reading, he sensed
the attention of his audience drift to the other
side of the sanctuary, to the angel statue.
He, too, felt its presence in an almost palpa-
ble way, a wave of energy or perhaps just his
own heightened awareness. He wasn't sure
what it meant, or if he was only imagining
the phenomenon. But it was definitely dis-
tracting, and it felt . . . strange.

Ben closed the Bible and paused to take a
sip of water. He heard the usual restless
shifting and muffled coughs. He opened the
folder on the pulpit with his neatly typed sermon. Then closed it.

He took a breath and looked out at the
group: so many familiar faces he had known
most of his life. They trusted him. They
looked to him to be a guiding presence. He
could deliver the sermon he had prepared
and practiced, which was a good one, he
thought. But it completely—and perhaps
consciously—ignored any mention of the

angel. The elephant in the room. The one with the golden wings.

He knew what he had to do.

"There's been much talk about miracles at this church the past few weeks," he began. "Much talk in this town and even places very distant from here. I'm sure that some of you have come to our church this morning because you've heard this news.

"Many now believe God is working through the statue you see, right here." Ben made a gesture toward the angel. "They believe that by offering their intentions and deepest hopes, their prayers have been answered. They believe that by touching the statue, their bodies have been healed. They believe they have been blessed with miracles."

Ben paused and looked around the sanctuary. His listeners were completely silent, staring up at him with rapt attention. He saw Carl, Digger, and Grace Hegman, and of course, Carolyn. In a pew up front, he saw Marie-Claire and Gerald, sitting side by side, holding hands. His mouth grew dry.

"I've listened to these stories, some of them completely amazing and defying any rational explanation. I've been shocked and often . . . overwhelmed. I would be the last one to ever deny that these reports are sincere. Nor would I ever attempt to dissuade those who truly believe they've experienced some . . . divine intervention. The question I've been wrestling with, though, is: are these truly miracles?"

He paused and took a breath. "Some of you are probably thinking, 'If anyone in this church should know, it should be you, Reverend.' But I'll confess, I've searched my heart and soul over that question and still . . . I don't know. I can't say."

Ben gazed out into his audience, sure that there were many who were disappointed by his reluctance to come to some definitive conclusion, to give a public rubber stamp to this phenomenon.

"I don't believe we can ever know for sure what's happened here. Perhaps this beautiful statue, so inspiring and evocative, has been an instrument that's helped to focus our faith. Making it far stronger, more intense. Like a tuning fork, putting us on the right pitch. Or a magnifying glass refracting a single beam of light until it's powerful enough to light a fire.

"Ultimately, I believe it's faith that fuels

miracles. Faith that finally saves us. In the Book of Matthew, we hear of the Canaanite woman who begs Jesus to heal her child. At first, she's brushed aside and ignored. But her faith is so strong, her plea is finally recognized. Jesus says to her, 'O woman, great is thy faith: be it unto thee even as thou wilt.' And her daughter is suddenly— miraculously—healed.

"The Bible is filled with reports of miracles. Far too many for me to mention here, even if I could remember half of them . . ." He paused while a few quietly laughed. "A quote from the poet Walt Whitman comes to mind, though. He wrote, 'A mouse is a miracle enough to stagger sextillions of infidels.' And I must agree. A mouse. A flower. A flash of lightning. A child's laughter. The sight of a bird in flight. Falling in love. Making a friend . . . The list can go on and on . . .

"I do know God created a universe that abounds in miracles. Our ordinary world, our everyday experience, is filled with amazing events we completely take for granted. We stumble along, numb and jaded, blind to the beauty, the astounding experiences that fill our lives every day. We fail to recognize their true meaning, fail to see their essence, what they truly are—blessings and amazing gifts.

"Just as the infant sleeping in the manger on that first Christmas morning remained overlooked, unrecognized . . . except by the shepherds and three wise men. And even they would not have recognized him, but for the angels.

"But think of it. Think how that newborn baby, wrapped in rags and sleeping in a barn, would save the world and bring us eternal life. Think how lowly, how ordinary, how un-miraculous the scene must have seemed. How it would have looked to you or me, if we had been there."

He paused and stared down at the pulpit a moment, gathering his thoughts. He wasn't really sure if he had made his point or given them any insight at all. Yet, he didn't know what else to say.

"My friends . . . it seems to me that we don't need to search the world, or even search the Internet for miracles. We need only to meet the challenge God sets for us in this earthly lifetime—to truly recognize and appreciate the miracles that are part and parcel of each waking day. The miracles that surround us, but are often under wraps, in disguise. Perhaps that is one lesson of Christmas Day, of Jesus Christ's humble birth. One that can radically change the way we live in this world."

The sanctuary was nearly silent as Ben left the pulpit. He felt both drained and relieved. The choir began the next hymn and the congregation rose to sing along. He couldn't tell how his sermon had been received.

The rest of the service seemed to pass quickly. After the final blessing, he stood at the rear of the sanctuary, just outside the big wooden doors, shaking hands and exchanging good wishes for the holidays.

Molly Willoughby Harding was one of the first to greet him. He had often seen her husband, Matt, and their daughters on Sundays but rarely saw Molly, due to her work schedule. He had known Molly since she was a girl, had watched her bravely meet more than her share of life's challenges. She had made some mistakes but had learned from them and gone on to do better. She had raised two wonderful girls on her own, no small accomplishment.

Now she had found her place and

seemed happy. With all his heart, he wished her well. Molly greeted him with a hug. "Merry Christmas, Reverend Ben."

"Molly. How good to see you. How's business?"

"Oh, business is fine. Too busy, actually." She glanced at her husband who stood beside her. "We have some news to share. I'm expecting a baby."

"A baby? That's wonderful. God bless you both." He hugged her again and shook Matt's hand. "When are you due?"

"Oh, mid-July. We have a while to wait."

"And get used to the idea," Matt glanced at his wife with a tentative smile.

She looked at Reverend Ben and sighed. "It has been a surprise," she admitted. "But I really liked your sermon this morning. It gave me something to think about."

"Yes, it was wonderful. Very well said," Matt added. Ben got the feeling there was some tension between them about this unexpected new family member. But they were a strong couple. He felt sure they would work it out.

At least his message had touched one person listening, given them something to think about. That was the best he could hope for.

M OLLY WENT BACK TO WORK THE DAY AFTER Christmas. She was the first one in, partly because a number of her employees were off this week with their children home from school. At least she didn't have that problem this year. Amanda and Lauren had left early that morning on a school trip for the senior class, and Jillian had been invited to go to Vermont for the week with Sam, Jessica, and her two cousins. It was just her and Matt in the house now. Things had been tense between them ever since Christmas Eve, which was the other reason she had come in early.

Matt hadn't wanted her to go in, but she had insisted. She was still booked with parties, the grand crescendo being New Year's Eve. She had even hired extra employees, since so many of her key people were off.

"Hi, I'm here," Betty announced from the front door.

"Come on back. I just made coffee," Molly called.

Her friend's voice cheered Molly instantly.

Betty had offered to come help at the shop for the week, knowing Molly was short-handed. Even though she knew nothing about cooking, Betty had a great way with the clients and the staff. She also brought a new sense of organization to the business. Betty made up better schedules and typed out work procedures. She figured out the cost per serving of each dish and did much better pricing.

Molly wasn't looking forward to the week when Betty would return to her real estate office. But she had her now and so tried not to dwell on that.

The cup is half full, *okay? Can't you re-member that?* she scolded herself.

They worked together for a while, making pie crust, both of them absorbed in the soothing rhythm of work.

"So, your Christmas Eve party turned out to be a big success anyway," Betty said at last. "Even though nothing went the way you planned. Just goes to show, you have to be flexible sometimes, right?"

Molly nodded. All she could remember now of that night was seeing her husband embracing Alex Cole.

"Betty . . . something happened that

night. I haven't told anybody, so please don't say a word about this to anyone."

Betty looked instantly concerned. "What is it? Is it the baby? Is something wrong?"

"Oh, no, thank goodness. The baby is fine." Molly patted her softly rounded stomach. "On Christmas Eve at the party, when I finally came downstairs, I had to go into the mudroom to get something. Root beer or something . . ." She took a breath. It was so hard to say the words out loud. "I saw Matt and Alex. Together . . . he . . . he . . . had his arms around her, and she was sort of . . . hugging him back, with her head on his shoulder. . . ."

Her voice trailed off, she couldn't say any more. She felt tears streaking her cheeks.

Betty's eyes widened and her jaw dropped. "Oh, no . . . Molly." She shook her head. "That couldn't be. You must be jumping to conclusions."

"I know what I saw," Molly insisted. "They were together. I saw it with my own eyes. She was crying, with her head on his shoulder."

Betty was quiet for a long moment. "I understand why you're upset. Anybody would be. But you're not being fair to Matt. You have to give him a chance to explain."

"I'm afraid to ask him," Molly confessed. "What if he tells me something I don't want to hear, like I'm right and he has feelings for Alex?"

"I don't think that's the case at all. But on the one in a million chance it is, wouldn't it be better to get this all out in the open rather than sit here, torturing yourself?"

Molly nodded. She rolled the pastry up into neat balls and covered each one in plastic wrap. Betty watched her, then did the same.

"You're right," Molly said finally. "I have to ask him. I have to know what's going on." She turned to Betty. "The girls are gone for the week. I'll ask him tonight."

Molly went home early, feeling relieved to leave the shop in Betty's capable hands. She showered and changed, then heated the elegant dinner she had brought home, salmon with citrus glaze, stir-fried vegetables, and little squares of toasted polenta with rosemary. Healthy, too. Dr. Cole couldn't find fault with this meal, she was sure.

She set the table with nice china and candles, trying to create a relaxed atmosphere. Relaxed enough to ask her husband if he was in love with another woman. . . .

Matt came in and kissed her on the

cheek. He seemed tired and flipped on the lights to read his mail without even noticing the candles. "What's for dinner?"

Molly answered, reciting the menu to him.

"Oh . . . okay. I had fish for lunch, though."

"It's healthy for you. Omega-three oils."

He nodded, skimming a letter. "Yes, I know."

She made up their dishes with an artful flair, set them on the table, and turned the lights down low. "Candles," she said, pointing them out. "I thought it would be more relaxing. We can have a nice, quiet, leisurely dinner without the girls here, right?"

"Right . . . it does seem quiet, though. Mind if I put the news on? I just want to see the headlines."

"Yes, I mind," she told him, trying hard not to whine.

He sat back and took a bite of salmon. "This is good," he said quietly.

"Thanks."

She could tell he didn't like the salmon. He didn't like fish very much. She should have brought home the lamb chops. Dinner wasn't going well. Was it so hard for them to be together without a houseful of noisy teenage girls as distraction?

"How was your day?" she asked. "Was the office very busy?"

"Pretty quiet," he said. "I was reading up for the conference mostly. There are going to be some excellent speakers, but I want to read their studies beforehand."

"The conference? What conference?"

He looked at her curiously. "The conference at Yale Medical School, on juvenile diabetes. This coming weekend. I told you about it. You must have forgotten."

He sounded a bit annoyed. Molly felt confused. She was almost sure he had not mentioned going away this weekend. But maybe she had been so busy, her hard drive overloaded with information, that it had never registered.

"I'm sorry. You're right. It must have slipped my mind." She tried a bite of polenta. Tasty, but it had dried out a bit.

"That's okay." He glanced at her. "Alex is going, too. She signed up a while ago, before she came down here."

Molly pushed her plate away. Dinner no longer seemed appetizing.

"Interesting. No, you didn't tell me about this trip. I'm positive."

"Of course I did. You must have forgotten,"

Matt said again. "Sometimes, I'm not sure you hear half of what I say, Molly."

"Believe me, I would have remembered that," Molly said.

"What difference does it make? Are you afraid to stay here alone, is that it?"

"No, of course not." How could she tell him now what she was really afraid of?

"It's just one night away. I'll be home Sunday night," he promised.

One night away with Alex was one too many in Molly's book. She felt like she was going to blow her top again. But she knew that was not the right choice. And there was no way now to bring up the question she had planned to ask.

After dinner, Molly stayed in the kitchen, cleaning up. Matt went into the family room and read a medical journal. He didn't even notice when she went to bed early.

THE DAY AFTER CHRISTMAS, BEN STAYED HOME and took a well-deserved day off. On Thursday morning, he arrived at church at the usual time. He called Carl into the sanctuary. It was time to take down the angel.

"Okay, on the count of three. Let's just lift it off the pedestal and put it back in the crate."

"Not by the wings," Carl warned. "You don't want to hurt her."

"Of course not. Gently now . . ."

It was a large piece, but surprisingly light. Several moments later the angel was back in the crate and the pedestal was bare.

Ben had mixed feelings about packing the statue up again, but he felt it was the right thing to do. Carl seemed genuinely sad to see it back in the wooden crate.

He watched as Ben covered it over with a piece of canvas and crunched-up handfuls of newspapers.

"People are going to miss that statue," Carl said solemnly. "It looked real good in the sanctuary, Reverend. It's a small thing, but it made a big difference."

Well said, Ben thought. It was a small thing that had made a big difference, all right. He would never deny that.

"The angel had its season, Carl." And perhaps even encouraged a miracle or two. "But it doesn't really belong in this church. I believe she's only visiting."

"What will you do with it? Keep it down in the basement until next Christmas?"

Put that way, it did seem wasteful.

"I'm not sure, I've got to figure it out," Ben said.

He had some ideas but he wasn't free to share them yet.

MATT LEFT FOR NEW HAVEN VERY EARLY SATUR-day morning, while Molly was still asleep. The house seemed eerily empty when she woke up. She heard her own footsteps echo-ing in the big rooms and didn't like the feel-ing. She dressed quickly and set off for her shop, not even lingering at home long enough to make coffee for herself.

Several parties were booked for the weekend, more on New Year's Eve, which was Monday, and even a few on New Year's Day, including Madeline Norris's brunch—Betty's pet project.

Luckily, Betty was still helping at the shop. Molly had expected her to overdose on a steady diet of nine-to-five catering, but her friend seemed to thrive on it. Betty had been right; she really was ready for a change. Molly didn't know how she would have sur-vived the week without her.

Molly opened the shop to find the mes-sage light on the answering machine blinking. She pressed the play button. "Hi, Molly, it's Sonya. Sorry but I just can't make it in today. Brian is sick with strep throat and I don't have anyone to stay with him . . . I think I might be catching it, too . . ."

Molly didn't know what to think. Sonya was never all that reliable. Then again, Molly knew what it was like to be a single mom. Hadn't she been in that situation herself not so long ago? Stranded at home with a sick child, or just stretched to find child care during a school vacation. She felt annoyed with Sonya for a second, but it quickly passed.

The problem was that Sonya was her best cook, which meant that now Molly would have to step up and do double the work in the kitchen. Hard, hot work at the stove, on her feet for the rest of the day.

Molly was just donning her apron, stretching the long strings around her expanding middle, when Betty came in. "Morning," she said cheerfully. "Did Matt leave for his conference?"

"At the crack of dawn. He didn't even wake me up to say good-bye."

"He probably wanted to let you sleep. I'm sure he'll call later." Betty poured herself a mug of coffee and took an apron from the hooks by the door.

"Sonya called. She can't come in today. Her son is sick."

"Oh, that's too bad," Betty said.

"I guess I'll just have to take over her work. It doesn't matter. There's no one home. I can stay here until midnight if I have to."

Betty's eyes widened. "You'll do no such thing. You can't do all that cooking yourself. We'll just have to improvise. That restaurant supply place you sent me to has some great stuff in the freezer section. We can buy something basic and doctor it up with some special sauces or something."

Betty was amazing. She caught on real quick. But Molly still didn't like the idea of serving anything less than the very best. "Betty, please. These clients are expecting duck comfit with ginger-plum glaze."

Betty looked insulted. "If you want to grow this business, you have to be flexible, Molly. You have to . . . let go a little. Now, let's get out those recipe books and see if we can figure something out. I'm going to check the schedules, too. Maybe you can ask Rita or Lisa to work a few extra hours and pick up the slack. I'm not going to let you stand at that stove all day."

Betty stared her down. Molly felt herself finally giving in. Betty was one of the few people who could talk some sense into her, that was for sure. She was also great at juggling the staff schedules and coaxing people to go the extra mile. That was a rare talent, one Molly knew she didn't possess.

"Okay, let's see what we can do."

Molly and the rest of her crew worked hard all day. She got home later than usual, but at least it wasn't midnight. She went straight upstairs and collapsed on her bed, which she hadn't even bothered to make before she left the house.

Matt hadn't called all day and she was too stubborn to call him. She had just drifted off to sleep when she heard the phone ring and then heard his voice on the answering machine.

"Molly, are you there? I tried your cell before. I had a bad connection. I'm not sure if you got the message . . ."

Oh, right. Sure. That was an easy out.

She wasn't sure she wanted to talk to him. She was too upset, afraid she would say something crazy. Then, just before he was about to hang up, she quickly rolled over and picked up. "Hey . . . I'm here. Sorry. I was sleeping."

"Sorry I woke you."

"That's okay. I wanted to talk to you. How was your trip?"

Three hours alone in the car with Alex Cole? Huh . . . ?

"It was fine. No traffic at that hour. The conference has been a mixed bag. These meetings are sometimes really boring, but the presentations are top-notch."

"I'm glad you're having such a good time." Her tone was flat, almost sarcastic.

Matt didn't say anything. She wondered if he was still there.

"Are you all right?" he asked at last. "You don't sound like yourself."

"I'm just tired. That's all."

"You're working too hard. You promised me you would cut back," he reminded her.

"It's the busiest week of the year. How can I cut back?"

"You're pregnant, remember?" His voice sounded tight.

She sighed and rested her hand protectively on her tummy. "Yes, I remember. You don't need to keep reminding me, Matt."

She hadn't meant to sound so sharp with him. *Great move, Molly. Make your husband mad at you while he's away for the weekend with another woman.*

"I don't know what you mean lately, Molly. I just don't understand you," Matt said wearily. "Don't you want this baby?"

Matt's voice sounded so sad and bleak, she wanted to cry.

"Of course I do . . . it's not that."

She did want the baby. She loved the baby already. Tonight she felt alone in the world, except for the baby's company. They were alone together and she was grateful. It was Matt who felt distant, at odds with her.

"What is it then? Can't you tell me?"

Molly couldn't answer. She felt confused and couldn't put her deepest feelings and fears into words for him. She was afraid she was losing his love. Even if it wasn't Alex, she felt a distance between them lately that she couldn't seem to bridge.

"Honestly, I'm just tired. It's not the best time to talk about all this."

He sighed heavily, and she wished with all her heart he was with her, so she could just put her arms around him.

"All right. We'll talk when I get home. I'll

call you tomorrow when I leave New Haven. Should I call you at the shop?"

"Yes, I'll be there."

"Why did I even bother to ask?" he said. "Good night, Molly."

She said good night and hung up the phone. Matt used to always say "I love you" when he said good-bye. Especially if he was away.

Molly thought this was a bad sign. A very bad sign.

"CAROLYN? WHERE ARE YOU?" BEN CAME DOWN from his study, clutching the printout of an e-mail he had just received. It was past eleven. Perhaps it wasn't very late for most people on a Saturday night, but tomorrow was a workday for him, and Carolyn was an early-to-bed type. He wasn't even sure she was still up, but then he heard the TV and went back to the den to look for her.

"Look at this. I just received an answer from the Roman Catholic Dioceses in France. I wrote to them about the angel. Remember?"

She nodded. "Yes, I do. What did they say?"

"I can't read it." He laughed and held it out to her. "Do you remember any French from college?"

"Oh, let me see . . ." She took the page from him and put on her glasses. "I think we have a French dictionary somewhere. Let's give it a try."

They settled at the kitchen table, and Carolyn worked at translating the letter. Some time later, she thought she had the gist of it.

"It starts with the usual things—thanks for contacting us, and so on," she told him. "But then they write, 'The church that was destroyed during the war has been rebuilt. The church officials do have a record of that statue and thought it had been plundered by the Germans. They will be delighted to receive their lost angel . . .' I'm translating literally here," she added.

"Yes . . . yes, of course. Go on," he said eagerly.

"They will reimburse you for any costs." She paused and looked up at him. "That's basically it. How will you get it there?"

"I'm not sure. Ship it, I guess, by air or by boat. I have to look into that part. But this is good news. I had been hoping I could send it back where it belonged."

"You never felt that angel really belonged in our church, did you, Ben?"

Ben smiled at her. "There was always

something about it for me that seemed to mark it as a visitor. A beautiful, strange visitor who had come to us for Christmas."

"And now," Carolyn finished for him, "it's time for her to go home."

ON SUNDAY MORNING, MOLLY PERMITTED HERself to sleep late. But by nine, she dragged her weary body out of bed, took a shower, and headed out again. Nearly ten hours of sleep had made little dent. She felt sluggish and sad about her fight with Matt the night before.

She wondered if she should call him this morning and apologize again. She decided she didn't want to risk another bad phone call. He would be home tonight. She would make sure she was home when he arrived. The girls would still be away and they could talk.

When she got to the shop, her staff was busy working in the kitchen and Betty was supervising. The night before, Molly had given Betty keys and instructions for opening up. She hadn't expected to get here this late, but the place looked under control.

Most of the dishes that would be served at the New Year's Eve parties tomorrow night needed to be cooked today, or at least prepped. The list was long and to Molly, it looked like a map for a forced march through the Sahara.

"Hi, there. We're doing very well, right on schedule," Betty said cheerfully.

Molly managed a smile. "Betty, I'm putting you in charge today. I don't have the energy to even think. Just tell me what I should do."

Betty laughed but seemed pleased by the compliment. "Let's just look at the list you wrote out last night. We're all on autopilot at this point."

They set to work at a reasonable pace. Molly knew she couldn't let herself burn out before they reached the finish line.

At lunchtime, they took a break. Smelling food all day had robbed Molly of her appetite, but Betty persuaded her to have a bowl of soup and some water crackers.

"Hey, why don't you just knock off for the day?" Betty suggested. "Matt will be home in a few hours and you ought to take a nap before he gets back. Did you sleep okay last night? You look beat."

"Thanks a lot," Molly said wryly. "You know how to make a girl feel good, don't you?"

Betty gave her a sympathetic look. "If I don't tell you, who will?"

"I didn't get much sleep. I was upset," Molly confessed. "Matt and I had sort of a fight on the phone. It was really my fault, too. I tried to apologize. But I know he's still mad at me."

"Did you speak to him at all today?"

Molly shook her head.

"You're too stubborn, Molly."

"I know, but he said we would talk tonight. I didn't want to dig the hole any deeper."

Betty sighed. "Well, maybe it's just as well."

"Betty . . . what if he doesn't come home tonight? What if he makes some excuse and stays over again?"

"Don't be silly. Of course he'll be back. The weather report is predicting snow, but I'm sure Matt will make it home. He grew up in Worcester, remember? He knows how to drive in snow. I still say you ought to go home in a little while and rest before he gets there."

Her advice made good sense, as usual. But Molly hated being all alone in the big empty house. "I don't want to wait around for him all day. I'll go crazy all alone. He might be back late tonight. I'll hang out here and get some work done. He said he would call when he was leaving New Haven."

"Okay. Suit yourself." Betty shrugged and finished her soup. "Guess I'll get back to work. I think we're making progress."

Molly nodded. "Yes, we are . . . I don't know what I would have done this week without you, Betty. You saved my life."

"Don't be silly. You're just getting all mushy on me. Save it for New Year's Day, when this is all over, okay?"

Molly sniffed and nodded. "Okay, will do," she said. "But listen, I've been thinking about something. I want to run it by you."

Betty sat down again and looked at her curiously. "Some new recipe you'd like me to taste test?"

"More important than that. I'm really going to miss you at the shop next week," Molly began. "It's going to seem so quiet."

"Tell me about it. I can't even picture myself back in the wonderful world of real estate deals. Hard to believe, right?"

It felt like the perfect moment to ask her the question. Molly went for it. "Betty, I've been thinking. You said you wanted a change and you seem to like the catering life. Would you like to come into the business? I mean, officially . . . like a partner or something? Willoughby *and Bowman* Fine Foods?"

Betty didn't answer. But her blue eyes slowly widened and so did her smile.

"You really mean it? That would be . . . great."

Molly breathed a sigh of relief. "Great for me. You're so good at schedules and managing the staff and figuring out the costs of everything. And knowing when to be realistic and not try to make everything perfect. All the things I'm bad at," she said with a laugh. "I think we make a good team."

"So do I. And we have lots of fun, besides."

"That goes without saying." Molly reached over and squeezed her hand. "What about the real estate office? You won't give that up completely, will you?"

"Oh, that place practically runs itself by now. I think I can supervise from around the corner. I have a few agents in there who have been with me for years. I'm sure I can work something out with them."

Molly's heart felt lighter. She had solved one major problem in her life. She could keep her business and not be completely overwhelmed by it. Even better, she had some good news to tell Matt tonight. It would prove to him that she was trying to change, to work less.

She just hoped it wasn't too late.

THE LAST OF THE HOUSEGUESTS HAD LEFT THE orchard that morning. Sophie and Miranda had immediately set to work, vacuuming, mopping, doing laundry, and putting the house back in order.

"They're calling for snow tonight; could be heavy," Sophie told her granddaughter as they pulled the sheets off the beds in one of the extra bedrooms. "I'm glad everyone is already on their way home. They won't get caught in it."

Miranda felt her spirits dip in the sudden quiet. The full house had been a big distraction. Now there was nothing to tug at her attention. She had completed most of the Valentine's Day order and didn't have much work to focus on. Images of Adam filled her head, and it was hard to think of anything else.

"It's nice to have company," Sophie said, "but it's nice to be just us two again." She studied her granddaughter, and her brow wrinkled in concern. "You look a little low, honey."

"I'm just not sure what comes next," Miranda said honestly.

"Did you make a decision about the acting job?"

"Yes. I turned it down."

Sophie dropped the pillowcase she had been holding. "You did what?"

Miranda shrugged. "It felt great to be offered the role—it was a complete ego boost—but I realized that I didn't want to start up my acting career again."

"Why ever not? Isn't this something you wanted for years?"

"It was. But it's not anymore. When I really thought about it, it just felt as if that chapter in my life had closed."

"Are you sure this isn't connected to Adam?" her grandmother asked.

"It is in a way," Miranda admitted. "At first I thought that taking the role would be the perfect cure. I could leave here, go on tour, and get away from all my memories of him. Then I finally realized that I could take an acting role on the moon and I wouldn't escape my feelings."

"Oh, honey, I'm so sorry," Sophie said.

Miranda sat down on the edge of the bed. "It's not all bleak," she said. "I also realized that I didn't want to give up the life I have here—and the start of my new business—for something that feels like an old dream."

For a moment Sophie didn't respond. She pulled down a window shade and straightened out the curtains that framed it. "I have to admit, I'm glad you're not leaving. I would have gotten along here somehow, it's not that. But I would have missed you."

"I would have missed you, too, Grandma. I would have missed this place."

Sophie gave her shoulders a quick, affectionate squeeze. "Someday you'll leave. I know you will. But it wasn't time yet."

"No, it wasn't," Miranda agreed.

"You must be eager to get back into your studio. Are you way behind in your work?"

"Not really. I have a few orders left to get done by next week. Nothing overwhelming."

"Why don't you go down to the city and see some friends? I'll bet some of them are taking time off from work?"

Miranda had a group of friends in the city, fellow actors—and former actors, like herself. But she wasn't in the mood to socialize. She didn't want to sound disagreeable though. Her grandmother was only trying to help.

"Maybe I will. I'll see. You just said there was going to be heavy snow," she reminded Sophie.

"Oh, right. Well, it won't last forever." Sophie yanked the top sheet taut and Miranda pulled on the other end as they made up another bed together.

Her grandmother folded a blanket corner to corner, pressing it against her ample chest. "How about New Year's Eve?" she persisted. "You must be invited to a party. You go out and enjoy yourself. Don't worry about me. I've got my own plans with Vera Plante and some other ladies from church. Vera's finally home from the hospital. We're all going to her place. We're going to watch the ball drop in Times Square. I hear Dick Clark is coming back as the emcee. Isn't that something?"

Miranda gathered up the extra pillows strewn around the room and set them in a pile on a chair. "I'm not sure what I'm going to do. I'll figure something out."

She wished she could just go to bed and pull the covers over her head. She had no sense of excitement about the new year. No hope that anything good would happen for her.

BY LATE AFTERNOON, THERE WAS STILL NO CALL from Matt. The snow had started to fall in Cape Light. Betty turned on the shop radio to hear a weather report. The storm front was coming up the coast. Boston was hit hard and Connecticut was even worse.

"Matt might be stuck," Betty said. "You ought to call him."

Molly nodded. But didn't call.

A short time later, the shop phone rang. It was Matt. He and Alex hadn't even left New Haven yet. "We wanted to hear the last speaker," he explained. "We both know him. He was one of our professors in med school. When we came out, there was all this snow piling up. There's zero visibility, and the hotel says the roads are awful. We're going to stay over another night. It's just too dangerous to try to drive . . ."

Molly couldn't believe this was happening. Matt spending another night with Alex? But what could she say, come home anyway? Drive through a snowstorm? If you stay there with her another night, I'll never forgive you?

Instead, she said, "We heard it was bad down there. We're getting some snow here, but it's not that heavy yet."

Matt talked to her a few minutes longer then said good-bye.

Molly felt numb as she hung up. "Matt's staying over again with Alex," she told Betty. "See, I told you something was going on. You didn't believe me."

"Molly, look outside." Betty turned her shoulders so that she faced the window. "Would you rather he was driving in that mess? Or stuck in a car on the highway somewhere?"

"Yes, I would," Molly ranted. "As long as Alex wasn't in the car with him."

Betty rolled her eyes. "You're so stubborn."

It was almost five. The phone call from Matt and her emotional reaction had worn Molly out. She glanced at Betty. "I'm beat. Guess I'll go home. Would you mind closing up?"

"It would be my pleasure," Betty replied.

Molly glanced around the shop. "We're almost done here. The finishing touches can be added tomorrow."

"You're coming in tomorrow? Molly, please. Take a day off. Take a look at yourself. I'm worried about you."

Molly shook off her friend's worried tone. "I'll just come in to send off the crews and make sure the parties are set up right."

"I can check the parties. You don't have to do that, too," Betty reminded her. "How about you pick the most important one—or two? I'll handle the rest."

Molly nodded reluctantly. "Okay. I guess that would work out."

Betty watched her as she pulled on her hat and wrapped a scarf around her neck. Her wool jacket no longer fit well over her pregnant tummy; she could only secure the middle button.

"Hey, how about if I drop by later and we watch a movie or something?"

Molly appreciated the offer. Especially since Betty had been working hard all day, too, and was probably beat. "Thanks." She touched Betty's shoulder. "I'm just going home to conk out."

Betty nodded. "Okay, good plan. Listen, watch your step outside now. The snow might be slippery."

"I'll be okay," Molly promised. She made it out to her car and quickly cleaned off the snow. Then she drove home through the snowy, twilight streets.

She ate a quick bite, standing up at the kitchen counter. Cheese and crackers, washed down with ginger ale, her favorite meal lately.

She was dressed in her nightgown and robe by half past seven and lying in bed, watching TV. She told herself she wasn't waiting for Matt to call, but she couldn't stop herself from imagining romantic scenarios of her husband with Alex Cole. Molly wanted to call him but wouldn't let herself.

Matt was away. She was alone and pregnant. *He should be calling me. End of story*, she kept reminding herself.

CHAPTER ELEVEN

THE SOUND OF THE PHONE WOKE MOLLY WITH A start; she felt foggy-headed and disoriented.

The TV was still on, a home shopping show. A woman wearing too much makeup and an iridescent pink sweater was spraying stain remover on a T-shirt.

"Hello?" Molly's voice came out in a croak.

"Hi, honey." It was Matt, finally. "I've been trying you at the shop and on your cell. Didn't you get my messages?"

"No. I've been home all night." She didn't mean to sound accusatory. It just came out that way. "What time is it?"

"Oh, about eleven. I just got up to the room. There's a big group here from the conference. Everyone is stuck. Alex and I had dinner with some pediatricians from Boston."

"You and Alex seem to be having a nice weekend together."

"Molly, what are you talking about?"

"I'm talking about you and Alex. Is there something you want to tell me?"

"Tell you? Like what?"

"Like you're having a . . . a relationship with her."

There, she had said it. She hadn't meant to say anything like this. Not until he got home and they were sitting face-to-face. But it felt good to get it off her chest.

"A relationship . . . Are you crazy?"

He sounded genuinely shocked. She wasn't sure if that was a good sign or a bad one. He could be shocked because he was totally innocent. Or because she was calling him on his indiscretion.

Neither of them spoke for a long time. Then he said, "I am not even going to dignify that question with an answer."

She knew he was mad now. Matt always

got a formal tone when he was really angry. She was just the opposite.

"I asked you a simple question, Matt. I don't know why you won't just answer it.

"Because this time, Molly, you've gone too far."

Had she gone too far? Her great feeling of relief was quickly replaced by a wave of horror.

If he really wasn't involved with Alex, he would be now. She could see him, calling Alex as soon as they hung up and confiding everything about his shrewish wife.

This time, Molly saw Matt crying on Alex's shoulder as clearly as if they were both standing right in her bedroom.

"Molly . . . are you still there?"

"Yes, I'm here," she said quietly. She braced herself for what he might say next.

"We need to talk about this when I get home."

"Yes," she agreed. "When you get home. Whenever that turns out to be."

"Good night, Molly," he said curtly. He hung up, not even waiting for her reply.

MOLLY NEARLY CALLED BETTY THE NEXT MORNing to tell her she couldn't make it in. She had been up most of the night, crying. And wondering if she should call Matt back and apologize.

Somehow she managed to get up, get dressed, and drag herself out of the house to do what she had to do. Snow had fallen throughout the night, but the streets were already clear from the plows that had been working steadily.

Although she had some trouble backing out of her driveway, her big SUV finally made it through the drifts, and she quickly reached the open road and headed for the village.

Betty was at the shop before her and had already started the last-minute prep on assorted dishes. Molly helped along with Sonya, and they started packing the vans.

"Did you hear from Matt last night?" Betty asked, once they had sent the crews on their way.

Molly nodded curtly. "We had another fight. I asked him if he was having an affair and he wouldn't answer me. What does that tell you?"

"It tells me you made him mad. But it doesn't prove anything."

"Betty, I know you're trying to help, but I

know what I saw on Christmas Eve. And that combined with his . . . attitude . . . I don't think I'm imagining all this."

"Well, at least you got it out in the open," Betty said. "When he gets home, you'll just have to sit down and have a serious talk."

"*If* he comes home. Maybe he wants to have New Year's Eve with . . . her."

"Oh, Molly, don't be a nut. Just go home and take care of yourself a little. He'll be home soon, I'm sure of it."

When Molly didn't answer, Betty said, "I know it all seems pretty bleak right now, but you'll work it out. I still think Matt is loyal to you."

Molly sighed. "That makes one of us." She picked up her schedule and checked the address of the party she planned to check on. She felt so weary, she had narrowed it down to one.

"I'm just stopping at Woodruff's. Here's the rest of the list."

Betty took the sheet and looked it over. "No problem. This looks very do-able."

Molly leaned over and impulsively hugged her. "I don't know what I would have done without you this week, Betty. How can I ever make it up to you?"

Betty laughed softly and hugged her back. "Just stay married, will you?"

Molly nodded and sniffed. "Okay, if you say so." She picked up her purse and set off for the party. "I'll check in with you later."

"Yes, make sure you do. Drive carefully," Betty added.

Molly waved and went out to her car.

The Woodruff house was in the village, less than a half mile from her shop. Even with traffic moving slowly on the snowy streets, Molly was there in five minutes. She pulled into the driveway and parked behind her catering van. She saw Rita dressed in her uniform, emptying out the van. "How's it going?" Molly asked her.

"So far so good."

The front door opened and Mrs. Woodruff waved to her. "Hi, Molly, come on in. Everything looks very nice."

Molly was pleased to hear that. She didn't need any problems today. Betty had given her the right advice. She needed to get home and take care of herself—and wait for her husband.

"Be right there," Molly called back.

She was halfway up the walk when she suddenly felt her feet fly out from under her.

For a split second, her arms flailed as she tried desperately to regain her balance. Then with a yelp of alarm, she landed flat on her back. Mrs. Woodruff ran out the door and Rita ran from the driveway.

"Molly, are you all right?" Mrs. Woodruff knelt down next to her. Rita was on her other side.

Molly felt stunned. She couldn't talk at first. She felt a searing pain in her ankle. She started to sit up and the slight motion made her leg feel even worse. She bit down on her lip to keep from crying out.

"My ankle . . . I think it's broken."

"Just stay right there, dear. We've called nine one one. An ambulance will be here in a minute . . ."

Molly nodded. Then she felt a sudden cramp in her abdomen that made her curl up in pain.

"Oh . . . no." She sighed and bit her lower lip. What had she done? *The baby . . . Please, God, let my baby be all right. Please. I'll do anything. I can't believe I've been so . . . so stupid.*

She felt tears fill her eyes and she started to cry. The hot tears slipped down her cold cheeks.

Mrs. Woodruff took her hand. "Let me call your husband, dear. How can I reach him?"

"He's been in Connecticut. He should be on his way back by now," she managed. She recited Matt's cell phone number. "I hope you can reach him."

"I've called Betty," Rita said. "She's on her way."

Betty arrived just as the ambulance pulled up. She rushed to Molly's side and hugged her. "I'm coming to the hospital with you, don't worry."

Moments later, Molly was rolled away on a stretcher and loaded in the ambulance.

Flat on her back and strapped to the stretcher, Molly stared up at the ceiling of the ambulance, wondering how she had ended up here? Simple, she was just too stubborn. She wouldn't listen to anyone.

What if she had harmed the baby? Would she ever forgive herself?

She closed her eyes and started to sob again. *My poor little baby. I'm so sorry*, she said inside her head. *I've been so stupid and careless. I love you so. . . .*

Oh, God. Please don't let anything be wrong . . . please?

Miraculously, she fell asleep.

* * *

Betty sat with Molly in the ER and helped her deal with the doctors. Fortunately, Molly's pregnancy gave her some priority with the triage nurse, and they didn't have to sit for hours, waiting for attention.

"The ankle isn't the big problem. I would say it's broken and you'll need a cast. We'll get to that. I'm more concerned about the cramping. You need to have a sonogram, right away," the admitting doctor told her. "This way we can see what's going on."

Her leg hurt something fierce, but Molly barely noticed. She was desperate to find out about her baby.

The doctor glanced at her chart a moment. "Is your husband here?"

"He's been out of town," Betty answered for her. "He's on his way back right now."

Mrs. Woodruff had reached Matt on the first try, and Betty had spoken to him after they reached the hospital while Molly was being admitted.

"Sorry, but we can't wait. We have to take care of this right away."

Molly nodded. "I understand."

"Do you want your friend to come in with you?"

Molly glanced at Betty. "No, that's all right. I can go alone."

She did want Betty in a way, but in another way, she knew that if Matt couldn't be here with her, she had to face this on her own.

Betty squeezed her hand just before the doctor rolled her away. "I'm praying for you and the baby," Betty said quietly.

"Thanks. I am, too," Molly admitted.

The room with the sonogram equipment was dimly lit. The technician, a woman about Molly's age, rolled up Molly's blouse and smeared cold gel over her stomach. She smiled kindly and tried to make small talk to put Molly at ease. But Molly was too nervous to respond.

"First pregnancy?" the technician asked as she looked over Molly's chart.

"No, my third. I have two daughters. Teenagers, actually."

"How nice. Do you want me to tell you the sex of the child?"

"I just want to know if the baby is all right." Molly felt tears pressing at her eyes again, but she fought hard not to cry.

"Yes, I'm sure you do," the technician answered softly.

Molly would have given anything to have

Matt with her. She had been so awful to him. How could he still love her after some of the things she had said?

"Are you ready to start, Mrs. Harding? This won't take very long . . ."

There was a sharp knock on the door, then it opened. Molly saw the doctor first, then Matt standing just behind him.

"Dr. Harding, the patient's husband," the doctor said quickly to the technician.

"Come right in, Dr. Harding. We're just getting started."

Matt barely glanced at the technician. He walked quickly to Molly and tried to hug her, though it was difficult. "Oh . . . honey. What happened to you?"

"I'm a complete idiot. That's what happened. . . . Oh, Matt . . . I'm so sorry . . ." She started sobbing and couldn't stop. "If anything's happened to the baby . . ."

"Shhh . . ." he soothed her. "Let's just find out what's going on, okay?"

Molly nodded. She loved him so much. She didn't even care anymore if he had gone off with Alex. She had been so awful, she couldn't blame him. She just wanted the baby to be all right and everything to be all right between them again.

Matt stepped aside and the technician started the test. Molly closed her eyes. She couldn't bear to watch. She squeezed Matt's hand, barely able to breathe as the technician examined the image on the screen. It seemed to be taking so long. Molly felt her heart speeding up, and she tried to take slow, deep breaths to calm herself.

Finally, the technician started to describe what she saw.

"I see the heartbeat. It looks strong. The baby is all right. You have nothing to worry about. The cramps are just a reaction from the fall. The placenta is lying a little low. You'll have to stay off your feet awhile. But there's been no harm."

"Thank God . . ." Matt's head dropped on her shoulder, and she felt his body shake.

He was crying. She reached her arms around him, crying, too.

A few hours later, she found herself in a hospital room with a fresh cast on her leg. Her obstetrician had examined her and thought it best if Molly stayed overnight for observation.

Matt sat by her side. "So, are you going to do what the doctor says this time? Bed rest? No working for a while?"

Molly nodded. Matt looked doubtful.

"No, I really mean it, Matt. I've even asked Betty to be a partner in the business. She said yes, too. Isn't that great?"

"It is good news," Matt admitted. "If it will really make you cut back on your workload and not take on double the business now."

"I will cut back, I promise. I had the scare of my life today," she confessed. "I would have never forgiven myself if anything had happened to . . . to our baby."

Matt didn't answer for a moment. "So, you want the baby now?"

"I've always wanted the baby," she said. "It's just that you were always so darned cheerful and had an easy answer for all my problems. I felt like you weren't really listening to me, like you didn't really understand how this baby is going to change my life. Going to change our lives," she corrected herself.

He stared down at her, looking more sympathetic. "I think you're right. I didn't get it at first. I didn't understand what you were so worked up about. But I understand better now."

"Maybe this fall was a good thing," Molly said. "It made me see I was on the wrong track. I want to raise this child with you, Matt, not with an army of babysitters and nannies. We're so lucky to have this chance."

"Yes, we are," he agreed. "You don't have to convince me of anything."

He took her hand and looked into her eyes. "While I was away, I had some time to think. If Alex Cole's presence is that upsetting to you, I'll end the partnership. Though there's absolutely no reason for you to be jealous of her, Molly. Honestly."

That was a major concession, Molly realized. It meant Matt would have to shake up his practice and look for someone else. And he would have to tell Alex that the partnership he had offered her was over. Would he have even offered this concession if he were in love with Alex? Somehow Molly didn't think so.

"No," Molly said. "You don't have to end the partnership, not for me."

"How did you ever get the idea I was involved with Alex? She has a boyfriend. They're very serious. In fact, they're supposed to get engaged soon."

A boyfriend? That was news.

"Where is this boyfriend?" Molly asked a bit suspiciously. "How come this is the first time I'm hearing about him?"

"He's in Africa, working for Doctors Without Borders. I suppose we'll meet him soon. He was supposed to come for Christmas— and give her a ring—but unexpectedly he had to stay. She misses him very much," he added.

"Oh . . . so maybe she was upset about this boyfriend on Christmas Eve?" Molly asked.

"Very upset. He called on her cell and she started crying afterward. I didn't know what to do. I just gave her some tissues."

"And your shoulder, maybe?" Molly added.

Matt looked surprised. Then he nodded, looking embarrassed. "Yes, and my shoulder. Maybe. For a minute. How did you guess that, Molly?"

"I saw you two together, in the mudroom. I guess I got the wrong idea," she confessed.

"Is that what started all this? Why didn't you just say something?"

"I tried . . . but . . ." She sighed and shrugged. "I'm sorry I accused you . . . and for all the nasty things I said."

"I'm sorry you got so upset. . . . I guess you must really love me if you're that jealous."

"Yeah, I guess I do. Did you ever doubt it?"

She smiled at him. "Do me a favor? If any other gorgeous, brainy babes need to borrow a shoulder, have them check with me first."

Matt nodded. "Absolutely."

They heard a flurry of excitement in the hospital hallway. A nurse peeked into the room. "Here—to celebrate the New Year. It's almost time."

She handed Matt a small bottle of ginger ale and two plastic glasses. He brought them over to Molly's bedside.

"Time to ring out the old and ring in the new." He poured out the small bottle of soda into the two cups and handed her one.

"Ginger ale. How appropriate. Did they know I was checking in?" Molly joked.

"I guess this is the best we can do. I'll make it up to you."

Molly smiled. "As long as I'm ringing in the New Year with you. I don't care where we are."

Matt lifted his cup and looked into her eyes. "To the New Year, Molly. To all the love we've shared in our marriage and with our beautiful girls. And to our new baby and all the love that is yet to come."

"That was just perfect, sweetheart," she

said giving him a kiss. And she meant it, too.

A perfect way to start off the year.

MIRANDA THOUGHT SHE HAD TO BE THE ONLY person in the world working on New Year's Eve. Except for firemen and policeman, and doctors and nurses in hospitals, perhaps.

Her grandmother had gone to her get-together at Vera's house, and Miranda had rented a movie. But the film hadn't held her interest very long. She flipped through the channels on the TV, looking for something to watch. It was hard to avoid all the images of cozy couples, kissing and hugging as they anticipated midnight.

She couldn't help wondering what Adam was doing. Celebrating with his fiancée? Thankful to be back in his real life? Probably not sparing a thought about her.

She clicked off the TV and went out to her studio, needing the distraction that only work could bring. She wasn't sure how long she had been out there when a sound at the door startled her. She jumped in her seat and turned around.

Had her grandmother come home early? She had said she might. Miranda knew that

Sophie had been worried about leaving her alone.

"Grandma? Is that you?"

"No, Red Riding Hood, it's the Wolf . . ."

Adam swung open the door and stepped inside. Miranda felt her heart skip a beat, but she couldn't move a muscle. He smiled at her, his eyes alight with the warmth that she had missed so much. She couldn't stop staring at him.

He looked the same, but different, wearing a soft leather jacket, jeans, and a thick blue sweater. She almost didn't recognize him.

He walked toward her. "I called the house. No one answered. I wasn't even sure I would find you here. Why aren't you at a party or something?"

"Why aren't you?"

She still couldn't believe it. She wondered for a moment if she was hallucinating. She had never expected to see him again.

She stood up and faced him, feeling the impulse to throw her arms around him and hold him close.

But, of course, she couldn't. He was almost married.

"We saw you on the news. They said your memory was returning."

He nodded. "Yes, I remember everything now."

"Wow. That's amazing. So, tell me everything. What do you do for a living? How did you end up unconscious in the orchard? Do you remember how you got hit on the head?"

"Okay, okay," he said with a laugh. "Just give me a minute. I'll answer all your questions, or as many as I can. I'm a cab driver, in Portland. That's my day job, at least. I've been doing it these last three years while trying to make it as a writer. The day before I ended up here, I had an appointment in Boston, to meet my agent. I came down from Portland on the train. We met at the Charles Hotel, in the Regatta Bar. Hence the matchbook cover we found in my pocket. I left Boston late at night and the police figured I must have been mugged in one of the stations where I had to switch lines. The trauma of being attacked and a blow to the head caused my memory loss. I got on a train and blacked out. When I came to, I realized I had no wallet, no money or ID. I panicked. I remember standing between the cars, trying to get some air. I remember that the train stopped in the middle of nowhere. I heard the conductor coming and I just jumped off."

"You jumped off a train as it was passing the orchard . . . that's how you ended up here?"

"That's why the police never found an abandoned car. I don't own one. I drove an orange cab though. That's why I remembered an orange car and the number fifty-three. It was the number of my cab. And that's why when Dr. Carter asked how I got to the orchard, I told him that I jumped. I know it sounds pretty bizarre, but I was totally disoriented and practically paranoid."

It did sound odd but Miranda supposed it was possible. Some of the trains that ran through the area were very old, with diesel engines and old-fashioned cars. It was possible to stand between the cars or even hop off.

"That actually makes sense," she mused. "The trains always stop near here—it's an unmarked crossing. The conductor has to get out and check the crossing by sight."

"I remember jumping, landing on frozen earth. I was cold and scared out of my mind. I started walking. I didn't recognize anything. There were no lights or houses. I saw the hill in your orchard and thought maybe if I got to the top, I could see lights or something. I guess I collapsed when I got to the top. That moment I still can't remember."

"But didn't people miss you?" Miranda asked. "Didn't anyone start looking for you? I mean, besides Lisa?"

"I have a married sister in Chicago and my mother lives in Florida now. I speak to them every few weeks. Even if they had called and left a message, they wouldn't worry not hearing from me for a few days. Since I worked for a cab company and kept odd hours, no one thought much of the fact that I didn't show up for work. They called me, of course. But they were more annoyed than worried about my absence. It's not unusual at all for cabbies to just walk off a job without notice."

"So it was only Lisa then," Miranda said.

"Even Lisa didn't notice I was gone. Not at first. Didn't you wonder why it took her almost a month to find me? She was only two hours away in Portland."

"But why wasn't she looking for you? You're engaged, aren't you?"

"We were. But a few weeks before I got lost, she broke up with me, gave me back the ring. She said it just didn't feel right. I think she met someone else she liked better but wouldn't admit it. I was pretty devastated at the time. It may have even contributed to the memory loss. Maybe I just wanted to forget."

"Then why did she come looking for you and tell everyone you were still engaged?"

"She told me that at first she just came to find me—to help out, as a friend. She knew that I didn't have any family in the area, or anyone who would really miss me. Then once she started talking to the police, she had second thoughts about dumping me. She wanted to get back together, so she told everyone we were engaged. She hoped that by the time I remembered what had really happened, she would have won me over again."

He moved closer and took Miranda's hands in his. "But even if I could forgive her for trying to trick me, I could never be happy with Lisa again. I couldn't think about anyone but you, Miranda. As soon as I remembered the truth, I knew I had to come back to you."

He gazed down at her, a tender light in his dark eyes. Before she could say a word he pulled her close and kissed her. Miranda melted against him. Though they had held each other this way before, this time it was very different. There was no shadow, no cloud. He was free. His past was no longer a mysterious question.

It was the reunion Miranda had dreamed of but believed would never happen in a million lifetimes. When they finally parted, she had one more question for him.

"So those nightmares, they turned out to be nothing after all. Why do you think you kept having dreams like that?"

"They weren't exactly nightmares, or even chronic guilt feelings, or whatever Dr. Carter said. I was remembering images from the book I wrote—a mystery set in Boston. I had been working on it so long, spent so much time in that world, that somehow it was what surfaced in my dreams, instead of my real life."

He hugged her close and kissed the top of her head. "You seem relieved to hear I don't have a shady past, Miranda. I was hoping to hide out in your studio again."

Miranda hugged him. "That would be fine with me. You can stay here . . . forever."

MOLLY WAS HOME BY NOON ON NEW YEAR'S DAY. Matt had come early to the hospital to pick her up. When she hobbled up the path, she saw a bunch of balloons tied to the railing on the front steps. "Aren't you supposed to wait for balloons until the baby is born?" she asked.

"The girls are so happy you're all right, they can't wait to see you," Matt said.

She couldn't wait to see them either and when she came in the door, the three of them nearly knocked her off her feet with hugs and kisses.

"Jill, I swear you got taller," Molly said, flopping down on the sofa. "Didn't she grow again, Matt?"

"Mom, it was only five days. How could I get taller?' Jill already had Molly's crutches and was testing them out.

"It was a spurt. You had a growth spurt," Molly said, feeling extra motherly.

Sam and Jessica and their two boys had brought Jill home from Vermont, and Matt had persuaded them to stay and celebrate New Year's Day. Her parents had called the hospital last night, and were coming later, too, to check on her. It was going to be a full house.

Jessica was in the kitchen but Matt dragged her back out to the living room.

"Nobody's cooking. We're just having

takeout. Pizza, wings, Chinese food, the works." He stared at Molly. "I mean it, too."

Molly raised her hands in surrender. "Don't look at me, I love the works. Let's get out every menu in the junk drawer."

"Pizza . . . and a football game. The perfect start to the new year. All right," Sam said. He was already watching a game and had only come out for a break, to say hello to his sister. He carried a plastic bowl in each hand, one filled with pretzels, the other with chips. He set them down on the coffee table, oblivious to Molly's daggerlike stare.

Then she sat back and sighed. She had learned her lesson. Life was too short.

The doorbell rang and Matt rose to answer it. Molly heard Betty in the foyer and Matt's New Year's greeting.

". . . and there was all this food in the shop, left over from different parties. I thought you guys might like some of it, so you won't have to shop or cook."

"That was very thoughtful of you, Betty," she heard Matt say. "We're going to order out, but we do have a big crowd here. We'll have an even bigger spread at halftime," he said with a laugh.

Molly saw Matt head for the kitchen with two big shopping bags while Betty came into the living room. She gasped at the sight of Molly on the couch.

Betty walked over and gazed down at her sympathetically. "Look at you. Are you all right?"

"This is nothing. You should see the other guy," Molly said automatically.

Betty grinned and held out a bunch of flowers. "For you."

"Gee, thanks . . . These are pretty."

"You're welcome. Can I sign your cast?" Betty asked.

"If you can find any room. The kids have been playing tic-tac-toe on it for a while."

Betty took a marker and signed her name and added a "get well soon" message. "This is going to slow you down some," Betty said, looking over the hunk of plaster. "How are you going to run the shop?"

"Over the phone," Matt answered for her as he came back in the room. He glanced at Molly, as if expecting an argument, but she didn't say a word. He spotted the flowers and took them from her.

"Thank you, Betty. Let me put these in a

vase." He left the room again, leaving the two friends alone to talk.

"So, you just got back from Mrs. Norris's New Year's Day brunch," Molly guessed. "How did it go?"

"Perfectly. She introduced me to this woman who organizes a big hospital fundraiser every year. She wants to meet with us."

Molly didn't say anything, just smiled. Of course Betty would make new business contacts everywhere she went. She was a natural at that.

Betty sat down and took a pretzel from the plastic bowl on the coffee table. "Guess what else? This really nice man was chatting me up the whole time, and he asked me out on a date. Very attractive professional type, not too old, not too young." She shrugged. "We'll see."

Molly could see Betty was excited. She felt happy for her.

"It was a nice surprise," Betty added. "I had no idea I could meet men doing this."

"I didn't mention that? It's definitely a perk."

Betty laughed and leaned closer. "So it looks like you and Matt sorted everything out?"

"We had a long talk last night. Turns out I was way off base about Alex. She's in a serious relationship. I felt like an idiot . . . a relieved idiot," Molly corrected herself.

Betty smiled. "I'm not surprised to hear that."

They heard a raucous cheer from the family room. "Sounds like the Patriots are winning," Molly said.

"Want to join the party?"

"Why not? Hand me those crutches, will you?" Molly sat up and maneuvered her way to the edge of the couch. Betty handed her the two crutches and helped her up.

"Gee, Molly. I really feel bad for you. What a time to break a leg."

Molly sighed. "I think it's just God's way of putting the brakes on. I wasn't really listening before. In a strange way, I think the accident was a sign. Know what I mean?"

"Yes, I do," Betty said, guiding her toward the back of the house. "I have a good feeling about the new year, Molly. And I'm glad I'm here, spending New Year's Day with you."

"Me, too," Molly said. "We didn't have much of a celebration last night in my hospital room. So this is really our New Year's party."

Betty gave her a look of mock horror. "You do realize there are plastic bowls of chips in there? And dip made from sour cream and soup mix. And any minute now, there will be greasy wings and non-gourmet pizza."

"Yeah," Molly said happily. "And it may just be the best party of all."

On Wednesday, the second day of the new year and the first official workday, Carl Tulley set to work, putting away the rest of the Christmas decorations, and Ben began work on his January schedule. With the holidays over, he wanted to spend more time visiting the local nursing home, and he had promised to organize a new drive for the community food bank.

He looked up from his desk as Carl entered his office. "'Scuse me, Reverend," Carl began. "There's some folks in the sanctuary, say they're looking for the statue and want to know what's happened to it. I told them it was put away, but they said they need to talk to you about it."

Ben sighed. Perhaps he would have to put some notice in the newspaper. He couldn't be answering these questions every day.

He walked into the sanctuary, preparing some official explanation. Then he saw that the visitors were Marie-Claire and Gerald. They sat in the last pew, patiently waiting for him.

"Why, hello," he greeted them. "Happy New Year."

Gerald rose and shook his hand. "Happy New Year, Reverend. We didn't want to bother you, but we're looking for the statue. The sexton says it's been put away in storage somewhere?"

"Back in the basement," Ben explained. "I've had some correspondence with a bishop in France. From the parish in your village, Marie-Claire," he added. "The church has been rebuilt on the same site. They even used some of the original stones. I'm making plans to send the statue back home. They've missed her."

The couple looked at each other and smiled. "Perhaps we could accompany it," Gerald said. "We've been planning to go back to France soon anyway."

"We came here today to ask if you would marry us in this church, in the sight of the statue," Marie-Claire explained. "But now that it's going back to France, to the place where it protected us, that would be even better."

"Yes, it does seem even better," Ben said. "It seems ideal. My sincerest congratulations on your engagement. That is good news." He shook Gerald's hand again and hugged Marie-Claire. "I wish you every happiness."

He had a feeling his good wishes weren't even necessary. These two seemed to be destined to be with each other, their union blessed from above.

Ben walked the pair out and they parted on the green, making plans to get in touch once they settled their travel plans.

Ben walked toward town on a path that edged the harbor. He paused and gazed out at the blue-gray water and turquoise sky. Seagulls cried and wheeled above, swooping down and up again, like white kites in the wind.

Did the statue possess miraculous powers? Ben still wasn't sure.

He did believe there was a grand design to all experience, a pattern so vast and complex, one could hardly discern it from close-up, everyday life. It was like trying to view a huge mural with your nose pressed against the wall.

As for the angel, the way it had surfaced after all these years from the boxes in the church basement—if its only purpose had been to reunite Marie-Claire and Gerald, then it truly had worked a miracle.

Ben was willing to grant it at least that.

EPILOGUE

⌒

ON THE MORNING OF JULY FOURTH, MOLLY'S whole family went into town very early. They set up folding chairs at the edge of the Village Green to watch the annual reenactment. One of the first battles of the American Revolution had been fought in Cape Light. Every year, the local history buffs loved to dress up and play it out all over again—the ragtag Colonial army battling the British redcoats. Everyone in the town gathered to watch.

The girls all spotted friends and ran off to meet them. Matt and Molly sat together. Matt drank coffee and Molly sipped herbal tea.

"I'm not sure that Chinese food we had last night agreed with me," she said. "I seem to have some heartburn."

"Not uncommon at your stage. Your stomach is pushed up by the baby, and the acid—"

Molly raised her hand. "Too much information, Doc. I'll just live with it. In a week this will all be over."

July eleventh was her due date, and at her last exam the doctor had said that everything appeared to be right on schedule.

Matt took her hand and pressed it to his lips. "You've done great. It won't be long now."

"I can't wait for this baby," Molly admitted. She rubbed her huge stomach with her hand. Tests had revealed the baby was a girl. Molly was thrilled. If Matt was disappointed, he didn't show it. He seemed eager to have another daughter, joking about his harem.

Everything was ready for the baby. Her room, her toys, her cute little clothes.

Everything except her name, which they couldn't agree on.

It was getting down to the wire, but Molly hoped they could negotiate it in the next few days. She wanted to know by the time the baby was born.

"Look, they're starting . . ." Matt stood up and pointed to the far side of the green. The first shots were fired, and Molly covered her ears from the popping sound. A row of red-coats marched across the green in formation while colonists hid behind rocks and trees, then jumped out and fired their muskets.

Molly stood up, shading her eyes. Her brother Sam was out there, as usual, running around in a three-cornered hat and brandishing a musket. She teased him about it mercilessly, but never missed a chance to watch him battle the British, dressed like Paul Revere.

"Do you see Sam?" she asked Matt.

"Not yet," he said. "Wait . . . I think I see him. Over to the left, by the boat rack?"

Molly turned to look and felt a deep, unmistakable pang. It took her breath away.

She grabbed Matt's arm. "Honey . . . I think it's starting."

He nodded, without looking at her. "Yes, it's started. It's well under way."

Gunshots fired, a fierce popping sound. A fife and drum duo marched by, the drummer's head wrapped in fake bandages.

"Matt, I mean my labor has started."

"Your what?" He finally turned to look at

her. His face went pale. "Your labor? For pity's sake, Molly, why didn't you say something? Quick, where are the girls? Wait, let me fold up these chairs. . . . Oh, leave the chairs, we'll get them later . . ."

Molly put her hand on his arm. "Matt, calm down. I have a long way to go. We have plenty of time."

"Not necessarily, Molly. This isn't your first. Your labor could go very quickly."

"That's true. But I'm not going to have the baby right here."

"I'll say you're not. Come on." He stuck a chair under his arm, stepped over the rest, and bustled her off toward the car. The green and the nearby parking lot were packed, and everyone seemed to be walking in the opposite direction. It was hard to work their way through the crowd. Molly kept a sharp lookout for her girls. They all had cell phones, so she could call them from the car and round them up that way if necessary.

Luckily, Molly spotted Jessica. "Jess, we're on the way to the hospital. The girls are around, but they don't know what's going on. Can you round them up and watch them for a while?"

"Absolutely. Oh, I'm so happy for you."

Jessica ran over and gave Molly a quick hug. "Good luck."

"She'll be fine," Matt insisted. "If we can get her there in time."

Molly rolled her eyes at him. "We'll get there in time."

When they reached the car, Matt insisted that she sit in the back. "You'll be more comfortable if you need to stretch out, and it's safer back there."

She didn't like sitting in the back with him in the front, but it was necessary. Her labor pains were getting stronger and coming much closer together than she remembered with either of her other children.

They drove out of town and reached the highway. It was over an hour to Southport Hospital. Molly hadn't thought much of the drive before, but suddenly it seemed like a long way.

"Are you all right, honey?" Matt asked, turning to check on her.

She nodded, gritting her teeth. "I'm okay."

"Should I try to time your pains?"

"I'd rather not know," she admitted. She tried some breathing exercises, but they didn't seem to help much. "Just get us there."

"I'm trying, honey." He had no sooner said the words than the traffic slowed and came to a complete stop.

"Oh no . . . Is there an accident?"

Matt shook his head. "I think it's just beach traffic."

Molly's head flopped back against the seat. She didn't want Matt to know, but her labor pains were starting to come very close together. She closed her eyes and willed herself to hang on. She didn't want to end up a headline in the newspapers: *Woman Gives Birth on Highway!* How incredibly tacky. It wouldn't be good for business.

It felt like the longest ride of her life, but finally the hospital came into view. Matt drove to the emergency entrance and practically carried her through the door. "My wife is having a baby. I mean, really having a baby. Like, immediately!"

Nurses came to help Matt. They put Molly in a wheelchair and took her up to the maternity wing. She waited in a small labor room only a few minutes before the doctor on call examined her. "You're almost fully dilated, Mrs. Harding. It won't be long now."

Molly turned to Matt and gripped his hand. "This is it. She's here . . ."

"I can't believe it," Matt said. He had tears in his eyes and brushed them away with the back of his hand.

Molly wanted to kiss him, but her legs were set up to push and she could barely move.

It all seemed a blur after that. She did whatever the doctor—and her body—told her to do. She felt Matt beside her, hovering, stroking her hair, holding her hand while she squeezed his fingers so hard, she was sure he was going to scream out in pain, too.

Finally, she heard the baby's first cry and saw the doctor lift her in the air. "Here she is. Isn't she beautiful?"

"Just like her mother," Matt said, his voice filled with awe.

A nurse wrapped the baby in a blanket and set her down on Molly's chest. Molly held her close and ever so gently kissed the top of her tiny head.

Then it was Matt's turn. He cradled the infant in his strong arms, tears of joy running down his handsome face. "Oh . . . she's amazing," he breathed.

"Yes, she is," Molly agreed.

Molly was wheeled into a recovery room, and Matt followed. A few moments later, the baby was brought in. A nurse handed her down to Molly. "She can stay for a few minutes, then I have to wash her up and make her an ID bracelet."

Molly nuzzled the baby's silky cheek. She felt as if she were kissing an angel. "Oh, she's delicious."

"She's perfect," Matt declared. "She's simply a miracle."

"But we still don't have a name for her. That doesn't seem right."

"We have a lot of names, Molly," he reminded her as he sat on the edge of the bed. "We just need to pick one we can agree on."

"I have another one. It just came to me. What do you think of . . . Betty?"

Matt didn't answer. He gazed down at the baby and gently touched the tiny fist curled around the edge of Molly's gown. "I sort of like it. It's a little old-fashioned sounding. . . ."

"Classic," Molly corrected.

"But I don't mind that either." He looked into Molly's eyes. "If you want to call her Betty, then it's all right with me."

"Thank you, Matt. It means a lot to me."

He leaned over and kissed her. "This has to be one of the happiest days of my life, Molly. Thank you for giving me such a beautiful child. I'll always cherish and protect her.

I'll always cherish and protect you," he added. "But you already know that."

She nodded, her vision blurring as tears filled her eyes. How had she ever doubted him? That dark hour seemed years past.

"I love you, Matt. I love our life together. I love our children and I adore our new baby." She sighed. "I know I can be difficult at times . . . but you're good to put up with me."

He laughed softly. "You make my life interesting. From the first minute I met you. I would be bored to death if it was any different."

"Not a chance. I think you're stuck with us now," she teased him.